Lena Wood

ELIJAH CREEK & THE ARMOR OF GOD

Vol. III

BOOK 5: The Haunted Soul
BOOK 6: The Angel of Fire
BOOK 7: The Carpet of Bones

info@braughlerbooks.com

Cover art and map illustrations by Daniel Armstrong

Printed in the United States of America

Published by Braughler Books LLC., Springboro, OH

Second edition, first printing, 2019

ISBN: 978-1-945091-29-2

Library of Congress Control Number: 2018963617

Ordering information: Special discounts are available on quantity purchases by bookstores, corporations, associations, and others. For details, contact the publisher at:

sales@braughlerbooks.com
or at 937-58-BOOKS

For questions or comments about this book, please write to:

info@braughlerbooks.com

Braughler™
Books
braughlerbooks.com

in honor of
The Sword Bearer
&
all those who do battle at the gates

THE HAUNTED SOUL

BOOK 5

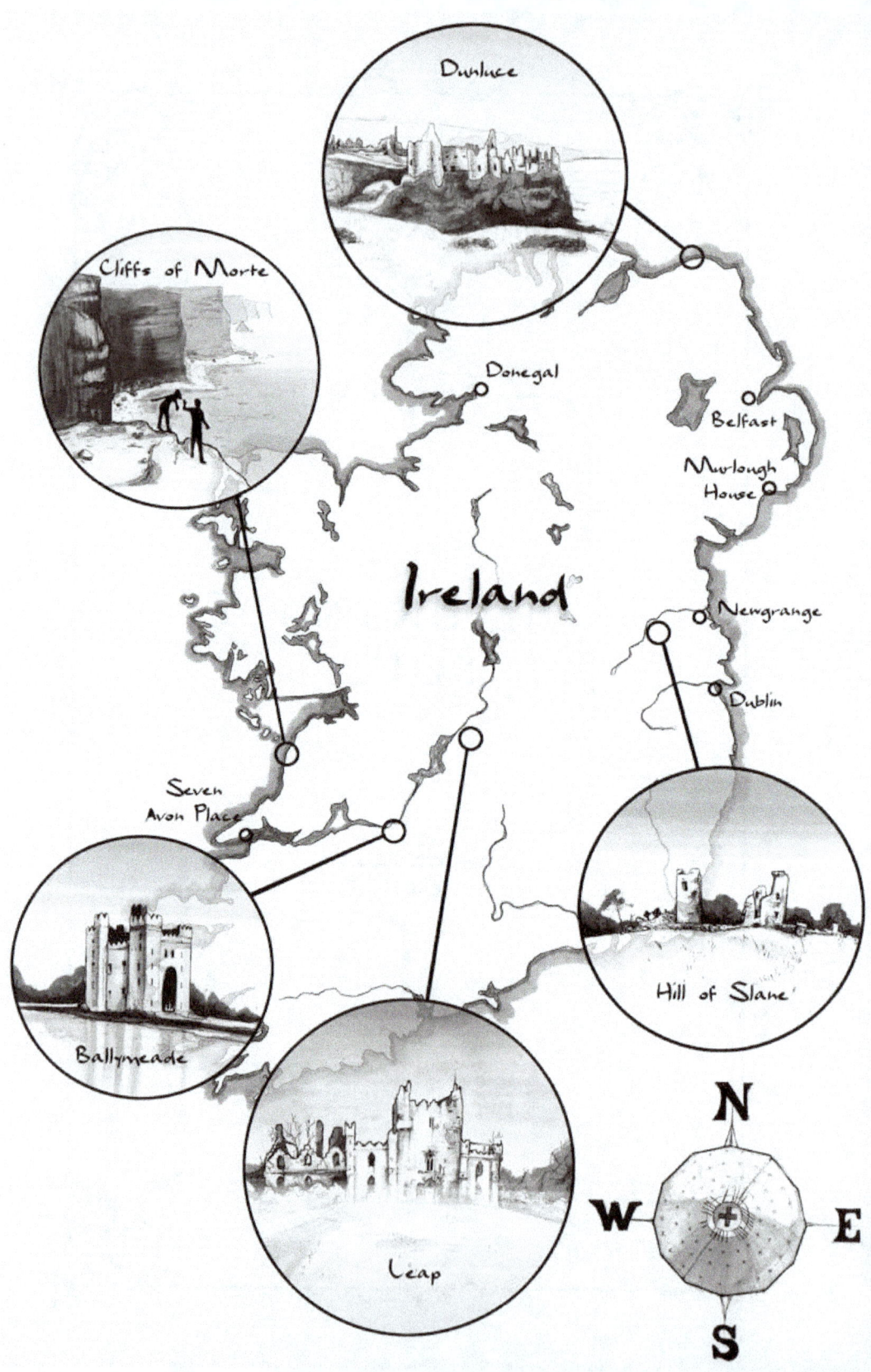

Dunluce

Cliffs of Morte

Donegal

Belfast

Murlough House

Ireland

Newgrange

Dublin

Seven Avon Place

Hill of Slane

Ballymeade

Leap

N

W E

S

You believe that there is one God. Good!
Even the demons believe that—and shudder.
—James 2:19

It's hard to say when I started to really believe in God. I guess I knew from when I was four years old down in Georgia and woke up in the middle of the night for no reason. I went out to the porch just in time to see lightning strike a tree. I kind of knew I was supposed to see it, so it didn't scare me. I didn't run inside and wake Mom—I never told anyone. Maybe it was him saying to me even way back then: *Know who you're dealing with, Elijah Creek.*

The armor quest and Reece's confidence in God pumped up my belief in him. Skid's Quella helped too. But what nailed it for me was what Dr. Eloise calls the Presence, the feeling I'd get that he was watching me from trees and sky—from everywhere; or when it seemed he stood by my side as real as Skid. I can't describe it except to say that it empties you out and fills you up at the same time. So I sort of always believed—kind of hard not to, really. Just look around.

God had to be the scariest being imaginable, scarier than all the terrors in the world combined. He was the Master of Breath with the power of the distant stars in his control.

So why would I want to be around him? That was the thing I couldn't get. I knew how dangerous he was—I'd seen it first-hand—but I was anxious to know him better, to move in closer. Why? Beats me, but there it is.

As for when I first believed in Satan, I can nail it down precisely: I was over three thousand miles from home on Halloween week of my freshman year. It was around 12:30.

CHAPTER 1

I was reaching my hand into the fire, trying to snatch something out of it. My mom screamed at me, but I kept saying, "I'm okay, I'm okay!" I wasn't being burned, but they didn't believe me. "I'm okay!" I insisted.

"Elijah?" Mom's worried voice called to me as if from far away. She shook me awake. "You were having a nightmare. Elijah, hon, it's all right. You're in your room."

I sat up—my head wobbling, my eyelids drooping.

"Dad needs you at the nature center right away, but it's not an emergency." She tousled my hair. "It's a *good* thing."

"'Kay." I forced my eyes open and surveyed the backyard. Through my open window, I saw the pool, as quiet and blue as the sky above. Beyond lay a plot of bare land. The Camp Mudjokivi trustees had bought up the spot that once was Old Pilgrim Church. Dad wanted to make it into a sand volleyball court—his idea being to attract college kids for twilight pool shindigs while campers trekked through Owl Woods on night hikes. I rubbed sleep from my eyes, threw back the covers, and stood, swaying like a drunk. "I'm okay."

Mom laughed. "You said that already. Dorian just called and asked me to drop by right away. He sounded mysterious on the phone." She walked out of the room, twisting her hair up and clipping it. "It's probably nothing. He loved teasing me as a kid. My brother, the bane of my existence!"

School was set to start in a week, and I dreaded it more than

usual. The five of us had spent half the summer roaming Council
Cliffs State Park. Roaming: it's what I like best in the world.
Then Reece got hurt. The doctors had to cut a bone out of her
leg, sand it off, and put it back in. Mei had been sent back to
Japan by her parents, who thought we were some weird religious
cult for kids. According to Reece, Mei's parents had found some
ideas for clan names that Mei had written in her journal—names
like Warriors of *Gi,* Fighters for God. To an outsider this might
seem weird, but we were just regular kids looking for an old suit
of armor with the power and history of spiritual warfare tied
up in it. Mei's parents didn't understand. They tried to get her
to break off from our group. When she wouldn't budge, they
shipped her back to Japan.

Reece missed Mei a bunch, and our clan was down to four
again: Reece, Skid, Rob, and me. I didn't get why God didn't
fix everything. Several times I'd even asked, *Why are you doing
this to Reece—taking her friends away, keeping her on crutches?
She trusts you. You're number one with her. Doesn't that count for
something?* I even said once, *Hey, if that's what it means to be on
your A-Team, no thanks.*

Dad met me in the reptile room of the nature center, wearing his usual khakis and Camp Mudj T-shirt. "We have buyers,
Elijah. The money's yours, son."

I perked up. "For the baby snakes? Cool!" We high fived.
"Really?! How much?" I peeked in on the writhing mass of
speckled blue racer babies, which were under maximum security
alert with a padlocked cage and a sign on the reptile room door:
"Authorized Personnel Only"—meaning Dad, Bo, and me.

Dad admired our stash of rare snakes. "We're still dickering
on the price," he answered.

"Dicker high, okay?"

"You earned it, Elijah." He broke into a chuckle. "You know

what *I'd* pay cold cash for: seeing you tear up the hill again—your fists full of baby blues—and Rob bounding sideways into the lake like a human pogo stick."

I thanked Dad again and headed back to the house. My dad's the greatest—ever. I want to make that clear before I tell this next part. I don't mean anything bad by this, but after that night earlier in the summer when he couldn't answer my questions about God and the other world out there, there was a shift in my thinking. Dad didn't have all the answers, especially answers to questions that I'd come to think were pretty important. I needed to know.

. . . . .

"Can I borrow that Quella sometime?" I asked Skid when we met by accident at the store. We were loading up on school supplies. The twins needed glue and colored pencils, and they'd graduated from round scissors to the pointy, dangerous ones. I hoped Mom was ready to part with her good drapes and anything else they could get a blade through.

"The Quella?" Skid asked. "Sure. Why?"

"Well," I stammered, getting shy all of a sudden, "you guys keep bugging me about church. I want to know what I'm getting into beforehand."

He pulled it out of his jacket pocket and handed it over. "Look up *saved,* Creek. That's what you're shooting for."

"Okay. Thanks."

Later that week—almost a year since we'd first gone into Old Pilgrim Church—I went up on Devil's Cranium and built a little fire, just enough to read by. This wasn't a vision quest; I was learning that God's showing up didn't depend on you sweating and showering and starving yourself. You could knock yourself out, and he might leave you sitting there in the dead quiet to think it out all alone. It was his call. Reece thought he'd be showing up in the Word to tell us what to do next, which was good enough for me.

It was funny, reading about *saved* in the Bible. There were a bunch of short paragraphs in different parts to hunt down and ponder a long time. It wasn't like a schoolbook. Learning about *saved* was kind of like my first prayer walk, only I wasn't walking a snake-infested meadow at dawn.

"He will save his people from their sins," I read.

Sins? Well, God, I used to lie, but I've steered away from it after finding the belt of truth. As for other sins, I haven't killed anyone except Salem. I haven't stolen anything except for that leather key ring from Mitts Bros. Department Store when Aunt Grace worked there. Once was all, and I lost the key ring the next day at school. I was seven and dumb at the time. Sorry 'bout that.

"Whoever wants to save his life will lose it, but whoever loses his life for me will find it."

Huh? What's that mean? I'll have to ask Reece or Skid.

I read, "What good is it, my brothers, if a man claims to have faith but has no deeds? Can such faith save him?" and "For it is by grace you have been saved, through faith."

Then in the book of Romans, it said, "If you confess with your mouth, 'Jesus is Lord,' and believe in your heart that God raised him from the dead, you will be saved." I considered the words in the mellow twilight of late summer.

From high on Devil's Cranium, I looked across Telanoo, which I had fully claimed as my own. No one else wanted it, no one used it, and I'd covered pretty much all of it looking for the armor. If I got creeped out—like the time I heard a coyote at sundown on the west perimeter, or the time of the deep fog when I lost my way—I'd call to El-Telan-Yah: a name I made meaning "the God of Telanoo is Yahweh."

· · · · ·

School started. Our moms got it into their heads from the PTO meetings that we each needed to build "a well-rounded academic and extracurricular portfolio in order to have an impressive college application." Translation: get involved in clubs and sports. After my experience with last summers's crop of college-age camp counselors (slimeball creatures of the night, according to Rob), I wasn't spotting any ivy-covered halls of higher learning on my horizon. The only things the counselors had taught me was how to catch poison ivy, how to build illegal fires in a state park, and how never to get asked to work at Camp Mudj again. No thanks. But our moms wouldn't budge, so Rob signed on to the swim team, school newspaper staff, and drama club. Skid went out for tennis and Spanish club. Reece got into choir and started her own girls' Christian club called Devo. I joined the cross-country team. It was no surprise as school got underway that powwow time was going to be harder to come by.

I even broke down and took a language class. Magdeline Independent didn't offer Hebrew or Greek, which I was now interested in because of the armor and the Quella. The closest option was Latin, which Mom said would help me speak English better. That made no sense, but I didn't want to argue with Mom over a dumb thing like school. So I signed on.

We freshmen were given a red alert about the Latin teacher, Miss Abner, but upperclassmen tended to use scare tactics to keep the upper hand. Supposedly her classes were sheer terror. I couldn't picture it. She was ancient, less than five feet tall, and blind as a bat. She wore pink and purple every day and wore her hair combed up and piled on her head like a plate of gray sausages. People said that she wore contact lenses with her glasses but still couldn't see. And if she heard talking during class, she'd just send a random person to the office. You could be the next victim! Seniors claimed that she knew Latin because she had dated Caesar.

Miss Abner admitted all of her shortcomings on the first day of class. She sat behind her big desk, rubbing her hands together like a fly does before it starts in on a dead squirrel. "My faculties aren't what they used to be," she said in an uppity, high-pitched voice. "I can't see well, my hearing has deteriorated, and they tell me my reflexes have slipped," she smiled out the window, "but at least I can still drive."

We laughed uncertainly. Was that supposed to be a joke?

Her head bobbed at each of us as if she were counting us. She made a thin, straight smile. "However, my teaching skills have not depreciated in the least since I entered the teaching profession right after the war."

Someone behind me whispered, "Trojan War."

"Your test over chapter one is on the board. Begin."

We first-day Latin students—there were only thirteen of us—traded terrified glances. *Hey, did I miss something here? A test? This is the first day, isn't it?*

Dora Ann, a straight-A student who regularly cheated to keep her grades up, raised a trembling hand. "Miss Abner, this is our first class. I just got my textbook this morning!"

Miss Abner bent her rigid neck at Dora Ann. "Didn't all of you just come from study hall?" she surveyed us knowingly. "I expect my students to come prepared *every* day!"

Basketball player Mike—big, blond, red-cheeked, and meek as a lamb—raised his hand. "Well, ma'am, we just didn't know that. Our other teachers usually give us *assignments* on the first day and tests *after* we've studied those assignments."

Obviously Miss Abner didn't like being compared to the other teachers. And she didn't like Mike insinuating that she didn't know the teaching business. She pushed back her chair, stood, and whirled to the board. She grabbed up a piece of chalk and drew angry circles around the test questions. Then she turned and squinted at us. Surrounded by a white halo of chalk and with meanness written all over her face, Miss Abner bobbed her head at us maliciously. "You shall not do well in my class if you are not prepared!"

In the cafeteria Rob's table was full of guys, so I slid my lunch tray across from Reece and said hey. She was in the process of sitting down by Emma Stone, a tall freshman with choppy, brown hair and cute freckles across her nose.

I said, "Hi, Emma. Same lunch time. Cool." Since Mei was gone, Reece had chummed up with Emma. She was bubbly and friendly enough, but nosy and a big talker—not at all like Mei. I could tell that she was just a stand-in best friend.

Reece slid her crutches under the table. "I'd ask you to get my tray, Elijah, but the guys would call you a wimp or worse."

"I'll get it," Emma said and took off.

Reece called after her, "Pizza, salad, two milks, no cake."

The three of us talked over lunch about the usual stuff—what classes we liked and which teachers spelled trouble with a capital *T.* "Abner," I said dejectedly. "She's everything they say and more. We had a test already. I flunked. She even spied out our schedules and knows when we have study hall!"

Reece was shocked. "Are you serious?" She huffed sympathetically at me and then narrowed her eyes at Miss Abner, who was hunched over in the teachers' corner. "Peanut butter and crackers—that's all she eats. They say that she drives on the wrong side of the road because she can't see."

A guy down the table jumped in. "She drives the biggest Caddy ever made, and last year it came at me on Scioto Road—a big, white barge and nobody behind the wheel!"

"What do you mean?" Reece asked.

"Oh, she was driving, all right. But Abner's so short that she has to look through the steering wheel!" He shuddered. "I hit the ditch, cracked my windshield, and knocked my wheels out of line. And she kept right on driving!" He tossed his fork down angrily. "The cops won't stop her. *They* all had her for Latin when *they* were in high school! She's untouchable!"

"No kidding," I said seriously.

When Emma left for class and the table thinned out, I saw my chance. "Hey, Reece, um, I borrowed Skid's Quella and read some of it last night."

She perked up. "Really?"

"I read up on *saved*."

"Want to take the plunge?"

When I paused, she smiled at me, "Elijah, it's only a matter of time. It'd be nice if you had faith before we found the shield of faith. You'd be ahead for once."

"If I wanted to, how would I do it?"

"What'd the Quella say to do?"

"A bunch of stuff."

"Like what?"

I shrugged. "Believe."

"Done. You do believe in God, right?"

"Kind of hard not to, since—" I lowered my voice, "we're looking for his armor."

"What else?"

"It says to confess with your mouth and call on God's name, be baptized, stand firm to the end, repent, something about grace. One part was about losing my life to find it—that doesn't mean dying, does it?"

Reece popped the last bite of pizza into her mouth and shook her head. "Living sacrifice. It means following God no matter what." She thought for a second. "But it *could* mean dying. Some of Jesus' followers were killed because they believed."

"Like the Moravian Delawares," I remembered.

"Yes, and for thousands of years before them. Millions have died because of their faith in God. The Stallards told us that." She blotted her mouth, wadded the napkin, and tossed it onto her plate. Then she clasped her hands under her chin and gave me a huge smile. "I really admire you for being the first one in your family. You're a man of courage, Elijah."

Reece Elliston was the prettiest girl I'd ever seen, and I was so busy looking at her that I hardly caught what she said next: "I can tell you right now that you won't be living the regular life: go to church on Sunday, put a buck in the offering plate, and light a candle at Christmas. Nope."

"Uh-huh."

"The real journey is scary."

"Yeah," I agreed, clueless.

"You need to meet with my minister right away."

"Minister? Okay. But first I should talk to my parents."

"And church is cool once you get used to it."

"This week? There's no rush, is there?" I asked uneasily.

Reece huffed at me. "There may be." All of a sudden she was squishy again. Her eyes went melty. She squeezed my hand, snuck her hand back in her lap, and glanced around shyly. "I'm so proud of you."

. . . . .

I don't know why it was so hard to bring up the subject of my beliefs. Dad was busy, and I didn't think Mom would understand. So I waited and followed Dad down to the lake that night. We talked about nothing until it got quiet. He gave me a quizzical look. "What is it, Elijah?"

"It's something I've been thinking about for a while. About giving my life to God."

Dad nodded. It was his cautious nod. "I see. I know many

good people who are religious. Reece is, isn't she?"

"That's not the reason."

"All right. May I ask why you're thinking about this?"

"Lots of reasons, I guess." I looked out over the lake to Owl Woods. "He made the world—Camp Mudj and the wind and waves and trees and everything. He tells nature what to do, and it does it. I've seen it happen, Dad. And I've been out there at night with no one around, and he's there. I can't explain it. He—" I didn't know how far to go with this. I wanted to tell Dad about how he talks to me and the others through the Quella and the silence and sometimes in a strong, quiet voice. But I didn't want Dad thinking of me the same way Mei's parents did. "He just wants me to, that's all."

"And how will you go about it?"

"Reece is going to have her minister talk to me. I'll have to start going to her church, but they'll give me a ride."

"I don't see any harm in going to church. But we'll discuss it with your mom first."

Mom wasn't totally keen on my being a Christian, but said I was getting old enough to make my own decisions. She made it clear I was still "accountable" to them and that church shouldn't take up all my time or interfere with my schoolwork. She also asked why. It was hard to say what I'd been through the past year. My parents thought the Stallards were weird. They were right, but weird didn't always mean bad. Weird could be cool if God had something to do with it.

That very next night, Reece's mom drove us to her church. Their minister was the guy who'd had the great sermon about Indians, so I wasn't nervous to talk to him. We sat in his office in a circle of big fake-leather chairs, just him and me and Reece who was beaming from ear to ear. He showed me some of the same verses I'd found in the Quella.

"I've read those," I said.

"Good! You've already done your homework about becoming a Christian."

I gulped. "There's homework!?"

Reece cracked up.

"Oh, there's homework, all right," he chuckled, "but God gives the tests. And they're usually pop quizzes."

Visions of Abner flickered before me.

"From what Reece told me, Elijah, you've already passed a few of those tests. You're the first in your family?"

"Yessir."

"We need to make this official, and then you can keep on with what you've started. First and foremost, this isn't about following a man's list of rules to live by. It's committing to a relationship with the living God."

"Okay," I agreed.

He looked at me thoughtfully. "Have you been attending a church regularly?"

"No. Just the time you preached about the Indians and once in a pentecoastal church in South Carolina."

"Pentecoastal?"

I shrugged. "That's what they called it. There was a lot of yelling and crying and dancing, but it was okay."

He smiled at Reece. "He's open-minded. I like that. So, Elijah, what made you decide to become a Christian?"

"Reece and Skid and ... God himself. He called me."

He looked a little stunned. "Wow." He sat back in his chair and gave me a look so curious it was scary. "He called you."

"Yessir."

"How'd that happen?"

I didn't want to tell how God told me to find the armor and how I'd figured that God needed me to be on his side. "It's kind of personal," I answered, glancing at Reece, "but it's true. He called me."

"Wow," he said again. "Perhaps we'll talk about that in the future."

I said okay, but hoped he'd be too busy or forget about it. It would be almost impossible to tell my story without spilling the beans about the armor.

He called my parents to be sure it was okay for me to make this decision. Then he explained the drill for Sunday morning: I'd have to come up in front of everyone, but only to answer a few questions and prove I was serious. Then I'd be baptized, dunked under water as a sign that I was dead to my old life and starting a new one. (When Reece had mentioned my taking the plunge, I didn't know she meant literally.)

The minister prayed for me, and Reece got all teary-eyed.

· · · · · ·

Skid knew the drill about getting dunked. Rob bugged me for details with a shifty look in his eyes, and I wondered if he was thinking about becoming an official believer too.

That Sunday I dressed up in my one white shirt and the new pants Mom bought for the occasion. Then I was really nervous. Skid's family was there even though this wasn't their regular church. Rob sat by himself in the back and sneaked out a couple of times to get a drink and go to the restroom. It made me feel good, his being nervous on my big day.

Reece and her mom were there with Officer Taylor. Seeing him and Reece's mom give each other goo-goo eyes was traveling-freak-show weird, so I didn't watch.

The sermon started, and Reece whispered, "When they sing the last song, you go. I'll come with you if you want."

"I can handle it," I said, acting brave.

Leading herds of kids on night hikes or wrestling a handful

of baby snakes seemed like no big deal compared to walking up in front of hundreds of strangers. It gave me the willies, but it was too late to back out.

When the sermon ended and the time came, the music sounded way far off like I was in a bubble. The first verse was over, and they went into the chorus. Reece nudged me and smiled, "It's now or never."

Stepping out, I went a little bit blank. But in no time I was standing at the front, looking at a sea of faces. The minister put his arm around my shoulder and introduced me as a friend of the Elliston family. Mom and Dad watched me from the back with a kind of sad pride as if they were thinking, *It could be worse; he could be out stealing hubcaps.*

I said aloud that I believed Jesus was the Son of God and that I wanted him to save me from my sins and be the Lord of my life. Then I was taken to a back room where I stripped down to my underwear and put on a white robe while organ music droned in the auditorium. Then someone started singing a song that was perfect for me, about running a race and asking the Spirit to fall like fire and rain.

A guy knocked on the door of the dressing room, and I went out. In front of everyone, I stepped down into a big tank of warm water where the minister was waiting for me with waders on. He turned me around, and that's when I caught a glimpse of something yellow floating on the water.

The minister said, "Elijah Creek, do you believe that Jesus is the Christ, the Son of the living God?"

A yellow rubber ducky bobbed toward me from the edge of the baptistery. Peeking around the corner from the backstage part of the baptistery was a fuzzy, blond head and one big, prankish eye.

You're dead, Wingate. Dead!

I had rehearsed what I was supposed to say, but my train of

thought derailed. "Umm …" A hundred ideas flipped through my mind. If the audience saw me with a rubber ducky on my holy dunking, I'd never live it down. I'd have to convert to another religion. My best idea was to go under fast and hard enough to make a tidal wave and send the thing back to its corner. "Amen!" I threw myself backward with a splash. Before I went under, the minister blurted, "I now bap—!"

I forgot to close my mouth. It was over in a second, and I came up sputtering, dripping wet. But my tidal wave had worked; the ducky listed toward the corner of the baptistery.

The minister frowned at me and stammered, "I now … I just … I have baptized you in the name of the Father and the Son and the Holy Spirit. Amen."

I'd jumped the gun on his ceremony and went under too soon. *Did it take?* Snickers came from the top of the steps. *Not funny, Rob Wingate! You just wait … uh-oh …* The ducky had bumped the wall and was heading back. I slapped at the water, hoping to change its course. The minister thought I was panicking again. He patted my back reassuringly and whispered, "It's okay, son. You're okay."

I wiped water from my face. *Oh brother! Those people out there think I clammed up, that I'm afraid of three feet of water! Dad'll never let me lifeguard at Camp Mudj, ever again! Wingate, you are so dead!*

Strange, that my first thought as an official sin-free Christian was to murder my cousin in cold blood.

People clapped like I'd done something great. The minister said I'd now have a new life. I didn't hear angels sing or anything. I didn't feel much different other than being wet and ticked off at Rob. But I'd taken the plunge, and things would be different now, I guessed. Once I got changed and the last prayer was said, I stood down front with my parents and the minister. Everyone came by and shook my hand. Some people I'd never met hugged me and said welcome. It was kind of like when Grandma plants a wet kiss on your cheek: icky but nice.

Reece crowded in line and hugged me hard. She whispered, "It's okay that you got choked up. I cried too!" She hugged me again right in front of everyone.

CHAPTER 2

On Monday, my life was full steam ahead for God (except for a dark plot stewing in the back of my mind on how to get even with Rob). But scheduling powwows suddenly had a new complication: Emma Stone. She hung around all the time and wasn't like Mei, who would give somebody a minute of privacy with Reece. I knew without asking that it was only a matter of time before Reece would want to bring her into the circle.

When Emma went to get Reece's lunch tray, I mentioned, "Hey, you're not telling her anything about … you know."

"No," Reece said glumly. "But I wish I had someone to talk to about it."

"You have us guys," I defended.

She shook her head. "It's not the same."

"We need a powwow. How about Tuesday? We could have it at your house … if the lovebirds aren't there," I said, teasing her about her mom and Officer Taylor. We compared schedules.

Reece said, "Tuesday would work."

"Work for what?" Emma sat Reece's tray down.

Instantly I had a made-up answer: Mom needed Reece to baby-sit. But I couldn't lie. "Some of us hang out every now and then," I said casually.

"I'm free on Tuesday," Emma said.

While Emma dug into her lunch, Reece and I argued with our eyes: hers were asking, *Is there a possibility we could bring her in?* My eyes answered, *Not a chance.*

Somehow during the year, with all the publicity and the police storming Camp Mudj over church burnings, mysterious fires, grave diggings, and journals stolen from the police department—not to mention the Kate Dowland mystery and the very belt of truth in custody for a while—somehow we'd kept the armor of God a secret from the world. And that's how it would have to be. My eyes told Reece, *We can't risk it.*

Hers said in a lonely way, *I know.*

I said to Emma, "Rob may have a club on Tuesday. (This was true.) I'll have to get back to you."

That very day Reece, Rob, and I found notes on our lockers in Skid's handwriting: *POWWOWASAP.*

· · · · ·

We settled on the Tree House Village at 9:00 that night. All the tree houses were under roof but hadn't passed city inspection yet; we wouldn't be bothered.

The three of us had just gathered when Skid swooped in on his skateboard. Halfway down the path to the lake, he pulled a piece of paper out of his pocket and waved it in the air. At breakneck speed he zipped around the lake, ditched the board, and flew up the steps to the tree house. "I have a letter, people, and wait until you hear! We be gettin' some praise on!" He dropped down cross-legged and read:

Dear Children, We pray you are doing well in your first year of high school. Here's what we have on the shoes. It's obvious they are not from the Roman era but of Spanish origin. As to how they were engraved with Langundowagan, *the Delaware Indian word for "peace," here are our theories:*

In the early days of America, native peoples were sometimes taken to Europe, either by force as a curiosity to the conquerors, or voluntarily to get an education. Perhaps a Native American picked up these sandals in Europe in the eighteenth century where he heard the gospel. Upon his return to America—or at his death—he left his sandals behind in Europe, engraved with his native word for "peace" as a witness to his faith. Another spiritual warrior wore the sandals to Ireland where they joined the rest of the armor.

A more likely possibility is that these shoes belonged to Cabeza de Vaca, whom we mentioned before. In 1528 his boat ran aground near what is now Galveston, Texas. He met gentle tribes and preached the gospel of peace when many churchmen were adding to their numbers by cruel force. De Vaca went back to Spain, then South America, then back to Europe where he died. Since the Renaissance was a time of global travel, it's not a far stretch that the next owner of the shoes went to the British Isles, i.e., Ireland, where Dowland eventually purchased the full armor. This is the strongest Native American connection we have found.

Children, we realize that the shoes are perhaps the least glamorous of all the armor pieces, but certain hunters of religious or Indian relics might want them for the historical significance.

Yes, we do keep saying that the armor is not worth a great deal as a relic, but the world of archaeology is an unpredictable market. Items which had been gathering dust on our shelves for decades have recently caught the eye of certain collectors. All the more reason to keep the search to ourselves.

Skid looked up, said, "Okay, here's where it starts getting good," and continued:

On another matter ... all of you—but especially Elijah—seemed upset about the missing sword. What we feared about the sword may be true. From what we can deduce, there was a sword during the time of Paul. We may even trace a sketchy trail all the way back to creation. After sin entered the world, the Garden of Eden was barred from humankind with a fiery, ever-turning instrument of war. It must have been a perilous-looking thing, double-edged and glittering, a brandishing, slashing, thrusting weapon, even more terrifying in that it accompanied the angel-beasts known as cherubim. The sword, which represented God's word of judgment, was apparently visible at that time. Whether it was a physical sword can't be determined. (Occasionally—and not always pleasantly—the senses are exposed to this parallel universe we call the spiritual realm.)

Why it is not with the rest of the armor is most vexing. On a positive note: a "sword of flame" is described in a few little-known writings from around the world, and depicted in certain carvings and tapestries from abroad. Whether their inspiration was the actual sword itself is currently our most perplexing question.

Skid looked up. "Okay, now it gets to us."

We have a hint of a sword around 400 AD in Ireland and wending its way across Europe through the Middle Ages and then back again. The sword seemed to appear in concurrence with the renewed interest in the Word of God. Here is our plan. Skid paused and grinned. *We must start in Ireland right away. We have written to your parents in a separate mailing to ask permission and will do the same for your school.*

We are calling it an educational and cultural tour, which it most certainly is. Any of your parents is welcome to chaperone since they do not all entirely trust us. Please move quickly on passports. Rest assured that we will keep costs at a minimum. In the meantime would you look through the journals or contact Francine Dowland to get the name of the castle where the armor was purchased? We must know where we're going in order to get there!

All Our Best, The Stallards

Skid raised the letter and let it drift down on the breeze. Then he sat back, proud as a peacock—like he had something to do with it.

I couldn't believe my ears. "Ireland? They mean it?"

Skid punched his fists into the night sky. "To the Emerald Isle, my people!"

Eyes bugged, Rob said, "They already asked our parents?!"

I glanced at Reece. A look of doubt clouded her face. "Wait!" she said. "Shouldn't we check Dowland's house first? I mean, we never did, and the sword could be hidden in a dark corner. Actually the next piece is the shield of faith and then the helmet. The sword is last. I'll bet Darrell—I mean Officer Taylor—could get us into Dowland's house."

Rob said, "Remember what Francine said? There was no sword with Dowland's armor."

Skid huffed, "The Stallards don't give up so easily."

Reece was the least pumped about going to Ireland to search for the sword of the Lord. I wondered if her mom had the money. I worried that Reece didn't have the strength.

We made our way back around the lake, chattering about whether we'd get in trouble with God if we found the pieces out of order and about going back to the old Dowland place. The first chance I got, I pulled Reece aside and whispered, "About Ireland—it's like that time at Devil's Cranium when we all wanted to get to the ruin, but you didn't think you could make it. Remember what I said then: If I'm going, you're going."

She smiled weakly. "I hope so."

I called Francine several times, but no one answered. I wondered if she was on vacation, or sick. Or dead. After a few days, I ran by the police station to ask Officer Taylor if he knew anything. In the meantime Reece went through the Dowland journals for a clue about where to start once we got to Ireland. When she turned up nothing, Rob went over them again. He'd already been studying maps of Ireland, getting familiar with place names. "If a place is referenced in the journals, I'll spot it," he said with confidence.

· · · · ·

By pure miracle our parents gave the go-ahead. Aunt Grace was to chaperone and do research for her tea room. We were to leave the last week in October if all our paperwork came in.

We had a ton of things to talk about every day, but Emma ate with Reece and kept prying about when we could all hang out. Don't get me wrong; she was nice and cute too. But when it came out that the four of us were going to Ireland, she'd be on us like scum on a pond. Her parents were both doctors; she'd be able to scrounge up money for a plane ticket. As for me, I used the snake money to help pay for mine—funny how things work out sometimes.

Reece hadn't given us guys her final word on Ireland, and my attempts to keep Emma out of the loop were wearing thinner by the day. I strong-armed Rob into giving up lunch at the guys' table to start eating with us. I needed help in the chitchat department to keep Reece in top-secret mode.

We talked grades. "I have two big fat Fs in Latin already! All I've learned so far is Caesar's motto. It looks like this—" I wrote on a napkin *Veni, Vidi, Vici,* "which means, 'I came, I saw, I conquered.' But in old Latin when all the *V*s were *W*s, it comes out weeny, weedy, weeky."

Reece cackled. "What kind of a wimpy motto is that?!"

Rob said, "Sounds Hawaiian," and proceeded to stand up and go into a hula dance, singing, "Weeky weeky weeny weedy wooky cooky hooky," and so on until the whole cafeteria thought he was freshman psycho of the year.

Skid saw the proceedings and sauntered over to our table.

Reece was dying laughing as she said, "You're embarrassing us, Rob. Why don't you go back to the guys' table?"

Skid leaned coolly over to Rob. "You danced a beansy weansy

hula for the masses at Magdeline High. You can never go back."

· · · · ·

I thought Aunt Grace was going to Ireland with us until one night after dinner. My bedroom window was open, and I heard Mom ask Dad if she could go to Ireland instead of Aunt Grace. I stuck my head out. "That'd be cool!"

She viped up at me. "Elijah, you weren't supposed to be listening!" She poked Dad playfully in the chest. "Your son has radar." Then she turned to me, "Not a word, you hear?"

October rolled on with no news on Francine, which had me worried. Reece was still on crutches and tight-lipped about going to Ireland. My cross-country coach was miffed about my leaving the country. "You got talent, Creek," he'd said when I broke the news. "But you can't come in here, show your stuff, and …" He'd shoved his hands roughly into his pockets. "I may have to rethink you. Lack of commitment is bad for morale."

I had to be doing something about the next piece of armor. On a blustery October Saturday, I gathered our clan of four at Dowland's place, 26 Jewett Avenue in Newpoint. Officer Taylor had cleared it for us to have a last look around the house before it went up for auction. Two men were there, appraising the contents of the house.

"Shield *and* helmet *and* right arm," Rob whispered as we split up for the search, each one to a room.

"And sword," I reminded.

"Francine said there was no sword," said Rob flatly. "It's still in Ireland."

"We don't know that. She and Stan split up years ago, remember? He may have gone back to Ireland to find it!"

Deep down I wanted the sword to be in Ireland so we could go on an awesome trip and find it there. But I didn't want Reece fretting herself into a relapse over it. "We'll look around here.

Clean sweep—don't miss a spot."

I took the dining room, a small room with a pine table, a hutch painted blue, and an old mahogany desk with one drawer. The hutch had the usual: dishes on the top shelves, tablecloths and stuff stored in the bottom cabinet. I nosed around and checked for secret compartments.

Reece came into the room. "Nothing in the kitchen but cookware. The pantry's almost bare. Can I help you look?"

"Nothing here. Did you check for secret compartments?"

"No, but I didn't see anything unusual."

I saw my chance. "Reece … about Ireland … your mom's going to let you go, isn't she?" It was my way of putting it nice, but cut-to-the-chase Elliston didn't let me get by.

"What you're asking is whether I'll be well enough."

"Yeah, that's what I mean. Are Skid and I going to be hauling you around a whole country on a stretcher?"

She smiled. "That's better. I'm in therapy, hoping I can get down to using a cane. Mom and I are praying every day. You pray too."

"Don't try so hard that you relapse." I fiddled through a drawer of maps and papers and other junk. "I … really want you to go." It was then that my hand hit something: a gun. I pulled it out and laid it on my palm. The words "Victor 22 Cal.R.F." were inscribed on the barrel.

Reece and I locked eyes. "A gun!" she cried.

In a flash I remembered how Stan Dowland had written my name three times in his journal and crossed it off twice. I couldn't help wondering whether he'd carried this weapon when he stalked me.

"A gun?" an appraiser came from the living room.

I offered it to him. "It was in a drawer behind the papers."

He looked it over. "Huh. Twenty-two caliber, cracked handle, probably works okay. Not worth much, but I'll have Norton take a look at it." He headed toward the bedroom calling, "Norton, we missed a gun." He turned to me and nodded approvingly. "Thanks."

The four of us gathered back in the living room empty-handed.

Rob said, "The boxes in his closet were just old taxes and clothes." He looked around the living room at the piles of magazines and papers. "We could go through these."

Reece said, "That would take forever."

"We should shake out a few," he insisted, "to see if he hid clues or a map between the pages."

Skid said, "The bathroom and spare bedroom are no-shows. What about the basement?"

"Check it out, will you?" I answered. "Reece and I will go through some of these stacks."

"Aye, aye, Cap'n," Skid said. "Wingate, give me a hand."

Reece and I stayed busy, but we were both thinking the same thing. If she really couldn't go to Ireland, would I stay behind too, like I'd said? I'd thought hard about it and reasoned that if I was now a man of God, I had to be a man of my word. No matter how much it hurt. "About Ireland," I said quietly, "I meant what I said."

"That's what worries me," she said without looking up.

In a few minutes, Skid and Rob came pounding up the steps. Rob huffed, "Shelves of jars, a table full of dead plants under the back window, a couple of old mattresses."

I perked up. "Mattresses?"

Skid shook his head. "I thought the same thing, but we pressed on them and checked for rips or new stitching. Nothing stashed there. Nada."

"Anybody check the attic?" I asked.

Rob said, "The appraisers have been up there raking through

the insulation. Lots of people hide treasures and documents in their attics, but it's empty."

"You're sure? They missed a gun, you know."

Rob slumped. "If you want to go up there and get itchy and have spiders drop on you or get bird lice and have to go get medication, go right ahead."

Skid's smiling, green eyes slid from Rob to me. "Voice of experience."

"The garage," I said. "Let's check there."

Reece stood slowly. "If we don't find anything, don't be discouraged. We're getting our directions from God now, not Dowland."

I unlocked the door to the garage, opened it, and sighed. "There's nothing here. The car's gone. The burlap sacks are gone. He already buried the pieces." We wandered out to the backyard, a small lot that slanted up to a fence surrounded by trees and thick shrubs. "Maybe he hid them in there."

Rob said, "If we're supposed to look for the shield of faith in the opposite place—a place of doubt—his home would be the spot, all right."

"We're not following Dowland anymore," Reece insisted.

"But he's the one who hid the armor," Rob argued.

I strolled to the edge of the property and hooked my fingers through the chain-link fence. "What other clues do we have?" I peered through the fence into the underbrush. No disturbed ground. No lingering smell of fresh dirt. "Nothing here," I said with confidence.

We stood in the tree-rimmed yard, empty-handed. "God's supposed to tell us," Reece kept saying.

"How?" I asked.

"Let's think. And pray," she said. "You go first."

"What?" I asked.

"Pray. You're a Christian now."

"You mean out loud?"

Skid smirked, "Or use smoke signals."

Reece herded us into a circle. I shoved my hands into my pockets and dropped my head. "Okay." I cleared my throat. "Okay, God. We're standing here in Dowland's backyard in Newpoint—"

Skid snickered. "He doesn't need latitude and longitude, Creek. He's God."

Reece hissed, "Shhh!" but I couldn't let it pass.

Head still bowed but eyes on Skid's lower half, I brought my foot up behind his knee and yanked, throwing him off balance. His head shot up. He grabbed my sleeve. I threw him off. He regained his balance and lunged for me. I took off for the fence. Rob burst out laughing.

Reece yelled, "You guys!! Cut it out! This is prayer time!"

Skid hollered, "He's gonna need prayer!"

Adrenaline rushed through me. I grabbed the fence with one hand; my feet scrambled up, got wings, and sailed over. I turned around victoriously. Skid slammed his palms into the fence, defeated but grinning. He was thinking up a wisecrack when Reece butted in. "Let's just go back to Council Cliffs."

I climbed back over the fence. "We've wandered around those hills long enough."

"The raven is our only sign," she said in a frustrated tone. "God won't answer our prayers if we're not serious."

"I'm serious," I said. "Do you always have to stand still when you pray? Can't you pray on the move?" I thought a moment. "We've gone through those hills long enough."

"You just said that," she griped.

"I know," I said curiously, "but it seems important." The words echoed in my head again.

Reece asked, "What do you mean?"

"I don't know … hey … the trunk of his car! If he hasn't buried the pieces, they may be in the trunk."

Skid nodded. "Worth a shot."

I said, "Rob, go ask the appraisers where the car is."

While we waited for him, I caught Reece staring at me. She said, "Say it again."

"We've looked through those hills long enough?"

Reece turned to Skid. "Got the Quella? Look up 'hills' and 'long enough.'"

Skid said, "Okay. Here's what I have: 'Then the LORD said to me, "You have made your way around this hill country long enough; now turn north."'"

Rob came huffing and puffing across the yard. "They had it towed to a junkyard."

"Where?"

"North of here on Highway 137."

CHAPTER 3

Chills went down my spine. "North ... how far?"

"About a mile."

I took off.

"Wait!" Reece said. "Skid's mom is on her way!"

"Tell her to pick me up at the junkyard!"

Reece called to me again, but I was already over the rise of Crayford Avenue. "Cross-country training!" I yelled back. A feeling of urgency and dread swept through me. "Now turn north," came the words of the Bible. *Now.*

Halfway there I noticed a pillar of blue smoke. The dream came back: me reaching into the fire, mom yelling, me shouting, "I'm okay!"

North. I sped, gulped air. Cars sped past. My feet pounded pavement. I wheeled into the junkyard and crashed through the door of an office not much bigger than a gatehouse.

The man inside was looking through a grimy notebook. He jumped. "What the—!"

"You got a car here from Stan Dowland? From his estate? You would have just gotten it, an old blue sedan—"

"Yeah, yeah." He seemed annoyed that I'd scared him.

"I need something out of it. Did you know that there's a fire out there? Can't tell if it's on your property, but you may want to check it out."

He came out of his run-down office cussing. "People burning off weeds in this wind. Idiots!"

"Where's the car?" I asked. "There may be something important in the trunk!"

He was paying attention to the smoke. "Grass fire." He muttered more curses. "Looks like it's come over my line. It'll smoke out the rats. We'll be crawling with 'em."

"The car!" I asked again.

He dialed the fire station, gave his location, slammed the phone, and took off down the dirt road. "Grab a shovel!"

By the time we'd reached the back of the junkyard, the smoke had grown to black billows stinking of burning rubber. The fire had reached a stack of tires. "You stay back," he ordered. He cussed at the rats scampering our way and batted them off the path with his shovel. "We got trouble."

"I have to look in Dowland's car," I insisted.

"Not if it's near the fire. I haven't siphoned the gas out." Here came a handful of men alongside the burning field, waving shovels. Desperately I scanned the lot for Dowland's dusty-blue wreck.

"Where is it!?" I demanded. Then I saw it just beyond the burning tires. A siren wailed in the distance, but there wasn't time. Flames filled the windows of the car and licked the ground underneath. The tires smoldered and hissed. I ran toward it.

"Get back, kid! It could explode any minute!" he yelled.

I got as close as I could and looked inside. A window shattered from the heat. Flames bellowed out in my direction. I reeled backward. The seats were ablaze. The junkyard man drew his shovel in front of me. "Get back!"

"I have to check the trunk!" I ran to the back of the car, aimed the point of my shovel at the lock, and rammed.

"This could blow, you fool!" he screamed.

"I'm okay!" I yelled. I aimed and rammed again and then again. "I'm okay!" My hearing went into radar mode, each sound separate and distinct: the crackling of the flames, the hissing of tires, the boiling smoke, sirens and fire engine horns blaring, then a car horn and people screaming.

I rammed the shovel once more, and it stuck. I put my whole weight into it and pushed. *Crack!* The handle broke. In shock I stumbled backward. *No good!* The blade was still lodged under the trunk lid. I threw down the handle and looked around frantically for another tool.

"What are you doing, kid?!" came the voice of the junkyard man behind me. "Trying to kill yourself? Whatever's in there isn't worth it."

Leverage. I need leverage. I grabbed a cement block with one hand and yanked for all I was worth. *Got it!* I flew toward Dowland's car, winding up for a throw as I went. Somehow I swung that block in a perfect arc over my head. It came down with a blow dead on the shovel head with such force that the tip broke, but the trunk lid flew open.

Hot, acidy smoke billowed from the trunk and filled my nose. Instantly I couldn't breathe. I reeled back, choking. The people screaming behind me were coming closer. *I'm okay!* I covered my nose with my T-shirt, gulped in a breath, and reached into the smoke, my eyes burning.

I felt around on the hot floor of the trunk … rough carpet, a cardboard box, and burlap. *Burlap!* I grabbed, pulled out something wide and heavy. *Shield!*

Flames roared and voices screamed, "It's going to blow!!"

"Get out of there!"

"Elijah, NO!"

The junkyard man grabbed the back of my T-shirt and yanked. Blindly I stumbled backward and then turned and ran, my eyes and lungs scorched. People ran up to me, Skid and Rob and Skid's mom among them. The men with shovels stared at me like I was crazy.

"I got it, man! I got it!" I said.

"The shield and helmet?!" Rob gasped.

A bolt of horror shot through me. *Helmet?!*

I turned back to the burning car. Skid grabbed my arm. "You're not going—"

Boom! The ground shuddered. Flames shot out from under the car in all directions. The crowd cried out in one voice and pulled back. Yellow flames engulfed the black, brittle frame of Stan Dowland's car.

"The helmet and sword ..." I moaned. "What if—"

Reece was beside me now. "C'mon, let's get this in the car before people start asking questions."

It was a ritual by now to take our treasure to a secret spot and examine it. We had peeked into the bag and cheered. It was a shield, all right.

"Devil's Cranium," I whispered on the way back home.

Skid swore his mom to secrecy. When she dropped us off at the Camp Mudj maintenance building, she pulled me over and said firmly, "Elijah, I'm not your mom. But here's fair warning: you pull a caper like that again, and I'll sic your mother, your father, and Dom loose on you all at once."

"I'm okay," I said.

"Then why are you covering your arm?"

I lifted my hand. The hair on my forearm was singed off, and a blister rose around a nasty-looking red patch. It stung like the dickens. "I'll put aloe on it. I'm okay."

"By the grace of God!" she barked. "That armor is important to you kids. But I will not stand by and watch my son's best friend fry himself to a crisp! I'm a mother! We have a code of ethics!"

Marcus Skidmore's best friend? Me? He told his mom I'm his best friend?! I beamed.

She slapped my shoulder with the back of her hand. "You

take me serious now."

"Yes, ma'am. It won't happen again."

"You got that right!"

The four of us loaded the golf cart with food and gear and a first-aid kit. I drove by the house to let Mom know where we were going. She met us at the door with a strange look on her face. I thought Carlotta Skidmore had already ratted on me.

"What's up?" I asked uneasily, hiding the burn.

She said, "Elijah, I need to talk to you—alone."

She knows. Carlotta snuck over here while we loaded the cart and ratted on me. This means a permanent grounding for sure.

"What'd I do?" I asked, bracing to get viped and grounded.

"It's not you, hon." She looked over my shoulder to the others. "You're in the middle of something, aren't you?"

Reece waved from the front seat of the cart and said, "It's okay. We'll wait at the lodge."

Skid drove the cart off, and I followed Mom into the formal living room where Dad always brought me for the big talks. The house was empty. A weird feeling crept over me. *What's wrong?* The nightmare of Rob's parents' near split popped into my head. I asked, "Where's Dad?"

"He's with a group of campers. Have a seat."

We sat together on the couch, my heart thumping, my mind spinning, and my arm in searing pain.

Are Mom and Dad splitting up? Or is it Francine? Did word come that she's dead? Since she was our only lead on the sword, is the trip cancelled? Or is it my Latin grade?

"It's not bad news, Elijah. It might even be good news." She took a deep breath and so did I. "You know those false walls your Uncle Dorian and Aunt Grace uncovered at The Castle a while back?"

"Yeah …"

"Well, Dorian found some documents in there. Papers about the history of Magdeline … and possible information about our biological mother."

I sat back, relieved and excited. "You know who she is?"

"Not yet. But we have something to go on for the first time in our lives. We grew up in Magdeline but never lived in that old house. We can't imagine why our family secrets were hidden behind a false wall. I haven't told the girls yet. I don't want to get their hopes up. But I thought you should know. If you catch snippets of our talking, that's what's going on—," she tugged on my ear, "we can't get anything past you anyway."

She settled into the couch, curled her feet up under her, and broke into a big, shaky smile. "I've wondered about it a lot. After your Grandma Wingate passed away, I thought that was the end of it. She was the only one who knew about our biological parents. If we find out anything solid, I'll let you know. The search might take months and might involve my traveling some. That's why I'm going to Ireland. There's a woman there who may have information. We have other leads—in Scotland. But this one seems the most promising. We'll have to be patient with the process. Dorian and I have talked it over and agree that finding our mother is more important than your Aunt Grace sampling Irish teas."

Thinking about my own quest, I said, "I hear you."

"Let Dorian tell Rob in his own way."

"Sure." I heaved a sigh of relief. No bad news. And the possibility of a new grandma? Don't get me wrong, Grandma Creek was a bucket load of funny-old-person—enough for twenty kids—but it couldn't hurt to have another one.

. . . . .

Light mist was falling in Telanoo when the four of us stopped short of the summit of Devil's Cranium under a flame-red maple tree. I unloaded the pop-up tent and had it set up in a minute. "This will hold us all." We crawled in, and the red tent and leaves cast a glow over our circle of four.

Reece put on gloves and started to take the shield out of the bag. Then she stopped and sighed, "This was Mei's job. And … she always made the sketches too. Who's going to make sketches?"

"I will," I said.

Rob said, "Or … we could take pictures and mail them to Japan. She could make sketches and send them back."

Reece said, "Let's do that! Mei misses us like crazy!"

Skid said, "Not that we're ragging on your talent, Creek, but keeping Mei involved is a good idea."

Reece pulled out the shield of faith. It was about three feet across and round in shape, but the edges were angular, not curved. Rob counted the angles. "It has twelve sides."

Skid nodded. "Twelve tribes, twelve apostles."

Golden brads or knobs moved in a spiral pattern from the outside edge to a shiny disc with gray, metal crosspieces in the center. Surrounding the disc were slashes radiating out like ir-regular sunbeams made of the same gray metal. The surface of the shield was pock-marked and smudged.

"It's heavy," Reece said, "definitely metal; the back is hard leather or wood."

There were two leather straps on the back, one in the middle and one on the side to hold the shield with. I stuck my arm through the bands and held it in front of me.

Skid quoted, "'Take up the shield of faith, with which you can extinguish all the flaming arrows of the evil one.'"

Noting the singed hairs on my arm, I asked, "What's that mean—'flaming arrows of the evil one'?"

Skid checked the Quella. "The commentary says they are Satan's attempts to destroy us. The point is that faith in God will stop his destroying power."

"Then … the … evil one probably doesn't like it that we have this."

We got quiet. After a minute Reece asked, "Do you see any letters?"

"Not yet," said Rob. "But they may be encrypted. The Stallards said so."

I borrowed one of Reece's gloves and ran my fingers over the shield's war scars. Black dust stained my fingertips. "This is soot. These are scorch marks."

"Here's something else," Skid said, reading from the Quella. "It's talking about our reward being kept in Heaven for … 'you, who through faith are shielded by God's power until the coming of the salvation that is ready to be revealed in the last time. In this you greatly rejoice, though now for a little while you may have had to suffer grief in all kinds of trials. These have come so that your faith—of greater worth than gold, which perishes even though refined by fire—may be proved genuine.'" He nodded. "Deep stuff."

My fingers grazed the burn bandage on my arm.

"Hey look," Reece said, "the backing is loose."

Rob said, "Be careful that it doesn't fall apart."

She gently pried the metal covering of the shield from the backing. "Elijah, do you have a flashlight?"

I dug it out of the equipment box and clicked it on.

"There's something in here," she said.

We moved in. "What is it?" Rob asked eagerly.

"Metal braces … and an old piece of paper!"

Even Reece's little hand wouldn't fit down into the space. It took a good twenty minutes of shaking and poking to get it out without tearing the paper. At last, it came free and dropped out.

"It's like a page from a book," Reece said.

Rob said, "English letters, but it's another language."

"Maybe it talks about faith," I said.

Rob studied it up close. "This isn't paper. It's parchment. We have to get a picture of this to the Stallards!"

CHAPTER 4

Latin was a nightmare, as expressed in a poem scrawled in the back of my secondhand Latin book: *Latin is a language, as dead as dead can be. It killed all the Romans, and now it's killing me.* The problem wasn't my mind being weak on language. Basketball Mike was a brain, but he popped antacids before class every day; straight-A cheater Dora Ann dropped out after the first week. We went from being the unlucky thirteen to the twelve martyrs. But every day Rob walked by on his way to lunch, doing his hula dance and mouthing words like weeny, weedy, weeky. No matter how rotten class was, Rob's loony hula dance made it bearable.

Most days I'd recuperate from Abner's verbal lashings by running cross-country. I was the coach's favorite from day one because I could outrun everyone else and was already close to breaking the school record. It was sweet that I could chalk up all those jogs through Telanoo as "building a well-rounded academic and extracurricular portfolio." Maybe college was back on the horizon after all. Maybe I could major in roaming.

Since we couldn't get together much—what with all the portfolio building and Emma's raging curiosity—I called the Stallards myself about the shield and mentioned the idea of sending pictures to Mei.

Dr. Eloise freaked. "Oh dear, you haven't done it already, have you?!"

"No," I said.

"Then don't! You shouldn't develop photos at an outside

establishment. No part of the armor is to be seen by the public eye. One of you will either have to draw the shield by hand or … none of you have a darkroom, do you? … No?"

I mentioned the page we found in the shield.

"Is that so? Can you read any of the words?"

I did the best I could, and she thanked me for trying. "I've made a few notes. We'll see where this takes us."

The Stallards called back the next day. They were antsy to fly down but couldn't. "We are condensing our classes as it is to free up time for Ireland. Keep everything under wraps," she warned again.

Was it my imagination, or were the Chicago archaeologists getting more secretive and more worried about the quest?

Dr. Eloise's voice crackled through the phone, "Ah, before I forget, what have you heard from Francine Dowland?"

A lump formed in my stomach. "We can't find her."

Long pause. "Oh dear," she said darkly.

"I called and called and even asked Officer Taylor to help me," I defended. "It's like she disappeared."

There was another long pause. "We … we must not lose faith. Faith without works is dead, isn't it?" she said cheerily.

· · · · · ·

I'd started going to Reece's church, and nobody gave me grief over the rubber ducky caper. (I'd put revenge against Rob on hold for lack of time.) Going to church involved a lot of sitting still and listening, sort of like school. But since the teens banded together in the front center pews, I got to sit with Reece and her church friends who were mostly from other schools. All of a sudden, I had a new circle of friends.

The minister usually talked about Jesus and other Bible people and told pretty decent jokes. I always went away feeling really good on the inside, though I can't put my finger on why exactly.

As Halloween approached, he started a set of sermons on the occult. He mentioned The Crystal See by name, calling it a place of deception at best, a gateway to Hell at worst. He pointed a finger down over the pulpit and warned us kids point-blank: *"Necromancy* means contacting the dead, a practice among the nations since the dawn of time. And the question we ask is, does it work or are mediums frauds?" He paused. "The Lord never said it had no power. He said don't do it. In exchange for the remote possibility that one actually can give you supernatural knowledge from beyond, you expose yourself to the influence of demons. Demons impersonate the dead to control the living and lure them away from God."

Skid had told me that the spirit world was not a safe place. A wispy chill went down my backbone. Why? I didn't know.

The minister looked at the whole congregation. "When the Lord spoke about the end of days, he said: 'At that time many will turn away from the faith and will betray and hate each other, and many false prophets will appear and deceive many people. Because of the increase of wickedness, the love of most will grow cold.' He also asked this unsettling question: 'When the Son of Man comes, will he find faith on the earth?'

"Friends, it's an ominously simple formula he gave us: no faith in Jesus, no love in the world."

Well, I hate to admit it, but that mention of The Crystal See just made me want to stop by, just to peek into the spirit world and see what it was like. All this spirit stuff was new to me, and I wanted to roam around in it.

I mentioned that to Skid the next day at my locker, and he about took my head off. "Just see how people live who believe those lies, just once, Creek. My Dad's been to West Africa where voodoo was born—saw it firsthand. It's all filth and fear." He jabbed himself in the chest, his eyes blazing. "My ancestors were stuck in it. My distant relatives still are; it's my roots. Along dirt roads you got piles of black, crusty, oozing slime where people pour blood over their gods day after day."

"Weird," I said agreeably.

"You can put a different face on it, call it fortune-telling or a séance, but it's all the same. It's like worshiping a boo hag, but there's a real entity behind it, luring you in. Once you're in, it don't want to let you out."

He was getting more like his military dad every day. I backed off. "Okay, okay. I was just saying …"

He cooled off and helped me shove my books into the locker. "I'm supposed to look after you, that's all. Keep you on the straight and narrow."

·　·　·　·　·

By mid-October only Reece's passport hadn't come. There was still no word about Francine. But the Stallards hadn't canceled the trip, so permission was granted for us to be out of school for a week-long "educational and cultural tour of Ireland." The teachers managed to knock some wind out of our sails by assigning us homework for that week. Abner's two-page nightmare was for me to explain why the Roman hordes had or had not invaded Ireland during their conquest of the known world—in Latin, of course. How I was supposed to find this out while snooping through an old castle was beyond me. But question Miss Abner and you fry.

Reece came up to my locker by herself. I caught her shocked expression and expected the worst. "You'll never guess! Not in a million years!"

I knew it was good news.

"Guess where Mei is!"

I looked around.

"Not here. Better! In London! She's doing a homestay to

study English for six weeks!"

"That's great," I said mildly.

"Don't you get it? She can come to Ireland and go with us to look for—" she glanced around and lowered her voice, "the you-know. See how God worked it out?"

I didn't see.

"If she had stayed here in America, her parents would never have let her go with us," Reece bubbled over, "but now she can tour the British Isles with her parents' full approval because it's culture! Mom's calling the Stallards to make sure it's okay, but it will be. She's one of us again!"

"Who's one of us?" said a voice behind us.

It was Emma.

· · · · ·

Reece was going to try to go if her passport came in time. She broke the news to Emma, who started working the possibilities over lunch. "My family travels a lot," she fished for an invitation. "I have a passport," she hinted. Even when Reece explained that it was independent study with these professors we know, Emma kept trying to worm her way in.

"It's nothing personal," I said finally. "The Stal—I mean, the professors are working with us four. And Mei. It's been planned for weeks."

"Mei? She's not even at school anymore!" Emma shot a hurt look at Reece.

Reece said apologetically, "I'm still not positive that I can go—it all depends."

Emma pouted over her food a minute. "Well, Reece," she said slowly, "if it turns out you can't go ..." She grinned at me and fluttered her eyelashes, "I could take your place."

I swallowed hard. *Uh-oh.*

The Stallards had written to Francine Dowland but hadn't

heard back. It occurred to me that she could have been lying about the sword; she might have stolen it like she did the shoes of peace and the journals. *That former preacher's wife is probably a penny-ante thief. Who's to say the sword hasn't been here all along?* But I had no proof.

Reece was praying and cranking up her therapy but was still on crutches. If she didn't go, I couldn't either. I didn't tell Emma though. Things were getting complicated. *Is God really working it out?* I wondered. *Did he let Mei's parents send her home so she could end up in England and fly over to Ireland and meet us because the sword is there? Will Reece get to go? Will we find Francine? Will she help us? Where is the sword?!*

This was the biggest thing in my life ever, but I had no control over any of it. I could hardly sleep for the tension building up in me.

In a few days I got a call from the Stallards. "It's about Francine," said Dr. Eloise.

"Did you find her?" I asked, feeling queasy.

"She was staying in Louisville with friends. She wasn't much help. To make a long story short: the Dowland family visited several castles and antique shops on their tour. Toward the end of their trip, Stan took a day for himself while Francine and their daughter Kate spent the day shopping in Dublin. He returned with the armor, saying he'd seen it in a shop and couldn't get it out of his mind."

I thought a moment. "At least we know it's a one-day drive from Dublin. That should narrow the field."

She sighed. "Ireland is small, roughly the size of Ohio."

I got it. "So you can get anywhere and back in one day?"

"Precisely."

"What do we do?" I asked, wondering how they found Francine when the Magdeline police couldn't.

"She did provide us with a list of the castles and shops."

"We have to hit 'em all?!"

"It will be grueling. Approximately a thousand miles of driving. Not a lot of time for leisurely dining and sightseeing. But if we are to find the sword ..."

"We can do it!" I said, praying like crazy. *C'mon, please!*

"Elijah, I hesitate to ask such a personal question, but what about Reece? How will she fare?"

"She's good to go once her passport comes in," I said, faking confidence. "And you can ask her point-blank about her problem anytime. She hates it when people tiptoe around it."

"Excellent. One more point. Dale and I believe we should examine the shield before we go. We'll drive down this weekend and bring the shoes. Does your camp have a vacancy in one of the cabins?"

"I'll check. There's probably a room at the lodge."

"Any accommodation will be fine—we live simply."

The next day I was slogging down the hall toward Latin when Reece pounced on me like a cat and yanked me into a corner. In her shaking hand was a navy blue passport. "We're going!" she whispered. "We're all going to Ireland. The five of us together again! He worked it out for us, Elijah! He did it!"

A jolt of disbelief coursed through me. Reece and I stood there grinning at each other, speechless and overjoyed in our usual own private world, until I got a thick elbow in the back.

I whirled. It was that bulk Justin Brill with a slimy look on his face. "Hey, Nature Boy, I hear you got religion."

He leered at Reece. "Elliston, maybe he can lay hands on you and heal you." His mocking eyes shifted to me as he lumbered off.

CHAPTER 5

The day before takeoff, the Stallards arrived with the shoes of peace, which we all looked over again as if we'd never seen them. Dr. Dale had brought measuring instruments and some sort of chemicals to test the shield.

We met at the lodge, lit a fire, and gathered around. When Reece brought the shield out of the sack, the Chicago archaeologists leaned over and gazed at it like it was their own new baby.

"We've been doing research based on your description," Dr. Eloise said after a minute.

Skid flipped open the Quella. "The first mention of the shield is when God told Abraham not to be afraid. He said, 'I am your shield, your very great reward.'"

Rob said, "A warrior's shield was the most important defensive piece. It protected the whole body and even the other parts of the armor."

"Correct," said Dr. Eloise.

Dr. Dale reported, "The shield is average size—around three feet across—to fit an average person, meaning the general population. Faith must fit you just like shoes or a helmet. It must be of a size you can wield, but sufficient to protect you. Not too big or too little."

"A person can have too big a faith?" Reece asked.

"There's no such thing. What I'm saying is that God will give you sufficient faith for your fiery trials."

At the words "fiery trials," the others glanced in my direction.

Skid whispered "pyro" at me. I frowned back and mouthed, "Am not!"

Dr. Dale lifted the shield, looked at it sideways, and bounced it in his hands. "Approximately an inch thick around the edges, fifteen to twenty pounds." He went on as if talking to himself. "Earlier shields were edged in bronze. This one is *sheeted* in bronze, indicating a later origin."

"Or possibly a later enhancement," Dr. Eloise added.

He agreed. "The shape is more like ancient Sumerian, Assyrian—"

"Or Greek!" Rob chimed. "I've been doing my own research!"

"Excellent, Mr. Rob," chirped Dr. Eloise. "You are such a little man already!"

She meant it as a compliment, but the "little man" label deflated my short cousin. He managed a polite smile and rolled his eyes at me when they weren't looking.

Dr. Dale reported, "These steel enhancements are also later additions. These slashes could be stylized sun rays radiating from the disc—" He paused, studied them a minute. "Their irregularities seem to be a deliberate design."

Dr. Eloise agreed. "It could be our encryption."

"Now that you mention it, there seem to be six distinct patterns of rays separated by small spaces. If only we were back at our lab," he said longingly. They analyzed the lines a long time. "Nothing familiar to me," he said finally.

"Nor me," she said.

"Well, let's move ahead to the shape of the shield."

"It's twelve-sided, like the apostles!" chimed Rob.

Reece laughed. "The apostles weren't twelve-sided!"

Dr. Eloise let out a high-pitched "Skwagack!" like some prehistoric bird. We laughed at her laugh, then at each other, pretending we were still laughing at Rob, until we all were cackling. It suddenly hit us all: *we're really going! Even Mei. It's really happening. Our quest has just gone global!*

When we'd settled down, Dr. Eloise said, "We know what you mean, Rob. Back into the analysis of the shield."

Rob said, "It's curved to deflect arrows and javelins and to allow the armor bearer to rest the upper edge on his shoulder."

The Stallards were impressed. Skid got Rob in a friendly headlock. "He's our resident research-nerd-meteorologist."

"And actor," said Reece. She made an observation, "That cross in the middle. It's not like a church cross. The two sticks are the same length."

"Ah, the cross!" said Dr. Eloise. "A most ancient symbol. It predates Christianity and is evidenced in virtually every major culture. To some it meant the four directions, to others eternal life, the four winds, or four corners of the earth. Over the centuries the cross has been twisted, inverted, looped, and broken to give it some new or perverse meaning. Denominations have claimed their own designs. Everyone wants to claim the cross." She leveled her eyes at us. "They know in their hearts the cross has power; some just don't understand what *kind* of power."

"Amen," I said. Dr. Eloise's mysterious comments didn't put me in the blind panic they used to.

Dr. Dale continued the analysis. "The arm and hand straps, called the porpax and antilabe, are positioned to distribute the weight. A shield should be held waist high, the forearm parallel to the ground. The curved shape is designed for pushing ahead, and these spiraled brads deflect the thrust of a blade point. Its smaller size suggests that a warrior has a better chance of survival if he stands close to another warrior. In this way each is protecting the right flank, that is, the sword arm of the other.

Reece said, "A person's faith helps his friends."

"Yes. One disadvantage of a more cumbersome shield is that

a strong wind can pull it away, throwing its wearer off balance. For a long-distance military campaign in unpredictable weather, a huge shield is not necessarily the most practical."

Reece smiled at me, "Even a little bit of faith works."

Dr. Dale put down the shield, nodding slowly. "An excellent piece of armor, the shield of faith. One caution I must mention, however." His merry mood turned quiet and intense. "Shields have been known to shatter upon impact, especially on the front lines ... during the initial attack."

Only Skid nodded that he understood.

Dr. Eloise cleared her throat and smiled eagerly. "About the page you found ..."

Reece had it in a plastic sleeve pressed between two pieces of cardboard. She handed it over to Dr. Eloise. "We never touched it with our bare hands."

"Good girl," said Dr. Eloise, and then to me, "You did an excellent job with the language on the page. After hours of research, we believe we've identified it."

It was then I realized how tired they looked. I said, "I got a really nice room for you here in the lodge. First floor."

Dr. Eloise thanked me. Dr. Dale brought a book out of his raggedy briefcase and opened it. They compared the page with pictures in the book. Dr. Eloise's hand slowly went to her mouth in amazement. "Will wonders never cease ..."

"What is it?" I asked.

"It does appear to be a lost page from the most ancient manuscript in Ireland ... a book called the *Cathach*, which means 'warrior.' If this is genuine ..."

As if cued by the same director, the Stallards suddenly looked at each other long and hard. Dr. Dale said, "Hmm. This is at once a blessing and a complication. We must be cautious, for now we venture into another area of antiquities. A cutthroat business." He studied the page in his wife's hand. "But this could possibly lead us to the sword."

"Where is the book it came from?" Rob asked.

"In Dublin." She turned to Dr. Dale. "We'll need to acquire special permission."

"We have no time," he said with concern. "Perhaps a phone call of introduction before we simply appear at their door and ask to see the manuscript."

"What kind of manuscript?" I asked.

"It's a portion of the book of Psalms."

"Oh." Disappointment showed in my voice.

Dr. Eloise smiled tolerantly. "Yes, yes, just a book of dusty old poems, you're thinking. But these poems were transcribed by a spiritual warrior named Columba who risked his life to keep them. They have been used for warfare for centuries! I believe it's no coincidence that this book is stored in the very city already on our itinerary." Dr. Eloise closed her eyes. "Psalm 3:3: 'You are a shield around me.' Psalm 7:10: 'My shield is God Most High.' Psalm 33:20: 'We wait in hope for the LORD; he is our help an our shield.'" She smiled. "Words from the *Warrior*."

Skid said, "Preach on, sista!"

The shield was returned to its burlap bag. "Where is it to be stored?" Dr. Eloise asked.

Rob said, "In my attic. We had the armor at Reece's until our remodeling was done."

"We shall need to take the page to Ireland." Her eyes sparkled with wonder. "Thank you, children. This is the most exciting venture of our lives. We deeply appreciate you. Well," she stood, "we must hit the proverbial hay. Tomorrow: Ireland! Logistics have been discussed with your parents. And one more thing: if you have not prepared your heart, do so before departure."

"What do you mean?" I asked.

"It's particularly important that we keep perspective during this season of pagan Celtic festivals. In Ireland the holiday of Halloween is called *Samhain*. On this night the pagans say that the veil between the worlds grows thin. I don't expect trouble, but we are on a spiritual quest. So pray," was her answer. "Pray hard."

I was too excited to sleep. Mom was up too, making meals ahead for Dad and the twins.

"I'm going for a walk, Mom."

"It's midnight, and you're in your jammies."

"I'll change."

"Where are you going?"

"Owl Woods, maybe farther. Cross-country training."

"In the middle of the night? My, such a disciplined son I have!" she kidded. "Take your flashlight."

"There's a gibbous moon."

"Whatever. Be back soon."

I ran full tilt for over half an hour and ended up due west of Devil's Cranium in a big gully lined with smooth, stone walls and steep, dirt banks. I sat under a huge slab overhang. The moon broke over the hill and sparkled on a narrow, trickling stream at my feet. *El-Telan-Yah?*

Quiet settled over me—the Presence.

Thank you, I said with a knot in my chest. *Thanks for letting Reece go so I could go … You are letting her, aren't you? She's not having a relapse tonight, I hope. Because I made a deal: I can't go if she doesn't. And thanks for working it out so Mei could come … the long way around the earth. Did you really work all that out? Because that's really planning ahead.*

Sitting there in the moonlit dark, I felt as far from tomorrow as a person could. It wasn't real. *I hate to bother you, but it's just one little thing: could you lead us to the sword? We have no clues, so we're counting on you.*

What was to be my final purpose in finding the whole armor? I mulled over the professors' words and wondered, *If this is war, who's the enemy exactly? Who am I fighting?* I yearned to own a Quella. *One more thing, God. It would be handy to have a Bible where I can find things quick.*

The trickling stream like a ribbon of light led me deeper into the unexplored part of Telanoo. *If you want me to fight, I want to know my enemy. I want to see him. I mean it. I'm not just some kid fooling around with my beliefs, God.* Leaves fell around me like tiptoes. *I'm ready to go with the belt of truth and the shoes of peace, and now the shield of faith. I believe in you. I said so in front of a church. I've been baptized. You've washed away my sins. I'm caught up, right?* Cautiously I demanded, *So show me who I'm fighting against.*

All right.

His answer had a stern, deep ring. A ferocious shiver ran through me. What had I just asked for?

CHAPTER 6

Everyone met at my house the next day. Reece was the last to arrive. I don't mind saying that I was on pins and needles until her mom's car pulled up. She was shaky but used only a cane. I heaved a huge sigh of relief.

Lots of hugs went around, all the parents squeezing everybody else's kids and crying over their own. Mom and Dad kissed a long time; then we loaded into the camp van, and Uncle Dorian drove us to Port Columbus International Airport.

The Stallards got us checked in, and Dr. Dale handed out cloth envelopes on cords to hang around our necks. "You are to wear these travel packs hidden on your person at all times. Each packet contains a miniature map of Ireland that shows the locations we'll be investigating, plus contact names and phone numbers in case we get separated." He handed a card to Dorian. "You'll notice an addition to our itinerary."

Uncle Dorian looked at the card darkly. "Grafton Institute. What's there?"

"A book we must see." Dr. Eloise went on with the instructions. "In your packs you'll also find a little Irish currency: change for the phone or emergency fare. After losing our daughter on several occasions, we've come up with this plan. It saves time backtracking."

We said good-bye to Uncle Dorian, breezed through security, and boarded. Mom sat between Skid and Reece on the three-seat side of the plane; Rob was in front of them with Dr. Eloise and a really big lady. I sat across the aisle next to the window with Dr. Dale. The plane started to taxi.

A strange, dark fear crept into me. "We're going."

"Are you afraid of flying?" he asked.

The plane gained momentum, roaring and rattling. My fingers gripped the armrests. "No, but—"

"It's the lack of control we feel," he consoled me. "Eloise used to hate flying until she understood that she was simply afraid of dying." He shook his head at me as if that were silly. "Now before we fly, she simply plans on dying. She makes sure that everything is in order and spends the night in prayer—confessing her sins and seeking peace. Ever since she discovered this method, she's able to set off into the wild, blue yonder happy as one could be!"

I glanced over at Dr. Eloise. She was talking the ears off Rob and the big lady.

"When one feels out of control, Elijah, one must *not* fight it but determine to move through fear to courage." Dr. Dale looked at me directly. "Move toward your destiny, Elijah. If you retreat from it, you are beaten."

I wasn't into talking death while we hurtled along the runway at two hundred miles an hour. So I nodded and glanced out the window as the ground dropped out from under me. Across the aisle and back one seat, Skid—Mr. Height Fright—was into his Quella, probably reading up on Heaven. My mom—sort of white-knuckled herself—was giving him a mommy talk.

"Hey, Skidmore," I called back, "here's good advice: if you just *plan* on crashing and dying, you'll feel a lot better."

If looks could kill, I'd have been dead. Mom wasn't thrilled over my advice either.

Dr. Dale smiled a sleepy smile. "We're all in God's hands."

I leaned my head back—the plane zoomed up, up, up and then leveled off while my stomach kept going up another hundred feet. The captain gave us the weather and time of arrival in Boston where we'd switch planes for Ireland.

Dr. Dale pulled out a flask, the kind people keep whiskey in. "Coffee," he said and took a sip.

I got a whiff, or I'm not sure I would have believed him.

Earth dropped away. We angled up into the clouds. The outside world was nothing to me but a big silver wing cutting through blinding whiteness until the sun burst through.

"Thunderheads, children!" Dr. Eloise chirped.

The patchwork fields of central Ohio were gone, and the new landscape was miles and miles of clouds and light. I whispered to myself, "God's hands."

Once in Boston and waiting for our flight out, we sat at the gate with all kinds of people who spoke with Irish brogues. *This is really happening. We're really going!* We got snacks, and Dr. Dale refilled his coffee flask. The sun sank toward the horizon as we boarded. This time we all were on the same side of a much bigger plane.

In no time we were high over Boston at twilight. "The street lights!" Reece said, poking me between the seats. "They look like fairy trails!"

By the time we passed over Maine, the world had gone dark. Again I sat in the window seat over a massive wing, its silver blade taking swipes at the full moon. Mom drifted off when we passed over Newfoundland, so Dr. Dale lectured me about the first explorers to America. "The very first settlers were Indians, as we call them. But evidence is emerging in texts and artifacts that lends support to the theory that Christopher Columbus was not the first European discoverer. One of the first explorers may have been Brendan the Navigator."

"Never heard of him," I said.

"He was one of a number of Irish who called themselves the

peregrini—Brendan, Patrick, Columba, and others—wanderers for the faith who set out like Abraham, not knowing where God would lead but willing to go nonetheless."

"Peregrini?"

"You've heard of peregrine falcons?"

"Fastest birds on the planet."

"It's from the same root word, meaning 'pilgrim.'"

Suddenly he nodded off. Just as I started to think he'd stopped breathing, the dignified Dr. Dale began snoring like an outboard motor and didn't let up until the meal came.

As we dug into our little dinners, he leaned over. "Eloise has been having dreams."

This got my attention because of my dream about the fire. "What kind of dreams?"

"She sees ancient standing stones holding hands and crying out. She can't understand what they are saying. You are leading us through the stones, and then we are on a high hill."

"What's it mean?" I asked.

"We don't put too much stock in dreams, Elijah. One never wants to sink into divination. But occasionally they teach us about Scripture or show us an aspect about ourselves we need to face. In the last days there will be a resurgence of visions and dreams. But dreams are never the final word."

We got up and stretched. Reece asked to borrow my seat near the window. We moved down and Mom moved back a row. I told Reece, "It's dark out now, but you can have my seat the rest of the way and be the first to see Ireland."

Dr. Dale nodded off again; things got quiet. Reece turned to me and said bluntly, "Emma likes you."

It was too close quarters for a discussion like this. "So?"

"I wanted you to know that if … if you wanted to like her back … I'd still … we'd still be friends, I hope. Forever."

There was silence until I muttered, "She's out of the loop."

"What loop?" Reece asked.

"The armor loop, the clan loop, any loop you're talking about." I yanked the flight magazine out of the seat pocket and flipped through it. "She's in the lunch loop—that's *all.*"

"Okay. That's … good." She turned to stare out the dark window, and I caught a glimpse of her smiling reflection.

Everyone took turns catnapping until hours later when we had breakfast. Dr. Dale and I made small talk. He looked at his watch and beamed. "One hour. I've waited years for this."

I was stunned. "You mean you've been looking for the armor of God since before you met us?"

"Oh yes." He paused, took a sip of coffee, and held it in his mouth for a second. His Adam's apple bobbed as the coffee went down. "Many's the year."

I wasn't sure how to feel about that. It put him more in Dowland's court: an old guy who'd made armor-hunting his life's work.

"Why do you think I—I mean *we* found it?" I asked.

He scratched his stubbly chin. "It appears that the Lord has been preparing you for leadership since your birth. As the eldest child you are called upon to care for the twins. You've spent much time in the wilderness, like Moses, Paul, and the prophet Elijah himself, who came from obscurity and appeared on the scene a full-fledged messenger of the Lord. There are many striking similarities. And your faith is not an inherited one. You have reasoned it out yourself. Rather uncanny."

"Do you think I'm the old Elijah reincarnated?"

Dr. Dale sighed tiredly. "Son, we must have some long theological talks very soon! At this point in your life—on the cusp of adulthood and possibly a mission for which you are completely unprepared—you must be extremely careful to listen to the right voices. We would not want your little craft set adrift on the sea of life only to be immediately blown off course by ill winds, the foul storms of the evil one."

"Yeah, but ... don't the winds and waves obey God?" I was remembering the tornado and the big kahuna wave.

He took a slug from his coffee flask and nodded. "I'm speaking in metaphors—the ill winds of ignorance, the storms of life, the dark clouds of uncertainty."

· · · · · ·

In one haggard, pasty-mouthed clump, we de-boarded at Shannon International Airport. Skid was wrung out, and Mom got a sudden case of the jitters about searching for her mother by herself. We made it through customs and changed our American cash to Irish. As the sun came up, we loaded our stuff into a rental van, and Dr. Eloise flashed around an Irish newspaper with a weather photo on the front page. "We've lost a night's sleep, and a terrible storm is on its way. The rental agent warned us of possible heavy rains with winds of up to fifty miles an hour. But we may be able to outrun the worst of it if we hurry."

Rob was the first to notice that the steering wheel was on the right side of the car. He watched Dr. Dale buckle himself into the driver's seat. "Do you know how to drive on the right side of the car on the left side of the road?"

"Mm-hmm," he mumbled distractedly, trying his hands on the gearshift and steering wheel. "It's those blasted roundabouts." He turned on the ignition and said to Mom, "Jodi, are we to drop you off at a designated spot?"

Mom gave him a map. "Right there. I've marked the route in red. My contact is meeting us at the mouth of the Shannon River. Her name's Ruthie. She lives where ... my mother used to live. If the gate's not open, we're supposed to call."

Eloise made us all bow our heads. She prayed for Mom to

find success and peace and for us all to be safe on our adventure. "And finally, O Most High," she prayed, "as this most pagan holiday approaches, deliver us from the evil one!"

Dr. Dale pulled out of the airport parking lot, muttering nervously to himself, "Stay to the left, the left … left."

The storm blew in as we headed out. Through sheets of pelting rain, Ireland looked similar to Ohio: smooth hills, lots of farms, trees turning orange and yellow. But there were sheep farms everywhere, surrounded by stone fences; and when we went through our first village, it was clear we weren't in Ohio. Stores of all different colors edged right up to the street, with names like Jonah Rylee's Pub and Brian Spellissy's Books. The village streets were narrow and winding. But the biggest shocks were the remains of castles perched on lonely hills.

Dr. Dale was right about the roundabouts. You'd careen into the circle of highway going fifty—on the left side, hopefully—and keep going around until you found the right road. Then you'd shoot off with cars coming at you and cars beside you. We guys thought the roundabouts were cool, but Dr. Dale sweated bullets every time he saw a sign for one ahead.

Dr. Eloise tried to navigate and give a tour at the same time. "We're on N18—these ruins, children, are anywhere from—watch for signs for N69, dear—two hundred to—that's N21, we don't want that—put the wipers on high. I can't see a thing in this torrent—take the left lane. No, it's the right—one thousand years old!" She patted Dr. Dale's arm excitedly, "We must take a few hours—there it is, N69—to visit Newgrange, which is possibly the oldest man-made—oh, look out!—man-made structure in the world, predating even the pyramids. And the Hill of Slane. Dale, we must not miss that." She leaned to her husband and whispered, "I think that hill is the one in my dream. There was a picture in the flight magazine." She turned back to us. "You children will find it very compelling, especially you, Elijah."

Mom spotted a road sign for Limerick through the torrent pounding the windshield and said cheerily, as if to calm her own nerves, "How about you kids making up limericks about Ireland? You can tell them to me when I see you again. Elijah, be sure to call me in the next day or two, so I know where to meet up." She looked at her map. "Okay, we're getting close. It will be a one-lane road. There, there it is to the left."

Suddenly we were driving down a dirt road on a narrow spit of land with angry waves crashing on either side. Mom said shakily, "This is the only road in or out. Ruthie warned me that if we came during high tide and rough seas, the road might not be passable. The address is Seven Avon Place."

The storm worsened. Windshield wipers swished frantically. Everyone peered silently ahead as waves splashed over the road. The drive ended in thick, gray woods with two big, iron gates— one open, one locked. There wasn't a number or a house visible, just two overgrown roads disappearing into the trees. "Let's try the open gate," Mom said.

A tunnel of trees swayed overhead as if it would topple on us. When Seven Avon Place came into view, everyone went stone quiet. Before us stood the spookiest place I'd ever seen. It was a massive three stories of square stone under a low roof in a bare, muddy field. Tiny, dark windows sat in rows like strange eyes. The upper windows were barred.

"Is that ... it?" Rob broke the silence.

"Maybe it was the locked gate," Reece said encouragingly. "We should go back and try that one."

Mom looked at her notes. "Ruthie said it was a three-story, gray, stone building with small windows."

"There's no car," I said hopefully. "This has to be wrong."

Looking concerned, Dr. Eloise said to her husband, "Drive

around to the back, dear. If the cars aren't parked there, we'll try the other gate."

Behind the house a bare lot spread out to other big, drab, square buildings. A little green car was parked behind the house next to a greenhouse in ruins. Mom couldn't hide her shock and whispered to herself, "My mother lived … here?"

We drove back around front. All the windows in the house were dark except for one faint light in the top left window. Mom looked at her watch. "Ruthie said she'd be home."

Bracing into the wind, she got out, ran up to the door, and knocked. We all waited. No one came. She dashed around back and out of sight. While she was gone, a really tall guy opened the front door and eyed us suspiciously.

"That's not Ruthie," said Rob in a sinister tone.

"We're not leaving her here," I said protectively as I jumped out of the van into the storm.

Just as Mom came back around the building, a woman appeared at the front door. She was young and tall and had a baby in her arms. As I stood by the van shivering, Mom went up the steps. They shook hands and talked a minute. She ran back for her luggage, trembling.

"Are you sure you're going to be okay?" I asked.

"I'll be fine," she said and bit her lip. "I have to do this. Dorian's counting on me." She gave me a big, quick hug. "I'll see you in a few days," she said. "I love you."

"Love you too, Mom. Be careful."

When the door to Seven Avon Place closed, we pulled out. A horrible feeling swept through me. I wanted to jump out, go back, and protect my mom—but from what, I didn't know.

CHAPTER 7

We drove out to the main highway and headed toward Ballymeade. Dr. Dale said, "If anyone asks about the nature of the trip, let's call it 'independent study.'" He added sternly, "We are here to gather information, not to dispense it."

Dr. Eloise turned to Reece cheerfully. "And Mei is still meeting us?"

Reece grinned. "She called. She and her friend are flying over from London. They'll meet us at the castle."

Dr. Eloise cleared her throat, her eyes wide and worried. "Her … friend is coming with us?"

Reece said, "I don't think so. She's going to some big celebration; I'm not sure what."

Dr. Eloise scanned the countryside through the side window. "I wonder what Mei has told her host family about the purpose of her trip."

Reece said blankly, "I don't know."

A quarter mile before Dr. Dale pulled into the parking lot of Ballymeade Castle, we saw its four towers poking up through the trees. Dr. Eloise was thrilled. "I hope *everyone* enjoys history!"

Skid slid me a bored look. "Woohoo."

"Behind the castle is an authentic reproduction of an Irish village. Look for opportunities to ask questions. We are in essence retracing the steps of the Dowlands in hope of finding where the armor was purchased."

We headed for the gift shop to buy tickets.

Rob asked, "What kind of sword are we looking for?"

Dr. Dale said, "The Greek word in the Ephesians passage is *machaira:* a short sword, dagger, or saber—the type Roman guards would carry. But in the book of Revelation, *rhomphaia* is used, which is a larger brandishing weapon."

Skid whipped out his Quella. "'These are the words of him who has the sharp, double-edged sword. I know where you live— where Satan has his throne… . Repent therefore! Otherwise, I will soon come to you and will fight against them with the sword of my mouth.'"

Dr. Eloise nodded. "Christ was speaking to the people of Pergamum, a town in modern-day Turkey. The throne of Satan at that time was either the temple of the serpent cult of Asklepios or the altar to the god Zeus. That altar, by the way, still exists and is on display in the Berlin Museum." She sighed happily. "Perhaps on our next journey, we'll go see the throne of Satan. Would you like that?"

Skid said, "Ditto on that 'woohoo.'"

Answering our creeped-out looks, she said, "Oh, sillies, it's a piece of rock in a dusty, old museum. Its power has been transferred to other sites on the planet."

"Like where?" asked Rob worriedly.

"Another day," she said evasively. "The evil one is always on the move. Now, keep your eyes open for a small, dagger-type weapon or a hefty broad-bladed sword."

"How will we know if it's *the* sword?" Rob asked.

Dr. Eloise stopped at the gift shop door. "We'll know."

Dr. Dale reminded us quietly, "We go in as tourists. One on a quest never wants to appear too eager. Take note of weapons mounted on walls or in display cases. Often history is woven or carved into a room, so look for illustrations in tapestry, furniture, and architectural details. At a time when many people

didn't read, tapestries and stained glass were often used as giant
storybooks for the illiterate."

We got a map of the castle layout and were let loose. Each of
the towers was a stack of big rooms where lords and ladies had
lived. The center of the square castle was the Great Hall. Below
it was a big room called the Main Guard where soldiers used to
hang out. Reece didn't want to climb the steep, circular steps in
all four towers, so I offered to scout out each tower and let her
know the best rooms to see.

"I'll look around here in the Great Hall," she said. "You guys
can report back to me."

Before we split up, a guide came in—a little bald man with
a thick accent, a brown suit, and shined-up shoes. "Did you
notice the steps wind up steeply clockwise?" he asked. "That is
so the enemy could not climb them and have his sword at the
ready. One must use the handrail, ya see—quite the clever safety
measure. If anyone has questions—"

"Swords?" I said. "Do you have swords on display?"

"In the Great Hall is mounted the Sword of Estate, symbolizing the lord's authority to sit in judgment."

I ran to the far end of the hall, eager to see the Sword of Estate
but was frankly disappointed. It was long and plain and slightly
bent. I ran back to the guide. "Where did they come from, and
which one's the oldest?"

Skid gave me a cool-it-Creek-don't-blow-your-cover look. The
others split up while the guide showed me the duke's quarters.
The sword hanging on the wall was not double-edged or dag-
ger-like or glittering. The guide wouldn't even let me touch it.

Reece was studying the stained glass windows. On three of the
walls hung huge rugs so faded I could hardly make out details.
"What about those tapestries?" I asked.

"We have several." He went off on his canned speech. "And

that one, the oldest in the collection, shows Jacob's dream. The story is biblical, but the art style is medieval."

I studied the tapestry. Beside the man sleeping on the ground stood a faded horse and a rider wearing armor. Even in the dreary light of the castle, I recognized a familiar twelve-sided shield with a cross in the middle. It took every ounce of willpower to stay calm. "Sir, what's the story behind the tapestry? Where'd it come from?"

"Ah, this work was created for the infamous MacMerrits—a bloody lot they were! Their history begins at Dunluce on the northern coast. The castle is not restored as this one is," he said proudly. "Dunluce has fallen into ruin. But what an impressive ruin it is. Do you plan to visit it?"

"Tomorrow!" Reece said, reading the itinerary from her travel pack.

I gave her the warning eye. *Don't give out information.* I ditched the tour guide and went hunting for the Stallards who were on top of the west battlement. I led them back down to the Great Hall. "Isn't that the shield?"

Dr. Eloise dug in her bag and brought out a tiny pair of gold binoculars mounted on a stick. "Not ordinary opera glasses," she said to me slyly. "I've had these enhanced."

Flash photography was prohibited, so Dr. Dale used a little spy-looking camera to get shots of the tapestry. Rob was in awe. "We've only been here a few hours, and we have a solid lead on the armor!"

Dr. Eloise folded up her opera glasses. "The aging and damage is severe. I can see no detail on the helmet or sword. It does look like our shield though. Good work, Elijah."

I said to Reece, "Wanna see a tower? I think you'll like the south one best. It has a duchess room and clothes hanging on the wall. We'll go all the way up to the battlement and watch for Mei—if it quits storming."

Being in a real castle was cool, but I can vouch that it's no great place to live: it's cold and dark, and you could break your neck on those narrow, slippery steps.

We watched for Mei from the tower. When Reece started worrying, we went down to the gift shop and found the rest milling around, sampling blackberry jam. Rob was sniffing out teas for his mom.

"What kind of school assignments do you have to complete?" Dr. Eloise asked to pass the time.

"Photo journal for the school paper," Rob said. "And I want to learn Irish brogue—jes' far me own self."

"Travel article for social studies," Skid answered.

Reece beamed. "Oral report for speech. I don't even have to write it. But I'm keeping a journal for my Devo club."

"Oh, eeeeeeasy," said Dr. Eloise. "They'll write themselves!"

I grumbled, "Mine's on why the Roman hordes did or didn't invade Ireland, and it has to be in Latin."

Dr. Eloise's hand went to her mouth. "Oh! Dear me!" She backed away with a whimper of sympathy and wandered toward the dungeon.

We strolled the path through the folk village, posing in front of thatch-roofed houses and acting medieval for Rob's camera. That's when I spotted two dark-haired girls walking the path toward us. "Mei!" I called.

Her face lit up. She ran full force to Reece. They hugged and cried themselves silly. The next thing I knew, the five of us were in a circle, jumping and acting like girls. But I don't mind saying I felt proud—my clan was together again.

Mei introduced her friend, a pretty, medium-size girl with a serious face and light hazel eyes. "This is Sahara Dahlman." We all said hello. "She is here for a festival." They smiled at each other. Then Mei said, "It's like our festivals in Japan."

With a cool British accent, Sahara said, "It's the druid holiday of *Samhain,* what Americans call Halloween. We fly over every year to celebrate the goddess." She glanced uneasily at Reece. I got the idea Sahara and Mei had been talking about Reece's religion—and maybe even the quest.

The Stallards' smiles froze on their faces. "How interesting," Dr. Dale said. "Well, is anyone hungry? Our body clocks are out of kilter. Please join us for a meal, Sahara."

"Thanks, but Mum's waiting for me in the car. We're needing to be off to the Hill of Ward for the festival."

The girls arranged to meet up with Sahara after her festival.

We went into the town to a coffee shop the professors described as "just darling" and got caught up with Mei. Dr. Eloise wanted to know about Sahara's holiday.

"She will dance in a play about the myth of the Irish sun goddess. The actors light a fire on the hill and dance around it. *Samhain* is like our *Obon* festival in Japan, when the spirits of the dead return. Sahara's mother says the walls between the worlds grow very thin on the Hill of Ward. Halloween was born there." Mei took her teacup in both hands, looking embarrassed. She said shyly to Reece, "I have learned many things about religions this year. I don't know what to believe. Sahara's religion is very much like the one in Japan."

Dr. Dale asked cautiously, "Does your friend know why we have come to Ireland?"

Mei answered, "I just told her we are searching for an ancient sword. I told her I'd see my best friends, and we would visit a castle." She looked like she was wrestling with something but couldn't get it out.

"What is it, dear?" Dr. Dale encouraged.

"Maybe it doesn't matter, but when I explained about the

sword, Sahara's mother told me a story about long ago, that the druid father of the goddess began to worry when belief in Jesus came to Ireland. He told her to go throughout the world and collect all the mysteries and magics and to hide them so the Christians could never find them. I am sorry, but I think maybe the sword might be hidden forever."

Dr. Eloise said lightly, "Take care what you believe, children. Take great care, for you see every region has its tales. Is it a coincidence that many tell of sacred swords? Britain had Excalibur. Japan had the sword of Atsuta. And Ireland tells of a sword coming from afar. Cut through the fairy tales, children, and you will find their origin."

I said, "The sword of the Lord from the Garden of Eden?"

She nodded mysteriously, then steered the conversation to chitchat where I lost track. Dr. Dale was looking long and hard at his half-eaten salad. Then he put down his fork. It was the last bite of solid food he took for the next week.

CHAPTER 8

Mei bought postcards to make a scrapbook of Ireland. Rob offered to share the pictures from his photo journal. Then we piled into the van and headed north.

Skid asked, "Aizawa, are you still obsessed with driving?"

"Oh yes!" she said. "When I graduate, I will come back to America and get my license. Then I will drive and drive!"

Reece chirped, "We'll drive across America!"

To pass the time, we started collecting funny traffic sign sayings: "Traffic Calming" meant merge. "Soft Verge" meant to stay on the pavement and not pull off. "Don't Rubbish the Tipp" meant don't litter in Tipperary County. It was great being together again, just like the good old days.

Around noon we stopped to stretch our legs and see some famous scenery: the Cliffs of Morte. We walked up a smooth path toward a gap in a wide, *U*-shaped hill with an old castle-type watchtower up to our right and massive knolls up to the left. As we approached the overlook, sheer cliffs stood in ranks and receded out toward the horizon. Round and green on top, they suddenly dropped off hundreds of feet straight down to churning waves and jagged rocks.

Skid's face went slack. "Oh man …" He fell back a step. "Whoa … whoa."

I answered Dr. Eloise's curious look with, "He's afraid of heights."

"Perhaps he should wait in the car," she said.

"No!" he said abruptly, fixing his eyes on those terrifying cliffs. "You guys go on," he said. After some useless pleading, Reece and Rob and Mei set off for the overlook.

"It was after Dowland's dog attacked us," I explained to Dr. Eloise. "That's when he caught height fright."

She came between Skid and his view of the cliff. "You came face-to-face with your mortality that day, didn't you? Some fear is reasonable, Marcus; we have to respect danger. But phobias are from the evil one; they keep you from optimum functioning. This is an unreasonable fear, Marcus. You can't possibly fall from here. The edge is yards away. See those slabs of stone leaning against the dirt bank, forming a waist-high barrier?" She pointed to the overlook. "See that wall of dirt and stone between you and the edge? There is *no real danger.*"

He looked over her shoulder to the cliffs for a long time, fighting for air. I waited to see what he would do.

"The evil one would love to paralyze you, Marcus," Dr. Eloise said patiently.

He breathed hard. "I need some time. You go on."

We left Skid and went to the main overlook to enjoy the view. Dr. Dale gave us a lecture on Ireland's unusual geography: "Unlike most islands, Ireland is lower in the center and higher around the edges, rimmed in many places with such cliffs. These are perhaps the most spectacular."

We went back to check on Skid; he was eyeing a break in the fence and a path that led down to a big, rock ledge with no rail. Three men in orange suits were hanging onto each other's sleeves and peering over the edge to the sea below. A sign on the fence read "Danger." Obviously, a lot of people couldn't resist the urge to go look straight down.

"Oh, dear Heaven!" said Dr. Eloise again.

"What?" I asked.

"Did you see the car in the parking lot with "Guarda" written on the side? Those are Irish policemen. These cliffs have a bad reputation for claiming lives," she paused to smile at Skid, "of those careless enough to hazard a stroll over to that edge. Winds from the Atlantic can be fierce and unpredictable, occasionally strong enough to blow stones from the sea to the top of the cliff."

A policeman walked past us. I asked what happened.

He shook his head sadly. "Poor bloke got off the tour bus, walked over for a look-see, and was gone. Fifth one this year." He eyed the swift, gray sky. "Frightful stiff wind a moment ago, still as death now. Puts the fear of God in ya sideways, don't it? Stay this side of the fence, folks."

He turned to go and then nodded to Skid and me. "But if ya venture out there to get a straight-down look like so many do, stay on yer bellies, lads, and mind the wind."

Everyone but Skid went up to the observation tower.

I half expected another topography lesson from Dr. Dale, but his crinkly eyes were focused on Skid, who looked small and lonely. Under his breath Dr. Dale said, "'My enemy will say, "I have overcome him," and my foes will rejoice when I fall.'"

"What's that from?" I asked.

He seemed startled that I'd overheard him. "Words from the *Warrior,*" he answered quietly. "Do you feel it? Do you feel the darkness falling?"

His question set me back.

"He wants one of us," Dr. Dale said quietly, as if he were listening to someone.

"Who wants who?" I asked.

"The evil one, and … I don't know."

I looked out over the dark sea churning below us. It was a little eerie, but nothing more. I didn't feel darkness falling.

Dr. Dale wanted to stay up there awhile longer. When we

came back down, Skid had passed through the break in the fence but was clinging to the post for dear life.

"What are you doing!?" Reece screamed at him.

"I'm done with it," he said. "I'm done."

"Done with what?" she demanded to know.

"His fear of heights," I answered for him.

"What's he going to do, Elijah?" Reece cried, then to Skid, "Someone just died on that ledge!"

Dr. Eloise calmly watched.

Reece threw her a glare. "You're not going to stop him?!"

Dr. Eloise called, "Marcus, it's obviously safe to crawl to the edge and look down." She turned to us. "Why don't you join him?"

Reece grabbed my arm. "No, Elijah!"

Dr. Eloise said calmly, "You must learn the difference between realistic and imagined danger. If you crawl out to the edge, you are safe. If you walk out, you are not."

We swapped glances. *Should we?* I wondered.

Skid closed his eyes and gulped. "I have to conquer this."

Mei said, "We can't let him go alone."

I looked at Rob. He bit his lip. "Good chance to experience coastal wind patterns."

"Okay," I said. "Let's do it."

Skid was gripping the fence, his eyes glued to the rim of the cliff. We made him let go and join hands.

Dr. Eloise said, "You can walk out for six paces—no more. Follow my instructions precisely, children!"

In a straight line, we counted off our steps: one, two, three, four, five, six. Reece tossed her cane aside. Mei and I helped her down, and then we crawled on our bellies. Skid was almost to the edge when his head dropped down on his arm, his lungs heaving for air. Mei scooted up and put her arm around him.

"You can do it, Skid! We'll go with you."

"You're safe on your belly," Reece said. "We're safe."

He rose up on his forearms and dragged himself forward inch by inch, his legs useless behind him. "I gotta do this ... do this." A yard from the edge, his head dropped again.

"Fear not!" Dr. Eloise called from the safety of the fence, her words almost lost in the ocean wind blast.

I pulled myself to the edge and looked down. "Wow, Skid, it's great!" Dark waves came in huge swells, turning white as they crashed over rocks and broke into fierce, white foam. It made us dizzy to watch. If someone had fallen just moments ago, his body had already washed out to sea.

I yelled over the wind, "The ocean waves are rolling in slow motion, Skid! Birds are flying underneath us! It's great! It's awesome! You'll regret it if you don't have a look!"

"A few more inches, Skid," Reece said. "You're so close!"

"We're together," Mei said.

"Be a man," Rob joked.

Skid dragged himself the last few inches, got his head over the ledge, looked down, and made a sound like he'd been punched in the gut.

"Isn't it beautiful?" Reece cried. "See the white birds against the dark-green water? Isn't God amazing?"

Dr. Eloise called, "Marcus! You did it!"

He breathed hard and said reverently, "It is awesome." Between gulps of air, he started to smile. "Whoa, baby!"

"Cured?" I asked with a grin.

Hypnotized by the swirling water and swooping birds, he murmured, "This is seriously cool."

"Time to go!" Dr. Eloise called.

We rolled over, sat up, and scooted a few yards away from the edge. The air suddenly went calm, as if the trial was over.

When I judged it was safe, I stood up to dust the dirt off. The others followed.

"Oh, quickly now!" Dr. Eloise said frantically.

I'd taken a step toward Dr. Eloise when I heard a *whoosh* and saw her pitch toward us. She grabbed the fence to catch herself. The wind had changed course.

I had no time to yell for everyone to drop before the blast slammed into us. It threw me back a step. I knew I was okay, and Rob and Skid were safely between me and the fence, but ... *Mei! Reece!* I spun around toward the cliff.

The blast had blown Mei backward a few feet and sat her down hard. But Reece had turned for one last look at the cliffs; the wind hit her full force in the back. Already unsteady without her cane, she stumbled forward. I bolted for her. Suddenly I was looking down, my toe over the edge, the angles of the cliff telescoping below me and vanishing in dark-green swirls. My fingers clamped like iron onto Reece's arm. *We're going over. Together, headlong, the wind slamming our faces. Birds screech and bank out of our way ...*

I saw whirlpools rising toward us as we plummeted. I saw it as if it were really happening. Behind me Dr. Eloise shrieked. I threw myself backward, pulling Reece with me—the wind fighting me for her. I spun her around and shoved her toward Rob. For a second I faced the wind and the horrified faces of Mei, Skid, and Dr. Eloise. I tottered back; my heel pressed down over nothing. Then I felt rock under my foot where there was no rock. Somehow I found the strength to fall forward onto my knees. I scrambled on all fours away from the ledge. We all rushed back to Dr. Eloise; her face was a pale mask of terror. When we'd gathered on the safe side of the fence, Reece flew into my arms and cried.

Dr. Eloise hugged Reece long and hard and whispered

comfortingly to her. "Hot chocolate for everyone," she said to the rest of us. "We're all right. Elijah, if you'll run up to the tower and get Dale, we'll all get off this cliff."

We crowded around a table in the cozy Cliffs of Morte Snack Shop. Celtic flute music played in the background while souvenir shoppers milled around. Dr. Eloise broke the news to her husband. He listened without batting an eye, and his words from the *Warrior* came back to haunt me.

Trying to be jovial, Rob said, "We should add one more rule to Skid's dad's life lessons. Lesson Nine: When it's not safe to walk, crawl!"

Skid made lame jokes about being cured, and Mei kept asking Reece if she was *daijoubu*. Reece sat beside me and wouldn't let go of my arm. She, the mouth of the group—Miss Sarcasm— hardly said a word. She just sipped her hot chocolate and stared darkly at the table.

CHAPTER 9

With the radio tuned to a talk station so Rob could practice his Irish brogue, Dr. Dale drove us through low, rusty hills littered with rocks. "This is called the Burren, but it's certainly not barren." We got an earful about the unusual variety of plant life, for the sake of Skid's travel report.

Reece hardly said a word. Her excitement about Mei and the search for the sword had washed out to sea.

We got out to stare at rocks. Reece pretended to look for flowers, but I knew better. She wanted distance from the rest of us. I followed her to the stone fence. "You okay?"

"Fine," she said, but her heart wasn't in it.

"Lots of rocks here," I said stupidly.

She straightened up and looked at me with a long, sad, searching look. "The winds and the waves obey him." It wasn't her usual Bible voice; I thought she was going to cry.

We were an hour farther up the coast before I understood what Reece meant, but Rob was sitting between us, so I couldn't bring it up.

It made no sense to me that on the week of Halloween most of the B&Bs were full. In America people don't travel far, except up and down streets for treats. We stopped at houses of every shape and size with big driveways and labeled "B&B." A few had vacant rooms, but not enough for all of us. We had to settle for a place with no green shamrock on the sign out front, meaning it was not recommended by the tourist board. It looked fine to me.

Dr. Dale pulled in. "This will have to do. We can't be searching for lodging after dark." He winked cheerfully at Dr. Eloise.
"After that sand spider incident in our tent outside old Babylon,
how bad could this be?"

She shuddered. "Shall we not talk about that!"

We wanted details, but Dr. Eloise frowned forebodingly.

The lady of the house reminded us of Miss Flewharty. She was
thin and brittle in a print dress and gray sweater. Her son was
just plain weird: a moon-faced kid who slumped and shuffled
and stared at the girls.

The lady ushered us into the entry hall. "Yer rooms are upstairs, but could ya wait here? I'm a-hoov'rin' the rug. Won't take
but a minute." She dashed up the stairs.

Dr. Eloise leaned over to her husband. "They're unprepared.
Not a good sign."

We guys stayed in a cramped, chilly room with bunks and a
twin bed. A narrow homemade shelf held an electric teapot and
cups. We had a stained sink, a closet made from old paneling,
and a tall, drafty window, which looked out to the main street.
Rob and I took the bunks. We were unpacking when there was
a knock at the door.

"Who is it?" Rob asked in a singsong voice.

A whisper penetrated the door. "It's me, Eloise."

She slipped in clutching a bag, said "Shhh!" and dumped
the bag onto Skid's bed: dish soap, disinfectant spray, a scouring
pad. "I can't let you boys sleep in this squalor." She set to work
scrubbing out the teapot and cups, thumping dust out of the
tea bags, scouring the sink, and beating the pillows. A toxic
cloud of feathers and spray chemicals hung in the air as she
made us tea and warned us about the basket of snacks on the
nightstand. "Individually wrapped, but who knows how long
they've been there?"

I asked if I could call my mom.

"Tomorrow, dear. There's a stiff charge for using the phone. She huffed. "No shamrock indeed! And that boy! Acts like a Peeping Tom! I've told the girls to chock a chair against their door. It wouldn't hurt for you to do the same."

She wished us a crisp good-night and slipped out, sticking her head back in to whisper, "We're across the hall. Don't go to the girls' room now. Breakfast tomorrow at 8:00. I'm sorry, boys. This is our last unapproved no-shamrock lodging place or my name's *not* Eloise Stallard!"

Skid pressed a fist into her shoulder. "This is spiritual warfare, Dr. E—the trenches. We're up for it."

The door closed. Rob unplugged the teapot and whispered uneasily, "One problem. Her name's *not* Eloise Stallard."

We talked in whispers, though we were probably the only people in the house except for Irish Flew and her weird son. After a snack of ammonia-flavored tea and old cookies, we jumped under the covers and turned out the light.

We couldn't sleep, so Skid turned on the radio. As part of the Halloween season, a lady was telling a story, her voice lowered to make it sound eerie:

"It was in the 1700s. Jack the blacksmith, a notorious drunk-ard, had run up a huge debt over the years. No pub would give him a drink. One night a little man at the bar said," (the lady went into a German accent) "*Mein freund,* I'll give you money for a drink, but I'm the devil, unt I'll need your soul.' Jack took him up on the deal, had his drink, and then scooped up the devil and put him in his pocket.

"He dropped a cross in his pocket and said, 'Ha, ha! Now ye won't be able to escape.' But the devil escaped and ran up a tree. Jack carved a cross into the tree so the devil couldn't get down, fer he was afraid of the cross, ya see. He begged Jack to let him down. Jack said, 'I'll let ye down, Old Scratch, but ya must promise never ever to claim my soul.' The devil agreed. So Jack the blacksmith went back to his loathsome ways and died an early death. At the pearly gates St. Peter said, 'Jack, ye're a terrible man; ye can't come in,' and sent him to Hell. The devil said, *Mein freund,* I can't claim your soul. I'm a man of me verd. You must vahnder zee oontervurld for eternity.' Then Jack said, 'Ah, but 'tis so dark out there in the underworld.' So the devil picked up a glowing ember and threw it at Jack, who was eating a turnip like any good Irish chap fresh out of Hell. He cut a hole in the turnip and put the ember inside to light his way through the underworld. So that's the story," the lady told her listeners. "When the Irish immigrated to America, they brought Halloween with them. But instead of hollowing out turnips for Jack lanterns, the Americans recommended pumpkins."

The program went into a round of Irish folk music, and Skid turned it off. "Skidmore," I said in the darkness, "that story's just made up, but this stuff about the devil. What's ... real?"

"Most of what you hear is not real," he answered. "Red horns and tail and pitchfork, making deals for your soul—most people don't know squat about the truth."

"And you do?" Rob asked.

"I have voodoo in my background."

"Is that where you learned it?" I asked.

"Everyone has an opinion about the devil, Creek. You don't go to backwater slaves or anybody else for answers. You go to the Quella. It doesn't say much about what he looks like—serpent, dragon, angel of light. But it tells a lot about what he does. You can look him up tomorrow. But Satan is real, we're clear on that. Demons are real and Hell is real. Dad says, 'Dabble in it, boy, and get sucked into the abyss.' That's what Dad says."

"But we're *men* now," said Rob boldly. "We're world travelers;

we can handle it."

"Nothing to do with manhood, Wingate."

It got quiet for a minute. I asked Skid, "Your parents believe the same as you, right?"

"Yeah."

"I don't think my parents believe in God and Heaven and Hell much. They don't talk about it."

Skid said, "My dad's always asking: 'When does a man of God start his eternal life? When does he cross that line?'"

Rob said, "Your dad's not much help in the answer department, is he? Big on rules, weak on answers."

"Hey, your dad's no prize, Wingate."

I heard Rob turn over and settle in for the night. With the Irish accent he'd been working on, he said, "Don't cha be dissin' me dad, Marcus, or ye'll find yerself a-shiverin' out there on the quay in the blinky of an eyelet."

I told the guys what Dr. Dale had said at the Cliffs of Morte about one of us being targeted by the evil one.

"Who?" Rob asked.

"He didn't know."

It got quiet for a long time. I thought I heard shuffling in the hall. I crept to the door, listened, unlocked it quietly, then flung it open. But no one was there.

I wanted to stay awake sorting through questions like: What is the veil between the worlds, and does it really get thin on Halloween? If Satan wants someone, how does he go about getting him? Could all the magics of the world be hidden in Ireland, even the sword of the Lord? And I wanted to keep an ear on the door, but jet lag got the best of me.

· · · · ·

We survived the night at the no-shamrock inn and met for breakfast downstairs. Irish Flew had a huge spread: eggs and sausage, different kinds of bread, and strong dark tea. Eloise didn't eat much, and from the way she looked at her plate, I figured she was leery of food not approved by the tourist board. Dr. Dale had tea and juice but no solid food. They arranged for Skid and Reece to be at their table, partly to give them pointers for their school projects. But my hearing being very acute, I was able to pick up whispery questions about what Rob and Mei believed. Skid said under his breath that Rob hadn't yet done the saved stuff it talks about in the Bible. I couldn't pick up what Reece said about Mei, but Dr. Eliose mentioned God's patience.

At our table Mei filled us in on life in London. "It's very wonderful. I attend Sahara's school to study English and European history. It's very difficult! But I prayed to see you again, and God answered my prayers! Sahara is so nice. They live very differently, so it is a good culture experience."

"What do you mean—different?" I asked.

"Her mother has a husband and a boyfriend. Her father has a girlfriend. They all live together with the children. This doesn't happen in Japan! They have an herb garden and sell magical mixes and amulets and oils."

She took her cup of tea in both hands and sipped. Shyly she said, "I missed you all so hard that I cried. Tell me what is happening in Magdeline. I want to hear!"

We filled her in on our clubs and sports and how I got burned rescuing the shield of faith. I showed her my scar, which had healed over. I'd missed having the whole group together and felt a pang. *We only have a week, then it's back to Magdeline, Emma ... and Miss Abner with her Roman hordes.*

On the way to the north shore, we stopped off to get gas. While the others went into a card shop, I cornered Dr. Dale. "Hey, um ... ," I asked, "did you believe what Mei said about all the mysteries and magics being hidden away?"

"No."

"But it bothers you."

"The influence of myths over her spirit concerns me. The problem with pagan religions is this: there is little or no revelation and much fabrication."

"You're talking college level. I'm a high school freshman."

"Of course. Revelation means truths about God revealed by God himself as opposed to fabrication: stories made up from experiences and folk tales."

"But I noticed you quit eating after Mei said that."

All he said was, "We'll discuss it later." I wondered if he was on a vision quest.

We drove along Lough Foille, a huge inlet bay of ocean. We argued about how to pronounce it until we passed Ballykelly Forest where Rob went into a spiel about how every place is named Bally-something.

"Bally means 'town,'" said Mei. "I'm learning three Englishes: American, British, and Irish. Too much vocab!"

Now that she'd warmed up to us again, Mei did more talking than Reece. Being an artist, she was interested in all the greens of the Emerald Isle. "It is very beautiful here, but I must brag about Japan. There is no green as beautiful as rice fields in August. Someday you must see them."

We reached the high and rocky north coast, edging along the cliffs above the North Atlantic. The sun was shining, and the ocean was blue. The storm had blown over, and we were in high spirits, except for Reece. Around a curve Dunluce Castle suddenly came into view: a huge, ragged, stone ruin perched on the very edge of the cliff.

I whispered to Reece, "This could be the place!"

No answer.

We parked above the castle in a parking lot surrounded by a

wet, sloping, green meadow that smelled like sheep. I held Reece
back from the others. "What's up?"

"Nothing." She struggled along, her cane sinking into the
soggy ground with every step.

I stuck by her. "C'mon. You mad at me?"

"Of course not. We have a sword to find. Let's get to it."

Dr. Eloise gathered us at the gate. "This place appears to be
nothing more than a shell. There is no roof, no windows, or
furnishings. We have read that a secret passage goes down to
the sea to a cave where sailors often hid. It's unsafe and therefore
locked." She glanced knowingly at Dr. Dale. "We'll take a look
around and then regroup here in thirty minutes."

The girls went off together. Skid and I walked around the
outside fence and peered down into a deep chasm that separated
us from the castle. He said, "I bet at high tide it fills with water.
That's one serious moat."

We wandered through what used to be a house and chapel
but were now only broken walls of sun-washed stone. Rob found
us and gave us his version of the info sheet: "It's believed that
the two round towers and some of the outer walls were built
by MacMerrits, who controlled the north coast in the 1300s,
blah blah … soft basalt made up of round boulders, inclined to
erode … Sorley Boy MacDonnell. Ha, funny name … In 1636
a new owner built a manor house for big parties. The duchess
hated the sound of the sea and with good reason: one night
during dinner the whole kitchen and the servants working in
it fell into the sea."

We found the drop-off place and looked down a long time.
I don't know why it didn't bother me after what had happened
the day before. I couldn't get Dr. Dale's warning out of my mind
though. Who did Satan want? What if it was Reece?

Rob went on, "The duchess made an inventory of the castle:

a harp, rooms of furniture, curtains, and weapons, which were shipped to their new home. But it doesn't say where that is."

Suddenly it struck me that Dowland would have stood here and read this page. "If Dowland was shopping for armor, this would have grabbed his attention."

Skid looked doubtful. "It's a stretch."

Reece wouldn't go near the wall overlooking the sea despite my efforts to cheer her up. "It's a great day. The sun is shining, it's warm, and we're all together again, just like summer. Can you believe we're here in Ireland?"

She looked at me, her lip quivering. "Even the winds obey him, Elijah."

"I know what you meant back there in the Burren. But God wouldn't do that to you. Wind blows over the ocean all the time. You have to put it aside," I told her. "You only have a few days with Mei; then she'll be gone. And we have to find the sword. We have to."

"I know that," she said coldly and walked away, leaving me with a hollow feeling in my chest.

There was nothing in the gift shop but postcards and mugs and key rings. I asked the man behind the counter about the old cache of stuff from the MacMerrit estate.

"Sadly, the furnishings are long gone. After the restoration of 1660, Sir Randal MacMerrit returned from exile and moved to Ballymeade. The clan broke apart during the next two centuries and died out at Leap Castle."

Francine hadn't mentioned Leap Castle. "Where is that?"

"You'll find 'er in the belly of Ireland. At one time the most haunted castle in all of Europe, she was. Gruesome history around the chapel, which housed its own relics and religious articles."

"What about swords and stuff like that? I like swords."

He smiled. "Sorry, lad. Any to survive would be in museums,

private collections, or disposed of."

"Thrown away?"

"A warrior and his sword are not easily parted. If a soldier was killed, his sword might be buried with him or ritually drowned in the bogs."

We gathered at the sunny, grassy floor of the manor house ruin and shared what we'd learned. The Stallards were out of breath and smeared with mud.

Rob said, "Where have … you were in the secret tunnel?"

Dr. Dale bent over, braced his hands on his knees, and huffed. "We have clearance."

"What was down there?" I asked.

"Picked clean," he said. "We figured it would be."

Rob said, "The sword was with the rest of the armor at the time of the MacMerrits—like in the tapestry at Ballymeade. It must have gotten separated after they lived here."

"Sketchy," Dr. Dale said in an exhausted voice, wiping his brow. "The trail is too sketchy."

CHAPTER 10

We stopped at a "chippy" in Ballycastle for fish and fries, or chips as they're called in Ireland. Rob went off on another tangent about how everything in Ireland is named Bally: "Ballymeade, Ballycastle, Ballykelly—it's crazy!"

Dryly Skid said, "Interesting observation … Ballyrob."

For the rest of the trip the nickname stuck.

"We have a nice place to stay tonight," said Dr. Eloise as we zipped along a side road, "a retreat house. It's an hour south of Belfast—a historic house on a nature preserve near the bay." She showed us a pamphlet about Murlough House.

"It's pronounced *Murlock,* with a soft *K* sound." Dr. Eloise demonstrated how to push air from the back of our throats. "It's the same as *lough,* which is Gaelic for 'lake.'"

We'd circled around half the country already. Now we were on the east shore, easing onto a narrow gravel lane with seawater lapping the bank on both sides. It looked suspiciously like the entrance to Seven Avon Place. Dr. Dale pointed out places of interest in every direction.

"Aren't we supposed to call Mom sometime?" I asked.

Dr. Eloise said, "Are you worried, dear?"

"That was a dark place we left her at."

"Dark indeed." Dr. Eloise traded glances with Dr. Dale.

"Ireland's gloomy," Reece complained.

At the end of the road, we plunged into a driveway surrounded by tall woods with nice landscaping and mowed grass along the sides. "It's a park like Camp Mudj!" Mei said cheerfully.

Reece said anxiously, "I hope our room is better than the first night. That was awful."

By now I was feeling sorry for Mei—with Reece being so down. We leaned forward anxiously in our seats as we approached a clearing and turned the curve.

Mei gasped with joy. Murlough House was a huge, three-story, beige stone manor, but with big windows, a pretty lawn, trimmed shrubs, and a circle drive with a couple of vans parked out front. A big, square entry jutted out from the front.

"We're staying here?" Mei squealed. "It's a mansion!" She hugged Reece, who smiled weakly.

Rob ran up and knocked while Skid and I unloaded luggage.

A red-haired lady swung the door open wide. "Hello! You're the group from the States, is that right? I'm Cynthia. I'll show you to your rooms."

The entry hall was wide with nice wood flooring and fancy rugs. There were chairs along the walls and big landscape paintings in golden frames. Our rooms were on the first floor.

"We have dorm rooms upstairs, but there are so few of you that we thought you'd enjoy our homier accommodations."

Mei had a fit about their room: pink flowered bedspreads and curtains, high ceilings, and tall windows that opened out to show flowering bushes and evergreens. Reece said grudgingly, "At least it's warm."

"And cozy!" added Mei. "And beautiful."

The guys' room was the same except the flowered stuff was blue and purple. Cynthia showed us the bathrooms and showers. "Towels are warming in your rooms. We were just having a snack in the kitchen, if you'd like to join us."

A dozen or so college kids were gathered in the big school-type kitchen around plates of cheese and smoked meat, crackers

and bread, and cookies. They were friendly and talkative, intro-
ducing themselves as being from all over the place: Oklahoma,
Germany, Florida, Canada, Taiwan. Dr. Dale told us to circulate
and then left suddenly. Dr. Eloise told us that he was very tired.
We grabbed plates and dug in. I edged over to Dr. Eloise. "Who
are these people?"

"This is a mission house, Elijah, which means that these young
people are here to share their faith."

I didn't get what she meant, so I milled around and asked a few
of them why they were in Ireland; they all said pretty much the
same thing: God had called them here. One explained, "We run
after-school programs for children, day camps, prayer journeys
for church groups, family retreats—whatever needs to be done."

They seemed like family even though they didn't look or act
alike, and they all had different accents. The kitchen was sort
of dark and cold, but I got a warm feeling while listening to
their stories of how God brought them to Ireland even when
they didn't have the money or their families objected. One guy
had been in jail before being a Christian; another had been an
atheist. They told how God had turned their lives upside down.
I didn't want to go to bed. These guys were nothing like last
summer's counselors.

Needing to keep a low profile, we told them about the castles
we'd seen and how this was an independent study. They all had
advice on what to do in the time we had left in Ireland:

"You have to eat at a chippy. You just have to!"

"Don't eat the black-and-white pudding!"

"If you're in Dublin, don't miss the *Book of Kells.*"

"The Rock of Cashel is my favorite spot."

"Been to the Cliffs of Morte? Awesome, huh?"

Cynthia let me in the office to call Mom. I dialed Ruthie's
number. It was almost 11:00, but no one answered. I tried again

to be sure I had the right number.

Dr. Eloise came in. "Did you get through?"

"No one's home."

She frowned at her watch but said in a soothing voice, "We'll try again in the morning. She's in God's hands."

We helped clean up the kitchen, the college kids excused themselves, and we hit the showers. Just as we bedded down for the night, music drifted down the hall: a guitar and voices. Skid's voice came out of the dark, "Night devos."

"Huh?" Rob said.

"Devotions—singing, praying, reading the Bible."

I tucked my hands behind my head and listened. Some of the songs I didn't know, but one was the same as from Reece's church. I mentioned it to Skid out of curiosity. "How do these people from all over the world know the same song?"

"Good news travels fast, Creek. You've got a lot to learn about how all this God stuff works."

"How do you know how 'God stuff' works?" Rob snipped.

"I got wise to it at an early age. It's big."

"Bigger than your ego?" Rob jabbed.

"A little bigger than that, Ballyrob." He laughed good-naturedly. "You the man, Wingate."

Maybe it was jet lag, but I slept better than I had in days.

· · · · ·

We were on our way out the door into a drizzly new day of sword searching when I remembered Mom. "Wait! I have to make a call!"

Ruthie answered and put Mom right on.

"How's it going?" I asked, relieved to hear her voice.

"It's going," she said weakly.

"Are you okay, Mom?"

"Mm-mmm."

I lowered my voice. "Hey, if there's something wrong on your end, tell me in code, and we'll come and get you. If you're in trouble just say, 'Have you talked to Dad?'"

She half chuckled. "Really, hon, I'm dealing with difficult issues, that's all. Are you having a good time?"

"Yeah. It's awesome. Today we see a five-thousand-year-old tomb; then we're going up on some hill. Tomorrow is Dublin."

Dr. Dale came in and asked to talk to Mom. He told her we needed a few more days and that we'd stay in touch. Then I got back on. "We have to go."

Mom said, "I'll see you soon. Be safe. I love you."

"You too." I hung up and felt dumb for getting spooked.

Once we got on the road, Dr. Eloise turned to me: "How's the Latin research on Caesar coming?"

I scratched my head. "I don't know where to start."

At the next small-town museum, we pulled over. "Pile out!" she barked. "For Elijah's sake!"

They had some pretty cool stuff—though nothing about Roman hordes. But what stopped me in my tracks was a standing stone on display with inscriptions carved in it. I snagged Skid as he sauntered by. "Hey, does that look familiar?"

"Yeah, it's called a rock."

"No, the slashes in the stone."

In three seconds he had it: "The shield."

When we called Dr. Dale over, he said, "Ah yes, standing stones. They're all over the British Isles. It says in the brochure they were used to mark boundaries and calculate solar and lunar measurements."

"The slashes look like the rays on the shield," I said.

He examined the stone more closely. "My word. I believe you have something! Eloise?"

They went to talk to the lady at the desk, and by the time we were ready to leave, they had the lowdown. "The script is spelled *O-G-H-A-M* and pronounced *Oh-yam*. Prehistoric Ireland had no written language, so this one was devised or adopted to keep general records. She'll mail us a copy of the alphabet."

"Irish language is too complicated for me," I said. "The words don't sound anything like they look. At least Latin looks like what it sounds like."

We stopped at a coffee shop for Dr. Dale to refill his flask. It was crowded, so I wandered back out to the street and stood under the awning out of the drizzle for some peace and quiet. Dr. Eloise wouldn't have it; she poked her head out the door. "Stay with the group, Elijah. We shouldn't get separated. Are you … all right?"

"Dr. Eloise, can I ask you a question?"

"Certainly." She came out and stood beside me.

"Do you think we went into that visitors' center because we were … supposed to, so we could find those letters?"

"Yes, I do. But if we had not gone in, he would have found another way to tell us. God is not limited by our choices."

"And one more thing," I changed the subject. "Maybe you noticed that Reece has been in sort of a bad mood?"

"She's been unusually quiet. That near fall at the Cliffs of Morte disturbed us all."

"Well, she wonders if … if since God rules the wind and the waves, if maybe he tried to …"

Her face went slack. "Oh, dear Heaven!!" I followed her back into the coffee shop where Reece and Mei were buying muffins. "Reece, dear heart, if God had wanted you dead, we'd be calling your mother with the sad news of your demise! We'd be planning a memorial service! God does not *try to do* anything! He only *does* things!"

Reece shot me an acid look for telling on her.

Back in the van we got another load of lecture from Eloise. "About the Cliffs of Morte and life in general, children, God may spare us from tragedy or he may not—"

"It's his call," I interrupted.

"Exactly. If God wants to kill us, he can … no, that's not what I mean … though he could. Not that he *would.*"

It was Dr. Dale's turn to interrupt. "What Eloise is trying to say is this: the evil one's best trick is to attack the character of the Almighty. Bad things happen, but God is good. He is good! He will—in the end—make all things plain and wipe every tear from our eyes. We have to trust him."

CHAPTER 11

We wound through the drizzly countryside, Skid giving us a running travel commentary for his assignment. "One can't truly see Ireland without a side trip to Newgrange," he said authoritatively. "The road to the ancient—what is it we're seeing, Dr. D?"

"A passage tomb. A tomb accessed by a long tunnel."

"The road to the ancient passage tomb leads the happy traveler through stone-bordered fields of quiet, green pasture. The damp, fresh, pungent fragrance of wafting October air is a refreshing change from the tangy, coastal breezes of Belfast."

"That's very good, Skid!" Mei said.

"Corny as Kansas in August," said Rob, snapping pictures here and there.

We pulled into the parking lot of Newgrange. Rob yelled, "My limerick's done!" He held up his paper proudly and read:

> *There was a young man from Bally*
> *Whose sisters were Ally and Sally.*
> *They all moved away,*
> *And the towns where they stay*
> *Are named Bally and Bally and Bally.*

This prompted another "Skwagack!" out of Dr. Eloise.

At the end of a long, woodsy path sat the visitors' center.

Dr. Dale went to the information desk and came back saying: "The next bus for the tomb site leaves in twenty-five minutes. We have time for a short film that will explain what we are

101

about to see."

"The gift shop looks nice," Mei hinted.

"After the tour we'll get a bite and shop," he said.

Skid had been unusually quiet, and I'd caught him in deep-thought mode a couple of times. When we got seated in the theater and everyone else was talking, I asked, "What do you think of the trip so far?"

"Pretty cool. Pretty cool."

"And?"

"And what?"

"Something you're not saying."

"Don't know how to put it," he shrugged, stretched his legs out, and crossed his arms. "I've traveled a lot, Creek. Been all over. Seen sights, met missionaries, been to churches—I didn't get it. After talking to those college guys at Murlough, I'm startin' to get what's happening."

The room got dark, and the movie started. Pictures of outer space dissolved into the sun and then closed in on the spinning earth. The narrator explained that all life depends on light, and the ancients feared the dying of the sun every winter when the days shortened. According to him, they worshiped the sun, prayed to it, and built monuments to it all over the world: Stonehenge, the pyramids of Mesoamerica and Egypt.

The movie showed the tomb at Newgrange and all its unsolved mysteries. Who built it? How'd they haul all those rocks—some weighing twenty thousand pounds—dozens of miles to make massive tombs? Why? What did the mysterious carved symbols mean? It struck me that prehistoric civilizations used technology we still haven't figured out.

Sitting there in the dark, I had the urge to ask El-Telan-Yah: *What are you trying to tell me by bringing me here? Is the sword here in the tomb? Am I supposed to be getting something else?*

When the movie ended, Rob leaned over to Skid, "That movie was like your dad: lots of questions, no answers."

Skid slid a threatening eye toward Rob. "We're heading toward a tomb now, Ballyrob, *a tomb*. Watch your step."

"I'm soooo scared!"

Rob and I got a kick out of Skid's big, hairy threats.

Dr. Dale overheard Skid's threat and suggested an immediate opportunity for us children to get some exercise.

Dr. Eloise said, "Let's start by making our way to the bus. It's a five-minute walk."

We walked across a narrow bridge and stopped to watch the swirling, muddy waters of the River Boyne rush under us. The Stallards talked history and kept an eye on Skid and me. As we waited for the bus, Reece came over, and I braced myself to get snipped at for ratting on her to Dr. Eloise.

She whispered, "What did you think of Sahara?"

"We only saw her for a few minutes. She's okay, and I like the accent. But when she talked about rituals and goddesses, I got a strange feeling."

Reece went on. "The reason I asked is—" she glanced over at Mei to be sure she was still out of earshot, "Sahara and her mom are teaching Mei witchcraft. Mei told me last night. Mei thinks that our beliefs are like that. You make up what you want to believe. Should I say something to the Stallards?"

"I don't know. They're not real subtle."

Reece huffed in agreement.

"Hey, by the way, I didn't mean to get you in trouble, but you were ..."

"I know. I'm trying, okay? I don't know what got into me, doubting God like that. Something just came over me."

"Dr. Dale said one of us may be targeted by the evil one." I was hinting that maybe he had tried to take out Reece or me.

But when my heel had tipped back and hit rock where there was no rock before, what was that all about?

"It's probably you he's after," she said matter-of-factly. "Satan hates it when anyone gives his life to God. Salvation is often followed by a spiritual attack."

A chill went through me. "No one told me that."

"Would you have backed out?" she asked.

"No," I said halfheartedly. We watched the swirling waters rush under us. I said to Reece, "I think it's Mei he's after. We don't have much time with her. Do your stuff."

"What stuff?" she smiled curiously.

"Be yourself."

A bus came to pick us up. I sat by Reece in the front seat; Skid pulled Mei down to the seat behind us. I turned to him. "You said you're starting to 'get it.' What did you mean?"

"Oh yeah. People from everywhere going everywhere to spread the word. It's happening already—millions of kids going around the world every year, building houses and churches, teaching little street kids, giving out food and clothes. The college students at Murlough House? That's us in the future, but our mission will be different." He squeezed Mei's neck. "You too, Aizawa. We're the new wave."

I didn't know what he meant by mission and new wave, but it filled me with a strange kind of hope. If you had told me a year ago that I'd be in Ireland on a quest for a mysterious sword with my four best friends, I'd have said you were loons.

In a few minutes, we were standing outside an enormous, grassy mound held in place by a twelve-foot-high wall of white stones. Around the bottom of the mound was a band of rocks as big as refrigerators. The guide, a friendly chubby guy in his twenties, did his spiel about the mysteries of Newgrange. As he led us into the tomb, he warned us tall guys about cracking our heads on the ceiling. The narrow passage was about sixty feet long; huge standing stones made the walls. At the end were three chambers with strange carvings covering the walls: leaves, flowers, diamonds, ovals with lines, and tri-swirls.

Nearly thirty of us visitors crowded into the center where the three small chambers met. We listened to how skeletons and pottery had been found in the chambers. Then the guide got to the main point. "On the shortest day of the year—the dark day—the sun rises directly into the stone window above the passage and lights up the chamber. Today is not the winter solstice, so we'll have to demonstrate the amazing effect using artificial light."

He turned out the lights. For a second it was pitch-dark; then a weak beam moved down the passage. When it got to us, it lit the entire room. "When the real sun comes shining in, it's bright and golden—amazing," he said. "Anyone can sign up for the winter solstice tour. But there's a ten-year waiting list and no guarantee it won't be cloudy."

When the other tourists filed out, we stayed behind. The Stallards wanted to ask the guide a few questions. That's when he turned off his spiel and got real with us. "I've stood here when the light comes. A lot of people don't put much stock in spiritual things, but when I'm standing here and the light comes ... you feel something, as if someone is here."

"The sun goddess?" Mei asked, intrigued.

"Some think so," he said politely. "I believe differently."

"I know what you mean," I said. "When I'm alone in my woods, he comes. But not just when it's sunny. He comes day or night, cloudy or clear. Anytime."

The guide grinned. "That's what I'm talking about."

I turned to Mei and pointed upward. "The creator."

Mei nodded thoughtfully. *"Souzousha."*

Dr. Eloise glowed. "Deuteronomy 4:19 says, 'When you look up to the sky and see the sun, the moon and the stars—all the heavenly array—do not be enticed into bowing down to them and worshiping things the LORD your God has apportioned to all the nations under heaven.'" She went on into another verse.

Leaving Dr. Eloise in her own little happy cloud, Dr. Dale said to the guide, "We don't want to keep you longer or miss our bus, but I'm intrigued by what motivated the ancients to build these structures. They must have lived in huts or tents. Yet to honor their dead, they created this enormous mound. It seems that from the very beginning, the ancients knew there was eternal life. Enoch, the seventh from Adam, didn't die, so they knew it was possible to live forever."

"Getting to the next life was important to these people," the guide answered. "Something else might interest you folks. See how this grave is a long passageway with three chambers, one to the left, one to the right, and one ahead? Well, here's how it would look from the air if you had x-ray vision." He knelt down and drew in the dirt. "Here's the mound of earth, a large circle, and here's the passage tomb inside."

Reece gasped. "A cross-shaped passage to eternal life?"

Dr. Dale said in amazement, "Three thousand years before Jesus was crucified!"

The guide nodded mysteriously and looked at me. "Coincidence?"

When we got out of the tomb, I turned back to the guide. "Hey, when people first discovered this tomb, all they found was bones and pottery?"

"That's about it."

"No armor?"

He shook his head. "Bowls … a few Roman coins."

"Roman? Did the Roman hordes attack here?" I added,

"I have a research paper to write."

"Some say Caesar invaded and occupied. Some say he didn't."

"Well, if he didn't, why not?"

He shrugged. "Too far to haul all that battle gear? Not enough plunder? For one thing, Caesar didn't like the druids and their ceremonies."

"Thanks." I shook his hand. "I don't guess you could you say all that in Latin and stretch it out to two pages?"

On our way back down the hill, Dr. Eloise said, "One more thing we have to clear up, children. Many people marvel at the intelligence and ingenuity of the ancients. Where did this technology beyond our own come from? Were aliens involved, some ask? I believe those inquiring minds are working under a false assumption: that mankind is evolving. According to the second law of thermodynamics, we are *de*volving, running down. Let's mentally travel back through time several millennia to people who lived for hundreds of years and built monuments like these. What do you have?"

Rob said, "Super-intellects?"

"Super-strong super-intellects?" I suggested.

"Super-cool ancients!" Skid threw his hands out.

"That's precisely my theory." She looked back sadly at the mound on top of the hill overlooking the River Boyne. "Superior intellect is not always wise. Death cults as practiced by the ancient Egyptians and Sumerians—all those who built great tombs filled with possessions for the next world—they didn't understand that you can't take it with you."

· · · · ·

We stopped for lunch at a pub and got a table by a fireplace—to take the chill out of our bones, as Dr. Eloise said. Dr. Dale ordered soup. The rest of us got big sandwiches. Halfway through the meal, Dr. Eloise said, "Children, we are going to skip our trip to the Hill of Slane this afternoon. Dr. Dale needs to rest. So I'll be driving from here on out."

We all shot him worried looks.

"I'm fine, I'm fine," he said. But his usual spark and energy were gone. His walk was slower, and his back was a little bent. Dr. Dale was acting his age, which worried me.

"Devolving?" Rob joked.

"A little," he said with a half smile.

Reece said, "Can we do anything to help? We'll be quieter. We can do the searching and asking questions."

He patted her hand. "Don't change a thing."

"I can read maps," Rob offered. "I'll be the navigator."

"Thank you," said Dr. Dale. "A half day of rest when we arrived would have braced me for the roundabouts and the spiritual uncertainties. A bit of a strain, that's all."

He was tired, but some big worry was going on in that high-IQ brain of his. Did he worry that the sword was one of the magics hidden for all time? The thought kept creeping into my mind. And what good is armor if you have no sword to defend yourself? None, if you ask me.

We stopped at a couple of antique shops—with no luck—before heading back to Murlough House. Dr. Eloise turned over all their pamphlets and gave us the rest of the day to work on our projects. "Read up on Patrick of Ireland, Elijah. You might find helpful material, a new slant to your topic." She helped Dr. Dale to his room.

Chilling in my blue and purple flowered room, I cranked out a limerick about how hard Irish is:

> *Skid said, "Lough rhymes with tough."*
> *Reece said, "Lough rhymes with through."*
> *Then I said, "Somehow*

Lough must rhyme with bough."
But it's Irish. So lough rhymes with rock!

I thought it was cool until I tried to read it out loud and sounded ridiculous. So I gave up, took a nap, and tried not to worry about Dr. Dale.

The college kids came bounding in that afternoon. They were about to ask if we'd like to help fix dinner that night when Dr. Eloise burst from her room. "We forgot! It's *Samhain!* Tonight! To the Hill of Slane!!"

CHAPTER 12

Looking weaker than ever, Dr. Dale was still behind the wheel, his wife barking road numbers as we whipped through the roundabouts for the next two hours. We zoomed past a small sign: "Hill of Slane." He slammed on the brakes, turned back, shot up a narrow street, and pulled up to a metal gate. Through the gate and nearly at the crest of the hill lay a cemetery and the remains of a church, the stones black with mold and age. "Patrick's hill of destiny," Dr. Eloise beamed at me.

Except for a couple of crumbling church towers and Celtic crosses poking up everywhere, it could have been Old Pilgrim's graveyard.

From the Hill of Slane, we could see in all directions: rolling farms green as summer but soft and mellow under the butter-colored sky. Not a sound could be heard. Everyone was awestruck.

"It's so beautiful!" Reece said reverently. "So awesome … to be here … together."

"Hi, Mom," I said under my breath toward the southwest. "Hi, Grandma."

Rob turned to me, looking puzzled. "Yeah, we could have a new grandma in a few days? That is too strange."

Standing as still as the tombstones around us, we watched the sun disappear and the sky turn to amber. My eyes left the sunset to glance at Reece standing beside me. Her face was pure gold. Behind her, circled crosses were silhouetted against the yellow sky with hazy, dreamy hills beyond. It seemed to me that I'd slipped into another world.

Reece's eyes, fixed on the sun's disappearing, welled up with tears. Her sniffles turned to sobs. No one had to tell me what she was thinking—she was sorry she'd been so angry at God. I put my arm around her. She folded herself into me and cried some more.

"Look southward," came Dr. Dale's voice from behind me. "See that clump of trees? That's the Hill of Tara. Sixteen centuries ago the high kings of Tara ruled from that hill. Once a year the king would order all fires extinguished. Then on the eve of his druid festival, the priest would light a fire. No one dared defy the custom. But in the year 433, young Patrick climbed this hill and lit a fire to signal the coming of the true light to Ireland. He set his face against the traditions of a whole country—a dangerous thing for one so young and alone."

"What happened to him?" Reece pulled away and wiped her eyes.

Mei was all ears.

Dr. Eloise took up the story. "He was immediately summoned to the king's court, as the story goes. But the king was greatly impressed with Patrick's gospel message and allowed the young missionary to live. It is said that the druids warned the king …" Dr. Eloise lowered her voice, "'If you let that fire burn, O high king, it will never be put out.'" She looked across the land with a satisfied smile. "And so it is. The fire of truth still burns."

Dr. Dale looked at me. "And so it must continue until the end. The fire must not go out." He turned and walked away.

Rob discovered a crumbling spiral stair to one of the small towers. "Come on, guys! It looks dangerous, but it's not. Reece, you can make it."

In a minute all four of them were up there clowning around. Skid peeked out a window from the top, enjoying his new love of heights. "Hey, Creek, come on up!"

"Maybe later." I skimmed the darkening land. *Here one young guy took a stand and changed the world. One guy.* House lights sparked to life one by one ... and another light high on a hill ... like the fires of Council Cliffs. I called Dr. Dale over. "What's that?"

He sighed. "That is the Hill of Ward."

"Where Sahara is?"

"Yes. A pagan fire is lit tonight; worshipers invite unknown entities to come through the veil. Here and around the world ... on this night and every night. Fires lit to gods who are inventions of the mind, or worse: demons in disguise."

Spread out before me was a black world, a crimson sky, and a decision. Reece had been right when she'd said, "You won't be living the regular life: go to church on Sunday, put a buck in the offering plate, and light a candle at Christmas."

Watching that fire on the Hill of Ward set a fire in me. Those people were bowing to nothing and calling it something, worshiping evil, convincing Mei that it was all well and good. I stood where Patrick stood, watching what he'd seen sixteen centuries before. I felt what he felt. I watched the fire grow.

"Do you have a match?" I asked Dr. Dale.

I dragged fallen limbs from the trees above the old church, broke them over my knee, and stacked them in a teepee shape on the paved path. All I had for tinder were some damp twigs and leaves. *It'll never catch.* There was trash in the van, but it wouldn't be enough. *Creek, what resources do you have?* Down beyond the gate were a few houses. *Yeah, sure, a foreign teenage guy knocks at your door on Halloween night and asks to borrow stuff to build a fire. That'd go over big.*

Then I remembered how the Mad River Boys did it. I went to Dr. Dale. "I need to siphon some gas out of the van."

Dr. Eloise wrung her hands while Dr. Dale helped me rig up a siphoning hose. I got drinking straws from our fast-food trash bag and stuck them together with surgical tape from the first-aid kit. I used his coffee flask to catch the gas. The other four convinced Dr. Eloise that I knew what I was doing and had years of training, that I wasn't a pyro.

In the end it wasn't much of a fire—even with a couple of flasks of gasoline thrown on for good measure—but it was a fire. I kept it going while the Stallards explained to Mei the big difference between Sahara's fire and my fire.

Stars popped out all over the universe. If you know one thing about astronomy, you understand that some old god of the sun couldn't hold a candle to the creator of a whole doggone universe. The Stallards didn't have to drive the point home to any of us. God did it himself with a cosmic show of force: the Milky Way, billions of suns. He even threw in a meteor shower for good measure.

Dr. Dale got a flashlight and beamed it on his open Bible. "This is a passage from the *Warrior.*" His voice was thick and powerful as he read: "'Why do the nations conspire and the peoples plot in vain? The kings of the earth take their stand and the rulers gather together against the LORD and against his Anointed One... . The One enthroned in heaven laughs; the Lord scoffs at them... . O LORD, how many are my foes! How many rise up against me! Many are saying of me, 'God will not deliver him.' But you are a shield around me, O LORD; you bestow glory on me and lift up my head. To the LORD I cry aloud, and he answers me from his holy hill!'"

Silence fell around my crackling fire. Skid looked at me, his green eyes wide and watery in the semi-dark, his voice low and awed. "This is what I meant, man. We're the new wave."

I understood in my head about good waging war on evil. God

and Satan. In some way, though, I was still out of the loop. But all that was about to change.

On the way back, Dr. Dale told the others about Patrick and Brendan and Columba, the *peregrini* who wandered the world—never sure where they were going, or if they'd return.

The college kids had saved leftovers for us, and we stood around in the big kitchen, chowing down until the wee hours. I did a lot of listening that night.

Later when they were having devos, I crept down the hall toward their meeting room. I eased myself to the cold floor, leaned against the wall, and listened. None of them were great singers, but together it was the nicest sound. Over and over I pictured myself on the Hill of Slane again. I watched the sunset; I kept holding onto Reece; I gathered wood. I felt the flames shooting heavenward with Skid's words ringing in my mind: *we're the new wave.* We'd made no headway finding the sword that day, but I wouldn't have traded my moment on the Hill of Slane for a million bucks.

· · · · ·

It was the morning of the fourth day. We'd had four hours of sleep, but the Stallards were up and packed by 8:00. Dr. Dale was gray with exhaustion, but his eyes were clear and intense. There was a mysterious calm around him, like he knew something we didn't. We thanked Cynthia for our breakfast of eggs and thick Irish bread with tea, then we loaded the van.

Dr. Eloise jumped behind the wheel. "Driving in Dublin will be suicide!"

"Greaaaat," Skid said smoothly.

Rob took navigator position, and Dr. Dale sat in the back. We pulled onto the main highway and Rob barked, "A25 to Newry where we catch A1 to M1 and all the way to Dublin."

Skid quipped, "Man the lifeboats, my people," then went off

ad-libbing another travelogue. "After a grand breakfast of sumptuous eggs and hearty tea, we depart for Dublin. Pungent air
awakens the lungs, and quaint villages invite the eager traveler."

Ballyrob threatened to hurl up his sumptuous eggs and hearty
tea if Skid didn't shut up.

"To spare our lives and our sanity," Dr. Eloise threw her voice
in our direction as she whipped us around the roundabout and
shot off onto A25, "we'll park on the outskirts and take a lovely
little train into the heart of the city. We'll have a look at the
Cathach, the oldest surviving manuscript in Ireland, written
down by Columba. The *Warrior,* Dale, the *Warrior!*"

We made it to Sandyford station where we boarded a silver
commuter train. We zipped through the outskirts and got off at
St. Stephen's Green, a nice, woodsy park with a lake and stream
right downtown.

Skid started in again. "Around the green, Dublin's downtown
traffic bustles along through the quaint but modern city of stone
and brick, trimmed in dark, rich colors. No, my friends, Dublin
isn't a high-rise metropolis like Chicago, but the friendly faces—"

Reece cut him off with a singsong, "I'm in Dublin with Me-i,
I'm in Dublin with Me-i."

They hugged and giggled. I breathed a sigh of relief. The evil
one had let go of his gloomy grip on Reece.

"Another museum?" Skid muttered as we headed into a huge,
gray stone building.

"Now, now. This is for our artist, " said Dr. Eloise, smiling
at Mei. "But I believe we'll all appreciate the art of manuscript
decoration. The *Book of Kells* is perhaps the world's most exqui-
site book. A quick look, then we must track down the *Warrior.*"

The museum had a film showing how people made books
from scratch twelve hundred years ago: pens from quills, pages
from animal skins, paint from plants and minerals, ink from

charcoal. Back then making one lousy book was two tons of work. They made it a whole lot fancier than they needed to because it was the Bible.

After the hard driving, we were glad to be hanging out, strolling along cobblestone streets, checking out the Irish city folks. I was starting to feel a little guilty that we weren't chasing down the sword, when I noticed a sign on a window: "The Cathach—Coffees Teas Books."

"Hey, let's go there. Maybe they have books about the *Warrior!*"

It was a tiny café with a few tables connected to a bookstore—even smaller—with floor-to-ceiling shelves and a ladder on wheels. A circular iron staircase led down to a basement. The owner was standing in his little office in the back. He stepped out. "May I help you?"

"We're looking for books on the—" I tried to say it right, "*Caa'thuck!*"

"Gesundheit!" said Rob.

The owner looked down his rimless glasses at me. "That sort would be downstairs. Liam will aid you." He stepped back into his doorway like a guardian soldier.

I peered down the stairs and saw a handful of shoppers jammed in the boxy little room. "It looks crowded down there. I'll go."

Rob said, "We'll check out the menu. I'm starved already."

A polite-looking guy not much older than I, with dark hair and green eyes, was restocking shelves.

"Do you have any books on the *Cathach?*" I asked.

He looked blank. "I don't know."

"Since your store is called that name, I thought—"

"We deal in history, folklore … divination."

"It's part of the Bible, the Psalms."

"I doubt we have anything on it," he said flatly.

"Would you mind looking?" I pressed. As he ran a finger along the titles, I pulled out a book and started idly flipping through it. "Yeah, some experts told me the *Cathach* was used as a good-luck charm for battles. But we're interested in it for *spiritual* warfare. Fighting evil," I said proudly.

I flipped through another book. I became aware that he'd stopped moving. I lifted my eyes from the page. Liam's hand lay quiet on the wall of books, and he stared at the books.

His head rotated mechanically in my direction. His dark eyes drilled into me. His lip curled in disgust, and this total stranger seethed at me with a kind of hate I'd never seen: black, pure hate. From his mouth came a deep rattle of a voice: "You'll never find it."

A quiet roar filled my head—blood rushed through my brain. I seemed to go numb. But a corner of my mind stayed perfectly clear. I knew without looking that there were only two of us in the basement. The other customers had left. But there was a third. Two bodies, three beings. It wasn't Liam talking. It was something else. Liam wasn't referring to the *Cathach*. He was talking about the sword.

Still sneering, his eyes slid back to the wall of books as if nothing had happened. I backed away without a word and went up the steps in a daze.

"Any luck?" Reece met me at the top. One look at my face and she said, "What happened?!"

"Nothing," I muttered. "They didn't ... uh ... don't ... have anything."

Her eyebrows shot up excitedly, a simple, sudden gesture that nearly made me jump out of my skin. "Well, don't go to pieces, Elijah! We'll see the real thing this afternoon. This is a side trip; our real quest is the sword."

"Yeah." I glanced around to see if we'd been overheard.

Skid came over. "You look shook. I can't believe the prices either; I could buy a new skateboard for one book the size of a piece of toast! Let's go."

"Yeah," I murmured weakly, "let's go."

I couldn't think. The hate from those eyes and that growling voice hung on me like a stench. I wanted to wash it off. I wanted to be baptized again.

"Cheer up, Creek," Skid insisted. "Isn't it weird that a store by the name of a book has no copies of the book, and even no books about it? Weird."

"Yeah."

"I know you're hungry, children," said Dr. Eloise, "but we need to try to view the *Cathach* if we can. It shouldn't take long. Elijah, aren't you feeling well?"

"I'm okay," I said.

We got directions to the Grafton Institute from someone on the street. Everyone was so friendly; the Stallards said getting around Ireland was easier than other places they'd been where few speak English or where Americans are generally disliked. "Most everyone here has a distant relative in the States," said Dr. Eloise. "We Americans love Ireland's people. What a nice arrangement between countries!"

I was going through the motions, my mind still on what happened in the basement of the bookstore. *It was a demon. A demon.* My mind in a fog, I tagged along behind the others down a tree-lined street to what looked like a town house. A fancy sign out front read: "Grafton Institute."

Dr. Dale paused, his hand at the door knocker. "Eloise, we are doing the right thing, aren't we?"

"I think we have no choice," she answered. "We have one more lead, Leap Castle, which seems to be long abandoned and under renovation. After that it's a dead end."

He looked at us. "Let us be cautious not to reveal any secrets about the sword. Let Eloise and me do the talking."

Dr. Eloise seemed torn. "They're antiquities people. What if they've heard of … the armor?"

"It would certainly complicate things," he answered, gripping the door knocker. "We've had this on our hearts for years—we've searched and made inquiries. We would have crossed paths with these people before, if they knew anything."

"Yes, of course. They're not a part of the network. We've been thorough and careful, haven't we?"

"Very."

He knocked. In a minute a heavy, old gentleman in a black suit came to the door. "We're closed today."

"I'm Dr. Dale and this is my wife Eloise. These are our students. I spoke with someone on the phone about an important matter, about the *Cathach*."

Skid and I swapped glances. He'd made it sound like Dale was his last name. He didn't want to be traced.

"I didn't take a call. We'll be open fifth November." He started to close the door.

"Wait!" Dr. Dale pulled out the page enclosed in the plastic sleeve. "You must see what we found!"

The door opened again. The man's eyes fell on the page. He did a double take. Dr. Eloise put her hand on the door. "We believe it's authentic." Dr. Dale put the page back in his briefcase.

Reluctantly the man let us in. "Cravens is the name." He took us to his office, and Dr. Dale laid his briefcase on the big desk.

Cravens started asking questions. "Where did you get this page, if you don't mind my asking?"

Dr. Eloise said, "We'd like to see the *Cathach* first, please."

"Certainly. Now what organization did you say you're with?" he asked cleverly.

They dodged instead of answering. Cravens wanted answers first. They wanted to see the book. Finally he caved and led us to a back room to a stack of flaky old pages like the *Book of Kells*, locked under glass with special lights. Cravens unlocked the case, gently pulled out the book, and laid it on the glass. He asked to see the page again. As Dr. Dale placed it on the glass, Cravens's eyes were glazed with excitement, his expression deadpan. "Are there more pages?"

"Not from this source."

"What source would that be?"

Dr. Eloise glanced at her husband, pulled the gold opera glasses out of her bag, and viewed the *Cathach* from where she stood. "We found the page in a spoiled old thing, a piece of armor. It's been fiddled with, redone, no story, no papers on it. The page was used as stuffing in the back of a shield, of all things! We tracked the language to Irish Gaelic and … voilà!" She paused. "We love antiques—European things especially. We'd be happy to turn the page over to …"

I gasped.

Up to this time Cravens had hardly noticed us, being intent on the lost page.

I cleared my throat as if there was dust in the room, which was dumb because dust is not allowed in fancy archive rooms. Dr. Eloise, cool as a cucumber, turned to me smiling. "Catching a cold?" But her eyes shot me a cautious look. *Don't blow my cover.*

"What we'd really like in exchange—" Dr. Dale started.

Cravens broke in. "This a private institute, small. We're not heavily endowed."

"No, no, I'm not talking money. We were curious about the origin of the shield from which we extracted this page. We'd love to have an entire set from the period, a helmet and sword and so on, for our entryway. Even just the shield and a sword would look marvelous over our mantle. So if you had any information in your extensive archives about a shield … or a sword connected with the *Cathach*—"

Ever so slowly Cravens began to change. His big jowls quivered for a second. He went rigid. I felt like a witness to a drug deal. Nothing was said for a very long moment. The doctors and the archivist locked onto each others' faces, looking for signals.

Cravens glanced at us kids suspiciously. "You're from America," he said at last, "and you came all this way for a mantle decoration?"

"This is primarily an educational tour." Dr. Eloise smiled at us. "Antiquing is merely a diversion."

Cravens didn't buy it for a minute.

Something was up. Dr. Eloise glanced at Dr. Dale and blinked in code.

Cravens bent over the page again. "It's authentic. One of the missing pages from the *Cathach*. We had no idea any of them still existed." He strolled around the table, circling us. Our eyes followed him; we didn't move. He said in an oozing voice, "Yes, yes, the world has its unsolved mysteries, doesn't it? The farfetched, the mythical, on which no respectable man of science would waste his time or risk his career. Myths," he said in my ear as he circled. "UFO landings," he said to Skid, and around the circle, "Noah's ark … the lost city of Atlantis … the lost pages of the *Cathach* …" He moved around to Dr. Dale and hissed, "The armor of God …"

The Stallards tried hard not to wilt.

He completed the circle and stood facing us in the dim archival light.

Dr. Dale said matter-of-factly, "Interesting myths aside, we're simply looking for a sword of a period that might match the shield we have."

"You have the other pieces?"

"Of what?"

A smile slithered crossed Cravens's shadowy face. "I believe they'll find Atlantis one day and the Loch Ness Monster. I believe it."

"Me too!" blurted Rob. "Nessie's probably a plesiosaur—"

I elbowed him hard.

The hefty man drew his hands behind him and bent over the lost page. "And I believe that wandering the world is a relic that is not a relic, a thing that spans all time, a thing that comes together only with great power, then disappears like a wanderer in the bogs, only to reappear again—when it's ... ," he locked eyes with Dr. Dale, "needed."

"Quite an interesting theory you have, Mr. Cravens," Dr. Dale said with finality. "We've taken enough of your time."

Cravens went on greedily, "A treasure of immeasurable wealth. No man can purchase it, for it cannot be appraised."

Smugly, Dr. Eloise spoke into the handle of her opera glasses, "Thank you so much, Mr. Cravens of Grafton Institute. If we happen upon anyone in the scientific community, we'll be sure to let them know of your interest in UFOs and Nessie and those other—" she chuckled lightly, *"legitimate fields of scientific study you mentioned.* I'm sure your colleagues would be delighted to know that." She closed the glasses with a loud click and dropped them into her purse.

Skid and I swapped looks. *She has a tape recorder in those glasses?!*

Dr. Dale picked up the page and slid it into his briefcase. "If we ever decide to sell, we'll give you a call."

Cravens followed us to the door. "And if I find a certain sword, where might I contact you?"

"Good day," said Dr. Dale.

CHAPTER 13

We wound through side streets of Dublin, the Stallards glancing back every now and then to see if we were followed. We slipped into a pizza place and got an upstairs table in a back corner. They ordered smoked salmon with crème fraiche. I got good old American pepperoni. When the waitress left, Dr. Eloise said sarcastically, "That went well! He knew, Dale, he knew! What were the chances?"

"Perhaps greater than we previously thought," said Dr. Dale nervously.

They were pretty upset. None of us knew what to do. But Reece popped up with, "We still have Leap Castle. Have faith. God wouldn't let us come all this way for nothing."

Afternoon on the streets of Dublin got balmy with good smells of coffee and food. Music of every kind drifted on the air. Dr. Eloise said, "Let's cheer ourselves with the street entertainers."

Some little kid stood on a corner and sang at the top of his lungs; I dropped a coin into his basket. There was a fire-juggling act on one corner and a flute player on the next. A crowd gathered around a folk rock group of three guys with guitars and a portable sound system. They had shaggy hair and were in jeans and black leather jackets. We edged into the crowd to listen. The words of their song were about life not being what you think, that even love is a broken alleluia. It was sad and beautiful. Reece had tears in her eyes.

This quest wasn't what I thought. *What's going on? Why's this*

strange stuff happening: Mei living with a witch, Reece and me
almost dying, Dr. Dale giving up food and acting mysterious? And
some entity telling me I'll never find the sword.

On down the street, another crowd had gathered at a big
intersection to hear a man yelling. I thought it was a politician
trying to get himself elected. Dr. Eloise warned, "Stay together
now. It could be a militant faction."

A man in his thirties held the microphone. His face was square
and serious, his eyes sad and piercing. People stood behind him
with posters that said "YOUR SIN WILL FIND YOU OUT"
and "REPENT AND BELIEVE THE GOSPEL." The preacher
paced and yelled above the street noise, "I am not asking you
to join a church or to follow some list of rules. I am begging
you to give your life to Jesus! The Day of the Lord is coming!"

Some people walked past smirking. Others looked embarrassed for the guy. One woman stood there crying until she was
handed a pamphlet. The preacher looked directly at me. "He
may be coming soon. Give him your heart!"

"I did!" I said back. "I already did!"

Everyone on that street stopped and stared at me. The preacher
himself seemed shocked, but he shouted, "Amen!"

Humiliated, I whirled around and disappeared into the crowd.
Reece and Rob called my name, but I kept on walking.

What's going on? God? Why's everyone talking to me? I'm in a
foreign country. No one even knows my name, and they're talking
directly to me!

I stopped at another corner where a woman in old-fashioned clothes sat playing a little harp in front of a church door.
I leaned against the wall a few feet from her, tossed a coin into
her basket and looked around me, wondering how I ended up
circling a country looking for a sword that the whole world had
lost track of.

After a while I doubled back to find the others. I found one of those pamphlets in the gutter and picked it up. It said: "Eternity … where will YOU be?" and the address of the gospel meeting on St. Stephen's Green.

No one in our group mentioned my yelling out, but they gave me odd looks. A drizzle settled in. We went to a pub for hot chocolate. I sat at the end of the table next to Dr. Dale. When the others got engrossed in their souvenirs, I pulled out the pamphlet and showed it to him. "I want to go to this."

He studied it. "This is downtown. We were going to take the train back to the station and the van to Murlough House."

"I know, but I have to go to this. I don't know why."

Everyone debated who should go and why until it was a big mess. Finally I said, "I'm going by myself, and that's it."

Dr. Dale sighed. He was tired and disappointed in the dead ends. "Can you get the train back?"

"Sure," I said uncertainly.

"You can catch a cab from the station." He pulled out his wallet and gave me some bills. "If this is something you have to do, here's money for your dinner, train and cab fare."

After a long discussion and more worried looks from the others, we parted ways. I watched the train pull out toward Sandyford. The sun was behind the buildings already. Streetlights flickered on, and the crowds just got bigger. *Don't people go home here? They roll up the streets of Magdeline at dinnertime.* I kept my bearings toward St. Stephen's Green and wandered, engulfed in pure loneliness and confusion. *You'll never find it.* That voice—I couldn't get it out of my mind.

Just before 8:00, I went inside a red brick building and sprinted up the steps to the second floor. A plain-looking man with a red face welcomed me. I recognized him as one of the people holding a doomsday poster.

"Good evenin' and welcome, lad."

"Thanks."

"What's yer name?" he asked.

"Uh … Telanoo. George Telanoo."

I felt terrible going to church incognito, but after the meeting with Cravens, I couldn't be too careful. It was the first time I began to understand why the Stallards had changed their names.

"Nice to meet ya, George. Warn't you the lad who—?"

"That was me. I'm … uh, saved, so …" I shook my head, indicating that I didn't need to be baptized or anything.

"That's grand. So yer comin' to hear the man again?" He nodded approvingly. "He puts the fear of God in ye sideways, don't he?"

"Um, yeah. Fear of God … sideways … yeah."

It wasn't a usual church but a meeting room—bare except for chairs lined up and a small pulpit. At the back was a snack table of cookies and tea. Off the room was a hallway where moms were taking their little kids.

I picked up a program and took a seat at the back. A lady with a guitar got up and started playing. People joined in with hands raised and eyes closed—sort of like Skid's pentecoastal church meeting but not as rowdy. I didn't know the words, and I'd have felt fake doing the hand raising and eye-closing thing. It was a song about the end of time—darkness and famine and sword. *Sword?? Is this why I'm here? Does someone here know about the sword?* I flipped open the program to see what the song title was. Halfway down the page were the words: "The Days of Elijah."

I tried not to freak.

The street preacher's sermon was interesting partly because of his cool Irish accent. But mostly because he preached about the Elijah in the Bible, how he went up against Baal-Zebub, the lord of the flies, the prince of demons, all by himself. And how he called fire down from Heaven. I hung on every word. Other people liked the sermon too, and went forward to be prayed over or to give their lives to God.

Afterwards the preacher and the red-faced man talked a minute. They looked over at me. The preacher came over smiling. "Nice to have you at our service. You from around here?"

"The States."

"I see. First time to Ireland?" "Yessir."

"You're the one who spoke up today, sayin' you're saved."

"Yeah, but I'm new at it."

He smiled. "Do ya need a word from the Lord?"

After that moment in the bookstore, I sure needed something. "Yeah, maybe …"

The preacher took my hand, closed his eyes. He prayed for God to bless me and use me in a mighty way. He asked God to ease what was troubling my heart, so I guess my face had been telling on me.

On the train back, I recalled my last night in Telanoo when I prayed to see what I was fighting, to understand why we had to find the armor of God. A shiver of cold coursed through my veins. Then I remembered Dr. Dale saying that a warrior's shield can be shattered during the initial attack on the front lines. My faith sure felt fractured.

Once off the train, I stood at the station near a street lamp, watching how people hailed cabs so I'd know how to do it. I hailed one, jumped in, and gave the cabbie the address. I kept an eye on his expression in his rearview mirror and made small talk about the weather until I got back to Murlough House. I gave the mini version of the service and went to my room. The others knew better than to follow.

I wanted to tell someone about what happened at the bookstore, but couldn't bring myself to do it. They'd think I'd lost my mind. I wasn't so sure myself.

I clicked off the light and lay there in the dark, eyes wide and staring at nothing, afraid to sleep. Night devos went on down the hall, and I prayed that they'd keep singing until I fell asleep. But even the songs couldn't drown out the words meant for me and me alone: *You'll never find it.*

How'd that thing get into my world anyway? How'd he know where I was? Had Sahara's fire opened the veil to the dark side, and did he watch me build my fire for God on the Hill of Slane and follow me all the way to Dublin? Was he right about the sword?

I buried my face in my pillow. *God, why don't you tell me where it is?*

CHAPTER 14

We couldn't find it. We drove back roads, got blocked in by cows, and pulled over in graveyards to search the lonely, isolated hills of central Ireland. Leap Castle could not be found.

Slightly offended, Dr. Eloise said, "These directions are vague. Obviously this isn't a popular tourist stop. Don't expect much of a gift shop."

We stopped at a pub and asked directions from an old farmer. He gave them, but his accent was so thick I couldn't understand him. The Stallards thanked him and pulled out.

Dr. Dale turned to his wife. "Did you get that?"

"Nary a word. But his finger pointed down that road." We drove for a couple of miles.

"Have you children been working on your limericks?" she asked, trying to lighten the mood.

"I have mine," Reece flipped open her journal and read:

Me write a limerick? What do I say?
I'm happy to see my friend Mei!
The land is so green,
The greenest I've seen.
I like the museums—
I'm glad we got to see 'em.
The food is tops,
There are lots of coffee shops.

"I know this is too long, but I'm the mouth of the bunch!"

"Hey, that was it!" Rob said.

We turned around at the next farm road and backtracked to square stone gates whose iron doors stood open against a white sky. The van bumped down the rutted gravel drive. A solitary tower rose ahead. The castle came into full view, and Dr. Dale slammed on the brakes. For the second time in a week, we'd come upon a place that left us speechless. Nothing I can say in the way of description would explain what I felt.

Leap Castle was an ivy-covered shell of smoky plaster and stone surrounded by lonely blue-gray hills. It was flat along the front and two stories high with a three-story tower in the middle. There was ugliness in its wide tower: a single church window over the door and a narrow window above that. Two pointed decorations at the front corners looked like horns, or ears. Some buildings have faces—a door for the mouth and window-eyes looking down at you. Leap Castle was blind. No eyes, the central church window a slack mouth, its stony ears perked and listening for something across silent hills.

A shell of a left wing threw the whole house off balance; its six windows were broken out. Stone fences angled out toward us in front of the wings. The chimneys were ready to topple. Mist crept along the front; dead trees stood inside the roofless left wing; moss crawled up the walls; ivy dripped from the tower. It was as if the earth was reclaiming it—digesting it day by day.

"Whoa … ," Skid whispered, "this is one sinister place."

"Gift shop closed for all eternity," Rob remarked.

"You got that right, Ballyrob," said Skid—dead serious.

"A spiritual vacuum," murmured Dr. Eloise.

"*Kowai!*" Mei said. "Scary!"

"This is our last place to look," I said gloomily. I couldn't imagine finding the sword of the Lord here.

"It looks like it was bombed," Reece said.

"Destruction by fire actually, almost a century ago," Dr. Eloise commented. "Before we go in, we pray."

I heard the whisper in my head: *You'll never find it.*

"Good idea," Dr. Dale agreed.

As they prayed, I listened but kept an eye on the castle. In one way Leap Castle had nothing of what would usually scare a person: no glowing lights in the window, no swampy moat, no tall threatening towers. It was a blind nothing standing in silhouette against a white sky. The place seemed to open its stony arms: *Come on in. Nothing here. Looking for something, eh? You'll never find it.*

Not a soul was around. The front door was locked, but a soggy gangplank had been propped against the front left window. One by one we sidestepped up the rain-slick boards. Mei and I kept hold of Reece until she made it to the threshold.

Dr. Eloise spoke in a hushed tone as we looked around the weed-infested room with no ceiling. "From what I gathered, this castle was a stronghold for the powerful, warlike clan, the MacMerrits—the last to surrender to the British in the 1600s."

My ears perked—*feet crunching on gravel.* I ran to the gang-plank. Coming down the path was a medium-size man with long, gray hair. "We're closed!" he barked at me.

Dr. Dale rushed to the opening. "Good day, sir! We saw no one around. We're from the States. Touring castles." He pulled out a handful of bills. "A few minutes of your time?"

The man eyed the money. "I have to be leavin' soon."

Dr. Dale put the bills in the caretaker's hand. "I see from the two new windows over there that you're renovating. That must cost a few bob, eh? The children here are students on an educational tour. Ten minutes and a little history of the place?"

The man's frazzled expression mellowed. "The history, well ..." He started in with dates and names and when the clan died out, which I pretty much glossed over as we followed him from the left wing to the main room. "Below the keep here is a network of dungeons cut from rock. A treasure is supposedly buried here by a lord who went mad and forgot where he hid it. Tales of torture and death fill our history."

"Have you seen the dungeons?" Rob asked.

"The passages are bricked up."

"So no one has seen inside since they were bricked up?" I asked eagerly.

"I reckon not, lad. It's all rot and decay under the keep."

"This is historical fact?" Dr. Dale asked.

"The passage is there." His face screwed up in a humorless grin. "The treasure *could* be a tale, mind you," he surveyed the walls, "but me grandfather was here his very self when they cleared out the *spiked* dungeon, there off the chamber of the Bloody Chapel." He pointed to an empty corner. "That's where they'd throw their enemies, one atop another and leave 'em to die slow and horrible in the bloody awful company of corpses. Fact. When the place was gutted in the twenties, they hauled out three whole carts of bones."

We moved to the corner and looked down the deep square hole. The owner eyed Reece and Mei slyly. "Leap Castle: where the MacMerrits brought their brides and their prisoners. I guess yer history lesson here is, ya shan't mess with the MacMerrits."

"But they all died out, didn't they?" Rob asked.

"There's a few left. Most've scattered to the winds."

Even Skid's face had gone slack looking into the spiked dungeon. "The Bloody Chapel?"

"Where one of the clan killed his brother at the altar in the middle of services."

"Killed his own brother?" Reece asked in horror.

"Ran a sword through 'im."

"Sword?" I asked. "What kind?"

"No idea, lad." The owner saw he had our attention. "But of all the tales of me ole castle, none is so unnerving, none so chillin' as the foul-smellin' demon that haunts the tower stair—an evil creature, one that embodies all the old horrors of the place."

"Are we speaking historically?" Dr. Dale asked critically.

He shrugged. "A lady of the manor dabbled in the black arts, and she swore to seein' it."

Reece asked, "Have *you* ever seen or heard anything?"

"Felt a deathly chill once right before me ladder tipped. Almost broke me neck."

Skid shook his head skeptically. "Yeah, you hear that all the time—people feeling cold when evil spirits are around. What's up with that?"

"Dunno," the man said honestly. "I gave it thought after it come over me—put meself in a devil's head to figger him out—and here's what I come up with." He shifted his weight to one side. "If I was so unfortunate as to be one of the damned, yet so fortunate to escape the pit for a short while, I'd surely find a place with nothing of flames and screaming about it. If I couldn't find a body to occupy, then I'd welcome cold and silence and emptiness ... if it were me escaping from the pit of Hell." He looked directly at me. "Wouldn't *you*, lad?"

Uncontrollable fear shot through me. I fought the trembling so the others wouldn't see. The unnatural chill and the walls washed in the pale light of the lone church window took me back to Old Pilgrim's basement.

The Stallards wouldn't let me pick through the place—the floors and some of the walls were unstable. The castle had been scavenged by treasure hunters and ghost seekers. I asked about the walled-up dungeons. Dr. Eloise answered with a question, "Honestly, Elijah, who would bury such a wonderful sword?"

"The guide at Ballymeade said it was done all the time," I argued. "A sword could be buried when its owner died."

She smiled mysteriously. "Well, the owner of our sword is very much alive."

Still, it killed me to get in the van and drive away. "If it's not there, where is it?" I cried. "Maybe it was the sword MacMerrit used to kill his brother. We should have asked the guy about *that* sword. Maybe those walled-up dungeons are where all the magics of the ages are buried!"

Dr. Dale simply said, "We will not find it here."

We drove southwest into the sun. Silence hung like fog in the van—we were all thinking the same thing. We'd exhausted our resources. I expected the Stallards to say something cheery or uplifting, but Dr. Dale kept his eyes on the sunset. After a while he looked at the map, "We need to find lodging soon."

We found a shamrock B&B and settled in for the night. Since it was our last night with Mei, the Stallards let us kids hang out in one room until late. Sahara would be meeting her at the airport the next day. After a card game or two, the conversation turned to God. Reece read some Scripture about how everyone needs God, and people who don't know him dream up other gods to fill the gaps in their hearts. She explained how Jesus died on the cross to pay for our sins and fill those gaps. I sat on the bed with my back against the wall and watched Reece do her thing—her face glowing with love as she talked about Jesus. Skid threw in stuff too. I wanted to have a say, but I was new at it, so I mostly listened with a lump in my throat, a hollow darkness in my gut, and an echo in my head: *you'll never find it.*

Mei was having a really hard time. "I know in my mind it is true. I understand about the God of the universe. I know the world was not an accident. I believe in *Souzousha.*" Her head dropped. "But my heart is torn in two. My parents, my family, and my friends in Japan—no one else wants me to believe."

Reece hugged Mei and explained what the Stallards had said about having a little shield. "A little faith is okay to start with. A little shield works just fine if we stand side by side."

"Hey," I said finally, "before we turn in, let's have a devo. How 'bout a verse from the *Warrior*?"

Rob answered, "Dr. Dale said that the pages of the *Cathach* go from Psalm 30:10 to chapter 105:13."

"I'll read the last verse since this is our last night together." I smiled at Mei, "For a while, anyway."

Skid punched in the numbers and read to himself. "Hmm."

"What's it say?" Mei asked eagerly.

Skid handed the Quella to me. I read, "'They wandered from nation to nation, from one kingdom to another.'"

I looked at Skid. He nodded. "That's us, Creek. The new wave."

· · · · ·

I was anxious to see Mom again, but I wasn't crazy about telling her our quest was a total bust. I kept myself pumped at the prospect of getting to know a potential new grandma. Rob and I hadn't really talked about it. I didn't want to get my hopes up. But as the next morning rolled around, I started imagining a new grandma. It'd be strange, but my life at this point was as loopy as a roundabout.

In the thick fog, we barely found the one-lane road to Seven Avon Place. Our van seemed to be drifting on a cloud toward nothing. Trading glances as we crossed the narrow spit of land, we silently worried that Dr. Eloise would miss the road and drop us all into the icy sea. Ghostly trees appeared ahead and soon covered us over. We drove down the lane in silence.

A square, gray shape appeared. There were no lights on.

"I'll get my mom." I ran up to the door and knocked. For a

long minute no one answered. I peeked through the side windows. Empty. I didn't knock a second time; I tried the door. It was unlocked. I stepped in on cracked marble tiles covered with dust from fallen plaster and neglect. Tall rooms to the left and right stood empty. It was freezing cold.

"Mom?"

I swept down the hall in the same way I cover ground in Telanoo—eyes and ears on alert. The layout was similar to Murlough House, a wide hall running through to the back with rooms right and left. *The kitchen! If anyone's here, there'll be tea and cookies laying around, stuff in the fridge.*

The kitchen at the back of the house was bare—no stove, no refrigerator. *This hasn't been used in ages! Where's my mom?!*

I covered the first floor in a matter of seconds: dining room, a kind of ballroom, a huge laundry room, bathrooms. All bare. Panic rose as I shot up the stairs and covered the second floor. Creaking doors opened to empty rooms. *Ruthie and that man and that baby don't live here! No one lives here!*

I sailed up the next flight of steps and ran into another large, empty room with bars on the windows. "Mom!" I yelled. *Knock, knock* echoed in the empty room. I waited. *Knock, knock, knock.*

My mom's voice came through the wall. "Elijah?"

"Mom!" Horror swept through me. *She's trapped in another dimension!*

Her voice came loud and clear. "The other stairs, Elijah, the servant stairs. Go back down."

"Get a grip!" I yelled at myself. I ran back to the second floor and found another set of steps at the back of the house. A door squeaked open above me; I dashed up.

The woman who met me at the top hardly looked like my mom. Her face was drained of color, her hair was in a messy knot, and her eyes were swollen and sad.

Weakly she said, "Hi, hon."

"Mom?!"

She came to me and dropped her head on my shoulder.

"Did you find her?" I whispered.

She whispered back, "We'll talk later."

Mom let me into a warm little apartment with nice homey decorations. Breakfast dishes still sat on the table. Ruthie was rocking her baby.

Mom thanked Ruthie and hugged her a long time.

I picked up Mom's luggage by the door and headed down the steps. "Let's go."

· · · · ·

Saying good-bye to Mei was tough. While we'd been working on our school projects, she'd made each of our first initials on squares of real parchment with fancy designs like in the *Book of Kells*.

After a bucket full of apologies for being weak on English, Mei gave us her limerick:

> *Ireland I have never seen.*
> *I like travel with* Amerika-jin.
> *A very long* ryokou
> *To haunted Leap-*jou
> *Is scary at Halloween!*

We gave her a round of applause.

"I may never see you again," she moaned to all of us.

"Yes, you will!" Reece cried back.

Mei handed out her gifts. "Don't forget me! Please come to Japan. I need your help to tell my friends about God."

"We will, I promise!" Reece said. "We'll come!"

The Stallards swapped looks.

Sahara showed up, and we all gave Mei one last hug. I hugged her extra hard and whispered, "Have faith in *Souzousha*."

We reluctantly handed Mei over to Sahara, went through security, and were airborne in an hour.

Skid was so impressed with his fancy letter *M* that he announced, "People, I may have to upgrade my name like Rob did. Yeah, I think I will. I'm too old for nicknames."

Our plane shot up through the green mists of Ireland, and in a minute a whole country disappeared.

When we leveled off at thirty thousand feet, I said, "Um, Mom ..."

"I know. You want to know if you have a new grandmother. My ... mother is alive but in very bad health."

"Did you meet her?"

Her head wobbled tiredly. "I saw her, but she didn't see me. She wouldn't have known me. When we get home, I'll explain everything to the whole family. I have to get my thoughts together, okay?"

"Sure, Mom." I wanted to ask more—like if we were coming back to see Grandma—but she was too broken up.

The mood was quiet. Reece wrote in her journal. I fiddled with the beautiful *E* Mei had made me. Dr. Dale started eating solid food again. I fell asleep, and the next thing I knew, we were over green valleys and long, rust-colored mountains: the Appalachians. In a couple hours, we'd be home. It was over.

I saw Skid writing and asked, "Hey, is that your limerick, Marcus?"

"It stinks."

"Let's have it. Mom'll want to read them all."

He'd written one thing each of us might say about the trip:

> *Rob: Ireland was one big, foggy day.*
> *Mei: In Ireland you taught me to pray.*
> *Me: I changed my name.*

Reece: Elijah lit the flame.
Elijah: And the sword is still hidden away.

CHAPTER 15

Camp Mudjokivi looked strangely unfamiliar. Sand had been hauled into the future volleyball court. The leaves were mostly gone, the pool was covered, and a light snow had fallen. The twins had cut their hair with their new scissors while Mom was gone. Dad was ready to grovel for forgiveness for letting it happen, but she hardly even noticed.

After dinner Mom sat the twins and me down in the living room to tell her story. "About thirty-five years ago, a young Irish girl named Isabel had some very strict parents. She grew up to be a very pretty girl, and they thought she might get into trouble and embarrass the family. So they sent her away to live on an island, a place run by the church where they took girls with problems. She was so unhappy there that she tried to escape many times. Finally she succeeded. She ran off with a young man and got married. But he wasn't her religion, so when her parents found her, they took her back to the island. She had twins, a boy and a girl, who were taken and put up for adoption."

"You and Uncle Dorian," I said.

"That's right, and now she is very sick from all she suffered at that place. Sometimes old people have trouble remembering things. Well, your Grandma Isabel can't remember much any-more. I went to the old people's home where she lives and looked in on her. See girls, I know who she is, but she wouldn't know me." Mom made a strange smile and shrugged. "Who am I to her? A stranger, that's all."

"Did you take a picture, so we could see her?" Nori asked.

"She didn't look so well, hon. I can tell you she was slender and had some gray in her hair and a small face like me." Mom got a distant look. "I don't know what color her eyes were. I didn't get that close. But I did get to meet a wonderful young woman who helps people find their parents. Her name is Ruthie. Guess what? She took me shopping one day, and I brought you back a souvenir."

From behind the couch cushion, she brought two woolly toy lambs with silver shamrock necklaces fastened on. She put the necklaces on the girls. "Don't they look pretty! Well, you can know that you had a beautiful grandmother who would have loved you very much—" her voice broke, "if she had known you."

When the twins ran off to look at their necklaces in the mirror, Mom turned to me. "Elijah, your father and I want to talk with you about something."

Uh-oh …

When the girls were all the way upstairs, she turned to me and took my hands in hers. "I know you are interested in church things now, but …" She started shaking her head.

"What?"

"I can't tell you everything that happened to my mother, but this I know. We, her children, were stolen from her—by her church. She was kept a virtual prisoner in that awful place to work like a slave and make money—for her church. Separated from her husband, isolated from the outside world—"

Strange. Sounds a lot like Kate Dowland's story, I thought.

"She lost her mind and was sent to an asylum. That's where I went, to see her. All this was done by her church."

I see where this conversation's going. "Mom, mine's diff—"

She squeezed my hands roughly. "Listen! You'll soon be an adult, Elijah. You should be making your own choices. But

I—your father and I—strongly recommend that you not get involved with any kind of established religion. You're a good boy. You don't need a religion to teach you right from wrong. We've done that." Her voice sounded desperate. "You have a belief system that you developed on your own. As long as you are sincere in what you believe, Elijah, that's all that matters. You're a good son. Any problems you have in life, you can always come to us. Family's important. Anything that divides a family—whether it's a church or—well, it can never be a good thing, can it, to tear a family apart?"

"No," I said.

She patted my knee. "Good."

On the outside my life hurtled back to normal.

The Stallards sent a packet of castle pictures, museum pamphlets, a copy of the *Ogham* alphabet, and a letter. Dr. Dale wrote:

Dear World Travelers!

First order of business: with regard to your research paper, Elijah, I believe your Latin instructor may have set you up. There is no consistently held opinion on the extent to which Rome may or may not have subjugated Ireland. And consider this technicality: Ireland was called Hibernia at the time Caesar ruled. So in the literal sense, he most certainly did not invade Ireland. We relish scholarship but do not envy you this assignment. Good luck!

One interesting tack you might take, related to the pamphlet we showed you: one Roman soldier of note did conquer Ireland—Patrick. Remember? He was the son of a Roman official and a soldier of the cross. He conquered Ireland, not with the clash of metal, but with the sword of the Spirit.

Regarding the sword—if Patrick's fire is all we see of the Lord's flaming sword, perhaps it is enough. The fire burned brightly in Ireland: at Murlough House, on a street corner in Dublin, and one glorious night on the Hill of Slane. (I pictured Dr. Dale smiling as he wrote, slugging coffee from his gasoline-smelling flask.) *We are discouraged but not defeated. Spending time with you wonderful people was worth every minute.*

Thanks to you, Elijah, we deciphered the slashes on the shield. They are Ogham *script, as you thought. The word is* creidim, *Gaelic for "faith." You are a very discerning young man! Interestingly this alphabet was used only in the British Isles and only for a few centuries, the time of Patrick and the* peregrini, *including Columba, the one who fought—perhaps with our shield of faith—to have the Scriptures in his own hands. Isn't it curious, children, that in ages past men fought to the death to have even one painstaking portion of the Word? Today Bibles collect dust. Perhaps they understood what our generations don't. Yes, perhaps as a species we are devolving.*

If we can assist you in recovering the helmet, let us know.

All our best,
The Stallards

PS. The snafu with Mr. Cravens compels us to give an extra word of caution. If a stranger should come to Magdeline asking questions about armor, notify us immediately!

PPS. What about the arm? Was there not a right arm found at some point?

· · · · ·

Emma Stone was still a problem. She asked me a million questions about Ireland and ignored whatever Reece had to say. I hated to think it, but it seemed like she'd been helping Reece all along just as a way to get to me. Bummer.

There were two bright spots my first week back though: first, I won the cross-country meet by a mile. Coach still couldn't believe that I hadn't trained before. He said I was a shoo-in for regionals. Maybe state too. Coach and I were on solid ground

again. Bright spot number two was—ironically—Latin. I got
a B on my paper (which *proves* there is a God), but that wasn't
the best part. As I said before, Rob's class always went to lunch
right before the bell rang. He'd do his hula dance and mouth
words like weeky weeny weedy wooky. I never got tired of it, and
he never let me down. But by November Abner had caught on
that I watched the door and cracked up the same minute every
day. One day she kept squinting at the clock around that time.
I thought that she was sick of us, or just hankering for her daily
peanut butter and crackers. At exactly twenty till, she stopped
writing on the board and went to the corner by the door. I
knew what was about to happen. Rob sauntered down the hall
between Miranda Varner, who was Marcus's love interest, and
the infamous Justin Brill. I was ready to frantically wave Rob
a warning when I thought of the rubber ducky at my baptism.
Now's my chance! Here it comes, Wingate. Payback!

I grinned like a baboon just to egg him on. He was
wooky-weekying as big as you please when Abner jutted her
stiff neck from behind the door and caught him in the act.

"Disturb my class, will you?" Miss Abner raged.

A weeky-weeky smile froze on Rob's face. Justin log-jammed
behind him and grunted. Miranda sped ahead as Miss Abner
shouted, "Tooooo the OFFICE, Missster BRILL!"

Justin's brows knotted and his mouth went into an oval of disbelief. Rob's hula hands dropped to his sides, and he stepped away
from Justin like he had cooties. Blind-as-a-bat Abner marched
into the hall and stuck her finger in Justin's face. "How dare you
disturb my class! Don't think you've fooled me!"

Rob turned on one heel like a soldier, his jaw clamped shut
against an explosion of cackles. I shoved all my papers off my
desk as an excuse to duck under my desk and guffaw.

Every day after that, Rob would pass by as stiff as a private in boot camp, Brill would scowl in my direction, and I'd laugh to myself. And since Rob came out smelling like a rose, he still had one coming from me. Maybe I'd wait for his baptism and drop in an angry snapping turtle right before the amen.

. . . . .

November waned; I couldn't sleep for thinking about the sword. I had to get back to the junkyard to see if there were any metal remains in Dowland's charred car. That next Saturday I headed out on my bike, wearing a heavy jacket to keep out the cold drizzle. By the time I got to the junkyard, my hair was dripping, and my ears and fingers were numb. The gate was locked, but the fence drooped from where the men had leaped over to put out the fire.

Dowland's car was a blackened shell. The seats were piles of ash. The trunk yawned open to show more black ash in no particular shape. By the time I'd checked the inside, my jacket and jeans were smeared with soot. Mom would wonder what I'd been up to. I didn't want to worry her. She was spending a lot of time on the couch, staring out the window. She fixed mostly frozen dinners and didn't eat much. The girls didn't know what was wrong. Dad explained: "Mom is going to be sad for a while, girls. Her trip to Ireland was very hard. Be good helpers so she can feel better fast."

Dismal darkness fell around me in the junkyard. I had to get back or Mom would worry—if she even noticed I was gone. I stopped by Dowland's on the way back, but it had been sold, emptied, and locked. Dowland's legacy was a dead end. *You'll never find it.* The voice had never left, and I wrestled over talking to someone about it. But who? I couldn't tell Reece, not until I understood it better myself. Mom and Dad? Not a chance. There wasn't doubt one in my mind—I could never explain to them what happened. The Stallards were in Chicago. I didn't know Reece's minister all that well. Who could help me fight off the dark side?

Dom.

Once I'd worked up the courage to spill my guts to macho-military Dom Skidmore and take whatever he dished out, I bundled up and walked along Magdeline's dark, abandoned main street toward the Skidmores' condo. I wondered, *Since there really is another world, a spirit world, and since the creatures behind the veil can pass through to us, then it would seem pretty important to be protected from them. Are they watching me through the veil as I walk alone tonight? What kind of powers do they have? Do they know my thoughts?* I began to see the point of having the armor of God.

It's real, I said over and over to get it through my thick skull. *God, Satan, Heaven, and Hell. It's not just religion. It's real.* My knees got kind of weak. *If that's true, then why is there only one guy in my whole town who can help me?*

The whole idea knocked the wind out of me. For crying out loud, there're all kinds of people to protect us against crime and general meanness: Officer Taylor and other cops, the armed forces with their weapons and planes and bombs, detectives, CIA, FBI. We have parking meter cops and even dog cops! Forget the criminal hordes! What about the evil hordes beyond the veil? Who fights them—one person in all of Magdeline?!

A car pulled into the Skidmore driveway. I approached it. Dom was getting out when he saw me. "What are you doing out so late?"

"I need to talk to you—privately."

He studied me. "The car's still warm."

"That'd be good."

I'd practiced how I would explain about Liam, about the voice and the eyes of hate, how he might have been talking about the book. But I knew in my heart he wasn't—that the words weren't really coming from him.

Dom heard me out and nodded thoughtfully. "Old Serpent got you alone and scared the crap out of you, didn't he? He had you in his crosshairs and took his shot."

I admitted sheepishly, "I did ask God to let me see."

"See what?"

"What's out there … you know, the enemy."

"Better watch what you ask God for. You just might get it." His look went serious and dark. He paused. "Why do you think it happened?"

"So I'd know it's real?"

"You didn't know evil was real? Didn't know Hell and damnation was real?"

"I wasn't sure. My parents don't talk about that stuff."

"Well, now you know. No turning back."

"Yeah," I murmured halfheartedly.

We sat there looking at the garage door lit up by headlights. He asked, "Do you wish you could go back and pretend that life was all about sports and cute girls?"

"Sort of," I admitted.

"No you don't. You're a deep kid, Elijah. You're made of strong stuff. Hold your position."

I told him I'd had a dream here and inkling there and still wasn't sure what it all meant.

"Guess you need a Quella."

I nodded. "I'll start saving up."

"Better yet—" he popped one out of his glove box and tossed it to me. "Your mission has just taken a hit. Start gathering intelligence."

"Wow. You mean it?"

"Hold your position now."

"Yessir."

CHAPTER 16

Mom's disposition was changing. She griped about my phone calls to the Stallards. She got moody when I went to church with Reece—even though she said it was my choice—and harped on me about neglecting my homework. But going to cross-country meets was just fine with her.

It was after she walked in on one of our rare powwows at the lodge that she lowered the boom. She called me and Dad into the living room again. "Elijah, I guess I didn't make myself clear before. Your trip to Ireland was a great adventure, but the search for those old armor pieces—is over. You didn't find what you were looking for. That's all right. But now we want you to concentrate on your future: your studies and extracurricular activities."

What?! I looked at Dad. He didn't exactly agree—I could see that—but he wanted to keep the peace. He wanted the old Jodi Creek back. *She'll change her mind,* I thought hopefully. *She'll get over it.* It seemed like I was standing on the Cliffs of Morte again. Mom's words were like a North Atlantic blast.

She went on, "And more responsibilities at camp." She smiled. "Someday Camp Mudj will be yours! Don't think that we're not grateful to the Stallards for all the time they've spent with you. But they're just a couple of strangers interested in relics. They're not spending all this money on you kids for nothing; they want something in return."

Now you're sounding like Uncle Dorian, I thought angrily.

"So are we clear?" she asked.

"Ditch everything, that's what you're saying!" I snapped.

"Not everything! Goodness, no. You have family and friends, camp, school, and cross-country. Your future!"

Only days before, Dom had asked me if I ever wanted to go back and pretend that life was nothing more than sports and cute girls. Now my weak-willed answer disgusted me.

The next couple of days, I felt like I was walking through an Irish fog. I gathered the others at my locker, grabbing Reece before Emma could glom onto her for the day. I told them what Mom had said.

"That's not the whole story," Rob informed me. "What she told Dad was a lot more gruesome. Did she tell you that Seven Avon Place had been called the Isle of Magdeline? And did she tell you that when the house was closed a decade ago, a hundred unmarked graves were discovered?"

No place is safe, came a voice in my head. *No one can be trusted—no one.*

. . . . .

I felt like a traitor dialing the Stallards' number from Reece's apartment so my parents wouldn't know.

Dr. Dale answered. I cut to the chase. "I have to know. What are you getting out of this?"

Long pause. "The truth."

"It has to be more than that."

"Does it?"

"My mom says so."

"It didn't go well for your mother in Ireland. We've done a bit of research on Seven Avon Place."

"Formerly the Isle of Magdeline," I said, agitated. "Mom said it was all the church's fault. She said I shouldn't have anything to do with church and that I'm good enough already."

Long pause. "I should have warned you. But," he cleared his throat, "I didn't know it would happen this soon."

"What would happen?"

"The testing of your faith. The tribulations."

"Reece's minister told me that God gives tests," I said. "Is that what you mean?"

"Yes—not finding the sword, your mother's objections. Good and evil are constantly at odds for your soul. God wants to save you; Satan wants to destroy you."

"How do you know who's doing what, and when?"

"Sometimes you don't. Not until later."

"Oh, great. Well, Mom said that anything that breaks up families can't be good. So the church can't be good."

"God created families, Elijah. It is not his will that they be divided." He took a long, tired breath. "Perhaps Eloise and I should have spent more time on the pitfalls of the armor quest. But this ... this is unique."

"Um," I hesitated, "there was another test."

"What do you mean?"

"You may not believe me ..."

"I will."

"I think the devil talked to me."

I thought he'd freak when I said that, but he just said anxiously, "Dear Heaven. I'm just considering the nature of your quest—arming a generation. What did the entity say?"

I retold the story, explaining how the voice from Liam said, "You'll never find it." There was a long pause. "Dr. Dale?"

"I'm still here. What did you say to ... it?"

"I left."

"Good. Never address the evil ones without the authority of Jesus' name, and never ever *directly* rebuke them, Elijah. Instructions about this are in the book of Jude and elsewhere in the Bible. You do have a Bible, don't you?"

"I have a Quella."

"Good, that will help you find the words you need quickly. When Donovan's in the States again, I'll have him contact you. He has expertise in this area beyond my own."

I wasn't sure how to break it to him except straight. "The reason I called is that my mom doesn't want me involved in the church or in the armor search anymore. It's because of how the church ruined my grandma's life."

"Elijah, there's the church and then there's *the church*. There are people who go into buildings with religious names on them every Sunday. Most people see that as the church."

"But I know it's not a building full of people." Reece had talked about this before.

"Oh, that it were that simple. The church, Elijah, is invisible. It is made up of those who love God with heart, soul, mind, and strength."

Did I belong in that category? I was way curious about God and his armor and what he wanted me to do in the world—not to mention being curious about the devil. But all this heart and soul stuff—that was asking a lot.

"It's a process, learning to love God," Dr. Dale cut in on my thoughts. "Don't judge yourself. You've started the journey, Elijah; that's what matters."

"So what about Halloween when the walls between the worlds grow thin? What's that mean?"

"You're quoting the pagans. The whole truth is that the veil between the worlds is *always* thin. When you call to God, he is there. By the same token, if you open a door to the abyss by letting evil into your life, you'll discover that it is eager to claim you. Good and evil do not rest; and like the winds on the Cliffs of Morte, evil does not forewarn you. So don't forget, the veil between the worlds is *always* thin."

"My mom says I have to give up looking for the armor. What do I do about that?" There was a long pause again. I felt guilty hitting him with so much bad news.

"Take some time, Elijah."

"And why did you stop eating on the trip? I'm sorry, but I need to know what's going on."

"I was fasting and praying," he answered.

"Why?"

His voice came through the phone stern and severe, "Because of Rob's disbelief, Sahara's pagan influence over Mei, Reece's health, Marcus's ego, and your lack of understanding of the simplest truths of the faith. You five are completely unprepared for the task ahead. Not one of you has the vaguest idea what kind of spiritual and physical danger you are in."

And here I'd become a Christian so things would be better.

CHAPTER 17

I went deep into Telanoo to a little canyon—smaller and more isolated than those in Council Cliffs. Rocks hung over, dripping with icicles like daggers, like crystal swords aimed down at me from Heaven. Some were taller than me. Here and there when the wind blew, a little icicle would break off and shatter the quiet. At the end of the ravine was a frozen waterfall, a wide line of icy trickles.

I leaned against the cliff, tucked safely behind the crystal swords. They seemed like a dirty trick: God showed me a thousand swords, but I couldn't have the one I wanted—his sword. It was time for a confrontation.

The wind was like ice; my fingers and toes ached. Darkness descended, and I waited for the Presence. I waited, but he never came. Everything I believed and felt was crumbling, breaking off, and crashing to the ground. *Maybe the world would have been better off without Patrick burning his fire of faith, without that Dublin preacher and his motley crew embarrassing themselves on the streets. Maybe the Stallards would be better off peddling Babylonian demon heads on the antiquities market instead of looking for armor pieces lost in a backwater town like Magdeline.* The more I thought, the angrier I got.

My grandma would have had a better chance on the mean streets than in a church-run slave camp. Mom would have been better off never knowing. Maybe Reece would be better off giving up on trying to be so cheery all the time. Face the truth. Her life will never be all that great.

Suddenly I was standing beneath the ice swords with my head thrown back. "Just who do you think you are? I'm not afraid of you and what you can do to me! You ruined my grandma! You hurt my mom! You crippled Reece for life! And Mei's in the clutches of a family of witches who, by the way, seemed really nice! You could have fixed it. I've seen you work! You could still fix everything if you wanted to. Well, I'm not holding my breath, Master of Breath!"

Silence.

I trembled, rage boiling up in me. "This is not what I wanted! You think you're going to mess up my life like the others? You think you can scare me with demons! You have another think coming!"

Silence.

The air seemed to thin out; it was so cold and brittle that I could hardly breathe. *There's plenty of air,* I told myself nervously, *it's just cold and it hurts my lungs.* My chest tightened, my heart ached. I fought off panic. *Is he going to kill me for smarting off?* "Are you?" I gasped out loud. "Are you going to kill me like Dr. Eloise said you could?" The wind suddenly rose. I ducked under the cliff to get out of the wind and wondered if an earthquake was next. Would the cliffs collapse and trap me, crush me, and send me off into eternity? He could do it if he wanted to. *No one can stop you!* I stumbled back, pressing my hand against the cold stone, bracing for what was to come. I expected to feel smooth rock, but my fingers found grooves. *What is that?* Clicking on my flashlight, I examined the stone. *Claw marks? A bear waking up from hibernation, starving and grouchy, taking a swat at the world? Yeah ... no.* These slashes were deep, chiseled with a tool. Clumped and irregular but definitely man-made.

Suddenly my mind changed course. *Could it be ... Indian!?*

The Moravian Delawares, the two boys who'd lived out their lives in Hermits' Cave. *What if they'd been here? What if this was a message from them? How cool would that be?* I forgot about my argument with God and studied the marks a long time. *I need to show these to the Stallards.* There were too many to memorize. *I'll come back,* I said to the message in stone.

Heading toward home, I kept the flashlight on the ground. *Well, God, if you won't talk to me, maybe the Indians will.* The frozen stream like a curving, silver arrow guided my way. In an hour I came up behind what would be a new sand volleyball court. *Dad'll have to put up a privacy fence,* I thought practically, back to my old self. *Who wants to go out of bounds in volleyball and fall headlong into a cemetery and get RIP permanently stamped on his forehead?*

By the time I hit the porch, I was too frozen to be mad at God and too excited about the Indian message to sleep. I showered until the bathroom was thick with fog, put on sweats, went downstairs, and kissed mom on the cheek like nothing had happened.

"It's cold out," I said.

"You feel warm."

"I used up all the hot water."

"You going to bed already? It's early."

"I'm beat."

"Are you feeling okay, hon?"

I hugged her. "Don't worry, Mom. I'm okay." Upstairs, I threw the covers back and jumped in bed.

Once the light was off, I was wide awake. A message from the hermits! A secret across time for me, Elijah Creek!

*   *   *   *   *

I was dressed and halfway to the shallow cave before dawn. This place was going to be mine alone. I'd think up a new name and not even Rob or Marcus would know about it. I'd taken a big piece of paper and one of the twins' big stubby pencils to make a rubbing. I'd noticed one of an Egyptian tomb in the Chicago museum vault and knew how it worked. I placed the paper over the stone and rubbed with the side of the pencil. The grooves appeared on the paper as white slashes on a gray surface. For good measure I made a sketch. I had the message in positive and negative form. By lunchtime these would be on their way to the Stallards. I called them from home when Mom was busy.

"It's Elijah," I said quietly. "I found some marks on a rock in Telanoo and I think it could be an Indian message."

"Is that so?"

"From the Moravian Delawares maybe."

"What makes you think that?"

"It's not far from Hermits' Cave, and the marks were made by people, but they're not letters." I was ready to hang up when something occurred to me. "You know what, the slashes kind of look like the sun rays on the shield of faith, only they're all bunched up. I'll send you the rubbing. But don't call me. I'll call you when the coast is clear."

· · · · ·

My clan was in limbo. Emma was still glomming onto Reece to get to me. Marcus would meet me in the hall with a what's-up expression, and I'd have to shrug. He was hanging with Miranda more. One night in December, I called Dr. Eloise for an update on the rubbing.

"AB-so-LUTE-ly fascinating!" she squealed. "It's rather a puzzle, since not all of the vowels are present and we're dealing with old Gaelic carved roughly into a rock. But we put together the best combination we could. Incredible! And how this message got from Ireland to the Midwest fifteen hundred years ago is … well, unbelievable! It seems to say: The right hand of God is a shield—a prayer."

"You're kidding."

"Serious as a heart attack," she chirped. "Remember the story of Brendan the Navigator, how he set out in a boat with his fellow *peregrini*, asking God to guide him where he should go?"

"You're not saying they got this far! To Telanoo!?"

"History hints that the *peregrini* may have made it to America, but no supporting evidence confirms that they reached so far inland—until now. For fear of sounding redundant, Elijah, please be very careful with whom you discuss this. And keep the site a secret for now."

After school and cross-country, I ran back to my hidden gorge, pumped up about the new mystery and determined to tell no one—not even Reece (because of Emma). What should I call my secret place? I took the Quella from my jacket to find where the Elijah in the Bible lived: Gilead.

I made a fire in Gilead. I'd forgiven God and wanted to talk again. *El-Telan-Yah, you're going to have to tell me what to do next. And while you're at it, could you explain that seven-thousand-mile wild goose chase? Okay ... you don't have to. I'm not meaning to be bossy. But I'm your kid, aren't I? And parents get a kick out of telling their kids what to do and lecturing them. Keep in mind that I'm new at this, so be easy on me, okay?*

For a half hour I paced around Gilead to keep warm. *I'm listening.* I pulled out the Quella and read again about the shield of faith, thinking I'd missed something. *What exactly does* faith *mean?* I punched in the question and read: "Faith is being sure of what we hope for and certain of what we do not see." *Okay. The sword is somewhere but I can't see it. Invisible. Like the rock that kept me from falling off the Cliffs of Morte? I didn't see it, but I sure believe in it!*

After a while I began to see. Not the helmet and sword—not

yet—but a ton of other great things in my life: the lessons I'd learned at Farr Island, a cool trip to Ireland—purpose still unknown, God working a plan so Reece and Mei could be together again. And other things, invisible things I could see only because of my faith: Jesus dying on the cross for me, my sins forgiven, eternal life. And the dark side. I looked up to the narrow strip of sky above the rim of my gorge. *Hey, speaking of the dark side, one peek through the veil was enough.*

I paced the gorge. *So the sword is invisible? Do I have to see it with eyes of faith? Or is it visible but hidden in a secret place? As darkness fell a quiet wave of confidence swept through me, and I was certain—without knowing how—that I'd put my hand on the thing I hoped for. One day I'd see what I could not see.*

Two words echoed in my head: *secret place ... secret place.* Excitedly I checked the Quella. The first two references meant nothing to me, but the third pierced right into my soul. I took off for home through the cold, bare woods of Telanoo, reciting his words over and over, my heart pumping: "'I will give you the treasures of darkness, riches stored in secret places, so that you may know that I am the LORD, the God of Israel, who summons you by name.'"

THE
ANGEL
OF
FIRE

BOOK 6

Old Railroad Lake

To Council Cliffs

N

Magdeline, OH

1. Magdeline Independent Schools
2. Marcus's Condo
3. Reece's Apartment
4. The Castle
5 Florence's
6. Blessed Assembly
7. New York Jewelers
8. Library
9. Courthouse
10. Bank
11. Furniture Store
12. The Crystal See
13. Foggiest Notions
14. Mei's House
15. Morgan Farm
16. Camp Mudjokivi

Charlotte Heights

Main Street

Paris Street

The god who answers by fire-he is God
—1 Kings 18:24

CHAPTER 1

You'll never find it. Never …

"SHUT! UP!" Tending my fire in Gilead on a dry, biting day in early December, I pushed the demon's words from my mind and scratched out a map in the dirt.

Over Halloween, my clan had spent a week with the Stallards on a thousand-mile search around Ireland for the sword of the Lord, only to come up empty-handed. Those raspy words from the mouth of a polite-looking book clerk named Liam still haunted me: *You'll never find it.*

The quest was once again at a dead stop. My clan had settled back into school with a kind of quiet resignation. No one accused me of leading us on a wild-goose chase across the Atlantic. No one even seemed all that upset. They just said to wait and see.

We'd exhausted Dowland's journals, swept his house, and scoured Ireland. But the rest of the clan didn't know about the voice, and I couldn't say anything about it. They'd only make matters worse: Rob would dive into research on demonology, Reece would start a round-the-clock prayer marathon, and Marcus would preach at me about the evils of voodoo. I was leader of the clan; the next move was my call. I wanted to downplay the voice in my mind. I just wanted it to go away.

The clan didn't understand that beings from the spirit world were watching my every move—watching all of us. I'd told only Dom Skidmore and Dr. Dale about what happened because I had to talk to someone or freak out. Neither of them had acted surprised, but I was still reeling. This spiritual warfare stuff was new to me. And with Mom being depressed and steering me away from the armor quest and anything related to church, I couldn't see putting another problem out on the table. Better to deal with it myself on my own terms.

So to my surprise, here I was back in Telanoo—a place I'd once dreaded but been drawn to again and again. Not that I counted on finding anything here; there was just no place left to go. God had spoken to me out here—the last time saying he'd give me some treasure hidden in a secret place. But so far nothing had turned up. I sure could use a word now, and I'm not afraid to say that waiting on God was beginning to wear mighty thin.

Stirring the coals with a stick, smelling my fire going cold, I planned out my final systematic sweep of Telanoo for the helmet, sword, and arm piece. I'd give special attention to the Unexplored this time, the section lying west of Devil's Cranium between Old Pilgrim's cemetery and the place where Dowland once stalked me all night hoping to steal back the helmet of salvation. My headquarters would be here in Gilead, the hidden gorge in Telanoo where I'd found carved in stone a mysterious Celtic inscription, more than a thousand years old and thirty-five hundred miles out of place.

The Stallards had suggested that this discovery would make headlines in the archaeological world and had stepped up warnings to me about antiquities hounds and other interested parties. So fame would have to wait. I didn't want hounds sniffing around Telanoo before I found the last of my armor.

In the dirt I mapped out a rough idea of the Unexplored. *Think like Dowland,* I told myself. *Where would he hide the helmet of salvation?* Marcus and I had figured out months ago that Dowland buried pieces in their opposite environments. The opposite of saved is lost, so where was lost to Dowland?

Right here, I answered my own question. *A wanderer could get lost in Telanoo easily. I have—a couple of times—and I'm a good tracker.* I studied my sketch in the dirt. *These hills don't follow a natural flow; ridges don't run parallel. The landscape doesn't make geographical sense to me.* But Stan Dowland—who didn't make much sense to me either—had been right at home here, trekking across this wasteland many a time, away from the church he'd lost, on his way to visit the daughter and grandson he also lost.

Lost. The more I pondered it, the more I realized that the helmet of salvation could very well be in Telanoo. I looked around with a satisfied nod. I'd search for it back here on my own and maintain my running regimen to keep Mom happy. Good plan. The key to finding it: think like Dowland.

I had no idea what would happen when the armor of God all came together. To be honest, I wasn't real anxious to find out. I'd seen enough old adventure and horror movies to know that when pieces to an ancient puzzle are found and fitted into place, either the sacred underground temple collapses in a heap of rubble, or creepy dead people come back to life and wreak havoc, or the volcano god gets ticked off and a whole island sinks into the sea. In space movies, the planet explodes as the last ship of ragtag rebels zooms off, inches ahead of the cloud of destruction. The result is always complete devastation with the hero escaping by the skin of his teeth—if he's lucky.

But this was real life.

Still, I pondered, *if I'm to believe the Bible, the whole planet does go up in a fireball. No survivors. Sometime before all that happens, the love in the world grows cold, and faith in God drops to an all-time low.* I looked up into the evening sky. *El-Telan-Yah? When the armor of God comes together—when I have the sword in my hand—are we talking global annihilation? Is that your plan? Because if it is, I have some things I want to do first. You've given me a taste of the world, and I sort of wanted to see more. And there's Reece …*

Staring down the quiet gorge—my fire the only sign of life, every rock lying pretty much the way it had for eons, every tree frozen stiff from trunk to tip—I had a hard time believing an apocalypse was imminent. My mind was quiet. I'd thought my way out of the dumps, and the demon voice had gone. I was in Gilead, far from the world's problems and close to El-Telan-Yah. The sun had sunk below the gorge's rim an hour ago. My fire sputtered. *Better not worry Mom,* I thought tiredly. I scattered the ashes and took off through the Unexplored, making sure I'd be home before darkness fell, reminding myself as I surveyed Telanoo to think like Dowland.

CHAPTER 2

As long as I could remember, Mom had organized the school's Christmas Village, but this year she stepped down and was spending a lot of time ironing and watching TV. The twins knew something was wrong and got more clingy and wild by the day. Since I'd been used to taking over at Christmas, I rustled up some hot dogs and beans for them before retreating to my room. Using my secondhand Quella—compliments of Dom Skidmore—I looked up sword and was surprised to find it's in the Bible four hundred times. I didn't know the Bible was such a violent book. Then I recalled that a copy of the Psalms had been named *Cathach,* which means "warrior." Dr. Dale had used it on the Hill of Slane to pray against the pagans who were letting evil spirits through the veil to this world. I had a lot to learn about the Word of God.

The clues have to be in the Quella, I thought. *Stan was a preacher; he'd have checked the Bible first, wouldn't he?* I looked up lost sword and found zip.

The very first appearance of a sword was on the east side of Eden. It was a glittering, slashing weapon used by the cherubim to keep Adam and Eve out of the garden after the serpent talked them into sinning. Reece had told me that no one knew where the Garden of Eden was anymore, so that was no help. And even though I was a Christian, an actual sword of fire and a talking snake seemed pretty far-fetched to me. I searched some more.

In the book of Judges, I found a story about Gideon, a mighty warrior who staged a sneak attack against the Midianites, hollering, "A sword for the LORD and for Gideon!" as a battle cry. Armed only with trumpets, empty jars, and torches, Gideon and his measly three-hundred-man army surrounded the camp and threw the Midianites into such confusion that they turned swords on each other and ran in panic. Gideon didn't use an actual sword in the battle—neither did God—but they won anyway.

It grated on my nerves big time that I couldn't pick up any direction from the Quella. I'd sat there on my bed scowling to myself, *Maybe the armor pieces are east of Dowland's garden,* but then I remembered that according to his ex-wife Francine, he never had the sword. Maybe that was true.

I kept having a nagging feeling that it might be buried in the dungeons under Leap Castle, hidden away by the bloody MacMerrits who'd dabbled in the dark arts and may have wanted all good magic to be stashed away from the Christians. People like that would want to hide the sword of the Lord.

Furious, I slammed my fist on the bed. Why hadn't I insisted that the Stallards let me look for the entrance to the dungeons at Leap? It might have been there under our very noses, and we walked right over it! I sank down in a kind of despair. It could be anywhere in the world! Or nowhere.

I wondered if not finding the sword had driven Dowland nuts, which worried me. Because I wanted it more every day. I couldn't get my mind off it.

When the Quella went dry for me, I took off for town in a foul mood, roaming down Main Street crazily looking for a clue. What greeted me was a second-rate town decking itself out with a ton of gaudy Christmas decorations: tacky tinsel snowflakes swinging from street lamps and colored bulbs slung around store windows and bare trees. Cheap plastic reindeer with lightbulb noses teetered on people's roofs. I'd just left home where the usual carnivorous bears and angel dolls had been dug out and set around all over the place in pairs—like dating couples. Silly. I was never crazy about the whole showy mess in the first place. But now that I understood Christmas was about God in a manger in the Middle East two thousand years ago, the holiday fluff grated on me even more. What was wrong with people anyway?

Then I turned the corner and was thrown back by the tackiest decoration I'd ever seen: a gigantic inflatable Santa Claus, almost twenty feet high, tethered by boat rope and steel stakes to the courtyard in front of the town library. That red and white eyesore—wide-eyed and reeling and grinning like an idiot—hogged the whole downtown.

I huffed and walked on past the Blessed Assembly of the Full Gospel of the Holy Ghost, Magdeline's only surviving church. Its dusty, unlit storefront window had a plain wooden nativity set and a scroll across the top that said "PEACE." I stood in front of the dim window and wondered if any of these members had gone to Old Pilgrim Church or had seen the armor of God.

Winding back toward home, I took the side street past The Crystal See, a seedy-looking cottage with dark windows and hardly any decorations except for two faded plastic angels—each holding swords—on either side of the door.

. . . . .

The next morning I left early and slipped into Florence's Greasy Cup, knowing I'd show up at school later smelling like bacon and rotgut coffee—hazards of the job. It didn't matter. I'd forgotten to shower anyway.

There were the Romeos—Walter, Obie, and Charlie—in the same booth as always. I sat in the booth behind them and ordered bacon, grits, and coffee. Nodding hello, I asked how things were going. We exchanged a few lines about the Kate Dowland case again. They knew that Francine had materialized from the dead after decades but were foggy on exactly why, which suited me. I didn't want people talking about anything related to my quest. Whether townspeople thought we were a bunch of silly kids on a treasure hunt or whether God had drawn some veil over their minds, I didn't know and didn't care.

"Guess you know Old Pilgrim Church is history," I said, stirring a bunch of sugar into my coffee. "By next summer it will be a sand volleyball court."

They went off on a tangent about how reclaiming old real estate can rejuvenate the economy.

I asked who started the church, who named it Old Pilgrim, and why, hoping to steer the conversation to a certain relic that once stood inside.

Charlie gave me the rundown: "Psh!" he flapped his hand at me. "Some Indian legend about teachers who came from the four directions with great lessons, calling themselves pilgrims."

My heart took a leap, but I stayed cool and just nodded. "Pilgrims, huh?" I knew the legend of the Four Teachers, the People of the Light teaching their medicine ways. Add that to my secret discovery of the Celtic inscription in Gilead, and I deduced that the teacher from the East might well have been Brendan the Navigator or one of the other *peregrini*. History was coming together right under my nose.

Charlie said, "The same man who helped start the church and named it Old Pilgrim after the legends also built The Castle. A world-traveling politician."

The Romeos debated the age of the church—a hundred, a hundred and fifty years before its doors closed forever—then took off on how The Castle was the last of the original houses in Magdeline, how that was a crying shame. They went on reminiscing about bygone buildings and the loss of The Roanoke and the old train depot and so on.

To turn the subject to the armor would have been suspicious, so I gulped down breakfast and took off for school, saying to the Romeos, "Later."

We dozen die-hard Latin I students were silly with relief that first semester was winding down. Basketball Mike was a shadow of his formerly easygoing self, cowering behind me and chewing his fingernails, waiting for Abner's next sneak attack. Before developing a nervous condition, he'd been our star center and Magdeline High's best chance at beating rival Whitcomb. It hardly seemed fair that the entire future of Magdeline's basketball team hinged on the bony finger of a frail-looking, three-fourths blind old prune who lived on tea and crackers, and whose "Incorrrrrrect!" rolled off her tongue like a death sentence. A few more of her pop quizzes and Mag High would be basketball history.

But after the initial Latin I shock in September, I'd discovered a new thing about myself. After what I'd been through—a year-and-a-half quest, the town gossiping against me, run-ins with the police, taking on Bloocifer and her babies, a futile trip to Ireland where I came eyeball to eyeball with a demon—Abner was hardly more than a minor annoyance, a fever blister on the lip of my life. I had bigger fish to fry—namely finishing what I'd started with the armor of God. Plus there was a huge social dilemma looming on the bleak winter horizon: the supremely stupid first annual masked ball.

CHAPTER 3

Reece and I had gotten closer since Ireland. After almost losing her over the Cliffs of Morte and that one golden moment on the Hill of Slane when I'd swear she turned into an angel for a minute, I had a hard time taking my eyes off her. It was good for my grades that we only had one class together.

But since returning from Ireland, I made a regular habit of not sitting with Reece at lunch because of Emma Stone. Reece never said anything negative about her new friend, but I knew her well enough to see she was torn. She appreciated Emma hanging around and helping with her lunch tray and books and stuff. Emma was cute and talkative and bubbly—and maybe so dense she didn't get what was going on between Reece and me. Or maybe she just didn't care. Who really knows what girls think?

Mei would always be Reece's best friend; I could see it in Reece's eyes when she read Mei's letters to me.

The guys' lunch table was full one day, so Reece waved me over. In two shakes Emma brought up the subject that I didn't want brought up. She flipped her hair and wrinkled her freckled nose at me. "Going to the masked ball, Elijah?"

Simple enough question, you'd think. But I had to weigh my words. Most guys had already staked their claims on girls, except for Marcus who was still playing way, way cool with Miranda Varner. I'd even seen her walking to class a few times with square-shouldered, brown-eyed Henry Dale and wondered what Skidmore was waiting for. I'd been hoping to get pointers by observing a man of the world in action. But he was no help at all. Thanks to Marcus, I was lagging behind; the pressure to make a move built with each passing day.

Reece was always up front about having to use crutches, but I couldn't figure whether I should ask her to a dance or not. Would she give me a look and say, "Hello? Earth to Elijah. I can't dance." Or would she turn martyr and tell me to take someone else, which was sure to start a drama I wanted no part of. (I just plain wasn't into dancing or dressing up like a freak and parading around in front of hundreds of my peers.)

If I did end up going, it would be as an Indian. People would give me grief, saying, "Where's your costume, Creek? You wear those khakis to school!" The judges would probably make a new award category just for me: the Dud Award.

Why couldn't we have a regular dance like other schools? Miss Flew, the drama director, that's why. Budget cuts in the theater department weren't going to stop her from forcing kids into costume and throwing them into a spotlight at every opportunity. Most guys hated the whole idea, but every last one of us got sucked into going in hopes of winning cool stuff provided by the PTO and city council: sports equipment autographed by national players, two TVs, high-priced gift certificates, and the grand prize—a motorcycle.

Was I going? Emma's gray eyes followed my every move like a hungry coyote. Buttering a piece of bread half to death, I muttered, "I dunno."

"I hope I get asked," she said obviously. "I want to go as a flapper." She began to describe her short dress with the sparkles and fringe and little straps and how gorgeous it was. "Hey, Reece, if no one asks us, we'll go in a girl gang, okay?"

My ears perked. Reece poked at her food.

Emma prodded her, "You are going, aren't you?"

"It depends," Reece said, not looking up.

I ate fast and took my tray back. Retrieving my book bag from the shelf near the door, I glanced back toward Reece's table. Emma had motioned Marcus over and was gushing and pointing to Reece. Her voice cut through the cafeteria noise, and I caught the gist: she was trying to fix him up with Reece and telling him what a cute couple they'd make.

· · · · ·

I couldn't seem to focus on any one thing for worrying about something else: Latin I exams, my social life, the dance, Mom's depression, the quest for the armor, and the demon voice. One problem muddied another. I couldn't call the Stallards for encouragement because Mom didn't want me involved with them anymore. She spent lots of time with Uncle Dorian, talking over what to do about their biological mother, Isabel, who'd been forced to give them up for adoption by a church-run workhouse in Ireland. Mom was against churches now and didn't appreciate Reece trying to keep me involved. She didn't like my calling Reece, and I felt funny myself now because of the whole masked ball thing. It seemed that the only thing Mom approved of was my hanging out with Rob in The Castle like we used to. But those days were over. She just couldn't accept the change in me.

I hardly saw Dad these days. Camp Mudjokivi was booked with winter retreats, and he had his hands full around the clock. I couldn't talk to Dom about demon stuff and risk drawing Marcus's attention. And powwows were a problem because of moms and clubs and sports moving us all on different tracks.

Marcus had been giving me strange looks, like he was trying to read me or something. When I asked him one day in study hall what he was staring at, he said, "That shabby-rugged-stud look you're going for lately—it needs work."

The thought gnawed at me that maybe he was really

strategizing about Reece and me. If Miranda Varner and Henry Dale got to be a thing, Marcus would be out of luck for the dance—unless he asked Reece. He was itching for a chance to win that motorcycle, just like the rest of us guys. Things were closing in on me from all sides.

Over dinner Mom carped about the giant Santa. "Who paid for that monstrosity, Russ? If it came out of city taxes, I am going to write a strong letter! That money could be used for toys for poor children. Someone should say something to the town council!"

Dad said meekly, "From what I hear, hon, the city's planning to buy a giant snowman next year."

"Cramming Christmas down our throats with taxpayer money!" Mom snipped. She turned to me. "Elijah, how's that Latin coming? Language arts are important for college. You have to think ahead. And how many days in a row have you worn that shirt?" She passed around a bowl of instant macaroni and cheese. "Girls, you need to clean your room before bedtime. You're not babies anymore. Take some responsibility around here!"

I suddenly lost my appetite. Passing up dessert, I went to my room to stew. *Take one thing at a time,* I coached myself. *Okay, which first? The sword.* I surveyed my options and came up with one: call Francine Dowland one last time. I waited until Mom had dashed over to Uncle Dorian's about some family tree thing. The twins were in their room. Dad had rushed back to his office. The coast was clear.

I dialed the number. Francine answered, "Hello?"

"Hi. Um, this is Elijah Creek."

"Who?"

"From Magdeline, Ohio. You sent me the shoes of peace a while back."

"Oh yes. I remember. How are you?"

"I'm fine. Hey, I had a question and wondered if you could answer it."

"Well, I'll certainly try."

"We went to Ireland and visited all those castles you told us about. We even went to antique shops and asked around, but we didn't find the sword or any clue about the armor."

"That's too bad."

"I wondered if there was anything else you maybe forgot to tell us."

She paused. "I don't think so."

"I was just wondering why—with all the castles in Ireland— you all stopped at Ballymeade and Dunluce."

"I told you that Stan wanted to trace his family's roots."

"And his family once lived in those castles?"

"That's right. The MacMerrits."

I sat down on a kitchen stool and quit breathing. "Did you say *MacMerrits*?"

"That's the name."

Stan Dowland was a descendant of the bloody MacMerrits?! The ones whose tapestry at Ballymeade showed the armor of God? The ones whose victims haunted Leap Castle?! Well yeah, it made sense when I thought about it for a second. We'd followed his trail around the country and heard that name at every stop, but the whole time I'd never made the connection that those were the roots he was tracing.

Francine explained, "Stan read somewhere in his family's rather unsavory history a story about hidden treasure. The story led him to buy the armor. The whole tale seemed made up to me; I didn't pay too much attention at the time. Things get hazy for me nowadays."

"I thought he bought it because it was the armor of God."

"Well, yes, he said that and even preached some sermons on

it. In the end, though, it was hopes of a treasure that possessed him."

"Really. And the sword?" I asked for the umpteenth time.

"There never was a sword."

"Well, ma'am," I pressed, "if it's the armor of God, there has to be a sword."

She sighed tiredly. "That very thing drove Stan to distraction! It made him bitter, I'm sad to say."

"Did you go to Leap Castle? I'm asking because there was a story of treasure in an underground dungeon there."

"Leap Castle ... ," she thought out loud, "not that I remember." She sounded confused.

I tried to jog her memory. "A sort of scary place in central Ireland. Off the beaten track in some lonely hills."

"No ... I don't think so."

"'Cause the MacMerrits lived there too. It was their last stronghold before they died out."

Francine let out a hollow moan, "Ohhh ... the end of the line. What heartache for Stan when Kate and Adam passed. Having no descendants was his bitterest pill of all."

She went on a while longer about herself and what she'd been doing all day. I figured she was lonely, so I let her talk—keeping an ear toward the door in case Mom came back.

Finally I said, "Well, thanks for your time, ma'am. If you think of anything, call this number." I gave her Reece's phone number and told her not to talk to anyone but Reece, who'd be available most evenings. (Okay, so my motives weren't the best. But it was one possible way to have Reece start a conversation with me, which might lead to the subject of whether she really wanted to go to the masked ball.)

Mom came up to my room miffed, and I expected the worst: that she'd found out I called Francine. "I just saw your track coach at the gas station. He said you weren't sure you'd be at the postseason run on Sunday afternoon."

"I'll go," I said grudgingly.

"Then what was he talking about?"

I shrugged, tired of Mom taking all the fun out of life. "Season's over, Mom. I do plenty of running around camp to stay in shape."

"Elijah, you have to be thinking about your future. Your grades are … ," she strained to say, "good, but a track scholarship would help with your college fund. We're not rich, you know. Our life savings is tied up in this camp. You'll have to shoulder some of your own responsibility for college."

"That's four years away."

"Three and a half."

I sank back on my bed. "I sort of wanted to go to the lock-in at—" I couldn't call it my church without getting viped, so I just said, "with Reece's youth group."

Mom viped anyway. "An all-nighter?"

"It's safe. They have games and movies, and it's chaperoned. There's free breakfast before church. I'll be beat on Sunday afternoon after no sleep. I won't feel like running."

"Well, if you have all that time to spend, use it on something worthwhile: your schoolwork or your running. That church isn't even in town; you have friends at school. I don't understand, Elijah. You know how I feel about this." Practically ranting, she paused a minute and mellowed. "By the way, sweetie, I was talking to Emma Stone's mother at PTO. She says Emma speaks very highly of you."

"Yeah."

"You need to socialize more, Elijah. With other people."

I knew what she meant by "other": other than my clan, other than church people, other than Reece.

Mom had always tried to protect me and the twins from bad news on TV and in the papers; up to this point, I went along. My world up through middle school had been pretty much confined to Camp Mudj, school, Council Cliffs State Park, and the mundane goings on in Magdeline, Ohio.

World trekker Marcus Skidmore had said many a time that Rob and I were too sheltered. I was beginning to think he was right. So when sociology class assignments plunged into world affairs—wars, corporate corruption, government scandals, militant religions, famines, and pandemics—and when the high school Bible study class prayed about world missionaries being murdered in their cars and blown up in their churches, I sat up and took notice. I paid attention to what was happening in the Middle East where the Stallards had met the Skidmores and in Japan where Mei now lived. Marcus had relatives in northern Africa. All those places were in The Window, as it's called.

I'd heard of terrible things going on around the world before, but for the first time I connected them with me. For the first time, I really truly cared.

Sometimes after Mom and Dad went to bed, I'd get up and watch the late news with the sound turned way down. Then I'd have to flush my mind of worry with a midnight B-grade horror flick. My favorite show was hosted by a middle-aged woman who was made up like a dead person and called herself Minny Kadavers. She had the best worst horror movies of all time. But after two hours of black-and-white blood and gore and the undead creeping around in my mind, I'd spin off on the real, live evil beings busting through the veil. Sometimes I'd fall asleep on the couch reading the Quella. Sometimes I'd creep up to my room and listen to night sounds until I heard Dad making coffee downstairs and knew it was morning.

One of the tackiest movies of all time was advertised for Friday night's show: *From Hell It Came*. It was the worst.

I gathered the clan of four at my locker with a plan. "Old movie night with Minny Kadavers this Friday, one you'll love to hate. But we can't talk business or church or the Bible or the armor; it has to be goof-off time." The clan wasn't the same without Mei, and we'd pretty much lost our purpose, but they agreed semi-excitedly. As we scattered for class, I tagged along with Reece. "You can bring a friend, you being the only girl."

"Emma's probably free," she said blandly.

"Why don't you bring Miranda?" I suggested.

"We're not ... I mean, I like her, but we don't hang out. She may not want to."

"Tell her Marcus is coming."

CHAPTER 4

I arranged the lodge furniture around the fireplace and wheeled in a TV. Bo was around as part-time chaperone, and there'd be senior citizens on retreat wandering out of the shadows to the fridge until the wee hours—sort of like the undead. Marcus and Rob got there first. When Reece showed up with Miranda, Marcus started showing off by being Mr. Polite, getting bowls of popcorn and cans of cold pop for everyone, offering to get more wood for the fire.

We settled in for *From Hell It Came*. The scene opens on a tropical beach where an innocent guy gets executed by his island tribe for some trumped-up charge. He vows to return from Hell for revenge. The natives bury him in a tree trunk and plant him in a radioactive graveyard. The guy comes back as a tree named Tabonga with a face that's supposed to be scary but looks more like a cardboard character from a preschool play.

Rob started off being offended at the bad acting and unconvincing sets; but he soon got into the swing of it, rewriting lines as it went along and making fun of the cheap scenery and flabby natives. "Hey, natives, here comes Mr. Cranky Tree! Run—if you can!"

Tabonga toddles around through a woods that's supposed to be a jungle but looks more like West Virginia.

He chases people who run faster than him, but for some reason he always catches them. "Yeah, that's smart, people," commented Rob, "head toward the quicksand where it's safe.

Oh no! Tabonga's got you! He's hugging you to death with his cardboard limbs! Oops! Into the quicksand you go!"

Rob kept us entertained with a running monologue. "Yeah, that's right, run to the edge of the cliff. Now turn and scream at the tree. There you go. Back up, a little more ..."

In the movie the main scientist guy can't keep his mind on the deadly radioactive creature for trying to get the main scientist girl to kiss him. When she finally plants one on him, he asks, "Why'd you do that?" She says, "I don't know. My metabolism." That scene sent us off in a loony direction.

Marcus threw his arm around Miranda and said, "I'm burnin' for ya', baby, but I can't tell if it's love or calories."

"Tabonga die!" Rob cheered in a big dumb voice, mimicking the natives when they lured Tabonga into a fiery pit, raised their clubs in victory, and wandered back to what was left of the village. Hokey background music swelled, and we were supposed to think the carnage was over. Then a big hunk of smoking charcoal with eyes climbed out of the hole and toddled off to hug more natives to death.

It was the worst. We loved it.

Marcus and Miranda kidded around a lot. Rob gave the movie thumbs-up for cheesiness and hinted he might show up at the masked ball dressed as Tabonga. He tried to rope me into going as Great Oak.

"I will," I joked, "if Marcus goes as The Cedars."

Rob squealed, "Yeah! We can be a whole forest!"

We guys talked about vying for most original costume.

(I was already living with the nickname Nature Boy and had no intention of parading in front of Mag High dressed as vegetation.) My real intent was to fish around for a reaction from Reece. She just picked at the popcorn in the bottom of her bowl. Miranda said she was going as Nefertiri.

Finally Marcus asked outright, "You going, Elliston?"

"It depends …"

On what? I wondered. *If she's able to walk? If I ask her? If Emma talks her into going with a girl gang? If she finds a costume? If I ask her and don't go as a tree?*

She gave no hints, which drove me crazy. We were already like best friends, and I didn't want to ruin that. But I also didn't want to show up as a freshman couple and be branded for life, which tends to happen in small towns. My hesitation didn't have anything to do with her disability. I just couldn't deal with any more intense feelings.

About the only thing she said to me all night was, "Elijah, are you coming down with the flu? You don't look good."

· · · · ·

I was in the living room trying to do homework (but actually staring at a picture of Leap Castle Rob had given me and thinking how I might have to go back there to dig through that dungeon) when the phone rang.

"It's for you," Mom called. I went to the kitchen. "It's Reece," she said darkly. "Girls shouldn't be calling boys."

My heart thumped. "We're friends," I said flatly.

Mom whispered, "If it's another one of those youth group things, you have to get that Latin grade up before test time."

I took the phone. "Reece?"

"I … you . . I don't know how to say this." She sounded really upset.

My gut wrenched. "What's wrong?"

"I wouldn't say it's wrong. Maybe a shock."

"What's a shock?" Was she going to the dance with Marcus?

"I don't know how to say it."

My heart sank. "Say it."

"Francine Dowland called."

My heart thumped again in a whole different direction. I wanted to ask if there was a clue, but Mom was listening from the sink. "And?"

"She remembered something."

"About ..." I was hoping she'd say sword or treasure.

"A relative of the MacMerrit clan."

"The MacMerrits?" I asked.

Slowly Mom turned and gave me the weirdest look.

Reece said, "Okay, I'm going to give this straight, so brace yourself. Francine said that Dowland had a relative he once tried to rescue from an awful church-run home for girls... ." She paused.

My heart leaped into my throat. "Hold on." I covered the mouthpiece and turned to Mom. "What's wrong?"

Eerily she asked me, "How did you know that name?"

"A castle we went to ... the people who used to own it had that name. Why?" A strange hollow in my gut and a roar in my head told me what was coming. I just couldn't believe it.

"Elijah?" Reece said from the phone.

"Hold on," I said, still looking at Mom, my mind fogging. My voice rose. "What about that name?!"

Reece answered, "It was the name of Dowland's relative."

At the same time Mom said, "It was my mother's last name."

"I'll call you back." I hung up on Reece.

My brain was in a whirl. Hold on a minute! *Crazy ol' Dowland and me—related? Through the bloody MacMerrits, who may have been the last to own the armor of God?* Chills rolled over me; a thousand questions raced through my mind. *Wait a minute! Hold on! How did we end up in the same town, his church and my camp occupying the same hill?! Did he know about this? Had he been stalking me because I was the last of his clan? Or because I found the armor?*

"How did you know that name?" Mom asked again accusingly, as if I'd breached her personal security.

I shrugged helplessly. "That last castle we visited was the MacMerrits' last stand. That's all."

She glared at me skeptically for a long moment, then slowly mellowed a little and said as if to herself, "Oh … I guess it's a coincidence … probably a common name over there." Suddenly she changed again, viping at me, her head tipped down, her eyes drilling and ready to strike. "You're not still on that armor kick, are you?"

I shrugged casually. "It's just a few more pieces, Mom. If they turn up, that'd be cool. But we're not having powwows about it. Everybody's too busy."

I retreated up to my room with my books and turned off the light. Lying in a pool of cold moonlight from my window, I took the picture of Leap Castle in my hand and studied its shape. I couldn't think straight. Not one thought lined up behind another. My mind shot across continents. *The bloody MacMerrits, a family with a chapel where a murder took place, a family who dabbled in the dark arts!* I thought about Dowland preaching the armor of God while really thirsting for treasure. I thought about Grandma Isabel trapped her whole life on the Isle of Magdeline in a church-run workhouse while I lived free in Magdeline, Ohio. My mind whirled around the gods of Mei Aizawa and her Wiccan friend Sahara versus the creator of the universe.

Mysteries of the past, mysteries of the future. The cross-shaped tomb of prehistoric Newgrange. The Day of Evil looming ahead. The shabby Blessed Assembly of the Full Gospel of the Holy Ghost and the defunct Old Pilgrim Church. A giant Santa in the center of town and angels with swords guarding The Crystal See. Words volleyed back and forth inside my skull: saved and lost, lost and saved. Lost … saved. From the beginning of time until the end … pieces of the past, tragedies and truth … buried piece by piece.

Then and there I hatched a plan to retreat to Gilead if things got bad in the world. *Think like Dowland.* Yeah, he'd hidden his daughter and grandson in Telanoo to keep them safe. In the same way, I'd save everyone I could before the Day of Evil. I'd bring my family and my clan into Gilead. Dad and the guys and I could hunt and fish and build shelter. Mom and Reece and Reece's mom would cook and haul water and wood. Officer Taylor could come along for protection; he and Dom could stand vigil. If I kept the fires low and scouted out new hiding places, no one would find us.

All I needed was the helmet and sword. And maybe a treasure to boot, like God hinted. With a cache of money, food, weapons, ammo, we'd be safe from the evil to come.

So okay, I thought logically. *So I'm related to Dowland. So what? It might not be a bad thing in the end. Think like him and find the armor. Find the pieces of the past buried like the ones in the ground.* From the back of my closet, I dug out an old, plaid flannel shirt that I'd yanked from camp's lost and found to wear while painting. It was faded—worn out in the elbows and around the collar. I put it on and stood in front of the mirror. I studied my angled jaw and deep eyes, which looked tired, dull. The resemblance was slight, but it was there.

Think like Dowland.

I was staring in the mirror, wishing I was in Gilead or scouring the dungeons of Leap Castle, when I heard a knock at the front door and then a familiar voice. *Marcus.*

Clomp, clomp. He was coming up the steps. I threw my room together and tossed stuff under the bed.

He knocked on my door. "You in there?"

"Yeah."

He eased the door open. "Got any weapons aimed?"

"Only a couple. What's up?"

"My dad made me come." He was half serious. "You going to the dance?"

My gut went into a knot. He was here to ask permission to ask Reece. I knew it.

"I dunno."

"You should go."

And take Emma, I figured he'd say next. I'd always known from the first, since last year when Reece wanted to bring him into the group, that they had something going on. *Fine, you take Reece. I'll take Miranda,* I thought vengefully. *One night with me, and she'll never give you a second thought. I'll be so charming that I'll out-Marcus Marcus, just wait and see.*

"Reece is going," he said.

"Oh," I muttered. *Here it comes. With me, he'd say. You waited too late, chump.*

He was looking at me with that cool, cocky grin. "She'll probably want to see you there."

I looked at him. "She's going?"

"With the girl gang. She thought that'd be best."

"Oh. I didn't know …"

"Now you do. And there's a surprise. I think it's for you."

Oh great, I thought. *The two of you have some mystery cooked up, and I'm out of the loop.* "You going?" I asked.

"Not as a tree."

I grinned. "Me neither."

He eyed me for a moment. "You okay? You're sort of green around the gills."

"Who are you, my mother?"

"Just asking, Creek. You're gaunt. You need a haircut." He walked out of my room, turned, and gave me an unsettled look.

"Don't wear that. You look like Dowland."

. . . . .

I avoided everyone at school the next few days, dragged myself through classes, then ran straight home to my room. I'd stare at the picture of Leap Castle, feeling like it was calling to me. I mustered nerve for what I needed to do.

One night between frozen dinners and waiting for Mom and Dad to go to bed so I could watch TV, I took a deep breath, feeling edgy but determined. I smiled to myself. *You're getting brave in your old age, Creek.*

I took one last look at Leap Castle, the tower with no eyes; the one top center window, narrow and vertically divided like a snout; the points on the tower like horns listening, picking up only silence and wind across low-slung hills. I kept trying to make the tower into a face in my mind. I could; then I couldn't. It was; then it wasn't. I slid the picture into my pocket and went down to the kitchen. Mom stood leaning in the crook of the counter, holding a cup of tea.

I didn't know how to break it to her, so I just came out with it. "I want to go back to Ireland, to Leap Castle."

Without a hitch she said, "Absolutely not."

"You could go with me and see your mother."

"If anyone goes, it will be Dorian," she said flatly.

"I could go to navigate. I know the country now."

"No, and that settles it."

"I'll be driving soon," I half threatened.

"You can't rent a car at your age."

"Then I could bike it."

She gave me her viper stare. "Not by yourself. Not with Dorian. We can't afford the ticket."

"Aren't you ever going back to see your mom?" I asked, the edge in my voice sharper.

"I don't know."

"I think you should. And take me."

She spoke to me slow—as if I were dense. "Elijah, you have to get on with your real life."

"I'm living my real life." I turned to leave.

"Looking for some old relic is a waste of your valuable time." She sat the cup in the sink and said darkly, "You'll never find it."

I stopped and slowly turned, afraid to look her in the eye. "Wh-what … did you say?"

Mom eyed me vacantly, her voice flat and unfriendly. "I said you'll never find it."

CHAPTER 5

I ran to Dad's office. He didn't even ask what I'd come for or wait for me to explain. "I'm really busy, son. It'll be a couple of hours before the new folks are situated in the lodge."

"Couple hours?"

"At least. They're trickling in."

"'Kay ... Dad, I—"

"Later," he said, not looking up from paperwork.

I practically staggered outside the lodge. I threw myself against the wall, staring blindly down at the lake and beyond the trees toward Gilead. *My mom just quoted a demon. I have to get away. I'll keep my door locked. I'll put in an appearance at the stupid masked ball, try not to make a fool of myself, figure if Reece wants to dance and how we might do it without making a spectacle, maybe win some cash, and then that's it. I'm out of here.*

I raided the camp's lost and found box for a costume, a requirement to qualify for a chance at the prizes—Miss Flew's rules. Rummaging through the box, I found an old brown blanket, some faded beach towels, a dozen T-shirts, odd tennis shoes, and at the bottom of the heap some pieces of leather from an Old West tanning demonstration. *It's this or nothing.*

The night of the ball I showed up at school with my bowie knife. I'd stopped off at the hardware store to get it sharpened before I went into Gilead, but the store was already closed. *Can't take a weapon into the commons, even if it looks like part of a costume. Dumb.* My outfit was a leather poncho cut open at the neck and cinched in at the waist by a belt. Other than my Indian pouch, that was the extent of my costume. I expected a reaction from Marcus, Rob, and Reece, but I didn't care.

I stashed my knife in a bush by the side door and slunk into the commons, staying to the dark periphery. The place was draped with miles of see-through gauze. White Christmas lights twinkled behind the papery veil all around, like a foggy sky full of stars. Tables circled the commons so the center could be a dance floor. The stage was dark, its curtains closed. Later on we characters would have to appear one by one on stage to be judged. I found the stag table in the corner with Justin Brill, Henry Dale, and some other guys. I took a seat, wishing I were invisible. There must have been a run on pirate hats, eye patches, and stuffed parrots at every costume department in the county. Most of the guys were scraping by for a chance to win the motorcycle.

Marcus showed up as Lawrence of Arabia, suave and dashing in flowing robes and headgear. Miranda was on his arm as the queen of Egypt. When he saw me, he floated over by himself. "You made it."

"In the flesh." I looked around.

He read my face. "Not here," he half whispered.

I shot him a look.

"She will be," he said coolly.

I sat there like a knot on a log, drumming the table, half listening to the music. People were already dancing. Emma flitted around the girl gang at a table with one empty seat. She hadn't caught sight of me, thank goodness. I watched the door.

Rob came in dressed as a samurai warrior, much to my surprise. A geisha girl with a black wig and a white painted face snagged him at the door, and they found two seats near the stage. He didn't see me in the shadows of the back corner. I didn't care.

What am I doing here? This is stupid!

Miss Flew started the parade of costumes. Winners in each category were to get gift certificates. A drawing would determine who got the sports collectibles, the TVs, and the motorcycle. I went up with the stag table: four pirates, a farmer, a lab tech, a business tycoon, and myself—an Indian scout. Applause was minimal.

Lawrence of Arabia made a sweeping entrance, showing off his sand-colored robes and swirling around like a professional guy model. He waited at the bottom of the steps for Miranda, who got hoots of approval in her straight white dress with gold collar, gold sandals, cylinder-shaped headdress, and makeup just like Queen Nefertiri in the history books. They were a hit.

Several more paraded down: Elf Queen, the Masque of the Red Death, doctors and candles, wizards and butterflies and tin men. Everything from a Napoleon to a green crayon made an entrance from the closed curtains. Each character accepted what applause he got, marched down the steps, and walked back to the tables in the semidark. Then the stage was empty, the curtain black.

I slumped. Reece didn't show. She wasn't coming after all. I glared at Marcus, but he didn't look in my direction. What was this, a dirty trick? The crowd murmured. Were the judges making their decisions?

Miss Flew disappeared backstage and then reappeared a minute later, flustered and eager. "Sorry for the delay. Ahem! And last but not least … Little Soaring Eagle."

The spotlight came on. The curtains parted. She limped into the light on crutches, her blond hair and fringed dress glowing white against the black curtain. The room got quiet. Her dress was trimmed in Indian designs across the shoulders and around the bottom. Her crutches were covered with tapered strips of white material. For a minute she stood uncertainly. Then she planted her feet unsteadily, raised the crutches, and spread her arms out. I came out of my slump; my mouth dropped. The crowd gasped. Cheers and applause thundered. Her crutches were wings.

Reece didn't smile, not a big smile anyway. But a quiet confidence lit her face. Her head tipped determinedly as she extended the eagle wings for flight.

Brill leaned across the table, "Hot, Creek. Reaaaally hot."

The other guys razzed me and said things I can't repeat.

Brill went on about birds of a feather, joked about the birds and the bees, and then whispered something else to the guys clumped around him. They looked at me, guffawed, and made coyote sounds. Heads turned in our direction.

Reece lowered her eagle wings and strained to see through the spotlight. She scanned the audience until her eyes stopped on me. Everyone stared at me, as if we'd had this planned all along. The guys around me stepped up their hoots and razzes.

I'd have to walk across the whole gym in my dumb scrap-leather poncho and greasy hair. Reece would be disappointed. I wanted to stand, but I couldn't. I wanted to go to the foot of the steps and escort her down, suave and cool as Marcus. But my backside seemed glued to the seat.

Uncertainly she moved to the steps. The music started. Couples got up to dance. I couldn't budge. I'd have to run to get to the steps before she came down. I'd look like an idiot. The next thing I knew, Marcus had whispered to Miranda, swept to the steps, and reached up to Reece.

My face burned. She paused, looking back at my corner confused and hurt, but finally took his hand. Over the music came an announcement about the judging, but I didn't hear it. Reece propped her wings against the stage, and Marcus led her out to the dance floor. Justin leaned over to his fellow pirate and whispered something really foul. He didn't know that I'd heard. He didn't know about the benefits of being Nature Boy, how I trained my senses to pick up sights and sounds. I got up and headed toward the back door.

I don't know what possessed me. I turned, marched back to the guy table, and watched the stupid grins drop off their faces as I grabbed their table and flipped it—candles, drinks, snacks, and all. They went sprawling.

I ran.

I ran outside into a sudden whirl of heavy snow and grabbed the knife I'd stashed in the bushes. Wind whipped my leather wrap. Snow stung my face. I took off blindly toward home, knowing I could make it with my eyes closed if I had to. Main Street was empty. The tacky Christmas decorations, clouded by the blizzard, didn't look half bad, even sort of dreamy. But I still hated them. I hated myself, felt lower than a snail trail. *I'll get detention. How can I go back to school on Monday? How can I face Reece?* I remembered yelling at her last year during the play and how she had forgiven me then. But that was a backstage fight, not a blatant walkout in front of the whole school. I plowed through the blizzard, mortified over and over again by the fresh memory. In Reece's moment of glory, I'd left her high and dry.

My hair and jacket turned white with big flakes as I trudged through town. Camp Mudjokivi's sign had come into view when I suddenly sensed something behind me. *I'm being followed.* I pictured Justin Brill and his pirate friends coming to take me out in revenge. I whirled around, instinctively grabbing for my knife. Two blocks back—at the corner where Main Street curves to the left around the bank—I saw movement through clouds of blowing snow.

It's a truck barreling through town, taking the curve too fast, lost control ... no, it's ... Abner in her big white Caddy! The school sent Abner to hunt me down, and here she comes in a raging fury! She'll never see me in the blizzard. She'll run me down, and keep on trucking! Clear the decks! The huge, faint shape hit the corner of the hardware store and bounced off. The wind was howling, but I was still surprised not to hear the crash of metal.

The thing wasn't a car shape. And it was flying. Not speeding, I mean actually *airborne*—bouncing off one building, hitting the street, and bouncing off the opposite side. I heard plate glass shatter. *What in the world IS that?!* The truth dawned as it hurtled in slow motion through the blizzard—a bulky mass of red and white, a giant pair of eyes. The inflatable Santa had ripped free of its moorings and was crashing its way through Magdeline—toward me, the only pedestrian dumb enough to be out on a night like this.

Sure it was just a big balloon, but it wasn't harmless. I knew that much, having seen kids shatter femurs and crack skulls trying to control an earth ball, one fifth the size and weight of this hog-wild, goony-faced spirit of Christmas.

I wasn't sure that I could stop it and didn't care, figuring Magdeline was getting what it deserved. But my conscience spoke to me: *it could really hurt somebody, cause a wreck, take out electric lines. Power could be knocked out. Pipes would freeze and bust.* I couldn't let that happen. My hand unsnapped the strap to my bowie knife. Santa was in a high bounce. The wind caught him, slammed him into the second floor of the furniture store, and knocked him back onto the street.

Taking a knife to city property was vandalism, no two ways about that. But I couldn't let this monstrosity of a decoration ruin my town. I stepped into the street like a gunslinger at high noon, my knife hand poised behind me for maximum thrust, thinking faintly, *Mom will be proud.*

Here he comes! … He was on me, then over me. With more joy and less guilt than I should have felt, I drove the blade straight up into his belly and ripped hard. Pfff! A whoosh of air hit my face. I yanked the knife out and dashed back to the sidewalk. Santa headed out of town, slower and sloppier with each bounce. At the curve right before the camp entrance, he flopped off to the side of the road, his arms flailing, head lolling like a spent drunk.

For a moment I forgot the stupid masked ball and wished like heck that Reece, Rob, Marcus, and Mei could have been here. We'd have laughed about this for years.

I headed home, chuckling devilishly to myself, *Merry Christmas, Magdeline, Ohio.*

· · · · · ·

Rob called first thing the next morning. "What happened?"

"Whad'ya mean?" I asked sleepily.

"The chaperones were ticked at you."

"Brill and the guys said stuff, poking fun at me and Reece. I couldn't let it go."

Rob made a sound of exasperation. "Trouble."

"I'll pay for damages. I'll catch more blue racers."

He grunted again.

I said defensively, "Brill's been asking for it for a long time. He never lets up on me. What did I ever do to him?"

"It's not personal. He's like that with everybody."

"Oh yeah, what nickname did he stick on you?"

Long pause. When he didn't answer, I dropped the subject, having made my point. "Hey, who was the geisha girl?"

"Emily."

"Good costume. I didn't even know her."

"Yeah," Rob said with a goofy tone to his voice.

"Who won the motorcycle?"

"Greg Moline."

"Hey, uh, did Reece—"

"She left early."

"Oh." I nodded thoughtfully into the phone, sat on the couch, and stared out at the snow.

"She danced with a half dozen guys and won Most Inspiring Costume. I think the judges made up the award at the last minute just for her. Where'd you go?"

"Home."

"Well, I gotta go. I thought you should know that the chaperones were in a huddle after you left."

"Okay. Thanks."

I threw on a turtleneck and the old flannel shirt, told Mom I was going for a run, and took off for Great Oak. Last night's blizzard had left four inches of snow over the countryside. Camp was a perfect blanket of white, the lake skimmed with silver. The sky was blue, the sun warm. I filled my lungs, my feet pounding pavement until the trail ended at the dirt path we'd made into Telanoo last summer. I ran to Great Oak, suddenly weary, my eyes watery from the cold, dry air. I cleared a spot in the sunshine, faced away from the path, and plopped down against the trunk. I smelled the frozen air and felt the warm sun on my face. I closed my eyes and let my mind drift to mundane things so I wouldn't have to really think: *The snow won't last long—a day or two at the most. Then I'll work on Gilead. Gotta have a place. There's too much pressing me down. Hope Reece is okay. The snow won't last today, not if the sun stays out. I should have asked Rob about the weather. He'd know. He likes weather.*

I heard the blare of a distant train, the wind swaying the upper branches of Great Oak, and dead leaves somersaulting past me on the ground. Facing east, I was sheltered from the wind. The buzz of the golf cart approached through the woods from the direction of the camp. *Bo's checking the path. It won't need clearing. The snow'll melt by late afternoon. Dad'll want me to do the nature talk for the Whitcomb Nature Club's winter hike. That'd be good—a perfect day for the old folks. Crisp and clean. I need to be out and about.* I listened as the cart kept coming—past where the paved path ended a few yards behind me. The engine stopped. *Rats. Bo spotted me; he must need work done now. I'm not in the mood. I'm tired.*

A small voice cut across the quiet. "I thought you were Stan Dowland sitting there."

Reece!

CHAPTER 6

I shot to my feet so fast that my head swam. I spun around. There she sat behind the steering wheel of the cart.

"Hey," I said lamely.

In a peacoat and jeans, her face pink from the cold, she stared at me a long time. I wondered if she'd stolen the key from the maintenance shed or gotten permission from Bo. *Had Mom told her I was here, or did she just know? Am I even awake? Or is this a nightmare, the spirit of bad Christmas parties past coming to chew me out?*

She snorted. "Faded flannel, all scraggly looking—some clan leader you are."

"What clan? The Nowhere Fast clan?" The bitter edge in my voice startled me.

"Oh, grouchy and mean too. That's just super!" she snipped.

She got out of the cart with the help of her de-feathered crutches. Her eyes never left me. "Everyone cheered me but you. Everyone clapped and said what a cool costume it was. Marcus danced with me—and Rob and a half dozen other guys—to show me I don't always have to be a freak; to say, 'Hey Reece, you can be like the other girls for one night.'"

"You're not a freak," I said, my mind chanting, *Don't mess it up, don't mess it up.*

"Everyone but *you*." Seething, she came right up to me and backed me into Great Oak, her eyes narrowing. "You owe me, Elijah Creek."

"Everyone in the gym was staring at me," I explained. Lousy excuse and I knew it. *Don't mess it up! Think!*

She shot back, "They were staring, all right. Staring at the huge gap between where I was standing and where you were sitting there with your ... your pirate buddies."

"They're not my buddies!" I shot back. "They're jerks."

I wasn't about to mention the stuff they were saying about her—about us. Not now, not ever.

She agreed nastily. "Yeah. Jerks who couldn't get dates because they were too scared and too full of themselves to get out on a dance floor and move around for five minutes with someone who'd been hoping and praying for weeks she'd get to come."

It took every ounce of willpower to stay put. Part of me wanted to turn tail and run into Telanoo where she couldn't get at me, and part of me wanted to grab her and grovel and say how sorry I was. My mind was a mess.

She interrupted my thoughts. "I want to climb Great Oak."

I looked down at her hard-set face. She was serious.

"That's not a good idea," I replied.

She didn't flinch. "You said you can see everything from up there; you told me that once. That's what I want to see: everything. You owe me."

"I don't want to be responsible for you dying," I said bluntly.

"If you don't help me, I'll try it myself. Then you will be responsible."

Reece wasn't going to budge. But maybe I could put her off until she settled down and got some sense. "Well, uh ... okay. When it warms up—"

"I want to go now. Pay up."

I objected, "Reece ..."

"Now!" Her mouth was set, her eyes drilling into me.

"Without me you can't get up to the first branch," I argued.

"Just watch me. I'll use my crutches as a ladder."

"You'll kill yourself."

"And it'll be your fault. I brought rope to pull myself up."

"You'll hang yourself."

"Your fault." She repeated it matter-of-factly and went back to the cart to retrieve a length of heavy rope.

I followed her, throwing out any excuse to make her stop. "What about your mom? Does she know what you're doing?"

"She knows." Reece pushed me out of the way with her crutch and went back to Great Oak. "Mom knows how much you hurt me, and she wasn't about to say, 'No, sweetie, you just stay on the ground; stay in the background and be a big nobody. Be a cripple; don't do what everyone else does.' She wants me to stretch my limits." Reece unwound the rope and shot me an angry look. "So I'm climbing a tree."

I studied the chinquapin oak, the biggest, tallest tree in Owl Woods. Instinctively I started evaluating the shortest gaps between branches, the easiest, safest way up.

"My arms are strong," she said with a kind of nervous anger. "If you help me get to the first branch, I can pull myself up to the next."

"Okay," I said helplessly. I made a stirrup with my hands and hoisted her up. She sat down hard and grimaced.

"Reece …" But I couldn't tell her that she couldn't climb. Not after last night.

"Okay, wait," she said, thinking. "Okay, you climb up and pull me up until my feet find a branch. That'd be the easiest."

"Shouldn't I be beside you in case you start to fall?"

"I'll hold on."

I climbed to the limb above her and looked down at her blond hair whipping in the wintry breeze, feeling the chill through my shabby shirt. "It's much colder at the top with the wind and all."

I knew how the cold affected her.

"Good," she said sarcastically. "I like wind; it's refreshing."

I'd climb one branch above, she'd let go of her branch and grab onto my arms, I'd pull her up and talk her onto the next limb: "move your foot left," "go right," and so on. She didn't weigh much, but the strain of having her life in my hands wore me down. By the time we were halfway up Great Oak, she was trembling from the cold and the pain. I was unsteady myself. Sure, I helped Nori and Stacy climb trees all the time … campers too, but never Reece, never to the top of Great Oak in Telanoo. No one had climbed it but Rob and me.

"Let's stop and rest. Hey, look how you can see the lodge from here!" I said, hoping she'd be content with this view of the camp.

She kept her eyes on the swaying top of Great Oak and gulped hard. "I'm climbing … to there."

"But from here you can see—"

"Keep going!"

By two-thirds of the way up, her fingers had gone numb, and she was shaking all over. The wind was swaying the narrow trunk—I was truly scared. My fingers were purple; my ears burned. "Hey, Reece," I laughed weakly, "we'll probably get stuck up here like two house cats, and the fire department will have to come get us down."

Concentrating on one hand and then the other, she hauled herself higher and didn't crack a smile. I don't think she even heard me.

I dropped down so we'd be eye to eye. "Listen to me!" I yelled over the wind. "This is too dangerous. I wouldn't come this high by myself, not in winter in high wind. Your fingers can't hang on. The branches are brittle with cold."

"Then you go back down, coward."

"Come on, Reece!"

"Coward!" she blurted again. Her blue eyes filled with tears that ran down her face. "You can climb trees to the top, explore Telanoo, face down Dowland, and pull me back from the Cliffs of Morte, but you couldn't take thirty measly steps for one moment to make me feel normal?" A hiccup caught in her throat. "All the work my mom did on my costume and—" she broke into sobs, "and you couldn't take a few crummy steps! Who's disabled now, Elijah? Who's the *real* cripple?"

Angrily, Reece wiped her eyes and reached for another branch. "A few more feet to the very top. I'm going!"

I didn't know what else to say. I'm not a man of words.

So I kissed her.

She reeled back, shocked. "What'd you do that for!?"

I was confused. I thought girls who liked you wanted you to kiss them.

She raged at me. "Elijah, in front of the whole school, you act like I don't exist, but then when we're up here in the middle of nowhere, you ... you ..."

I was bracing for a slug in the nose, gearing up to dodge her fist, and planning how to keep her from losing her grip on the branch and plunging us both down the full height of Great Oak, when she kissed me back. "Coward!" she said the third time. Then she hugged me hard like it didn't matter what I'd done.

Girls make no sense.

Reece wedged her foot into the next crook, pulling herself up. "Why didn't you dance with me?"

Nothing I could do would get me off the hook. "I ... I ... ," I stammered. There was no excuse. "It ... it was my metabolism," I joked lamely.

Her head dropped, and she broke into a giggle. Then she cried a little more and slugged me with her fist and said, "Tabonga will die."

We made it to the top of Great Oak without another word. It was as if we'd said everything we needed to with the word *coward*, two kisses, and a couple of slugs. "Look down," I said. Our eyes followed the trunk of Great Oak to where the golf cart sat, small as a toy. Reece clung to me for dear life. "Amazing, huh?" I said it so proudly you'd have thought I had something to do with the tree and the view. "Not as high as the Cliffs of Morte, but the greatest view around here."

She locked eyes with me, tears sparkling on her eyelashes. "I've wanted to be up here ... with you ... forever!"

"Me too," I said, and then added, "I mean, I didn't think it would ever happen. But I'm glad too. Hang on. Don't get distracted and let go."

In all directions—Camp Mudj, Telanoo, Council Cliffs, Morgan's farm, Magdeline—I pointed out landmarks, even the direction of her apartment. For me it was like seeing my world for the first time.

Reece kept looking around and around like she was trying to memorize every detail. "I feel like I could really fly. Oh, Elijah, do you see how it works out? If you hadn't ignored me, I wouldn't have gotten mad, and I wouldn't be here. He always works it out. Always. I wouldn't trade this for anything."

We wrapped our arms around the thin trunk and each other, shivering and swaying in the biting wind. The branches clicked and crackled, making an unnerving sound. Reece couldn't have cared less.

There I stood at the summit of my own private kingdom, Reece with me—really with me. Feelings welled up, and it seemed that anything was possible now. We were perched up here like eagles, unafraid and free. I'd found myself again; I knew who I was and what I wanted from life. I had God and Reece. When Mom was her old self again, the clan could restart the quest. And come spring, I might even get semi-famous in track if I trained well. Reece was like my good-luck charm. Life was okay again.

There's nothing like standing at the top of a tall, tall tree and looking around at your life. You really can see everything.

· · · · ·

By the time we got back to the foot of Great Oak, Reece was having trouble. She tried to pretend that she was okay, but I knew better. She looked up bravely, "I knew it wouldn't be easy. Give me a day to rest; I'll be fine."

"Are you sure?"

"Hey, it's just a little pain."

I'd hoped we could go sit under the natural evergreen tent of The Cedars, out of the snow, but she needed to get to the lodge and rest before her mom picked her up. I drove us to the front door as some adult group was heading in for a meeting. "It's busy. We'll have to go back to the house. You can call your mom from there."

We were settled on the couch with hot chocolate when Mom burst though the front door, mad as a hornet. She took one look at Reece and turned to me with an accusing frown. "Elijah, where have you been? It's been hours!"

I stood. "Hi, Mom, I went for a run like I said." I made a code face to say I had company and could she please tone it down. "But Reece came over—"

Mom didn't get the code. "Officer Taylor called about last night. What were you thinking!?"

Officer Taylor? The school called the police over a dumb table!? It was only because Reece was there that I stayed calm. "I'm sorry, Mom, but it was not a huge deal. I can't believe they called the cops. Those guys were acting like—"

As if she didn't hear me, she went on, "If this is supposed to be some kind of favor to me, it's rather twisted. We're going to have to pay for all that damage!"

"What damage? It's a lousy table!"

She counted off on her fingers, "You break the table with that little tantrum at school, then you go through town on a rampage and slash the Santa—sure I hated the thing too, but you don't destroy public property—then you knock over trash cans and break store windows like a common vandal! What has gotten into you?!"

"No … no, Mom … hold on."

"I will not hold on! Your dad's on his way, as if he needs this aggravation! Don't you move an inch!"

I was hoping Reece's mom would pick her up before Dad came, to save me more mortification, but no such luck. The twins were sent to their room—where they were probably hearing every word from the heat duct.

It was embarrassing trying to explain to my parents how I'd acted about Reece at the ball, how Brill's gang had stepped over the line, how I'd messed up being a gentleman but couldn't let guys talk bad about girls, especially Reece. I did the best I could to explain. Throwing the table was an afterthought, I said, because there were more of them than me, and it was my way of making a statement. But saying the whole thing out loud made me sound like a coward *and* an idiot. "I wasn't thinking about what people would think."

There was a glint of approval in Dad's eyes when I said the part about being a gentleman, but Mom said, "It doesn't sound to me like you were thinking at all!"

Officer Taylor came over as Reece's mom showed up. We all gathered in the living room to put me on trial. I told them what really happened in town. I even suggested that Officer Taylor check the ropes that held the Santa. "See if they've been cut or if they tore loose." I showed him the murder weapon I'd used on Santa to protect the town.

Mom shrieked, "You took a knife to school?!"

I backtracked to explain the knife—Mom shaking her head the whole time—then I went on.

"I saw the windows break—it was Santa, not me. Look around at the scene on Main Street; you won't find a rock or stick or anything used to break windows. It wasn't me. I'll swear it on a Bible if you want me to."

Mom rolled her eyes.

Officer Taylor shook his head. "Not necessary. A man's as good as his word." He wrote some things in his notebook.

Dad said, "Darrell, this isn't like our son; you know that. He's gotten himself into some unusual situations lately, but he doesn't flagrantly destroy public property. He's a good boy."

Taking a cue from Dad, Mom said, "He is a good boy. Elijah's usually very responsible. This incident is the result of too much stress in his life. He needs to cut back on his involvements—" Her eyes skimmed over Reece and landed squarely on me, "which I've been trying to tell him."

Reece's head tipped so her hair hid her face.

When Officer Taylor asked a few more details and seemed satisfied, I walked him to the door. He glanced over my shoulder, saw my parents talking in the kitchen, and said in a near whisper, his kind eyes resting solidly on me, "Rachel and Reece—they're strong."

"I know."

He tapped me on the shoulder with his knuckle. "You take care of yourself. Looking a little thin there; eat your meat and potatoes. Runners need protein. I'll file this report and see if we can confirm your story. Depending on what we find, we may want you to come in for further questioning."

Reece's mom helped her to the door. On her way out, Reece

slipped a note into my hand. "I brought this last night, but I didn't get the chance to give it to you." She smiled at me as if all was forgiven. "A poem from English class. I thought of you when I read it."

I slipped it into my pocket.

· · · · ·

That night after dinner, when Dad had gone back to work, Mom grilled me about what Reece and I had been doing in the woods. I slumped on the couch while she rattled dishes in the sink, interrogating me. "Why did she follow you all the way back there in the first place? When she came by and asked where you were, I had no idea she'd follow you, for goodness sake! And why Bo gave her permission to drive the cart, I'll never know. Whose idea was that? It's not policy to let the disabled drive themselves."

I came out of my slump. "She's my friend, Mom. I'm allowed to have friends. Lay off Reece."

She marched over and glared down at me. "Don't you use that tone with me. You're allowed friends. Of course. Don't be silly. But bad influences, no. Absolutely not. Being a church girl doesn't make Reece a good influence," she said acidly. "I'm not naïve."

"You've got to be kidding me!" I jumped to my feet. "Reece a bad influence? That's insane!"

"How dare you call me insane!" Mom screamed.

I hadn't thought that she'd take it personally. But I guess with her just finding her biological mother in a home for the aged, with her mind being pretty much gone, it hit Mom the wrong way. I hadn't meant it like that, but before I could apologize, she said, "When your father comes in, we're discussing your increasingly rebellious behavior. Until then, go to your room, Elijah!"

I stormed up the stairs and muttered under my breath, "I'll go farther than that."

CHAPTER 7

At 11:00 Dad was still out. I'd already begun to quietly pack my gear: tent, sleeping bag, bow and arrows, fire kit, leather poncho. Mentally I made a list of tools from the maintenance building I'd need: shovel, ax, rope, hammer, nails, lantern. My heart was beating hard. I hoped Mom wouldn't come in, but I was prepared: I had books spread on the desk as if I were in the middle of studying for tests. My closet door was open and ready in case I needed to hide the gear.

I felt bad sneaking around behind her back. But I'd had it. Something was working on her against my Christian life—and against the quest—plain as day.

I started a short list of food I'd eventually need: energy bars, canned meat, trail mix.

None of us had talked to the Stallards for a while, but they needed to know we hadn't given up. They were probably lying low because of potential antiquities hounds like that Cravens guy from Ireland. Reece could send a quick note saying that the quest continues. I dug out their address and jotted it down to give to her at school on Monday.

For weeks a picture had been forming in my mind: a stone hut built against the gorge wall of Gilead. A roof of sticks covered with plastic and camouflaged with forest debris, a canvas flap for a door. I'd take a day here or there to work on it, the same way I had with the road. With a little ingenuity and a few weeks of elbow grease, I could make a base camp.

From there I'd be free to sweep Telanoo for the last of the treasure. We'd have a place—a clan hideout where no one could find us—to stash the whole armor of God if Mom or anyone else got too hostile over it. It'd be a bigger surprise for Rob, Reece, and Marcus than my road through Telanoo. If and when the Day of Evil came, we'd all have a place to hide.

I'd load my stuff at first light on Sunday, drive it out to Telanoo as far as my road went, then haul it the rest of the way and have the cart back before anyone else was up. I'd finish chores and tell Dad I needed to be by myself. He'd understand. Mom would be glad I wasn't going to church. Then I'd get to work.

Part of me wanted to disappear altogether. I hated the prospect of facing the police again, of going to school, of owning up to the masked ball committee and Miss Flew about making a big scene. I was tired of Latin homework, monster Christmas decorations, and dumb dances designed to make guys feel like losers. I was fed up with Emma's peskiness but didn't want to be the reason for the end of Reece's friendship with her. I'd spent all my snake money to get to Ireland, and for what? A depressed mom who greeted me from behind her dark cloud every time I came home from church, stealing away the good feelings I'd worked up there. Home had meant something, but with Mom so gloomy all the time and the twins getting clingy and wild, that was crumbling too.

My high-flying feelings from the top of Great Oak had disappeared like a puff of smoke. *Too much stuff rattling around in my head! I need space. I want El-Telan-Yah to tell me where the sword is. He will. He's gotten me this far. I'll find out what I need to know in Gilead.* I got my clothes ready and threw on the only clean shirt I had—the white one I wore the day I was baptized.

• • • • •

For all its isolation and strangeness, I loved Gilead: an unnaturally deep crack in a high ridge—water-formed for sure. I recalled Reece's global flood theory and decided that might be the best explanation. My hiding place was near the end of the gorge. The rim was so overgrown that at its narrowest you could plow through a thicket and drop right into oblivion. I surveyed my hideout with satisfaction. *One day soon I'll bring the Stallards back here and show them the stone scratchings. We'll keep the discovery to ourselves, at least until we've found all of the armor of God.*

I stashed my gear in a dry spot under the ledge, breathed in cold, still air. I listened to the trickle of water from above which made a straight, tiny stream through the gorge. *This is home,* I told myself with secret satisfaction: Gilead, "rocky place" according to the Quella footnotes.

I skimmed the gorge for resources to build my hut. The first wall would be the side of the cliff itself, the straightest rise being several yards away from the trickle. In the other direction—toward the mouth of the gorge—lay a slab of stone five or six feet long and three feet across, slanting up a dirt bank. The stone was huge, but if I dug around it and dislodged it from the dirt, I'd be able to push it down the hill—maybe. I could shove a log under it and roll it into position. I might need the guys to help me fit it into place. But maybe not ... I spotted a nice smooth sapling right away. That'd be my rolling log.

With a lot of maneuvering and sweat, I could scoot it down to the floor of the gorge, fit it into a shallow trench perpendicular to the cliff, and brace it with smaller stones. It would be my second wall. I'd pile up stones from the stream to make a third wall and then construct a roof of plastic and forest debris. A canvas flap would make a fourth wall of my house in Gilead.

Planning ahead, I piled rocks on the hard dirt canyon floor in the path of the slab, in case it got away from me. If it hit the ground flat, I'd never get it upright. For an hour I gathered stones from the creek and piled them at the foot of the embankment to catch the slab.

Sweating in the sunny, windless cold, I ditched my poncho and knife and dug around the slab, wishing for better tools: a pointed shovel, even a trowel. I hadn't thought about a trowel. A flat creek stone would have to do.

Once I'd dug a considerable pile of dirt out from under the slab, I positioned my back against the trunk of a tree up the slope, braced my feet against it, and pushed. It hardly budged. "You're heavier than I thought."

I took a break, got a drink of water from my canteen, and cut down that sapling, lopping off the top and stripping the branches until it was smooth enough for rolling.

After a snack I dug further under the edge of the slab with the stone trowel. "You're not spoiling my plans, rock," I huffed. "I *will* have a shelter in Gilead: one cliff wall, one slab wall, one creek stone wall, and a slanted roof so rain won't puddle. I doubt rain will reach the roof. We're pretty far under the ledge. That's how it is in my head," I said to the rock. "You're part of my plan."

For another hour I worked it down the hill inch by inch, pushing with my legs until my thighs and back ached. It had to be below freezing—the snow still lying in shady patches—but sweat ran from my forehead and down my back. After several hours I'd edged the slab to where the slope of the hill fell away five feet above the gorge floor. A third of the slab hung over. One more solid heave and it would go. It hadn't moved exactly the way I wanted, so I repositioned the pile of stones beneath it. *If I'm gonna get this baby upright to make my wall, I can't let it land flat. Can't.* Studying some more, I calculated how it might fall on the stones, how I'd work a log under it, roll it into position.

Yeah, I'll definitely need the guys to set it safely and firmly in place. That part has to be done just right. I grinned. Wouldn't want to wake up in my hut with you on my chest, big fella.

I thought about Newgrange, Ireland's prehistoric tomb, and wondered how they did it—its ring of megaliths hauled from miles away, the passageway lined with standing stones. Dr. Eloise was probably right: the ancient people were superhumans.

Back up the slope, I positioned myself one last time against a tree and braced for one final push. *Heave-HO! Breathe. Again! Little farther …* It tottered; the bank crumbled under it on one side, and the slab started sliding away from my pile of stones. *Uh-oh.*

I jumped down, got underneath it, and raised my shoulders, hoping to tip it back toward the stones. *Push, push! To the stones!* I thrust myself back. But the slab's incredible weight suddenly bore down on me. *Coming down!* Was it in place over the stones? My knees wobbled; I groaned. *Not giving up! This close. One more heave, one more …* I felt my shinbones bowing under the pressure. Fear shot through me. *Breaking! Get out! Go!* Pressed down into a crouch I threw myself forward. *Move!* The slab scraped my backside and hit the back of my thigh. I tried to lunge forward. Down I went, landing on my knee and forearm. *Go, go, man!* I heard the grind of rock against rock, slab crushing stones, and my own primal cry as I desperately pulled myself forward, the slap of my belly hitting the ground.

In the blink of an eye everything had changed. The weight of the slab had nearly flattened my pile of stones, trapping my left foot in the rubble. I couldn't move, but I wasn't worried. I wiggled my toes. There was pressure on my foot from all sides, but it didn't really hurt. Awkwardly—because I was pinned facedown—I turned to evaluate my situation. The slab was frighteningly large from this angle, bigger and thicker than it had seemed before, now sandwiching me to the ground. I gave my foot a yank. No luck. *I'll have to wriggle my foot out of my shoe to free it,* I thought calmly, though I knew how tight the laces were. My foot was much bigger than my ankle. How could I work it through that small opening? I yanked harder. The sound of stone grinding on stone stopped me. The pressure on my ankle tightened. *Hold it. Stop and think.* Propping on my elbows, I looked back again. The slab was at such an angle that I couldn't see under it. It was poised to slide if provoked, to crush my thigh, then hip, all of me if it slid far enough. I wondered if the stones surrounding my foot were cracking under the weight. If I yanked too hard, would they crumble? *Careful. Careful.*

I lay my face on the cold dirt and rested. *Don't panic. You can get out of this. You will. They'll find you.*

I lay there for a long while not thinking, just listening to myself breathe. What a wonderful sound, breathing. I ignored the trickle of water. I couldn't think about water. Then I realized what time of day it was. The sun had gone behind the rim, the sky was rosy. Darkness would come quickly.

A terrible dread settled on me. I'd never planned for this. I couldn't reach anything: food, water, my sleeping bag, wood. Dad always taught in survival classes, "Shelter is first priority, especially on a cold night." But I wasn't thinking about shelter. I was thinking about fire.

No cedar branches to make a bed. Only cold, hard dirt. I remembered how Marcus and I had banked sand around Reece that night she went down on the Hermits' Cave trail, how I'd brought water for her to drink and talked to her to keep her spirits up until help came. I had none of that here. But what worried me was a winter night without fire.

"If it rains or snows and you can't find dry wood, you might have to endure a night without fire," Dad told survival campers, "but crawling up under a spruce tree makes great shelter."

The closest tree was leafless and seventy feet away.

"On frigid nights make a debris shelter of boughs and leaves and then burrow in."

I had nothing to burrow under. Even stretching my arm to its full extension, I still lacked a foot in reaching the cord of my sleeping bag.

"Keep your core warm, whatever you do," Dad would warn his students. "Frostbitten fingers are one thing. Hypothermia's another."

The cold ground was already leeching the warmth from my chest. I couldn't think about my foot or water or food until I had that sleeping bag. With a sharp stab of reality, I understood that this situation was not in survival manuals. The twelve inches between the sleeping bag cord and me was the distance between life and death.

A tool. I need a tool. A stick … my knife! I twisted around to see where I'd left it. It lay not far from my free foot.

With the toe of my shoe, I edged it up in an arc toward me, careful not to jar the other foot. *Easy, easy, drag it, not too big an arc. Keep it within reach. Careful, careful.*

Got it! Twenty minutes until complete darkness. Once night fell, I wouldn't be able to see the cord. Get the bag, then worry about everything else. You can do it, I encouraged myself. I reached the tip of the knife toward the bag. *Don't cut the cord, pull it toward you … easy, easy. Drat!* It rolled from under the blade and sprang back. I slapped the ground and cursed. Then I dropped my head on my arm and rested a minute. *You cannot panic!* Concerned that I'd get too anxious and cut the cord, I turned the handle out and grasped the blade, concentrating every muscle on reaching the cord while I could still see it. Stretching until I trembled from the strain, holding my breath for control, I touched the cord with the tip of the knife handle. Steadily the knife handle pressed and pulled on the cord until it was within my reach. I grabbed the cord with a bloody hand, not realizing until then that I'd sliced my finger. I yanked the bag over to me and pressed my face into it like a kid to his favorite teddy bear. I breathed it in. Quickly, forcing myself to stay calm, I unrolled it. By the time I'd worked the sleeping bag under and around me, it was dark.

I worried a little that my smells—especially the blood— would attract coyotes. I had matches and a piece of paper in my pocket—Reece's poem—but nothing else to burn except for my clothes and a few stray leaves. I could stay awake to listen for leaves to blow past and collect them. *Wouldn't be worth it. Save your energy. You might need it later.*

Later … The word echoed in my mind. I worked my ankle and my toes—overjoyed that I felt them. I tested my foot's range of motion; it was encased without an inch to spare in any direction. But no crushing pressure. *Later. How much later?*

Until someone comes.

·　·　·　·　·

I lay awake fighting cold and panic. If only I'd broken my leg free of the rock! I could've made a fire, got water, food, made a splint, and limped home. I looked longingly through the darkness to where my pack was, tossed in a recess in the cliff wall not far from the ancient scrawls which read "the hand of God is a shield—a prayer." I'd tossed everything—medical kit, plastic garbage bags for a dry bed, canteen—in a pile so it would be safe.

As I weighed my options, horror crept into my belly … into my bones. I could not have been in a worse situation.

Okay, look at the advantages. Find something good here. A survival camp should be protected from the wind; that's one thing. I'm tucked under a cliff; that's another. The gorge has a southeast/ northwest orientation, southeast being the open end. I'll get morning

sun. Good. And I'm strong. I can take extremes in temperature—I
wade barefoot in winter. People will look for me. Mom and Dad.
Reece and Rob and Marcus. They won't give up.

Facts came rushing past. I'd just told Dad that I had to get
away. I didn't say where or for how long. Mom knew I wanted
to go back to Ireland. But my toothbrush was still at the house.
My suitcase. My passport. I pictured my bedroom as I'd left
it. What clues would they find? Open books. The note on my
desk with Stallards' address. A list of food. They'd think I was
hitchhiking to Chicago! Would my mom call the police on the
Stallards? *By morning, there'll be a manhunt for me around town.*
Then they'll sweep wider. The Stallards will be in the papers. Their
picture … and mine. My picture! What if Cravens or one of his
cronies sees it and tracks down the armor? What if days go by while
everyone blames the Stallards?

What if weeks go by?

They might search Telanoo, but not here. They'll follow the road
to Devil's Cranium and check the ruin. They'll scour Council Cliffs.
But I'm not there. I'm here! No one knows I'm here. No one but …

"El-Telan-Yah?" I called into the cold, eerie darkness. "You
know I'm here. Send someone!"

CHAPTER 8

Water source. At first light after an awful night, I twisted my neck to look up to the overhanging cliff. A small section glistened with groundwater. I listened for drips. It had been a dry winter so far. I worried about my foot and told my brain to work my toes to keep the circulation going. I couldn't feel them.

Rearranging the sleeping bag around me, I thought about Camp Mudj. I'd have given anything to be there: the lodge floor, a back cabin, a tree house. I wouldn't need my warm bed or one of the dinners Mom used to make. I wouldn't need the sound of the twins running through the house or the smell of Dad's coffee wafting up the steps in the morning. Yeah, a bunk with a one of those raggedy brown blankets would be great. A peanut butter sandwich would be a feast. I'd never complain again. I wouldn't, not once I was back home.

I lay there listening to my own breathing for a long time.

Listen, God, you see the mess I'm in. Can't you just flip this stone off me? Send an angel like you did at Jesus' tomb, and give it a big heave-ho. Remembering Reece's prayer when she went down in Hermits' Cave, I thanked God ahead of time for whatever he wanted to do for me. He knew where I was. In one way that thought helped. In another way it was terrifying beyond words. I didn't want to replay the minute the slab had fallen, how things might have been different if I'd moved a split second faster. *It happened the way it happened. Can't change the past. Only the future.* A knot of dread and gnawing hunger filled my gut. *Only the future.*

If I'd broken a leg, I'd have been able to crawl and could have found small animal trails, or built a snare. I'd never dressed and cooked a rabbit or anything, but ...

Why are you thinking about how to fix food? about how to trap an animal when you can't even move your foot? Idiot. You're the trapped one.

I know.

As the day brightened, I thought about Reece, how she'd been in traction for weeks over the summer, how she must have felt trapped.

Cold. I think my toes are still moving. Thirsty. Water is more important than food. I'll need water soon. They'll come. Someone will come.

When—February? April?

I could live a week or more without water in decent conditions—but on my belly on hard cold ground, immobile? I thought about my knife, a critical tool for surviving, for cutting kindling and rope, for hacking boughs for shelter ...

I thought about my foot.

It's the only thing stopping you from getting out of here.

I know.

So?

So I'm not ready to part with it yet, God.

What was he telling me? I thought of other ways: I could start yanking and keep yanking until I broke every bone in my foot and pulled the bloody stump through the hole. Then I'd drag myself to the tree, make a fire, and hope that some doctor somewhere would know how to rebuild a foot from a pile of splintered bones.

The foot may already be dead. You don't know.

No, God, I don't know! I answered angrily.

I suddenly rose up on my elbows, startled. The tone. The

tone in his voice. I replayed it in my mind. He didn't sound the same. Of the times I'd heard him speak before, he'd always sounded strong—powerful but quiet. And of all the things he'd said, I'd always had a feeling, a knowing that he cared—that he loved me. He never sounded teasing, taunting, like Justin Brill on his worst day. Chills rolled over me.

You're not him.

Silence. He'd slipped away.

· · · · ·

Shadows moved as the sun tracked across the sky, its warmth settling on my back. *Fire is everything.* I fingered the knife, thought about my options, and blocked every voice speaking to my spirit. Random, disconnected thoughts floated through my brain. *I never found the helmet or the sword. I ached with regret. If they don't find me in time, if … if I'm gone, will the others give up the quest?*

I envisioned them finding my body gnawed by coyotes and bears, pecked by birds. I saw myself like Salem was when we'd found him at the ruin: stinking, eyes shrunken, covered with maggots. I saw the rescue squad bringing me out in a body bag. I saw Mom sobbing, clinging to Dad. I pictured Dad looking out over the hills, his jaw clenched as he watched the coroner drive away.

Blinking back tears, I imagined my funeral. Reece would be there. She'd rush up to my closed coffin and drape herself over me sobbing—no … no, she wouldn't. She'd stand there like a soldier, comforting everyone as they passed by, saying, "We know where he is," and lift her teary, smiling eyes heavenward. She'd probably start dating Justin Brill and bring him under her influence, changing his life like she'd changed mine. Reece would go on without me. She'd be fine.

I sniffled, remembered where I was—still alive for now. *Cut the drama, Creek. Save your brain cells for survival.*

I remembered the Quella. Where was it? I'd stuck it in the folds of my sleeping bag at the last minute. It must have gotten tossed aside when I flung open the bag. I looked around and there it was, almost under me. I grabbed it, turned it on eagerly, and scrolled down randomly, wondering who was behind my predicament: God or Satan.

I didn't know. My foot was encased but not crushed. Had to be more than coincidence that it had slipped into a foot-shaped space in the rubble. I took great comfort in that. Where do I start? *Rock.* I looked it up. The first reference was about the Rock of Israel who blesses people with the heavens above and from the deep that lies below.

I read from the *Warrior*: "The LORD is my rock, my fortress and my deliverer; my God is my rock, in whom I take refuge. He is my shield."

In one story people were thirsty, and Moses struck a rock and water came gushing out. Welling up with hope, I felt around for a stone. If I hit the cliff, would I get water? I found only one stone, and it was too big to hurl. It didn't seem like there were any messages in the Quella for me.

The hours wore on. The sun moved. I got up on one knee to stretch but could only get into a low lunge position because of the slab hovering over my thigh. I fought my mind against replaying it over and over, how I'd waited a third of a second too long. I lay there eyeing my backpack where there was food but no way to get to it. I scratched in the dirt with my knife, wondering if I should leave a message … in case.

Don't dull the knife. You might need it.… .

I shuddered. How would I do it? I could barely reach to my calf, much less apply a tourniquet. *That's a lot of muscle to cut through. And the nerves!* I'd probably pass out from the pain and bleed to death. *I could take it off at the knee. What good is any part of a leg without a foot anyway? I'll need a tourniquet. My belt.* I worked it out of the belt loops and poked holes, starting at about eight inches from the buckle and every inch after that. When I was ready, I'd tighten it around my leg, then tighter and tighter until all feeling was gone.

Thirst had settled in. *Get used to it,* I thought dully.

Through the day I'd call out every few minutes, "Hey! Help! I'm down here!!" No one could hear me. I knew that. I felt lonelier because of the silence that followed my yells. So I quit.

The day wore on. I tried pulling my leg every few minutes, kept telling my brain to move my foot. *Send blood to it. Keep it going.*

Mid-afternoon, I began to feel different. It's hard to describe. A kind of inner warmth and comfort settled over me, sort of like after eating a big meal. My belly screamed for food, but the comfort went through my whole body in spite of the hunger. I lay there for hours just thinking about the comfort. Nothing changed, but I wasn't as afraid.

As the sunlight turned amber, I screamed for help for a while, and then went back to the Quella. I read about Elijah all through the Bible. The first Elijah from twenty-eight hundred years ago lived a pretty crazy life before he was sucked up into a tornado. John the Baptist was called the second Elijah, a voice crying in the wilderness. The commentary said that at the end of time, two witnesses appear on the scene. One is perhaps the third and final man born with the power and spirit of Elijah. The last reference said, "Elijah was a man just like us. He prayed earnestly that it would not rain, and it did not rain on the land for three and a half years. Again he prayed, and the heavens gave rain, and the earth produced its crops."

The words faded. My batteries had died.

I bundled up and slept until I was awakened by a sound, deep and penetrating. Wildly I looked around. I was in no position to defend myself from coyotes or bears.

Bears hibernate.

I grinned. *Oh yeah. Well, coyotes. It may be coyotes.*

Or small animals that could creep under the slab and gnaw on you while you helplessly scream in agony.

You! Shut up!

The sky went red. I spotted the source of the deep sound. A great horned was perched in a tree way behind me, a rectangular box with wide-set tufts sticking up. *You'll be laying your eggs in a couple months, huh? Looking for a nest in the cliff?* We watched each other. She was evaluating me lying in the red twilight, ripe and ready as a caught rabbit. *Hey, you're the exact shape and proportion of Leap Castle.* I held up my knife, turning the blade slowly in the light as a threat. *Come after me, friend, and you'll be my breakfast.*

The light went, the cold returned, I fell into shadow. The trees turned black and featureless against fading light, then reappeared again once night came, gray and still with yawning hollows behind them, horrible in their blackness. I was anxious that an animal face might appear. I wanted nothing to appear, but I hated the hollow empty loneliness too. *Enough nights alone like this, and a person could go stark raving crazy.* I could almost see the shape of Tabonga among the trees, those fake arms and the long, droopy eyes. "Tabonga will die," I joked dryly. I thought about Reece climbing Great Oak with me only a couple days ago. I lay down my head tiredly and touched my left thumb and little finger together. *It's a sign of hypothermia if you can't do it, so I'm still okay.* I made my fingers touch and got a huge kick out of it. *Touch, touch, touch.* I tried wiggling my toes and couldn't tell if they were moving. All night I prayed like Elijah for rain.

. . . . .

It was the third day. I had maybe one more day until hunger pangs would start to fade. Until then my guts would be screaming. I couldn't sleep because of the other voice, the one louder than hunger, worse than dead silence, the one whose jeer, *You'll never find it,* still echoed through my head. It was a shock how four little words could mess with me.

I was the only person out here, but I definitely wasn't alone.

The thirst was terrible, and I wondered about the world record for surviving without water. Was it two weeks? a month? Could I beat it?

I hadn't used the belt tourniquet—hadn't made that decision yet—but it was lying beside me, ready.

Last night Leap Castle had come again and perched on her tree, her horn-shaped ears listening to the silence, her eyeless face staring down at me. Like she was saying, "I'm Leap Castle. I have the sword and you'll never find it."

Was I going insane?

What are you doing here, Elijah?

I raised my head. *Hey, you sent an angel to bake bread and bring water for the first Elijah when he was out in the wilderness. I read about it in the book of Kings before my batteries died.*

Silence.

Okay, well, to answer your question—nothing. What am I supposed to be doing?

I got a crick in my neck looking up for an answer. After a while I put my head down and tried to sleep, hoping that when I woke, there'd be food by my head like in the book of Kings. But I couldn't sleep. I kept peeking around. *You could send the raven like you did that other time in the Bible. Bread and meat would be good; I'm not particular.* I even wondered if the squirrel I'd seen scampering across the stream would bring the food. I wanted to see how God would do it.

After a while I got to thinking, *Maybe it's like Christmas Eve; if you don't go to sleep, Santa won't come. The presents won't arrive.* I was thinking crazy. I turned my head to the cliff wall and forced myself to sleep, in spite of the maddening sound of water trickling from the rim of the gorge. *Drip, drip, drip.*

Hours later I woke and stretched weakly. There was no food from God. *Hey, you fed the first Elijah. And by the way, Jesus didn't have it this bad when he was in the wilderness. He could move around. He could've gone back to town if he'd wanted.*

I thought long and hard about Jesus out in the wilderness with nothing. No food, no gear, no friends. No nothing. *Can't imagine why you'd do that. Forty days? That's crazy. The sheer willpower it took not to run home. And why? That's my question. Why? There's nothing out here.*

After a long while, I realized that the whole lot of nothing was God's very point. I wouldn't be out here if I wasn't stuck—no news flash there. *If it's you that trapped me here, just tell me what I'm supposed to do, and I'll do it. Then cut me loose.*

High branches waved, but nothing else moved in my narrow little world. I got it at last. *Uh-huh. Got it. Nothing but you and me.*

And me, came the shadow voice, the voiceless voice.

· · · · ·

I drifted in and out, tongue parched, mind clear, belly burning. I tracked the movement of the sun across the sky, dreading another night alone. The raven sailed past. *I'm saved!! He'll bring meat and bread, like he did to the first Elijah. Thank you! Thank you!* But the raven glided on as if he hadn't seen me.

"Come back!" I called. "Raven! Come back!" I screamed and yelled and did raven caws until my parched throat quit on me. I slapped the ground furiously. *Come back!*

Talk to me! I wanted to read the Quella bad and wondered if I could squeeze out a little more juice by switching the two batteries around. *Maybe the contacts are dirty. Maybe he wants me to figure out where the sword is, and I'm stuck here until I figure it out.* I switched the batteries around. *Come on, more juice. More juice.* Search options appeared on the little screen. *Yes! Yes!* I rose up on my elbows. *Okay, I'm starting with the four directions. Could you at least tell me which direction, so I can save battery time?*

No answer.

I looked up *north* and gave up after a few tries. There was nothing to the north of me anyway but farmland. Dowland wouldn't hide anything on another guy's farm—too risky. *Okay, I'm looking up* south, *and you know I may be running out of juice.*

The first fifteen references were no help. The sixteenth was Deuteronomy 33:23: "Naphtali is abounding with the favor of the LORD and is full of his blessing; he will inherit southward to the lake." The footnote said that *Naphtali* was derived from the word *struggle* or *fight.* The one who fights, struggles—that would be me—will inherit something. I remembered what he'd told me before: that he'd give me a secret treasure. Did this confirm it? Camp Mudj's lake was due south of Gilead. *The sword's in Silver Lake?! Southward to the lake and close to where Old Pilgrim Church once stood, where Stan Dowland had first buried the armor! It's been lying there while paddleboats floated over it all summer— right under my nose the whole time? Is the helmet there too?*

The Quella died again. I switched the batteries once more, but it seemed shut down for good.

Southward to the lake! I know where the rest of it is!

I cocooned in my sleeping bag and celebrated my moment of glory. I'd found it. So Dowland had given up on his little piece-by-piece riddle and decided to dump the pieces at random? Had he intended to put a clue to finding the helmet with the shoes of peace before Francine stole them from his house? Was there a clue to another mystery at the bottom of the lake? I didn't care. Magdeline could have all the mysteries and scandals she wanted. I had the armor of God!

In the middle of figuring out what had been going on in Dowland's demented mind, it occurred to me with a dull gnawing in my stomach that if I didn't make it out of Gilead, the others would never find the armor.

I don't want the secret to die with me, God. Don't let me die—for the sake of the armor. You can't let me die.

He doesn't need you.

I'm not talking to you! I said with contempt to the shadow voice. *I can leave a message scratched in the dirt or I can lie here and die.* I considered my options. *Hey, God, if you don't let me live, the secret will die with me. So forget about that message in the dirt I just mentioned. I changed my mind!* I was bargaining, knowing deep inside that the evil one was right. *God doesn't need me. He never did. I'm as helpless and useless as a roach under the heel of a shoe.* I looked heavenward and called hoarsely, "Is this your plan for me? Is it? Tell me!"

Exhausted, I fell asleep for an hour or so and woke with no feeling at all in my foot. I pushed and kept pushing until I felt pressure and burning. The pressure had been there the whole time, but I hadn't thought about it. *I can feel my heel. It's still alive.* Encouraged—even though a feeling foot was a bad thing if you're going to have to amputate it—I pressed my heel into the rock and enjoyed the pain. *My heel.* Suddenly I was back at the Cliffs of Morte that moment I'd run to grab Reece at the edge. I relived how my foot had tipped back over a six-hundred-foot drop into the North Atlantic, how my heel had felt rock where there was none. *He didn't want me to die then. Maybe he doesn't now. You want me to live? You do, don't you?* I laughed out loud, a raw, hoarse bark.

You sound like Dowland.

I'm not him! I answered the whisper. *I never will be him! I won't make his mistakes,* I insisted, though I'd never exactly figured what Dowland's mistake was.

If Francine was right, he'd never really been interested in the real armor of God—truth and peace and faith and stuff like that. Yeah, he'd preached sermons on it, but it had never sunk in. Dowland had gone loony trying to find a treasure he had within reach all along.

Insanity runs in the family, boy. Self-destruction is in your genes.

I'm not listening to you.

A treasure almost within reach—but not quite. Like your food and water. It's right there. You can see it.

I looked at my backpack. So near. Rage and regret boiled up in me.

Can't reach it, though, can you?

God, make him stop!!

For hours I mulled over what could have gone wrong with Dowland and with the whole town in general, why all the churches died out except for a sad little storefront congregation with the drab Christmas decorations and the long name. Magdeline, Ohio, had possessed the armor of God for decades and had never used it. It was an average go-nowhere-do-nothing kind of town, and that's what it would always be. Dowland never learned what Reece knew from the very first: that the armor itself wasn't the point. The power of our treasure was in the message, not the metal. A free treasure, anybody could claim it and be saved!

I don't want this secret to die with me. I rubbed my hands together, thawing my fingers. With the knife I scratched in the dirt: SOTERION LAKE deut33. The clan would understand. *Soterion,* Greek for *salvation.* They'd find the verse and figure out that the helmet of salvation or the sword of the Lord was in the lake. They'd understand. Relief and joy flooded through me. They'd find it. They'd complete the quest.

Lying there, stinking and freezing, my body screamed for water. I cursed at the raven for leaving me. Dreading what God had lined up for me later, I suddenly had a revelation as blinding as lightning: *it's more important that Marcus, Rob, Reece, and Mei find the armor than whether or not I live. Its purpose has to be fulfilled—arming a generation for the Day of Evil. That's the most important thing of all.*

I was shocked that the armor meant more to me than my life. *More than my very own life!*

CHAPTER 9

Do you want me to lay here and die, God? Or do you want me to saw off my foot and crawl home and never run again? Which one is it? Is someone coming? Are they searching Telanoo right now? Or are they questioning the Stallards? Is news spreading across the Midwest that a boy from Magdeline is missing and thought to be headed for Chicago? If I wait too late to amputate, I won't have the strength to go through with it. But what if I do it and five minutes later they find me? I don't know what to do!

Exactly.

I could almost see the evil one grinning at my predicament. He sounded a lot like Justin Brill.

I seethed. *Don't you get it? I'm not listening to you!*

But I *was* listening. And as I played the conversations over and over and over, the difference in God's words and his got more and more distinct. The difference was in the content and in the tone. I felt pure hate coming from the hollow messages. But I'd always sensed God's love for me in his words—even the time in October when God said he'd let me see my enemy and his voice was stern and a little scary.

I knew it in the same way that I knew how Reece felt about me, even when she was rolling her eyes over something about the Bible that I was too dense to get.

I recognized the disgust in the evil one's tone because of how Justin Brill was always making fun of me. *Wow. I would never have seen the difference so clearly if I'd never heard Brill's slams and name-calling: "Hey, Nature Boy, eat any roadkill lately? Hey, Creek, you and Elliston … mumble mumble … heh, heh, heh."* How he leered and jeered at Reece and me. I had something he didn't. He was jealous. And so was the evil one. He was jealous because I had God.

God had been using something bad to teach me an important rule: good could come from bad.

"See how it works out, Elijah?" Reece's cheery voice spoke from our golden time at the top of Great Oak. *"If you hadn't ignored me, I wouldn't have gotten mad, and I wouldn't be here. He always works it out."*

I rested my forehead on my hand and smiled in amazement. *El-Telan-Yah, do you mean that you let Justin Brill give me grief so I'd recognize the voice of the evil one when it spoke? Was that the plan all along? Well, that's pretty weird—but cool. Funny, I never thought I'd be grateful to Brill for anything. That's wild, how you can make bad stuff work out for good. Like Mei being sent back to Japan so she could be with us in Ireland. But now that I know, now that I get it, can you make the evil one go away? And if I die out here, please don't let Brill end up with Reece. That would be sick and wrong.*

· · · · ·

It was mid-afternoon and my spirits rose again. I scratched a map of the world in the dirt around "SOTERION LAKE deut33" without even knowing why. Seven continents, seven seas. I quit drawing when the shivering and fumbling of my hand got worse—a sign of hypothermia.

I fluffed the sleeping bag and tried to rise up and stretch more. I edged into the sunlight as much as possible while it lasted. For someone like me who couldn't ride in a car for a few hours without going berserk, this was my worst nightmare. Stuck like a butterfly in a bug collection. I rubbed my arms and my legs as far down as I could to keep circulation going.

The burning throb in my foot was beyond measuring. Every move was more awkward and, as I got colder, every effort more exhausting. I fought sleep for fear I wouldn't wake up. When I couldn't fight it anymore, I gave in and thought of Reece, how she turned the bad to good, her crutches into wings... .

She stood on the rim of Gilead, which was also the edge of the Cliffs of Morte. The wind whipped her hair wildly around her face. The others were there: Rob and Marcus and Mei and Sahara too. We stood safely back from the edge. Reece was an eagle and an angel. She had a message for us. As we waited to hear it, she lifted her wings. The wind caught them, and off she went over the edge. Mei screamed. My heart stopped. We ran to the edge, threw ourselves on our bellies, and looked down in horror.

Below us she glided like one of the gulls—swooping, banking off away from the cliff, circling back. When I saw that she was going to be okay, I dropped my head to the ground and cried with relief.

I woke sniffling. It was the dead of night. Drained from my feelings about the dream, it was a minute before I realized that there was tapping all around me. *Taptaptaptaptaptap.* I looked around at the dull charcoal sky. There was Leap Castle, perched in a tree much closer than before. *She's moving in.* The tapping was rain ... no ... it was sleet.

An ice storm? God, what are you thinking? Sure it's water, but frozen water. I can't get to it!

At the first gray light of dawn, I raised my head and looked around. Every branch, every dead blade of weed and prairie grass was glazed over. Frozen stiff.

He's teasing you.

I ignored the voice, switched the batteries in the Quella again, and checked the screen in the pearly light of dawn. But it was no good.

Reece's poem! I hadn't brought it out because I would have wanted to burn it for the heat. I knew I'd see the paper, handle it, and imagine the warmth. I wouldn't be able to resist. If I needed to use the knife on myself soon, I would want to sterilize the blade with fire. *Read now; burn later. I have to hear a human voice.* I dug the paper from my pocket and held it to the southeastern sky. I imagined that she was reading it to me.

"A poem from English class," she said. *"I thought of you when I read it. So here it is. 'The Light of Stars' from* Voices of the Night *by Henry Wadsworth Longfellow."* She cleared her throat and read:

The night is come, but not too soon;
And sinking silently,
All silently, the little moon
Drops down behind the sky.

There is no light in earth or heaven
But the cold light of stars;
And the first watch of night is given
To the red planet Mars.

Is it the tender star of love?
The star of love and dreams?
O no! from that blue tent above,
A hero's armor gleams.

And earnest thoughts within me rise,
When I behold afar,
Suspended in the evening skies,
The shield of that red star.

O star of strength! I see thee stand
And smile upon my pain;

Thou beckonest with thy mailed hand,
And I am strong again.

Within my breast there is no light
But the cold light of stars;
I give the first watch of the night
To the red planet Mars.

The star of the unconquered will,
He rises in my breast,
Serene, and resolute, and still,
And calm, and self-possessed.

I stopped a minute to rest my arms. Leaning the side of my face to the cold ground, I looked up at the pale sky for a morning star. A few night stars still shone. I watched them twinkle, wondering if any of them was the planet Mars. I let Reece's voice read the rest of the poem:

And thou, too, whosoe'er thou art,
That readest this brief psalm,
As one by one thy hopes depart,
Be resolute and calm.

O fear not in a world like this,
And thou shalt know erelong,
Know how sublime a thing it is
To suffer and be strong.

Dazed with emotions I couldn't even name, I pulled my cocoon around me and stared at my frozen world. Slowly the sky brightened. Light grew on Gilead's ice-covered trees, their limbs bowing under the weight. Then the sun came out and cast gold beams down the gorge. Little by little the ice came alive—sparkling, blinding, and beautiful. Every twig and leaf and stone was a glittering rainbow. I'm in Heaven. I couldn't speak or even think a word. No words like *golden* or *crystal* could describe it because it wasn't just beautiful. There was life in it, in every frozen drop of water, every limb, groaning and crackling under weight of ice. The sun rose brighter. Every branch and blade of grass and bush became a trillion diamonds of blue, turquoise, gold, orange—a zillion rainbows.

I lay there in awe, drinking in the light show.

And the trees started to drip. I got up on my elbows to watch and listen. He was answering my prayer—not just from a cloud a few thousand feet up—from the sun's fire ninety-three million miles away. He was sweating the trees, turning sleet into rain from across the solar system! The verse came to me from the first Elijah's story: The god who answers by fire—he is God.

I got it! I got the message of the ice storm, El-Telan-Yah. I'm frozen too; the slab is weighing me down, but there's still life in me. I got the message, but ... where's my water? I can't reach it.

Wait, came the answer.

He's teasing you ... .

Trees cried and crackled as the morning went on, dripping, dripping. Diamonds falling like rain—diamonds of every color. The sun went behind a cloud, a big puffy white one with a blue-black underside. The dripping and crackling slowed for the next several minutes. Then the melting stopped. The zillion rainbows went away. *He's in control. He makes it start and stop. He can do anything he wants. That's what he's saying.*

The cloud drifted away and my world lit up again. The trees started crackling once more. As the ice melted and fell to the ground, their limbs began to rise. It reminded me of church, when the congregation bows together for prayer and then raises their heads together. I watched for hours as trees ever so slowly lifted their heads and arms to the sky. I missed church—the row of kids, the chocolate milk and donuts at Bible study, the songs, the stained glass windows, the minister's jokes and stories and lessons.

I understood now why sun worshipers built tombs like Newgrange. Every inch of the natural world depended on the sun and responded to its fire. I looked at the picture of the world I'd drawn in the dirt and thought about Mei and Sahara and all the millions of people in the world who worship nature. *If you don't know him, sure, why not worship the sun?*

Where's my water, God?

Rubbing my legs to keep them alive, I read the poem over until I had it almost by heart. I couldn't believe how clear I was thinking, how sharp my memory was. I tucked the page into my shirt, slept, and felt warmth again. It was mid-afternoon. The feeling of comfort returned.

Splat.

A drop of water hit the ground two feet from my head.

Splat. Splat.

I reached out my hand. *Blup. Blup.* Water dripped into my palm! I looked up. The sun had reached an icicle suspended from a crack in the ledge. *Water!* Painstakingly I gathered drips of water in my hand. *Patience, patience …* I lapped out of my filthy palm and reached greedily for more. The icicle was two feet long and a couple inches thick at the top. Three glasses of water were up there waiting to drip into my hand!

That won't keep you alive.

Before I could prepare my mind for another night of darkness, the sun moved behind the rim of the gorge. It was December 22, the shortest day of the year. By 6:00 it would be nightfall. The same sun, which had lit up the passage tomb of Newgrange on the other side of the planet, had given me another day of life and clean drinking water. *Thank you, God.*

The light left. The dripping stopped. The sky turned orange, the shadows purple.

Sun doesn't always mean life. In deserts the sun means death. Today in Gilead, though, I had water from fire. Ice needs fire. Everything needs everything else to work. Fire is life. It purifies, cooks, destroys, warms, and sterilizes. Earth, wind, fire, and water—that's all there is. *That's all I am: earth and water.*

And soul.

Yeah. I know I'm more than this aching, stinking body. I'm eternal. Even if I die.

Now I'm not ragging on Dom's Eight Lessons or anything, but the lessons I was learning from God while trapped under that slab had to number in the hundreds. Or thousands. My mind was razor sharp; my body was screaming for release. My foot was probably dead.

I got a little more water from the rock above me. Reece read the poem to me again and again inside my head. I reviewed my life. I tried to remember as much of the Bible as I could, wishing I knew more. I thirsted to hear his voice. A thousand times I said to God, *Get me out of this and I'm yours.*

I wondered what Mom and Dad were doing about me. *They've questioned Reece by now. She'll think I hid out in Council Cliffs like the two Delaware Indian boys. When she went down at Hermits' Cave, we'd talked about how I could live out there. They're probably scouring Council Cliffs. How long will that take?*

· · · · ·

I woke up terrified, thinking I'd gone blind. I didn't remember going to sleep. It was dark. Leap Castle was back, closer than ever, her black, square body and pointy horn-ears haunting me. She was one measly owl, but her presence and her shape terrified me beyond words. She didn't move. It wasn't natural. *It's an owl, for crying out loud. Get a grip.* But I couldn't. Inside I screamed,

I can't take any more! I'm going crazy! At first light, if I'm alive, I will get that knife and do what must be done! If you don't want me to, you better stop me!

. . . . . .

"Elijaaaah!"

My mind surfaced in a flash. Had someone called my name? I listened through a blowing snow squall. It was day five.

"Elijaaaaah!"

Rob! It's Rob!! I'm rescued! I'm saved!

My heart leaped. I raised my head, arched my back, opened my mouth, and cried out. But only a short, low-pitched bark came out. I tried again. And again. I'd shot my dried-out vocal cords screaming a couple nights before. My voice was gone. Rob's calls got louder. I heard him talking to someone and guessed that Marcus was with him. Frantically I looked around for something to make noise with. I had nothing but the knife and a rock. Aching and cold, I got up stiffly on my one free knee and reached for the rock. When their voices got closer, I'd throw it into the stream and get their attention. It was one of my only three weapons—rock, belt, knife—but I had to be heard.

"Elijah!" Rob's call was close.

They're above me! The sun came out, and two long narrow shadows fell across Gilead. I barked, but they couldn't hear. *You can see me if you circle around to the other side! You can see my gear if you lean way over. Circle around, Marcus. Circle like we did at Hermits' Cave. I'm right below you!* I screamed inside. *You'll see me from the other side. Marcus! Rob! Drop down on your bellies like we did at the Cliffs of Morte. I'm right under you!!*

I lifted the rock and hurled it toward the creek. My pitch was weak and shaky. The rock fell short and landed in a soft bush. *Bmff!* For a moment I heard nothing. They were listening. Had they heard the rock? They mumbled to each other. The sun peeked out, their shadows appeared, and then they moved away. *No!!* Once more I tried to yell. Hardly a wheeze came out, not enough sound against the wind. *Don't leave!* I threw myself forward and slapped the ground over and over. *Slap, slap, slap! Listen to me!*

Marcus's voice called, "Hey, Creeeeek!" Then it faded out, "Where are you, Cree ... ?" In the distance other voices were calling my name. Dad had organized a manhunt, but they'd missed me. A few stray flakes landed on the back of my outstretched hand. I licked them off and dropped my head to the cold ground.

Fire. If only I'd had fire. Smoke. Flame. Smell.

The day passed. I stayed sane thinking of Reece's poem and what Bible verses I could remember. *No one else is coming. They've probably decided I was in Chicago. I'll die in the shirt that I was baptized in. That's why I wore it. That's why.*

All voices went silent for a long while, even my own.

Then ... *Hey, what about the third Elijah? In the Quella's footnotes, didn't it say that some believed that a third Elijah would come at the end?* As the light faded again, I switched the batteries once more, cleaning the contact points with a corner of my shirt. This time I got juice.

"'And I will give power to my two witnesses, and they will prophesy for 1,260 days, clothed in sackcloth.' These are the two olive trees and the two lampstands that stand before the Lord of the earth. If anyone tries to harm them, fire comes from their mouths and devours their enemies. This is how anyone who wants to harm them must die. These men have power to shut up the sky so that it will not rain during the time they are prophesying; and they have power to turn the waters into blood and to strike the earth with every kind of plague as often as they want. Now when they have finished their testimony, the beast that comes up from the Abyss will attack them, and overpower and kill them. Their bodies will lie in the street of the great city, which is figuratively called Sodom and Egypt, where also their Lord was crucified. For three and a half days men from every people, tribe, language and nation will gaze on their bodies and refuse them burial. The inhabitants of the earth will gloat over them and will celebrate by sending each other gifts, because these two prophets had tormented those who live on the earth. But after the three and a half days a breath of life from God entered them, and they stood on their feet, and terror struck those who saw them."

If I'm the third Elijah, I explained to God, *then I have to die in the streets of Jerusalem. I can't die here. And it has to be after a whole bunch of days of preaching on the streets like that preacher in Dublin. A thousand days.*

It gave me a weird kind of hope. I closed the Quella and stared across the stream, imagining what I'd say if I ever got to preach in Jerusalem. At mid-afternoon the comfort came the same as it had on the other days.

If you want me to cut off my foot and crawl out of here, I will. But you know what that means. I'll never run track. And I won't be much good to Dad at the camp. I don't get it. Do you want me to be like Reece so I'll have faith like hers? Is that your plan? Whatever you want me to do, I will do it! Just TELL ME!! Just don't leave me here wondering.

He's not listening.

"Yes, he is! He is!" I growled it over and over, slapping the ground until I was exhausted and my parched throat burned. I lay there picturing where I was, as if from above, as if I were a raven. I drew a map of Telanoo in the dirt: Owl Woods, the streams, Devil's Cranium. I raised up. *Hey ... if Devil's Cranium due east of me was the actual skull of Satan crammed face-first into the cliff side of Telanoo—which it isn't, that's crazy, but if it was—then he's looking through the earth right at me.*

A wild chill of horror shot through me.

Stop it, Creek! You're losing it. Keep your mind on what's real. This is not a cheap horror movie. Focus on what's real.

"Hey, Wingate," I said, "what's the weather like where you are? Hey, Mom, what's for dinner? Hey, Skidmore," I wheezed as I drifted off in the cold darkness for the last time, "you always thought I was a pyro? Wait till I come hobbling out of these woods! Fire will be my middle name."

CHAPTER 10

I woke to the sound of music. I thought it was a hiker. My brain asked, *Where's that coming from? A hunter with a radio? A hunter singing? Crazy. You're imagining it. But it's not a radio. Where is that coming from? It's …* It was coming from inside my chest. A quiet voice was singing that song from Ireland about the days of Elijah. *What in the world?* my brain asked and then answered itself. *It's my spirit.*

I lay there in my dirty cocoon, my body cold, my mind paper-thin but razor sharp while my spirit sang as happy as a kid at a picnic. I listened, amazed. *How awesome it that? That's my soul singing while I'm dying.* I cautioned my brain to hush. *Don't think too much. You'll stifle it. Shut up and listen.* The little voice got quiet and reverent.

Then another voice spoke. *Put it on.*

What?

Put it on.

He meant the armor. How?

Pray.

The singer got quiet and waited.

Okay, God … My mind started in: *belt of truth. The omen. Your word is truth, and it says that you are with me always. The truth for me was—I could see so clearly now—that even if I died here, I wouldn't die alone. He would never leave. I had my spirit to sing to me in the final moments if that should happen.* Still I was terrified. I went on.

Breastplate of righteousness. You guard my heart with your goodness. I don't have to be good enough. I never did. Nobody does. You're the Lamb over me.

I remembered that it was Christmas Eve day, when God's Lamb was born to die.

Next are the shoes of peace. Langundowagan. *O God, this is hard. How does a person have peace when he's slowly starving to death?*

Do not fear.

Well … okay. I'm trying. The next is the shield of faith. I do believe. I do have creidim.

I felt a little fake. Most of the things I was praying were things I'd heard Reece or Marcus or the Dublin preacher talk about—nothing I'd thought up myself. *But I still believe it,* I insisted. *I'm not just saying this stuff. Okay. Helmet of salvation.* Soterion. *It's southward to the lake and with the sword, I hope, and the arm piece. Lord, I wore that helmet once—all night at The Cedars—remember?*

I realized at that moment the only reason Dowland hadn't taken me out in Telanoo was that I'd kept the helmet on all night. I saw his intentions now, clear as day.

He hated that he'd never found the sword and that the armor hadn't worked like he wanted. He hated that I might figure out what he'd missed—like a spoiled kid who says, "I don't want it, but I don't want you to have it either." Maybe he'd thrown it into the lake because he knew that I was the third Elijah. Yes, he'd written my name three times in his journals and crossed out two. Whether Dowland had kept his hands off me because he thought the helmet was magical or cursed didn't matter. Truth was that the helmet of salvation saved my life—not in just a spiritual sense, but in a physical sense. God had protected my life through Dowland's superstitions. He'd saved me in every way, even before I knew him. *I'm saved whether I'm alive or dead. I'll go to Heaven.*

In a real way, I'd already been rescued. The peace that I'd lacked a moment ago flooded through me. *I'm okay. I'm okay no matter what. The whole armor works together. One piece helps the other. Hey, God, if I die, tell Reece where the helmet and sword are, okay? Tell her personally. She'd like that, and she deserves to know even more than me. Promise me that you'll let her see it.*

I started thinking about her again, how we'd kissed at the top of Great Oak ...

Sword, he reminded me firmly. *Put it on.*

Oh yeah. The sword of the Lord. Well, I'd hoped to see it. Just once.

I sighed at the silence, hoping that he'd throw me a hint. Okay, here goes. *I'll take the sword in hand even though I've never seen it. The sword is your Word; your Word is truth. Your words have power. By the way, I'd be reading it right now, but the batteries are dead. A little ironic, isn't it?*

I lay there thinking of Scriptures. *"Even though I walk through the valley of the shadow of death, I will fear no evil, for you are with me." "In the beginning God created the heavens and the earth." "God is light; in him there is no darkness at all."*

How I wished I were on my back! Like when I was a kid and would lie in the grass and watch the clouds floating past. *I'm helpless this way, defenseless.* I longed for a patch of sunlight to warm my sleeping bag. *Sun, where are you?* I looked up hoping the clouds would clear. Something caught my eye. I thought at first that it was a broken branch. Then I thought it was a piece of rope draped in the top of a tree near the cliff wall. *That's no rope ... oh no ...* Slithering along a branch with her midsection sagging between two limbs was Bloocifer.

You! I sneered.

I wished for my rock, the one I'd hurled into the bush to signal the guys. All I had left was the belt and knife. *If I throw and miss, I'll have nothing. I have to keep both for the amputation.* Frantically I dug at the ground for clods to throw. The dirt crumbled in my hands.

She saw me and stopped. We locked eyes—her cold, sideways, Liam-looking glare fixed on me as she moved down the tree. I could just tell that she hated me for caging her and stealing her babies. She wasn't afraid of me; she was sizing up my situation and thinking revenge. Did she know that I was trapped?

I was afraid, but it was a different kind of fear. It was around me but not in me.

"You're just a snake," I whispered, "a belly-crawling reptile. You're nothing to me. You're not poisonous. Sure, you could bite, and it would hurt like heck, but you couldn't kill me." *Blue racers are constrictors,* I reminded myself, *but they don't strangle. They kill prey by pressing down on them, swallowing them whole.*

Like the slab that's pressing you, killing you ever so slowly, she seemed to say.

I held up my knife. *You bite me; I'll cut you. We both lose. So go away.*

Unless … unless she waited a few days until I was too weak. Then she'd win. *Does she know? Does she smell my weakness?*

She slid to the ground, raised up like a cobra, and froze. Her tail rattled, a soft whirring sound.

Ten yards. She'd be on me in two or three seconds. "You're just a snake," I said grittily. "I caught you, and you'd still be in that cage if those jerk college kids hadn't been goofing off." Using my anger for strength, I went on, "I took your babies, sold them, and then I used the money to search for the sword of the Lord."

Didn't find it, did you?

You're hallucinating, Creek, I told myself.

Keep your wits, came a strong, steady voice.

I will.

You'll never find it, came Liam's voice from that bookstore in Dublin. *You're starving.*

"'Man does not live on bread alone,'" I answered out loud, "'but on every word that comes from the mouth of God.' That's the sword of the Lord. The Word. It doesn't matter what you do to me, Bloo. That sword will cut you and your kind to ribbons in the end."

Who was I talking to: a snake, a demon, Satan himself, or just my own raw imagination? It didn't matter. I was weak … but somehow strong.

I kept my eye on Bloocifer until my neck cramped so bad that I had to rest it. I showed her my knife blade, turning it in the light. *Though I walk through the valley of the shadow of death, I will fear no evil, for you are with me.*

When I looked up, she was gone. *Uh-oh. How am I supposed to sleep tonight? Tomorrow night? Or the next, if there is a next? She'll slither into my sleeping bag. I have no defenses!*

You have the armor.

It's not real! I threw my head onto my folded arms. *I need something real! A rock or my bow and arrow! I need something REAL!*

The silence was deafening. For an hour I waited for a word. Had I offended him and his armor? Had he left me? No, I could still feel him there, waiting patiently for me to figure out things by myself.

I'm sorry.

Your struggle is not against flesh and blood, Elijah, but against the rulers, against the authorities, against the powers of this dark world and against the spiritual forces of evil in the heavenly realms.

My mind was still on Bloocifer. *Snakes hibernate in bunches, sometimes in the sides of cliffs,* I informed God, t*hirty, fifty, even a hundred at a time.* With growing horror my eyes went up the side of the cliff. *They're above me, aren't they? They've been there the whole time, a whole nest of 'em, just waiting to come out to sun themselves on the warm rocks.*

They're all around, he answered matter-of-factly. He wasn't just talking about snakes. He meant the spiritual forces. I was learning by now that when God speaks, he often speaks in layers or riddles. His words are three-dimensional. They can mean two or three things at once. His words move.

They are not your first concern.

The snakes or the forces of evil? I asked. He meant both.

I figured as much. I'm starting to see, El-Telan-Yah.

What are you doing here, Elijah? he asked me a second time.

I'm starting to see.

The story of Adam and Eve made perfect sense now. I was sorry that I'd doubted it and even sorrier that I'd ever asked to see the dark side. I heard Dom's voice warning me: "*Better watch what you ask God for. You just might get it.*"

I fought off agonizing weariness—afraid that I'd slip into unconsciousness and not wake up. I'd had nightmares: I was Salem, shot with arrows ... I was Stan Dowland, filled with rage and regret, watching someone else wear the armor of God ... Reece and Brill were together ... my dad was giving up on me ... rocks were falling on me. I dreaded the dreams, but I couldn't keep my eyes open. When darkness fell for the sixth time, it didn't matter anyway. I was in a pitch-black Hell of bone-aching cold and thirst. Numbness was creeping up my leg. Animals could be chewing it off, and I'd never know. I hadn't felt sensation in my foot since ... I didn't know when.

Okay. This is it. If at first light I'm alive, I will take my knife in hand and do what must be done. I mean it this time. While I have the strength to do it. I pray that I have the strength to crawl out of Gilead, across Telanoo, and through Owl Woods to home. Home.

I'll hug Mom and Dad, hug the twins, hobble through town, find Marcus and Rob, find Reece and kiss her again. Then we'll all meet at Florence's for grits and bacon. Yeah.

CHAPTER 11

Whiiirrrrr.

My head shot up, wobbling; my mind panicked. *Whirring? What is it?* My eyes strained to see into the blackness. Night clouds lay low and heavy; there was no light at all. *Is it the wings of Leap Castle zooming in to gouge out my eyes?* I ducked. *Is it Bloocifer's rattling tail, warning me of a strike?* I grabbed my belt and whipped it out blindly in all directions. The whirring was loud and steady. Horror gripped my mind. Lights flashed before my eyes. Terror surrounded me. *No ... no, not that! It's all hundred of them!? Vicious blue racers circling me in the blackness, signaling attack! God, are you there?! ARE YOU THERE? DON'T LEAVE ME!*

The sound got louder with a *thoo-thoo-thoo* thumping rhythmically underneath the whirring—like eagles' wings pumping the air in flight.

It's ... a helicopter! A copter!

Fumbling and frantic, I whipped out Reece's poem and wadded it up. I ripped off my damp shirt. I got the matches from my pocket and struck one, setting the pile on fire. My hands scrambled in the darkness and found bits of straw and a few leaves to add to my pathetic little blaze. I circled it with my arms to protect it from the wind. *Come on, copter. Look down; I'm here!* My hopes soared. *I'm saved!!*

The helicopter roared over the narrow rim of Gilead and headed west. The little fire sputtered. *Wait! I'm here!* In a few

249

minutes the copter doubled back and hovered a few seconds, but my fire had died down to a quivering pile of red ashes. My world went black for the last time; the helicopter moved on. My head dropped to the cold ground. Blindly, I waved my hand over the warm embers, feeling their brief comfort. *What more? I asked desperately. What more?*

I heard movement in the dry grass across the stream. *Footsteps? Slow and cautious. Not human,* I judged with a kind of strange, distant objectivity. *It's a medium-sized animal, four-legged. A coyote. They found me. And there'll be more.*

I got the belt, worked it around my left leg just below the knee—that was as far down as I could reach—and yanked. *Awkward angle. Not tight enough. I'll rest a little and try again. Tighter. Cut off the blood that hasn't crystallized.*

"I'll need your help to do this," I spoke into the night. "Don't they call you the great physician? Well, give me what you got: anesthetic, a steady hand, whatever. That helicopter sweep was my last hope. But I'm not staying here with a nest of racers over my head, coyotes circling, and my family thinking I'm dead, while the helmet of salvation and sword of the Lord rust at the bottom of the lake. I have to do something. I've waited on you long enough."

To spite my impossible circumstances, I scraped the ground where I'd written "SOTERION LAKE deut33" and drawn the map. *If there's a message about the armor of God, I'm delivering it in person.* I didn't care that I was dirtying and dulling the blade. *I've got no fire to sterilize it, got no feeling anyway, so what does it matter?* I rested awhile and then drew the belt another notch tighter.

The faintest hint of dawn teased the horizon. A bright star burned above me. I wondered if it was Mars and quoted Reece's poem: *As one by one thy hopes depart, be resolute and calm.* I bundled myself for my last hours as a two-legged boy and slept, so I'd be strong at first light.

. . . . .

I felt a hand on my shoulder. "Elijah! Dear God! Elijah!" came a booming voice. "He's alive! Give me a hand, quick!"

The voice seemed vaguely familiar. I was awake. Rescued.

"Russ! We got him, man. We got him!"

There was Dom kneeling beside me and my dad running up behind. Beside Dad was Donovan of all people, the tennis-pro type I'd first met at the Stallards' office in Chicago, who'd helped us retrieve the breastplate of righteousness. Behind them came two rescue squad guys I recognized from when Reece had gotten hurt in Hermits' Cave.

Dad's voice was choked when he dropped down and looked me in the face, his expression full of shock and dismay. "We've got you, son. You're okay now. We've got you. Hang on."

"I'm okay," I croaked. "I need water."

A canteen appeared. I tipped my head around and they poured it into my mouth. Never, ever was there a better taste. Never. Beautiful, beautiful water.

Then came a flood of questions and comments. Dom asked, "How'd you get yourself into such a fix, boy?" and proceeded to order the rescue squad around, how they could leverage the rock up little by little, brace it underneath, and pull me out. He joked about how bad I stank. He and Donovan talked like they knew each other; they surveyed the slab and my tools and exchanged words out of earshot. Dad never left my side.

The squad did their thing—taking my vital signs, checking for broken bones, and getting me warm.

With a lot of heaving and yelling, the slab was raised and Dad pulled me out. Everyone marveled that my foot wasn't crushed. But when the shoe and sock came off, we all saw what a nasty shade of blue gray it was. Dad's jaw clamped, and he said, "Let's get him to Columbus. Come on!"

They had to carry me a long way because the helicopter hadn't been able to land in Telanoo—too rough and scraggly. They'd found a pasture on a neighboring farm. Once we were strapped in and the helicopter took off, I asked Dad, "How'd you know where I was?"

He nodded to Dom and Donovan. "They saw your fire."

· · · · ·

The doctors weren't sure they could save the foot. Dad cried. I said, "It'll be okay. Don't worry." Nurses referred to me as "the missing boy," so I figured I'd made the papers.

Mom went all to pieces once she got there with the twins. She cried and apologized for being depressed and yelling at me. She blamed herself for my running off.

I had to talk her down from that ledge. "No, Mom. It was an accident. I was doing survival stuff, and a rock fell on me. No one's to blame."

The twins hugged me hard and patted my head like I was one of their baby dolls. It was kind of cute. They were glad I wasn't *weebid*. Whatever that meant.

"I'm very un-*weebid*," I said with a weak smile.

Grandma Creek had come up before Christmas when she heard I was missing. She swabbed her eyes and planted a hard kiss on my forehead. "Don't you ever go off without telling someone, my precious boy, no matter how old you get! No man is an island!"

I was hooked up to machines, scrubbed down, whispered over, fed liquids, poked, and prodded. The sheets and pillows and warmed blankets were pure Heaven. I concentrated on the bed linens to take my mind off the searing pain in my foot as feeling returned.

Then I heard other voices as if from far away. Rob, Marcus, and Reece were out in the hall. Mom was out there telling them that they couldn't stay long, that I might be sleeping and needed my rest.

"Hey!" I croaked. "Let 'em in."

They circled around me with strange, uncertain looks on their faces. They'd probably heard the news that I might lose my foot. Rob peeked under the sheet and nearly retched when he saw it. Reece pulled a chair up close to me and grasped my hand. She pressed her head to my hand and closed her eyes, praying. Then her eyes opened on me, sad and scared and intense. "Tell us everything."

"I was working on a place," I rasped. "Gilead. For the clan. Big rock slid; I got caught under it. Six days."

They helped me get the story out. When they got the whole picture—that I'd been facedown on the cold ground without food and water except for one big icicle, that I'd kept my sanity with the Quella until it died, then with the Bible verses I remembered, and finally with the poem—Reece covered her face and cried.

Rob said guiltily, "We were right there! During the manhunt we called and called!"

I pointed to my throat. "Dried out. Couldn't talk."

Marcus didn't say much, watching me with a mix of disbelief and admiration.

Reece said, "When we heard you were missing, the three of us got together every afternoon and prayed. We prayed so hard right after school let out. Then when Christmas break started, we called each other at the same time. Church had a prayer chain going and my Devo club did too."

"Thanks." I paused, remembering the feelings of warmth and peace that came about the same time every day. "Every afternoon?"

"Like clockwork."

"Wow ... I felt that. About 3:00 every day. I felt that."

She huffed. "Well, of course you did. It's *prayer!*"

Marcus peeked at my foot under the covers and made a face. "Whoa. Serious damage. That has to hurt."

"Right now it feels like someone stuck my foot in boiling oil." Soberly I thought, *like one foot in Hell.*

Reece said, "We'll go so you can rest."

I grasped her hand. "Don't leave."

Marcus and Rob exchanged looks. I explained, "Talk to me, guys. I need human voices. Talk."

Rob said, "Everyone had a different theory about what happened to you. It was crazy."

"Stallards?" I asked.

"That's what your parents thought. They found an address and thought you'd run off up there. It's been in the news and everything."

"Not good," I said, thinking of Cravens. "Call the Stallards; tell them I'm okay."

"Dad already did," Marcus said.

Reece glanced out the door to see where Mom was and then turned back to me. "Your mom thought for sure that I knew something, that I was keeping a secret. She kept calling all of us to ask if we'd heard from you. They were sure you'd gone to Chicago. But I knew you wouldn't go off without telling ... *someone.*" She grinned shyly.

Rob said, "The police grilled the Stallards, staged a manhunt through Telanoo, questioned Justin Brill—"

"Brill?" I croaked out a laugh.

"You're kidding." Marcus shrugged. "Which was my theory. But Reece kept telling Officer Taylor that you were back there in the woods. When the manhunt turned up zip, it was her idea to fly over at night. She was relentless about it."

She leaned in even more intently. "If you were back there and alive, there'd be a fire, I just knew it. So I made the police fly over at night."

I laughed. "You made the police fly over?"

"I did," she beamed.

"True," Marcus confirmed.

"I burned your poem," I told her. "I memorized it first. Without the paper, the shirt never would have caught. Even then it only lasted a few minutes."

Marcus said, "I can't believe you lasted almost a week out there. I thought for sure Brill did you in. I thought he dumped your body in Old Railroad Lake."

My eyes closed and my teeth clamped down as a sickening wave of intense burning rolled though my foot. I smiled weakly through it. "Brill ... I need to thank him."

They all acted shocked.

"Thank him? Are you nuts?" Reece asked. "You should have heard what he said about you being gone! I was so mad that I slugged him with my crutch."

Marcus joked, "Great weapon. I gotta get me one of those." He shot Reece an approving glance. "And she looks so harmless."

I said, "I'll explain later about Brill. Long story." I suddenly sat up. "Lake ... I forgot to tell you," I wheezed. "It's in the lake!"

"What's in the lake?" Rob asked.

I glanced at the door. The parents and the twins were outside talking to Reece's mom. I whispered, "*Soterion.*"

Reece's eyes popped. "What?! The helmet's in the lake? How do you know?"

"Maybe the rest of it too." I held out my hand to Marcus. "Quella." He turned his over to me. I fell back to the pillow, punched in Deuteronomy 33:23, and handed it back.

His cool green eyes locked onto the screen. "Naphtali—"

"It means 'fighter,'" I interrupted.

He read silently, frowned, then said out loud, "Will inherit southward … to the lake."

"We gotta get it now," I said.

"But the lake's frozen!" Rob said.

The hallway crowd came back in, and we switched the conversation to how far behind I was in Latin and how long until I'd walk again. Rob joked that he'd be organizing a homecoming parade in my honor down Main Street.

As Reece stood to leave, I squeezed her hand and whispered, "We're not waiting until spring."

She nodded.

CHAPTER 12

The doctor, a bald guy with bushy eyebrows and a wide smile, stood at the foot of my bed and discussed my situation with Mom and Dad. I'd insisted on it; I didn't want somebody sealing my fate out in the hallway and me not knowing about it.

According to the doctor, I was—in a nutshell—sort of a natural miracle. He said, "His foot was frostbitten for an entire week. But the conditions were—how shall I say this?—ideal, under the circumstances. He was wearing good shoes, the shoe stayed dry, he was out of the wind, and the collective heat from the rocks kept his foot a consistent temperature. When flesh freezes, thaws, and refreezes, you have serious problems, deep tissue damage. Apparently, that didn't happen here."

The whole Creek family knew this kind of stuff from first-aid classes. Mom and Dad looked at the doctor in pleasant disbelief.

"You're used to the cold?" he asked me.

"I hike barefoot sometimes."

The doctor smiled at his chart and then at me. "That's part of it too. You'd already acclimated. A person from the tropics would have succumbed. I hear you had a top-notch sleeping bag; you're strong and healthy. Still, with the fluctuations in temperature over the past week, I fully expected permanent damage." He took one more look at the foot and touched it ever so slightly in a few places. "Hurts?"

"Like the dickens."

"We'll keep him a few more days; those toes aren't out of the woods yet—no pun intended—but healing is taking place." The doctor shook his head in wonder.

"People prayed for me," I said.

He looked at my parents and back at me. "I'll say. I'd have to consider the likelihood that *someone* was adjusting the thermostat in that gorge."

I smiled, closed my eyes, and nodded. The doctor was a believer.

When I'd been pumped with painkillers and left alone to rest, I drifted under a snow-white warm blanket and realized that I'd had exactly what I needed to survive: no more, no less. Not the bread and meat that I wanted, but good gear, three cups of water, and steady temperature. And the Presence.

．　．　．　．　．

Reece came by the next day with a Christmas gift: a leather Bible and new batteries for the Quella. "I don't want you to ever be without the Word again. And don't be discouraged or afraid because of what happened, Elijah. Whatever Satan tried to do to you by trapping you back there, he didn't get away with it. He's not going to stop us."

"I'm … uh … I'm not sure it was him."

She sat back, stunned. "What do you mean?"

I explained how the rock fell, how my foot was protected all around, and what the doctor said. "It seemed that my foot never actually froze. So there's no permanent damage. I'll be more susceptible to frostbite from here on out. I know that, but I'll be good to go." I got quiet and didn't know how to say it. "I'm sorry everybody was worried. I feel bad about it. I was dumb to try moving that rock on my own. But—and I mean this, I'm not just talking—I'm glad it happened." I flipped through the Bible and smelled the leather and new-book smell. "Wow, this is great. It's small enough to fit right in my hand."

"You said reading the Bible helped."

"Oh, man … at our next powwow I'll tell you all what happened." I choked up thinking about it. "When I get home, we'll have an old movie and pizza night. I'll lay it all out. I'll write it down for Mei too. Reece, thanks for the Bible. I'm sorry I don't have anything for you."

"You can owe me." She grinned and poked me. "You're one of those last-minute shoppers, huh?"

"Yeah, that's it. I was waiting for the after-Christmas bargains."

. . . . .

Mom kept me on the living room couch to monitor me and keep me from trying to rush my recovery. She treated me like a prince. What kind of food did I want? Did I want to watch TV or read a book? Did I need it all quiet in the house to rest?

She helped me catch up on homework—only when I felt like it—and called in a Latin tutor. She even hired a masseuse to work the kinks out of my neck and back. Yeah, for a few days I was a prince.

On the front burner of my mind, though, was how to get to the bottom of Silver Lake. I was more than ready to get a scuba suit and dive down myself, but that would be dumb. Reece couldn't. So I called Rob. "*Soterion*," I said. "What do we do about it?"

"The water temperature is thirty-eight degrees. The depth of the lake is fifteen feet in the middle."

"You measured it already?" I asked, amazed.

Rob was all business. "Dom has a wet suit, but not for icy waters. It might work though. Marcus said he'd fit in it."

I pictured Skidmore in a baggy diving suit dropping backward off Paddleboat Dock. "Deep-sea diving in Silver Lake. That's a hoot. Or hey, we could drain it."

"It would take a day and draw too much attention." Rob's

take-charge attitude surprised me. I wondered if he'd been thinking about what to do if I'd turned up dead.

Funny, though, I wasn't offended or threatened or anything.
It was a good thing. They would have gone on without me.

"Diving's the best idea," he said, as if that settled it. "Marcus
said he'd try to clear it with his dad and get things set up. We're
calling it Operation Naphtali."

"Okay, Cuz. You'll be in charge. Hey, by the way, do you
know how Donovan got involved in my rescue?"

"Donovan was here?"

"Yeah. You didn't know?"

"No."

"He and Dom … the way they were talking during the rescue
in Gilead. It was like they knew each other."

· · · · · ·

I was soon putting weight on the foot. I got a pile of get-well
cards from school kids and teachers and church people. Mom was
impressed and sort of baffled at how the church people brought
food over even though they didn't know her. It was like when
Reece was recovering. A ton of food just showed up.

I moved up to my room when I convinced Mom that I wasn't
going to die or do something stupid with my recovery.

On the night of Operation Naphtali, Rob came over after
dinner dressed all in black and wearing a stocking cap, like at
Farr Island. He had the walkie-talkies and handed me one. "We're
doing it now. You'll be able to hear what's going on. Marcus will
actually do the retrieval; his dad's here to help. Your dad knows
about it but signed off because he has a planning meeting. Dom
has all this equipment: underwater lights, ropes, everything. I'll
report in."

"Where will you look? It's a big lake."

He unfolded a map. "Here's the lake, and here's where Old

Pilgrim Church stood. I'm starting with the assumption that Dowland came from the church, took the shortest path to the lake, and hurled it toward the center. I drew a straight line to show direction. Marcus will start from this point on the shore and work his way toward the center. You'll hear from me in a few minutes, Navajo." He turned to leave but then turned back. "I ordered myself one of those Quellas."

I was totally impressed with my cousin. I hated missing the eyewitness action, but the search couldn't have been in better hands.

I lay in my bed and prayed, "Let them find it quick. It's cold out there, and Marcus is a city boy from the tropics."

In a few minutes, Rob called in. "Viking to Navajo. Out."

I grinned. "Navajo here. Out."

"Cong here," Marcus's voice came through the walkie-talkie with splashing in the background.

"Metatron here," came Dom's booming, overly dramatic voice. I laughed out loud. *Metatron. Come on.*

"Little Soaring Eagle here." It was Reece.

"Going in," said Marcus, and I heard a big splash.

Rob's voice came through. "Operation Naphtali underway. I'll report back in a few minutes. Over and out."

I lay there with the walkie-talkie on my chest, more glad to be alive than I could put in words. *Thank you, El-Telan-Yah. Thank you, thank you, thank you.* I lay there, a big squishy pile of gratitude, sensing a cloud of goodness around me.

After a few minutes, the walkie-talkie crackled. "Viking here. Status report. Cong is nearing the center of the lake. No retrieval at this point."

"He's been under for ten minutes, right? Over."

"Nine minutes, thirty seconds."

"Don't let him get too cold. He's a tropical guy, you know.

Can't handle the winter temps the way we Ohioans can."

"We're monitoring him. Viking over and out."

"Navajo over and out," I said, grinning from ear to ear.

I could hardly contain myself. I sat up and eased my still puffy, blistery foot onto the floor. I threw on my jacket, wrapped my foot in a T-shirt, got the walkie-talkie, and eased down the stairs on my backside. At the foot of the stairs, I stood. "Mom, I'm stepping out on the porch for just a minute."

She came running. "Oh, hon! No, it's too soon."

"For just a minute. I've been cooped up for days. See, it's much better. Rob's down by the lake. We're using the walkie-talkies. I want to wave at him."

Reluctantly she went back toward the kitchen. "Five minutes. And keep that foot covered."

I stepped out on the porch in the dark. It was an eerie sight, two guys and a girl all in black, looking over the lake while a faint green light moved slowly through its depths.

"Navajo here," I spoke into the walkie-talkie. "I'm on the porch. Status."

Rob and Reece turned and waved. "Viking and Little Soaring Eagle here. He's been out to the center once. Working his way back. It's very murky. Out."

I went back in so I wouldn't worry Mom but stayed in the front room and sat by the window, peeking through the curtain every minute or so. She brought me some hot chocolate. I'd felt a weird kind of guilty, hiding the good news from my mom. I had to tell her. *It's now or never.* "Mom?"

"What do you need, hon?"

"Um, Marcus is in the lake."

She looked at me like I'd lost my mind.

"He's searching for another piece of the armor."

She dashed to the window, took one look down toward the

lake, and gasped.

Before she could blow a gasket, I said, "Dom's overseeing the operation. Reece and Rob are there. And Dad knows."

She whirled around. At first she didn't believe me. Then hurt feelings showed up on her face. "Your dad gave you permission?"

"Mom, I got a revelation when I was stuck in the gorge. A verse from the Bible made me think that the last pieces might be in the lake. They might not, but we have to look."

Glaring down toward the lake, Mom did a slow burn. She had never understood what the quest was about. She couldn't see the big picture. I was puzzling over how to explain it when my eyes fell on the Christmas bears and angels sitting on the couch. I hobbled over and picked them up. "Okay, here it is. Here's why the search is important. These are real, Mom. Bears are real. And angels are real. We have angels at Christmas because angels came. The spirit world is as real as the real world, Mom."

"Honey, I don't deny that there could be something out there, life on other planets …"

"I'm not talking aliens or some things out there! I mean God and demons and angelic forces." I held up a bear in coveralls and an angel in a pretty satin dress. "This is a big joke, Mom. In real life both of these beings can use deadly force against you."

You'd have thought I was a preschooler talking about my imaginary friends. It wasn't sinking in. My own mom seemed like a stranger to me.

The dryer buzzed. "The laundry's done," she said, obviously relieved for an excuse to end the conversation.

I had one more thing to say. It was more good news, but she wasn't going to like it. "Mom, remember that song they sang at my baptism about me never being the same?"

"Yes, I think so."

"Well, that's true—and it's getting truer by the minute."

She left me holding a half-empty cup of hot chocolate and with a worrisome question on my mind: Which was worse, to worship the sun the way Mei did, or to believe in nothing, like Mom? I was working on it in my mind when the walkie-talkie crackled and Viking blurted, "We have the arm piece!"

CHAPTER 13

It took a few more minutes for Marcus to find the helmet. I stood out in the driveway—my foot bundled in the T-shirt, the walkie-talkie pressed to my mouth. "Navajo to Viking. Bring it to the house. I told Mom. All's clear. Over."

We clan members beamed over the pond-scummy helmet wrapped in soggy burlap. Mom studied it with the strangest expression. "Now ... just how did you know this was in our lake?"

I grinned. "God told me."

She looked worried.

Dom thawed out in the kitchen and tried to explain things to Mom. I was glad for the help.

"No sign of the sword, I guess," I asked Marcus as the four of us clunked and thudded up the steps.

"I looked."

Reece, Marcus, and I crowded around Rob in the bathroom while he washed the arm piece and helmet in the tub. Dr. Dale's comments came back to me, about how unready we were for what was to come after the quest. I could still hear the half-scared, half-angry tone in the old scientist's voice: "... *Rob's disbelief, Sahara's pagan influence over Mei, Reece's health, Marcus's ego, and your lack of understanding of the simplest truths of the faith. You five are completely unprepared for the task ahead. Not one of you has the vaguest idea what kind of spiritual and physical danger you are in.*"

From where I sat—on the bathroom floor, wedged between the toilet and the tub—we sure didn't look like spiritual warriors:

me with my breadbasket-size foot, Reece with her crutch, Rob dressed like a ninja, and Marcus shivering in shorts and T-shirt. We looked like the Magdeline chapter of Rejects Anonymous.

Once Rob got the scum washed off the helmet, it gleamed. My heart warmed at seeing that gold-tinted relic again with the mysterious symbols carved into the forehead.

Reece took a towel and swaddled the arm piece like a baby. Rubbing the metal forearm until the word appeared, she whispered, "*Koinonia.* Fellowship." She took the helmet and said with emotion, "*Soterion.* Salvation." She grinned big at Marcus and me. "We have to tell Mei!"

Rob said, "I've been reading up on these words. They're written in an early form of the Greek alphabet—except for that." He pointed to the second letter on the helmet. "It's the omega, the big O which was added later. It's now the last letter of the Greek alphabet. It means 'the end.'"

Marcus said, "Jesus called himself the alpha and the omega. The beginning and the end."

Reece ran her finger over the omega symbol Ω, hugged the helmet, then handed it to me. "You keep it for a while. Your room will be headquarters until you're better."

We took the pieces to my room and then went down to the kitchen to thank Dom for helping us. When the others left, I went to my room, turned on my bedside lamp, and propped myself up to study the helmet and arm piece. Things I hadn't understood before were clear to me now. *Soterion* meant a person's soul saved, not a soldier's life saved. The winding vine and spikes were Jesus' crown of thorns; the reddish dots were his blood. I went to sleep with the helmet and arm piece next to me and thought about the stories hidden in the armor.

· · · · · ·

I woke while it was still dark, clicked on the light, and lay there full of wonder studying the helmet inch by inch. *Why did you choose me?* I asked God.

The inside of the helmet was worn and ragged and still damp. In the strong lamplight, I noticed that the high inside part of the metal nosepiece wasn't metal at all. It was soft. I pressed in with my thumb. *It's like clay but with a thin coat of metallic paint over it.* Pressing around the spot revealed nubs of what looked like tiny fasteners that had broken off. I sat up, held it under the lamp, and looked closer. A small square piece of something had once been fastened to the inside of the nosepiece and had fallen off. It had to be the little scrap of chain mail with an encryption of Job 22:25: "Then the Almighty will be your gold, the choicest silver for you."

Dr. Eloise had explained that the Hebrew word for gold in that verse referred to metal in a crude state, or "dug out," as in a treasure uncovered. "The root word also carries the idea of defense," she had said. "It may be translated *gold*, or *treasure*, or *defense*. And it looks like you children have found all three!"

Something hard was embedded in the layer of clay. Using the tip of my bowie knife, I carefully dug out a red stone—a crystal or a garnet maybe. It was large—obviously not a real jewel—and shaped like a raindrop. I hobbled to the bathroom and washed it off, careful not to let it slip down the drain.

When I held it to the bathroom light, I saw that it was a pure bloodred. And though I'm not a jewelry kind of guy, I thought it was beautiful. It was cut with little triangle facets all around. *Looks like a piece off a chandelier or an old lamp. Wonder what it's worth?*

· · · · ·

Mom had errands to run the next day and insisted I come along. I wasn't anxious to be gaped at and asked questions about my condition, but Mom had finally noticed that my winter jacket was two sizes too small, and she wanted to fit me in a new one. I was to sit in the car while she went to the drugstore for my anti-infection medicine.

Across the street—where the old hotel had once stood before the tornado ripped through—was a barber shop and the recently opened New York Jewelers, both with apartments above. I had the gem in my pocket.

Wonder what it's worth? It's probably a piece of glass symbolizing the blood of Jesus, and they'll probably laugh at me. Could be a ruby or a garnet. What if they thought I stole it? I could lie and say it was a family heirloom. No. I sat in the car gazing across the street at a sign in the window: "Introductory Offer! Free Appraisals!" Behind the counter stood a man in his forties, clean-cut, wearing a business suit. *Rob's been doing research. My turn.*

I got out of the car and hobbled across the street. The door jingled as I went in; the salesman looked up. "Good morning," he said, straightening the ring trays and locking the case.

"Hi. Do you do appraisals?"

He nodded to the sign and looked at me as if I didn't have the sense God gave a duck.

"Oh." I pulled the stone out and laid it on the counter. "Is this worth anything? It came out of an old piece. Belongs to the clan."

"Clan?" He smiled coolly and asked in a northern accent, "That's what you call family around here?" He took the stone in his fingers and put a jeweler's loupe to his eye. "Let's have a look."

He turned it in his hand. Then he turned it over and looked some more. His cool, big-city smirk faded to a look of confusion. He leaned down, his eyes seriously boring into the gem. He stopped breathing. I got uneasy. He suddenly seemed aware that I was watching him and tried to recover his air of casualness. "Very pretty stone. Old." He looked me over and then went back to the stone as if he hadn't believed his eyes the first time. "Are you ... interested in selling it?"

"What's it worth? I mean, is it glass or a ruby or what?"

"It's not glass," he said cautiously. He was so stunned by the gem that I half expected him to tell me it was engraved with words or symbols. *Why hadn't I thought of that before? I should have looked closer, should have left the research part to Rob. Drat!*

"It's ... valuable," he said matter-of-factly. "You said you found it with other pieces of jewelry? Is the jewelry your mother's or grandmother's?" He was gathering information.

I wished I hadn't come, wished I hadn't let a stranger see it. *What were you thinking, Creek? It's from the armor of God! You never underestimate it. Haven't you learned anything?*

I took a cue from the Stallards' wheeling and dealing with Cravens in Dublin a few months before. *Okay,* I coached myself, *you came in here with one question, and you're going out with one answer. Simple as that.* "You said free appraisals." I nodded to the sign.

"Yes, appraisals." He studied the stone again. "It's an older cut, called a briolette. A style from—" he cleared his throat, "older times. A simple cut like this doesn't provide the refraction of newer, better cuts. We could have it reshaped for you."

Oh, so now it's inferior? Sorry, bud, I just watched you lose your cool over that stone. "Is it a garnet?"

"Possibly a corundum."

"What's that?"

His eyes went all wide and innocent. "A harder stone. I'll need to confirm the age before I can give you an informed appraisal." He nodded to the back room. "Would you mind if I showed this to my associate?"

A wave of panic washed over me. I was no idiot. He was planning to go back there, find a substitute gem, and do the old switcheroo. I held out my hand. "I just wanted to know what it's worth, ballpark figure. Free appraisal and all that."

He balked. "All right. Value. I could ... offer you five hundred dollars."

"Is that what it's worth?"

He faltered. "Maybe seven-fifty. It has a few flaws, but the color is very nice."

"What did you say it was?"

"It's a—" Sweat popped out on his face. "It appears to be a diamond, but the cut is unusual. It's an older cut."

"You said that."

He nodded toward the back again. "So I'd like to confer with my associate to give you a more informed answer. If he concurs, we could do, say ... a thousand."

I looked at the gem, glistening bloodred between his shaking fingers. "Diamonds aren't red," I said.

"Red ones are relatively rare," he said casually. He licked his lips; his mouth was dry.

Thinks he can pull one over on the dumb small-town kid. I faked total shock. "Whoa, did you say a thousand whole dollars!" This guy didn't know who he was dealing with. I had international connections, friends on the police force and in the world of science. I had all but the last piece of the armor of God. "Well, thanks. That's really neat to know! A thousand dollars ... wow!"

"Or more, if I might show it to my associate. Then if you decide to keep it, we could put it in a nice setting for you."

Yeah, right. "You could?" I asked in a dumb, gawky way. "Could you put it in ... like a silver dragon head with the red diamond as the eye or something?"

"Sure, sure, we could do that for you," he said with an agreeable frown, as if he were thinking out how to do it. "A striking idea."

He thinks I'm dumb and *have no taste!* Well, to give him a little credit here, I hadn't actually combed my hair that morning. I was wearing a coat with sleeves halfway to my elbows, old sandals, and two pairs of big, fluffy white socks to pad my feet.

I kept my hand out and added a country twang, thinking how Rob might do it: "Welp, I'll think 'bout that dragon head with a big red eye on a big silver chain around my neck. That'd be nice. Real nice."

Reluctantly he dropped the diamond into my palm and followed it with a business card. "Our designers can set the stone according to your specifications—a dragon or a magnificent brooch to surprise your mother on her birthday. As a first-time customer, you'll receive an extra twenty percent discount on the setting. Now if you'll just fill out this card, we'll put you on our mailing list."

"Maybe later. I need to think 'bout that."

"We do appreciate your business. You live in town?"

I limped toward the door, bouncing in my springy white socks. "Family's from down in Georgia."

"It was certainly nice to meet you ... ," he fished for my name.

"Known 'round some parts as George Telanoo."

Once out of view, I jogged painfully down the street. I wasn't about to get in Mom's car and have him trace our license plate. *This was a huge mistake. Huge. Why did he want that stone so stinking bad? Why would he lie and call it a red diamond? There's no such thing!*

I glanced back when I reached the corner. He'd come out of the store and was watching me. I saluted him with my index finger, ducked into a side alley, and thought fast. *The treasure? Dowland's lost treasure?*

I had to get to the car before Mom found me missing. I circled around the backside of the block, cut through the parking lot next to the tracks, and limped back up another alley. I peeked around the corner. The jeweler had gone inside. I watched for Mom to come out of the drugstore and waved for her to come pick me up.

"What are you doing on your feet, Elijah? It's freezing!"

"Can you drop me off at Rob's?"

"Absolutely not! It's back home to rest. You have to get healed before school starts!" She patted my knee and mellowed. "You're a little stir-crazy; after what you've been through, I don't blame you. We'll invite Rob over when we get home."

"Wait. Drop me off here at the library."

Mom groaned impatiently. "Elijah!"

"I have to!"

She pulled up to the curb.

"Thanks, Mom. I'll be an hour. I'll call if I need a ride."

"Don't you dare try to walk home!"

I called Rob on the library's pay phone and kept my voice down so the ever-suspicious Mrs. Otto wouldn't hear. "Can you get to the library?"

"Yeah. What's up?"

"I don't know, could be big. Bring paper and pencil. We'll need to take notes."

"Are you trying to get me to do your homework?" he asked skeptically.

"No, jerk. Make it snappy."

CHAPTER 14

We found the most out-of-the-way table in the library, and I laid the gem on a piece of white paper. "It was in the helmet. Right behind the nosepiece in a lump of clay that had been painted to look like metal. Right here." I pointed to my forehead. I told him about the jeweler's reaction. "I think it's worth a lot! We're not telling another soul, not even Reece or Marcus. Not yet."

Rob grabbed every book on gems he could find, careful not to arouse Mrs. Otto's wary lemur eyes. I kept watch on the door through the bookshelves, wondering if the jeweler had spied on me from a back window in his shop; I wondered if he was flipping through the phone book looking for Telanoo. I'd never be able to walk down the streets of Magdeline again, at least not past New York Jewelers. I imagined him keeping a camera handy, snapping my mug, and flashing it around town until he'd tracked me down. *Oh no!* The Magdeline Messenger! *The story of the missing boy—me—was on the front page last week. Would a big-city jeweler bother reading a podunk town paper? Will he think I found the gem behind the camp? Will he call in his big-city hit men, who'll break into Camp Mudj and hold my family hostage until I turn over the stone?*

I'd become high profile in my own town, and I didn't like the feel of it. Not one bit.

Rob rifled through books, slamming each one shut when it didn't deliver the information he wanted. In a few minutes, he shoved a book at me with pictures of gemstones. "Red diamonds.

They do exist, but they're very, very rare! Found first in India, then Australia, and often called pinks because they aren't a true red."

I held my gem up to the light. "This one is."

He peered up at it, then pulled the book back under his nose, and read on: "Some have an orange or brown cast … it doesn't say anything about a pure red diamond … no wait … it says here, 'No true red diamond has ever been catalogued.'"

I locked eyes with my cousin. "Notice it didn't say never discovered, just never catalogued."

We took turns holding it to the light and keeping an eye out for Mrs. Otto or any library people. I whispered, "Maybe this is the only one in the world; diamond experts know it's out there but not where." My mind flashed back to Grafton Institute in Dublin and how Cravens had paced like a caged animal at feeding time when the subject of the armor of God came up. I looked at Rob. "What did Cravens say? Something like, 'No man can own it'?"

Rob quoted, "'A treasure of immeasurable wealth. No man can purchase it, for it cannot be appraised.'"

"Did he mean the diamond or the armor?" I asked.

"Do you think the Stallards know?" Rob wondered out loud.

"If they did, why didn't they tell us?"

Mrs. Otto came tromping around on her way to the periodicals. I slipped the diamond into my pocket.

"Maybe this is what the Stallards have really been looking for all along," I said, trying not to sound suspicious.

"Do we have to tell them we found it?" he asked.

The Stallards had done so much for us. But in the light of our new discovery, my old suspicions returned. Why had they spent thousands on us?

Reluctantly I said, "I think we have to tell them about the helmet. But maybe not the diamond."

"Where will we hide it?"

I felt in my pocket to make sure the diamond hadn't fallen out through a hole in my raggedy jacket. "Not in any of our houses; our moms might find it when they clean."

"Not out in the woods," he began.

I butted in before he said it, "where I lost the helmet once. I won't lose another treasure. That's all we need to say about that." I practically broke out in a cold sweat thinking about how last night I'd washed off the diamond over an open drain.

"Where are we going to hide it?" Rob repeated.

"Where am I going to hide it," I corrected.

"Elijah!" he hissed. "Don't start that again! It belongs to all of us! You can't take it!"

"The fewer who know, the better. Rob, you didn't see the hungry look in the eye of that jeweler. If news gets out, it could be dangerous.

Mrs. Otto's hot breath swept down on my neck. "May I help you gentlemen?" she fired at us.

"We're sorry for being loud," I whispered. "We'll get quiet and work on our research."

"Did I overhear one of you talking about taking something, because as a point of interest, there's been a rash of stealing from the library," she said accusingly.

"We're not stealing, Mrs. Otto," Rob said politely.

"And for that reason," she went on as if she hadn't heard, "a security guard comes by periodically to do random searches on suspicious patrons."

A search? The red diamond's not even safe in my raggedy old pocket in the town library!?

"We're legit," I said politely.

After she tromped off, Rob whispered, "So where?"

"I'll tell you Monday when I figure it out."

He gave me a look.

"I have to think."

Rob and I parted ways. He took off for home. I flagged down Bo in the camp van on a run to the hardware store. *Where? Where can I hide it?* By the time I reached the Camp Mudj maintenance building, I had the answer. It was the only possible place. I slipped in the door, went to the cabinet where we keep fasteners, ripped off a piece of duct tape, and sealed the diamond in my belly button.

Rob was at my locker first thing. "Where'd you hide it?"

"Where no one will find it."

He snorted like a bull. "More than one person has to know."

Mysteriously I answered, "It's at the source of life and nourishment."

He thought about it a minute. "You gave it to your MOM?!"

I glanced down the hall. The coast was clear. I pointed to my navel. "You know, umbilical cord."

He made a face. "How'd you—?"

"Duct tape."

"That stuff will rot your skin after a while."

"It's not a permanent solution. But I can't leave it lying around, can't bury it, and can't hide it in the woods. There's no other place."

He giggled. "Hope you don't lose it in all that belly button lint. Hey, you could get a safety deposit box at the bank."

"I don't trust the bank."

"Don't go paranoid on us," he snapped, which was funny coming from my once scaredy-cat cousin. "What do we do about Marcus and Reece?"

I thought a minute. "We show them but don't tell where it'll be hidden. The only reason I'm telling you is in case somebody kills me. If that happens, you get to the morgue first and rip it out."

"You're a nut," he scowled. "That's not going to happen. You're just talking morbid 'cause you—"

"'Cause I almost died and got my bones picked clean by owls and ravens and coyotes? Yeah. It changes you, man. It changes you."

．　．　．　．　．

Mom got past her compulsion to hover over me every single minute, so Dad dragged her out to dinner and a movie. Nothing had been said about Isabel MacMerrit in a while, which was okay with me. I had enough on my mind.

The clan gathered for a powwow around the fire in our family room. For them it might have been business as usual. But after the week in Gilead, I saw my clan in a whole new light: hanging out with them was pure gold. I had three surprises for Reece, all in ring boxes. I handed her the first. She gave me a weird, embarrassed, half-angry look. The guys grinned.

"What's this?" she scowled and turned red. Then she opened it and broke into a big smile.

"It's a Trinity ring," I explained. "The three interlocking rings represent Father, Son, and Holy Spirit. It has a double meaning for the clan: a cord of three strands is not quickly broken. Late Christmas present."

She tried it on, stretched out her hand to show it off, and beamed. Then, just to pay me back for putting her on the spot, she kissed me right on the mouth in front of the guys.

They hollered, "Woohoo!" and "Yeehaw!" and acted like idiots. I went red and handed her the next box. It had the same thing in it: a Trinity ring. "This is from us three guys for Mei. You can send it to her as a reminder that we haven't forgotten her."

She bubbled over and hugged us all.

I handed her the third box. "This is a gift from the armor to all of us. Marcus hasn't seen it either, but I'll let you open it."

She carefully popped open the lid. Lying on a little cushion of satin was the perfect, raindrop-shaped red stone. She touched it with the tip of her finger. "What is it?"

"It's a red diamond," I said soberly. "Maybe the only pure red diamond ever to exist. I found it in a little secret compartment in the nosepiece of the helmet."

We took turns looking at the gem close up in the firelight.

"You're sure it's a diamond?" Marcus asked.

"That's what the jeweler said. It's got to be worth a bundle. But here's the downside: the guy practically groveled to buy it from me, kept going up on the price, insisting that he had to take it into the back room and consult with his associate about it." I nodded knowingly. "He was trying to pull the old switcheroo."

Marcus leaned in to me, glaring. "You showed it to somebody? A piece of the armor?! Man, this is a monster problem!"

"I know that. I'm sorry. But look at it; would you think it's a diamond? All the diamonds I've ever seen are white and shaped like … diamonds!"

Rob defended me. "He didn't know red ones existed. Did *you?*"

Marcus shrugged. "No."

I said, "First question: do we tell the Stallards?"

We discussed it a long time and couldn't come to a conclusion. The old archaeologists had given us free reign with the armor, trusting us with its secrets. But around the fire and with lots of quiet time between words, we each admitted that in the backs of our minds, we'd all questioned their motives. Weird as they were, the Stallards seemed too good to be true. (It did occur to me that they might not even be from this earth, but I chalked that crazy idea up to my recent encounters with the dark side of the spirit world, which can grab onto a person's imagination and not let go.)

Reece said thoughtfully, "After that day at Grafton Institute, they were more nervous than ever about news of the armor leaking out."

Worriedly, Rob added, "The high-powered recording devices and binoculars, how they could track down Francine when the police couldn't even find her ... they're not the crusty old professors we first thought."

"I hate to say this," I concluded, "but we need another opinion." I turned to Marcus. "Hey, is your dad friends with Donovan?"

"Not that I know of."

"He and your dad were both at the gorge when they rescued me. They talked a long time in private, but once I got to the hospital, I never saw Donovan again."

Marcus thought long and hard. "Dad never told me they knew each other, but ..." He sat up, intrigued. "Remember the night we went on maneuvers to find the breastplate, that night down by the tracks? I was curious why our parents agreed to let a total stranger lead us on that operation. Didn't that seem bizarre?"

I shrugged, "I was so antsy that I didn't care. What I'm getting at is this: if your dad knows Donovan who knows the Stallards, and your dad knows the Stallards from years back ..."

Rob said, "We should ask your dad about them."

I added, "We don't have to show him the diamond."

． ． ． ． ． ．

I was surprised that Dom Skidmore would drop everything and come right over. When he joined our circle in the glowing firelight, I got flashbacks of Farr Island and half expected another ghost story. We reminded him that we had all but one piece of the armor and were pretty sure that the whole thing was going to turn out to be valuable. We asked if he had the inside scoop on the Stallards and if they could be trusted.

He looked absently around the room like he was thinking hard. Then he put his hands on his thighs and blew out a big, decisive breath. He squinted briefly at me and barked, "Okay! Here it is. Point one: back during World War II—which was called the war to end all wars, but didn't—there was an archaeologist named Nelson Glueck. While war raged around the world, Glueck continued his work—in the interest of science, you see. The enemy didn't quite grasp that archaeologists have precise knowledge of landscape. And they dig. *They dig!* Caves and tunnels."

He gave us a few minutes to think about that.

"In that war—right under the noses of the enemy and with the full knowledge and cooperation of Allied Intelligence—secret escapes were being prepared in case things went bad and the troops had to flee." He sat back and let it sink in some more. I was drawing a blank. What did this have to do with the Stallards?

Rob's eyes got wide. "Archaeologists on secret missions for the government?"

Dom smiled. "More was at stake than a military victory in those days. If the Allied Forces had failed their mission, we might all be living under the iron fist of global oppression: death camps, firing squads, perverse medical experiments. Point two: throughout history, when persecution of the church is on the rise, people go underground. I don't necessarily mean under the ground as in cellars and caves. It could be in a small group around a dinner table, or sitting by the fire in a nice house on a cold winter evening." He winked at me. "Or in handmade shelters in remote natural hideouts. As we speak, tens of millions of Christians are worshiping God underground."

Rob began, "Are you saying—"

Dom shot him a look. "I'm not saying a thing. All I'm saying is that archaeologists are allowed into areas—even war zones or hostile countries—to do research and rescue antiquities. I'm saying archaeologists know where ancient tombs are. Caves. Tunnels."

Rob asked again, "So are you telling us that—"

"I'm not telling you a thing. All I'm saying is that the war to end all wars didn't. But one is coming that will.. Things are heating up for Armageddon—people's faith being tried, their rights slipping through their fingers—subtle and slow. Today in The Window, some folks have no freedom at all, and death is sure if they speak the name of Jesus. The Window will widen; more and more believers will have to make difficult decisions: 'Do I hide? Do I preach the Word and run? Do I take a stand and die? Or do I play the coward, keep my trap shut? Do I wait for the heat to die down?'" He shrugged.

"Hide where?" Reece asked.

He leaned forward, "Where in the world?"

Rob rolled his eyes at me, and I knew what he was thinking: Dominic Skidmore, long on questions, short on answers. I was sort of getting on his wavelength, though, and saw how you can pass on information by asking really good questions.

"Wait a minute!" Rob cried, looking around at us, his blue eyes wide and wondering. "Newgrange passage tomb! The forbidden tunnel under Dunluce Castle where the Stallards went because they had," he made air quotes, "clearance!"

Reece said excitedly, "There were other tombs at Newgrange. Unexcavated tombs the Stallards knew all about." She asked Dom, "Do you mean that the Stallards are making hiding places all over the world for the Day of Evil?"

Dom threw up his hands. "You didn't hear it from me."

I fell back on the couch, dumbstruck. "They were showing us around! Newgrange, Dunluce, the Christian retreat house in Belfast. They were giving us a tour! So are you saying their archaeology projects are all a front, a way to get into places and make caves and tunnels where people can preach all over the world and then disappear when the Day of Evil comes?"

Dom smiled. "Did I say that? I never said that." He leaned back, locking his hands behind his head. "The big picture, people, has always been about saving the world."

I sat bolt upright again. "Wait a minute! Saving the world? Hold on! Yancy and Peck, the guys who played the boo hags at Farr Island. When we visited the base, Peck signed off saying, 'Gotta get back to saving the world.' What did he mean by that? He wasn't talking military?"

Dom gave me a friendly fist in the arm. "I just can't say, Creek. I just can't say."

Rob asked excitedly, "Are there hiding places around here? And who's Donovan? What part does he play in all this?"

Dom started to make a comment but stopped and took a hard look at Rob. "You're not a believer, are you, Viking?"

Rob's mouth dropped open, he stammered, then cried in a singsong voice, "Uh-huuuh! I believe!"

Dom raised a cool eyebrow and looked in that instant just like his son. "Haven't made it public, Viking. Haven't claimed the name. Haven't joined up. No, sir, I haven't seen your sins floating around in the watery grave of a baptistery." He went eyeball to eyeball with Rob. "Wingate, I got no proof at all of your allegiance to the cause. None. From where I sit, you've been coasting. So in answer to your many questions—" Dom tapped Rob's chin with his knuckle, "I could let you in on the whole secret plan, give you names, addresses, show you the global grid. I could do that, Viking," he said with threat in every muscle, "but then I'd have to kill you."

CHAPTER 15

That death threat from Dom Skidmore was all Rob needed. We were at church the next Sunday. Rob told on himself to his parents and mine about the rubber ducky caper so I couldn't give him payback during his baptism. I was so looking forward to dropping some big animal in on him and causing a sensation that would make church history, but it wasn't to be. When he stepped down into the baptistery, Marcus and I yelled, "Go, Ballyrob!"

With a swelling in my heart, I sat on the third pew with the youth group and watched my cousin claim the name and go under. *Four of my clan of five are in. One to go: Mei. All of the pieces found but the last. One to go.*

. . . . .

I was called in to the principal's office first thing Monday. My mind spun. *What kind of trouble am I in now? Detention for the masked ball incident? Is Abner on a rampage because I whiled away the hours facedown and dying under a two-ton rock in the gorge when I could have been working on Latin declensions?*

Mr. Erwin was middle-aged with a round, ruddy face and manicured hands, a soft-spoken guy who had the respect of the students because he was the real McCoy. Nice but tough. He was wearing a light yellow shirt with a navy tie and gold cuff links. He had me sit in the big chair across from his desk, the seat often warmed by many an innocent Latin student and more often by the big, guilty behinds of the Brill brothers.

"We're so glad you're all right, Elijah," he began. "Everyone was worried about you. When a young person disappears nowadays, the way things are in the world … well, we're all thankful it turned out well. I would like you to speak briefly to the student body before the pep rally today. We meant to have your father come last year and speak on this issue of survival, but regrettably didn't get to it. It's a near miracle you survived, and I think the students may be more likely to listen to an actual story. You've fully recovered?"

My words came out in a rush. "Yeah, I'm fine but the whole school?!"

He tapped a pencil on his desk good-naturedly. "A few minutes is all we want, Elijah. We'd like to present you with an award as well."

"Today?"

"Waiting will only make you more nervous. That's been my experience."

"What do I say?"

"Tell us how you survived, the tools and techniques you used. A few pointers."

"Thanks, but I'm not very good at public speaking. I'm taking speech next year though." I hoped he'd take the hint.

My man-of-action-not-of-words argument didn't cut any slack with Mr. Erwin. By the time I got back to class, I was a wreck. *Me? Speak in front of the whole school!* At lunch I stopped Marcus in the hallway, looking for moral support.

He listened and laughed. "You get an award for lying under a rock for a week? Nice work," and turned to saunter off.

It was just what I needed to hear. "Yeah, no big deal, huh? Crack a few jokes." I gulped hard.

He sauntered back to me and leaned in secretively. "You still don't get it, do you, Creek? You're the leader. So lead."

The day whizzed by. I couldn't concentrate. I got a note on my locker in Reece's handwriting: *You'll be great. Knock 'em dead!* I felt sick to my stomach.

. . . . .

All of Magdeline Independent filed into the gym and filled the bleachers. It felt like a public execution. Mom and Dad were there to see me get a citizenship award. I could hardly breathe. The principal stood behind the mike and said something, but I didn't hear a word until my name came up, "... our own Elijah Creek. Give him your full attention. His trial could one day save your life."

Dazed, I stood, walked forward, and faced the crowd. "Shelter is the first priority," I said in the same way that I had begun dozens of camp classes before. Somehow this was different. My throat went dry. "You can live a week or more without water, a month without food. But in the cold, you have to have shelter. Preferably not a two-ton rock lying on top of you."

They laughed, and I relaxed a little. I explained what shelter I did have: the cliff, an excellent sleeping bag, and the slab, which had both trapped me and stored the heat and, in the end, saved my foot. "I'm standing here today in spite of that rock and because of that rock."

Reece applauded. Her Devo club and a smattering of others followed suit.

"And you need water." I told about how I didn't have water because the canteen was out of reach, how the icicle had formed and melted in a matter of hours. "And fire. Fire is everything: it heats, cooks, sterilizes, lights the dark, keeps wild animals away." I paused. "I saved what little fire I had until the last minute, which was a good thing. The copter might never have spotted me otherwise. I'd been saving it for sterilizing the knife. If no one came by that next morning, I'd decided to use my belt as a tourniquet and amputate my leg."

The crowd had been half attentive until that moment. They went stone still.

"I planned to wait until the temperature was below freezing and I was not in the sun before cutting off my leg. I would have tightened the belt to keep from bleeding to death, and then exposed the stump to ice to freeze the blood to crystals and hopefully stop the flow. Then if I had any fire left, I would have seared the stump to cauterize the arteries. Then I would have crawled home."

Mom's hand clutched her stomach. Dad looked stricken and proud at the same time. All eyes—even Justin Brill's gang—were locked on me. And suddenly I wasn't afraid. I looked at Reece. She nodded as if to say, *Go on.*

I took the mike off the stand and walked along the bleachers. "But that's how my body survived. It's also important to know how to keep your mind from going stark raving crazy alone in the dark; you need to know how not to let the fear swallow you whole out there in the wild. I'm telling you here and now to appreciate your families. Appreciate your blankets and chairs and running water and full refrigerators. They're luxuries a lot of people don't have."

I paced. "Coyotes were closing in on the last day, and I discovered that a nest of blue racer snakes was above my head in the cliff. I don't know how many: fifteen, thirty, a hundred."

A groan of repulsion went up from the crowd.

"One slithered down the tree to check me out but then disappeared. I had a hard time sleeping that night. To sum up, you need a fire kit, good shoes, a stash of food and water, a flashlight—because the darkness is horrible—and some kind of shelter, and this." I pulled the Quella from my pocket and held it up for the crowd to see. "I'll never go anywhere without this again. Anyone know what it is?"

Pitiful few hands went up: Marcus, Rob, Reece, and few from her Devo club. I walked the length of the gym in front of the bleachers, holding up the Quella. "It's the Word of God."

Most looked confused. A few teachers squirmed uncomfortably. Justin's bunch muttered. Mom and Dad smiled uneasily. Mr. Erwin put his hand on the bleacher like he was ready to spring up and put an end to my speech. I walked back to the mike stand. "If that helicopter hadn't spotted me, I probably would have bled to death trying to get home, even with my outdoor skills. Sometimes you just don't make it. But my soul would have made it. Because of this."

You could have heard a pin drop.

"And prayer. Every day at roughly 3:00 a strange calm settled over me. I didn't know until later that my friends gathered every day at that time to pray for me. I felt it. You may not believe me, but it's true; I felt it." I put the mike back on the stand. "There's more to survival than just staying alive."

Electricity coursed through me, energizing and calming me as I sat down. A knot of emotion formed in my throat. I'd just preached a sermon.

I could tell by the look on Mr. Erwin's face that I hadn't given him what he wanted. But I didn't care. He made me get up again and handed me a certificate, and everyone clapped. A few even cheered for me.

The crowd transitioned to the pep rally once the cheerleaders took over; but I wasn't into it. I was thinking about the street preacher in Dublin and how he'd taught me to preach without even knowing it. Sitting there surrounded by screaming students, I realized it was probably my last chance to preach to the whole school. I wished I'd said more.

As we filed out for homeroom, a few people stopped me

and wanted to see the Quella. Some said stuff like, "Good job!" and "Glad you made it, Elijah." Brill was lumbering on ahead. I slipped through the crowd and tapped him on the shoulder.

He turned. "Well if it isn't Nature Boy, crawling out from under his rock."

"Hey, Justin, I wanted to apologize for the incident at the dance. But, um … you don't talk about women that way, not in front of me anyhow." I reached out to shake his hand. He didn't respond, eyeing me darkly as usual. But this time I could see behind the dark to a kind of angry curiosity. I half smiled. "One more thing. I didn't mention it in there, but I found out something really interesting while I was trapped out in the wilderness: you sound a lot like Satan. Strange to say, but it's good that I know that. So thanks for the heads-up."

CHAPTER 16

We called the Stallards about the helmet and the arm piece. They were happy for us and eager to examine them but couldn't come down until their spring break in early March.

Over the next few weeks, I ate like a tick stuck on a big dog, gaining back the twenty pounds I'd lost in Gilead. Except for sensitivity to cold in my left foot, my body recovered. I decided—against the wishes of my mom and the coach—not to go out for track in the spring. They weren't happy, but I had good reasons. For one, I couldn't afford to show up on the sports page of *The Magdeline Messenger* on the outside chance that the New York Jewelers guy had an interest in small-town track.

I hung my hopes on the big contrast between that clean-cut "missing boy" on the front page of the Christmas edition and the shaggy hick who'd showed up in his store with a priceless diamond. I got a haircut and cleaned up my act.

Another reason I had to pass on sports: I kept the red diamond taped to my person at all times and didn't want it ripped off in the school locker room. Every morning in the hallway at school, Rob and I would exchange baseball-type signals, and I'd tell him without a word where it was: navel, underarm, back of the neck, behind the knee, in the shoe.

I didn't walk Main Street much anymore except to stop in at Florence's for early morning grits. If nosy strangers were to show up in town asking about jewelry, I'd hear it first from the Romeos, the Really Old Men Eating Out.

The clan decided to stash the armor in The Castle's attic again. I hated to part with it, but it would be safer there.

As my outer world in Magdeline closed in, my inner world grew like gangbusters. I read from the Quella every morning and night. When the weather warmed a little, I took my new leather Bible and the belt of truth back to Gilead to make peace with what happened. But I made sure to tell Dad where I was. I thanked El-Telan-Yah for the life lessons. There would be no hideout in Gilead—that much was clear. If the Day of Evil came, I'd be in the thick of it, not holed up under a rock.

I came back to camp with good news about the racers. Over twenty mixed in with other breeds had been resting in a big writhing pile above my head. Bo and a couple of naturalists did the retrieval. I'd had my fill for a while. But I got the payoff. My next plane ticket—wherever my destination—would be paid for.

Reece and I talked deep Bible stuff over lunch and didn't care who listened.

Seeing the sparks flying between Reece and me, Emma moved on to greener pastures.

Now that he was a true believer, Rob went crazy on sword research. We had Dowland's journals but figured they'd be no good. If the old man had found the sword, someone would have known. He wouldn't have kept it to himself. The journals got more random and disconnected as he reached his later years. Stanford Dowland, minister of Old Pilgrim Church, had lost the true meaning of having the armor of God. He had drifted over to the dark side until nothing was left of him but a gray, bitter wasteland. I'd gotten a taste of that a few weeks back and didn't want to go there ever again. Think like Dowland? No thanks.

· · · · · ·

The night before the Stallards came, I lay awake with the diamond held to the light, its beautiful red color and perfect shape hypnotizing me. *What's it worth? Where'd it come from? Who hid it in the helmet, and why? They could have sold it—maybe for a million bucks. Hey, I could be a millionaire! Me!*

I made a mental list of all the good I could do with the money: help Dad with the camp's debts; get Reece the best doctor in the world; buy myself a car; buy cars for Rob and Marcus and Reece too; fly Mei to Ohio for the summer; fly us all back to Leap Castle. I dreamed of all the things I could do with my fortune.

But what if … what if … the treasure has been the Stallards' goal all along? What if we're not talking thousands for the armor but millions for the diamond?

Old doubts returned—with a bigger price tag attached.

· · · · ·

This time Aunt Grace didn't mess with the whole froufrou Victorian stuff, and we didn't have to gussy up. The four of us met in Rob's room ahead of time and prayed about what to do.

Marcus led. "We're walking blind, Lord, walking blind. You promised to be a lamp to our feet and a light to our path. We claim it, Jesus! We're claimin' it, mighty Lord! You entrusted us with a treasure. Now we're trusting you to tell us what do."

We decided only to tell the Stallards if we felt unanimous about it.

Dr. Eloise came bursting into the Wingate Tea Room, hugged me hard, and fawned over me for surviving the ordeal. When she heard that I'd named the place Gilead, she burst into a lecture: "East of the Jordan River—the home of the first Elijah! A wild and rugged place it was in his time: hills of shaggy forests, awful solitude, dashing mountain streams, the haunt of fierce beasts! Only the hardiest sheepherders eked out a living from their stone hut settlements. To the sophisticated city dwellers in Jerusalem, the Gileadites were as unsavory as their geography—wild, uncultured, unkempt." She patted my shoulder. "He kidnapped you, didn't he?"

"Who?"

She smiled. "He's allowed. Not the best accommodations from what I heard, but you came back strong. That's often his way. He's forming a core of steel in there." She pecked on my chest with her finger. "Core of steel."

Dr. Dale shook my hand, his little old eyes looking deeply at me. He seemed unable to find any words.

As the others got seated, I asked him quietly, "Did the police question you about my disappearance?"

"They did."

"Any sign of Cravens? Are we still … under the radar?"

He smiled. "For now."

"And did you send Donovan?"

"Yes. Now let's have breakfast."

The clan endured me telling my war story again, each throwing in their parts about the prayer and the failed manhunt. I kept it short.

Munching scones and raspberry Danish pastries, I casually led into the subject Dom had told us about: a global network of hiding places prepared for the Day of Evil. I asked the Stallards, "Say, a while back you were talking about missionaries in The Window, how it's dangerous and kind of like spy work. I was wondering … if a missionary goes into The Window—or anywhere in the world—and gets into trouble there, what will he do?"

Dr. Eloise clacked her teacup down. "First, the code word is *seraph*. We don't openly call anyone in The Window a missionary. It's simply too dangerous."

"Seraph?" I asked.

"An angel of fire, a messenger from the throne of Heaven to the earth below. Our knowledge of the actual beings is scant.

Around 740 BC Isaiah the prophet saw the Lord on a throne, high and exalted. Above the throne were six-winged seraphs calling out to each other, 'Holy, holy, holy is the LORD Almighty; the whole earth is full of his glory.'" Dr. Eloise's voice rose in an arch of drama. "Their voices shook the very walls of the temple!" She looked at us with anticipation. "You might imagine that Isaiah was an emotional wreck at such a sight!"

"But he wasn't," I piped up.

"Oh, but he was! And to make matters worse, here came a seraph—a six-winged glowing creature—with a live burning coal from the altar of God and touched it to Isaiah's mouth!"

"Ouch!" Rob said sympathetically.

She smiled. "Growing pains, children. The coal signified that Isaiah's mouth had been cleansed from sinful talk. He was ready to grow up and be a spokesman of God." When the Lord said, 'Whom shall I send? And who will go for us?' Isaiah could answer with confidence, 'Send me!'

"All we know of seraphs is that they are fiery creatures equipped with pairs of wings to cover their faces and feet and a pair of wings to fly on divine missions."

I frowned thoughtfully. "Fiery creatures with wings, huh?" I snuck a glance at Reece. She smiled back.

"Isaiah's response to this meeting with a seraph was simply to say, 'I am undone,' or in your youth terminology, 'I am dead meat.' Seraphs are holy, powerful creatures who have a part in delivering the message before it's too late. So we call our missionaries seraphs. Please do likewise in the future." She sighed happily. "Aren't these scones just precious? I'd ask for the recipe except I rarely bake."

"Um," I tried again, "but what would a seraph do if he got in trouble?"

She dusted crumbs from her chin. "Run, hide, stand: whatever

God tells him to do. It would depend on the circumstance and God's timing."

"Hide where?" Reece pried.

Dr. Eloise referred the question to her husband. "What would you say, dear?"

"Any of a number of places." He turned to Rob and changed the subject, "Did we hear correctly that you made a public confession of faith in Jesus as your Savior."

"Yes, sir, I did. I'm in."

The Stallards didn't make eye contact, but they both made nice sounds of approval over the breakfast pastries.

CHAPTER 17

The Stallards followed us up two long flights of steps for a look at the helmet.

There in the dim, dusty light of the attic stood the polished armor. The helmet hovered above the breastplate, right arm, belt, and shield, which all seemed to be floating above the shoes. It was as if an invisible warrior were standing ready. Reece gasped. It took a second to register with me that Rob had draped one of the mannequins with black cloth and hung the armor on it. It looked awesome.

We circled around it. Dr. Dale said, "Nice presentation, Mr. Wingate. Very nice."

"I polished it with a soft cloth, being careful not to scratch it."

I watched the Stallards like a hawk, searching their faces, waiting to see if they'd look under the nosepiece, so I'd know if they'd known all along there was a treasure within the treasure. Dr. Eloise whipped out a notebook and pen. "Analysis of the helmet: bronze, a variation of early Greek style. Six strips of steel meet at the top, obviously a later addition."

Rob said, "It's just like the sketch Mei made for you. See the lines etched in the metal and how they arch around, connecting every other end of the steel braces." He took the helmet off the dummy. "Look at it from the top. It makes a kind of flower or star design."

Dr. Dale commented that it looked like the ceiling of a European cathedral, but which one he couldn't remember.

Dr. Eloise went on. "An ornate band circles the head. The band has gold and silver overlays and is engraved with vines and leaves."

I said, "The short spikes sticking out in different directions are the crown of thorns. Those red globs—"

"Enamel, I believe," said Dr. Eloise.

"That's Jesus' blood."

I stepped back when they looked at the nosepiece. Rob explained how the omega, which didn't fit with the earlier style of Greek letters, meant the end. Finally Dr. Dale noticed the inside of the nosepiece. "Looks like a piece was broken off."

Rob offered the little square of chain mail. "Here. We think it was compressed and fastened there. It fits." He demonstrated.

Dr. Eloise made a note. "Extra reinforcement for the forehead? Hardly seems necessary. Hmm." She made a note about how the sides and back were designed to protect the neck. She looked at it inside and out, commented on the murky smell of the lining, and asked Marcus about the retrieval from the lake. We talked about the symbolism, and they told the story of Jesus' death on the cross.

"Notice how elegantly simple they are," she said, "the story and the armor. No gratuitous gore recounted in the text, none of the appalling, haggard depictions you see on crucifixes; nothing of the depth of humiliation and agony our beloved Lord suffered. Yet the death is fully revealed in words and leather and metal: how he was falsely accused, convicted, stripped, whipped, crowned, mocked, spit on, taunted by enemies, abandoned by friends, nailed to a board, and pierced. Exquisitely precise, isn't it? No fluff, just fact."

I said quietly, "When I was trapped out there in Gilead, like a bug in a biology exhibit, I thought about things like that: how it must have been … for him."

Dr. Dale put a comforting hand on my shoulder. "How much more humiliating if everyone in Magdeline had been watching, laughing at you, leaving you there to suffer, your loved ones standing by helpless."

The idea made my skin crawl.

Reece said fiercely, "But nobody gave up."

I touched the crown of thorns, the red brads in the breastplate symbolizing the wounds in his hands and feet, the spear in his side. "They gave up on him, didn't they?"

Dr. Eloise said, "Yes, they did. They went back to their lives, certain their dreams had been dashed."

Dr. Dale examined the left shoulder of the breastplate. "You haven't found the left arm, I suppose."

Marcus said, "No sign at the bottom of Silver Lake. I doubled back twice. I'm ninety-five percent sure it's not down there."

"Maybe the arm is with the sword," Reece suggested.

I shook my head, "The sword would be with the right hand."

"Unless God's left-handed," she argued with a grin.

Dr. Eloise clucked. "Not to anthropomorphize the Almighty too much, but I daresay our creator is ambidextrous."

We went on thinking about where the missing left arm might be.

Dr. Dale said thoughtfully, "A reference in Isaiah ... about his holy arm. Marcus, if your Quella is handy?"

"Mine's here," I said eagerly, "and with fresh batteries." I punched in the words *holy arm* and read: "'The LORD will lay bare his holy arm in the sight of all the nations, and all the ends of the earth will see the salvation of our God.'"

"Yes, of course," Dr. Dale said, moving beside the armored mannequin to demonstrate. "See, I am extending the right hand of fellowship to my friend." He shook my hand. "But in war that same right hand fights the enemy." He detached the shield from

Rob's model and held it in his left hand. Wielding an invisible sword with his right, he re-enacted a sword fight. "See here. We, the soldiers for Christ, must wear the shield of faith, traditionally on the left arm, while we hold the sword in the right. Any ideas about why the left arm might be missing?"

"I know!" said Reece. "When we stand shoulder to shoulder with our shields of faith side by side, our left arms are protected by each other."

"You still need your left arm to hold the shield," Rob said.

"But not the arm piece covering it," Reece argued.

Dr. Dale said, "Good point. Here's another idea: we humans need the shield of defense. But when God comes to judge the earth, he will have no need to defend himself. He will come brandishing the sword—unconquerable, impervious to injury—leveling every foe in his path. No need of a shield. The devastation will be utterly one-sided. Symbolically we might say he will lay bare his holy arm in sudden and complete annihilation."

He put his hand on the shoulder of the armor as if to lean on a friend for support. Nearly whispering he said, "Imagine what it will be when the power that created the universe pinpoints his wrath on one tiny blue planet hanging on nothing in the cosmos."

The dusty air in the attic seemed to stir and quiver. I half expected the armor to move. It was the coolest kind of eerie.

Marcus said firmly, "Those demon hoards will never know what hit 'em."

Dr. Eloise whispered, "We must pray, children. We must warn the people."

"One more piece, and we'll have the whole set," I said with conviction.

Dr. Eloise smiled sadly. "Dear Elijah. We have exhausted our resources on the matter. The trail on the sword went cold ages ago."

"I'm not giving up. Going into battle without your weapon is a suicide mission."

Rob said in a scholarly way, "My research suggests possibly Serpent Mound just south of here. The opposite of the Word of God is the silence of evil. I looked for a place of dormant evil."

"Like Leap Castle," I offered.

Reece said, "The opposite-clue thing was Dowland's idea. He never found the sword, so it can't be in an opposite place."

Rob kept on. "It makes sense that the sword would be hidden in a place that has nothing good to tell us. Like that throne of Satan in a museum in Europe."

"Or Leap," I insisted, wondering if the owl hovering over me in Gilead was a sign.

There was a lull in the conversation. The Stallards sat tiredly on the wrecked Victorian couch, looking like a faded portrait from days gone by. I felt sorry for them, driving so far, working so hard. I looked at the others for a final word about the diamond. Do we tell them? my eyes asked. It was unanimous. I said to the Stallards, "So that's the end of the trail for every secret of the armor. There are no more secrets?"

Dr. Eloise sighed. "Well, there is another, but it is so fantastical that we hardly dare to mention it." She looked at Dr. Dale. "By which of its names shall we call it: the Stone of Abel, the Tear of Blood, the Netsach Prism? We've long assumed it was myth born to explain the Hindu practice of—"

"I have it," I interrupted.

They stopped dead.

I had transferred it from my navel to my pocket when no one was looking. I proudly held it out in my palm. "The red diamond."

They stared in disbelief. "How ... where?" murmured Dr. Eloise.

"It was in the nosepiece encased in clay and overlaid with metallic paint. I only found it because it had soaked in the lake for the last year. That little piece of chain mail with the encrypted verse had been fastened over it."

I let them examine it. Pressing their wrinkled cheeks together, they stood and held the red stone to the light, their eyes glittering.

Rob added, "You guys said the root word meant 'dug out.' So the treasure had to be dug out of the helmet. Pretty smart, huh?"

Dr. Dale looked at his wife. "Dear heart! Could it … is it … and if it is, what gemologist can be trusted to confirm its authenticity?"

"Oh, I don't know!" Her breathing shuddered. "No one!"

"Uh," I winced, "I already took it to someone."

Their eyes drifted from each other and rested on me, wide and fearful.

"I'm sorry, but I'd never heard of a red diamond. I thought it was glass. Doesn't it look like a hunk of old necklace or a piece from a chandelier?"

Dr. Eloise came over to me, folded my hand in hers as if to comfort me, and asked point blank, "Who knows?"

"New York Jewelers, the business that moved in when The Roanoke got blown away."

"And what did they say to you … when they saw it?"

"He wanted to buy it, made three offers, the biggest one being a thousand dollars. He kept wanting to take it to the back room to show his associate, said he'd be glad to recut it and put it in a piece of jewelry for me."

She nodded. "Aha! The old switcheroo. But you were not fooled."

"He tried to get my name."

"But you didn't!" Dr. Eloise froze. "Did you?"

"I told him my family was from Georgia and I was known

in some parts as George Telanoo."

Reece cackled and scolded, "Elijah! Where are you known as George Telanoo?"

"Dublin," I said sort of shyly. "At that little church meeting I went to. After the run-in with Cravens, I got skittish about tossing my name around." I asked Dr. Dale, "Is that lying? I don't want to lie, but you guys don't use your real names, so I thought maybe it'd be okay."

He explained, "It's a gray area, children. We were advised early on for the sake of the mission; there are drawbacks, certainly, but we take comfort in the knowledge that angels often appear incognito when necessary and for the ultimate good. Even Jesus hid his true identity until the proper time."

"Where will you be keeping the stone?" Dr. Eloise asked me.

Rob opened his mouth to answer, but I beat him to it. "I move it to a new location every day for maximum security. It's my fault that the news is out; I take full responsibility for keeping it safe."

For a long moment, Dr. Eloise sat on the couch with the diamond nestled in her frail hand, shaking her head in disbelief. "Of all the mythic tales about the armor, I was sure this one could not be real. It has been called the Tear of Blood for obvious reasons, the Stone of Abel from the murder of Adam's son at the hands of his brother Cain. God called from Heaven, "Your brother's blood cries out to me from the ground." God does not let bloodguilt go unpunished. The blood of his people speaks across the ages and will cry out in one voice at the end. So says the prophet Isaiah. Netsach refers to the winepress of wrath in Isaiah 63." She quoted: "'Who is this, robed in splendor, striding forward in the greatness of his strength?'"

Dr. Dale answered, "'It is I, speaking in righteousness, mighty to save.'"

"'Why are your garments red, like those of one treading the

winepress?'" she went on.

He responded, "'I have trodden the winepress alone; from the nations no one was with me. I trampled them in my anger and trod them down in my wrath; their blood spattered my garments, and I stained all my clothing. For the day of vengeance was in my heart, and the year of my redemption has come.'"

Dr. Dale faced the armor and said another verse: "'I will make your forehead like the hardest stone, harder than flint. Do not be afraid of them or terrified by them.'" He said to us, "This verse was the one clue we believed. But since the word for hard stone—*adamant*—can also mean 'sharp,' it seemed likely that the crown of thorns was the answer. Now that we see the stone really exists, wisps of stories throughout the ages converge. Hindus have legends of sacred rivers where red diamonds are found. We may deduce that this stone came from India and at some point in history was implanted in the armor. The Hindu practice of wearing a red dot between the eyes as a symbol of sacrifice and sacred service derived from this singular pure red diamond, probably dating from the earliest centuries BC."

Dr. Eloise looked lovingly at the stone. "Oh, the lessons in one tiny stone! They say a diamond is transparent. But one can't see through it entirely because it is always reflecting back at you. And it is a stone of judgment; how one behaves as owner of such a gem says much about his character."

Dr. Dale went on, "Made from the earth's mantle, born of fire, diamonds are rugged, created to survive in the most hostile environments. The red diamond is a superstone. The properties which make it unbreakable also make it beautiful. Such is the warrior. His hardships make him strong."

They both smiled at me. Dr. Eloise said, "You are different now, aren't you, Elijah? Your trial has toughened you?"

I nodded.

She put the Tear of Blood in my hand without a second thought, no trembling, no greedy fingers, no trying to talk me out of it like the jeweler did. "You will become stronger still. Children, surely you have already deduced that this stone is the only one of its kind known to exist. Unfortunately, the tantalizing news is out. The Tear of Blood is a holy grail, not just of the gem world, but of the antiquities world, and symbolically of the spirit world ... for the blood of Jesus is indestructible, shed in agony, beyond worth, still crying out from Jerusalem where it was poured out, still changing the course of history to its fiery conclusion.

"This little rock will be more sought after than Noah's ark or the lost ark of the covenant from Old Testament times. The armor of God with all its parts is not just a New Testament treasure. It spans all millennia, from the cherubim's sword in the garden to the mantle of Elijah to the timeless *omen* belt—all eras all at once. It cannot be catalogued, carbon-dated, typified, or classified. It is not meant to be displayed but used."

Marcus had been quiet, leaning against the wall with his arms crossed. "We're targets now, aren't we? Why didn't you tell us about the diamond before, about the risks involved in finding the armor?"

Dr. Dale's head dropped sadly. "We didn't entirely believe the myth. And why send you children searching for a fictional jewel or continue the quest out of wrong motives as Mr. Dowland apparently did?"

I agreed. "For him it became about getting rich and getting even."

Dr. Eloise added, "And nothing of the Spirit. We didn't want anything standing in the way of the real quest. So," she clapped her hands together under her chin, "the jeweler knows of the mythic stone. If he is foolish enough to let the word out, which he might be, then you must each keep a bag packed and your passports at the ready. Keep eyes and ears open." She eyed me. "And stay out of the headlines if at all possible."

"I already quit track. So … um, what is the Tear of Blood worth, do you think?" I kept a steady voice.

"Would you offer it to the highest bidder?" she asked.

"No."

"Would you sell if off, dismembering the armor of God for personal gain?"

"No."

"Then your question is purely academic."

CHAPTER 18

Spring was in the air. Things in my life had gone back to normal except that everything had changed. Rob stayed busy but was quieter than usual. I went through classes, sometimes in a daze, wondering what our futures held next. And the tiny stone I carried on my body began to feel as heavy as that slab in Gilead. It was on my mind every minute of the day.

First thing almost every morning at school, Rob would ask, "Where is it?" and I'd say, "Left shoe," or point to my armpit or navel. But after a while, I just couldn't hack the burden of having it with me every minute. So I made stash places: a tiny pocket on the back of the Indian blanket hanging in my room, a geode that I'd cracked open and sat next to my arrowhead collection, the knothole in the highest log on my wall, and so on.

I made a list of the stash places on an index card and had a paper clip pointing to the day's location so I wouldn't forget where I put it. That way if something happened to me, Rob would be able to find it. We had a pact.

Marcus was more withdrawn and moody. He was tired of waiting on God—like I had been before my week in Gilead. He still liked Miranda, but I now knew why he kept it cool with her. She wasn't a believer. I understood why that makes all the difference.

Emma had glommed onto Greg Moline after he won the motorcycle. So Reece and I hung out over lunch every day. I helped her with her tray and books and stuff, and nobody gave me grief.

People at school looked at me differently—partly because of my sermon that day in assembly but mostly because I'd lived though a week in the wild. I was unofficially dubbed Most Likely to Survive of the freshman class. Sometimes they'd ask to see the Quella or want to know what it was really like out there when I was trapped. I was still learning; God was still teaching me his thousand lessons.

· · · · ·

Spring dragged on until early May when things started to change quickly. I spotted Marcus with a letter in his hand, pacing like a panther in front of my locker. I hadn't seen him so unnerved since he'd crawled on his belly to the edge of the Cliffs of Morte.

He met me halfway down the hall. "They really cut to the chase this time." He snapped the letter open and read quietly as we walked.

Children,

Our worst fears are confirmed. Your foolish jeweler believed he could quietly inquire in the diamond community about the stone. The industry is abuzz, with word rapidly spreading to the antiquities circuit. Be on your guard! Our contacts in Dublin tell us Cravens has been in a fever since our visit. After that fateful meeting, we must face the appalling truth that there is an information leak in our network. No one else to our knowledge had believed in the armor of God outside our circle, or cared to search for it. We must wonder how Dowland knew.

By the way, Elijah, when we meet again might we get a sampling of your blood? We are a bit curious about your lineage regarding Native American roots. Your mother, we hear, is not having much luck on her side of the family tree either. Perhaps our genealogist can help.

Marcus grinned at me. "They want your blood." Then he went back to reading:

But back to the crisis at hand. Cravens's motives are clearly greed and fame. His feeble institute struggles to stay afloat; they need funding. Such is the case with many relic hunters worldwide. As for the diamond market, the existence of the stone has rocked the establishment.

As if we need further complication, those in the field of spiritual warfare believe the discovery of the armor is significant—one of many signs of end times. We must take great care of it for the time being so that its lessons will not be lost.

There is an upcoming conference of our core people in a location and time yet to be determined. With your permission we would like to take the armor. All of you may accompany us—of course.

We've submitted our resignations at the university and are moving our office to another city in order to be more liquid, financially and geographically. Thankfully we are not homeowners.

I interrupted him. "Wait a minute. They're going into hiding?"

"Sounds like it." He read on:

Don't be anxious for us. We're entering the next chapter of our lives, as are you.

Elijah, since the stone has been singularly connected to you (so cleverly disguised as the unkempt George Telanoo from Georgia!), we are—how shall we put this?—discussing what to do with you should things take a sudden turn. You made it clear to the jeweler that you were not interested in selling. Your evasive behavior surely piqued his attention. You, first and foremost, must keep a keen eye on your surroundings.

We don't suppose you speak any other languages, do you? Marcus, could you be of any help here?

Marcus looked up from the letter and chuckled, "How's the Latin coming along?"

I snorted. *"Cadens asinus undique portat nuper caseum."*

He shrugged. "Sounds pretty good. What's it mean?"

"The falling donkey on all sides carries recently cheese."

He gave me a look.

"I forgot to study for today's quiz. Abner almost had a stroke. Called me the most pitiable of linguists in her tenure. I don't even know what that means, and it's English. I'm not a man of words."

"You got that right."

Rob walked up and peeked over Marcus's shoulder. "What's up? Hey, a letter from the Stallards? Cool!"

Marcus went back to reading:

True, we could sell the gem and be done with it. But then we expose ourselves and the armor to the world. So, you ask, since our relic is not the actual spiritual armor we will wear in upcoming battles, why not just turn the thing over anonymously to a museum?

We cannot answer that question except to repeat that the armor may have stories yet to tell us. And—as much as we hesitate to mention it—there remains the gnawing issue of the missing sword. We have no words either of comfort or hope.

Finally, if you hear of trouble from our sector, disavow all knowledge of us and press on. The Almighty will lead you. However, do contact us if you see anything suspicious in your area. We'll send news of our whereabouts when we get settled. Above all, be strong and courageous. Angels of fire hover near, seen and unseen; seraphs fly to and fro worldwide. We can spirit you away in a matter of hours if need be. But in the end, the quest will be yours. You children began it, and you must carry it to its certain conclusion. We'll keep you posted.

Traveling light,
The Stallards

"'Certain conclusion?' What certain conclusion?" Rob asked.

"I think they mean God's plan," Marcus answered flatly. "We follow blind."

Before the week had passed, Reece heard from Mei. I knew something was up when she grabbed me in the hall and shoved me into our corner. "I don't know what this means," she said shakily. "In Devo club we keep coming across Scriptures about the islands. 'Be silent before me, you islands! Let the nations renew their strength! Let them come forward and speak; let us meet together at the place of judgment.' 'The islands will look to me and wait in hope.' And then I hear this quiet voice in my heart saying, *You need to go there. You need to go there.* So I'm thinking, sure okay, Lord—one of these days. Then I got this!" She pulled a letter from her purse. It was from Mei.

"Hold it," I said. "This is for the whole clan."

· · · · ·

Running ahead of the pack after school (it was raining, so Reece and the guys got a ride), I headed into Florence's but had to make a quick U-turn when I spotted the New York Jewelers guy buying coffee. I ran back outside, leaped into their back seat, and said, "Change of plans. Tree House Village!"

Like in the good old days, we gathered with camp snacks and hid ourselves away high in the feathery, light green trees of spring. Reece read Mei's letter:

Dear Reece, Elijah, Rob, and Marcus,

How are you? I am doing well. Thank you again for my Trinity ring. I wear it every day and remember my best friends. School is very hard. I am jealous that you will be out in a few weeks!

We have had a few earthquakes lately. Most are small, but one lasted many seconds and was scary!

I have been reading the Bible, and I have many questions. But

I do believe in Jesus. His story is true! I didn't understand that the time of all history is divided on the life of Jesus—BC and AD. Until I met you, I thought Jesus was a hero from fairy tales like Hercules. But he is real. I love to read about him very much. He was kind and strong.

Is he like my friends in Magdeline? I think so a lot.

I have found a church in my village. It is different from your big American church. It is very small, and the people have many struggles. I now see how dark and sad my village is. Our valley is a beautiful place with friendly people. But their lives are hopeless. People live with much fear. We pray to small gods, but it is just wishing. People are afraid of oni—*demons. Everyone goes to temples and shrines. It is just custom but so hard to leave. The family is very hurt if I stop the customs!*

When I started to read the Bible, God woke me up!

Please come and help me show my friends the love and power of God like you did for me. Thank you, Reece, for being my best friend. Thank you, Elijah, for saving my life. Thank you, Marcus and Rob, for being cool guys who will spend time with the gaijin *girl.* Arigatou gozaimasu! *Thank you very much!*

I want to come to Magdeline this summer, but I cannot. I must study! But if you come to my home, I am indebted to be a good hostess. This is important to Japanese people! Please come and rescue me from study!

Greetings to Stallards and all your nice parents.

Love and peace,
Mei Aizawa

PS. I know it costs a lot for you to come. If you cannot, it is okay. But I am reading the Bible, and I don't understand so much.

"He put on righteousness as his breastplate, and the helmet of salvation on his head; he put on the garments of vengeance." Then

it said, "So will he repay wrath to his enemies ... he will repay the islands their due." It makes me worried that God will use his armor against me because I live on an island. Can you explain to me? Can you help me?

Thank you, Reece. I love you all.

Reece crushed the letter to her heart. "We have to go! We have to!"

I said, "Sure. Okay." But I was thinking, *Impossible.*

· · · · ·

I sat on the steps of Mag High. It was an hour before classes started, but that morning I couldn't sleep. *Three weeks until I can shut the door to Abner's class forever. Three weeks to freedom: campfires, working with Dad, night hikes and owl calls, nature walks through Council Cliffs, hanging out with the clan, and climbing Great Oak again ... with Reece ... maybe.*

I held the Tear of Blood in my fist.

Reece got dropped off by her mom. She came up, sat down beside me, glanced at my closed hand, and made a sarcastic face. "Is that where you're hiding it today?"

I opened my fingers enough for her to see the diamond. It picked up the sun's rays and glowed. "I don't know what to do with it. Rob was right; duct tape is very bad for your skin." I didn't tell her I'd worn raw places around my waist and under my arms. I didn't tell her that the stone was wearing out more than my skin. It was wearing my soul down.

"Did you pray about what to do?"

"Um, not yet."

"Don't forget what you learned in Gilead every day at 3:00. Prayer works."

We sat there looking at each other in the cool quiet of morning. I studied her pretty face. I noticed her gold star earrings.

I reached up and pinched her earlobe. Then I pinched mine, thinking about the size and thickness.

She instantly knew what I was thinking. "Implant it? Oh, that would hurt. You'd have to get a doctor to do it. He'd think you were—"

I broke in, "A dumb kid starting a new fad."

"He probably wouldn't do it. He'd ask questions. Anyway, you can't let anyone else see the Tear of Blood. And you better not try it yourself. It would get infected and swell up."

I agreed. "I guess we won't be able to use the we're-dumb-kids excuse much longer. That's a shame. It works so well."

She grinned. "We're almost sophomores."

"Can't wait." We turned that over in our minds. Absently I felt behind my ear, the top part where the skin seemed sort of loose over the cartilage. It would be a good place. It might work ...

She reached out her hand. "Let me see the stone. Maybe the clue for the sword is on it or in it," she said.

I shook my head. "Rob put it under a microscope."

"It's beautiful." She took it and rolled it around in her palm. "Hard to believe people would kill for it though."

I looked at her a long time. "I've gotta do something with it."

"Your nerves have to be shot. You're the only person in the world connected to it. And the guy in New York Jewelers works right down the street. You pass him every day on the way home!"

"Not anymore. I cut through yards and follow the tracks behind the bank or across the Morgan farm."

"He probably wouldn't recognize you," she said encouragingly. "You looked a lot different right after you came out of Gilead—all skinny and grungy. You've spiffed up. New clothes. Nice haircut. More muscle. She squeezed my arm and smiled. "No more looking like Dowland—what a relief!"

We got quiet. I took the gem, slipped it into the tiny leather pouch I'd made, peeled the hunk of duct tape off my ankle, and secured it in place beside my ankle bone.

I stared out across the school lawn, disheartened. "We have the armor but no weapon."

"It's symbolic. Don't forget that. You do have the Word. The Quella."

"Yeah, but ..."

"I know." She sighed. "I'm tired of waiting too. So is Marcus. He's ready for action."

I shuddered. "Don't say that! The last time I complained about waiting on God, I ended up under a two-ton rock. Then I was really waiting! I say God can take all the time he wants! We'll deal with it."

"You know, though, looking back over the past year and a half, so much has changed, and pretty fast. Just think about it."

"Yeah. When Rob was baptized it hit me: four of my clan of five are in."

She nodded. "One to go: Mei. And all of the pieces are found but the last."

"One to go," I said. Hope started creeping back into my soul. Reece had that effect on me.

"Remember how we doubted every time, Elijah? We thought we'd never find a piece; then we'd find it."

"You didn't doubt, Reece. You never doubted."

"Sometimes I did."

Buses pulled in; kids piled out.

I stood and helped Reece up. "There's nothing we can do about the sword right now."

"But we can do something about Mei. You can complete your clan. She's ready. She needs us. And God keeps saying to me, 'You need to go there.'"

We climbed the steps and headed into Mag High. My hopes

still lagging, I said to her, "Ireland's one thing, Reece. But Japan? That seems impossible."

"Impossible," she murmured with a mysterious smile. She looked up at me and chirped, "Perfect!"

THE
CARPET
OF
BONES

BOOK 7

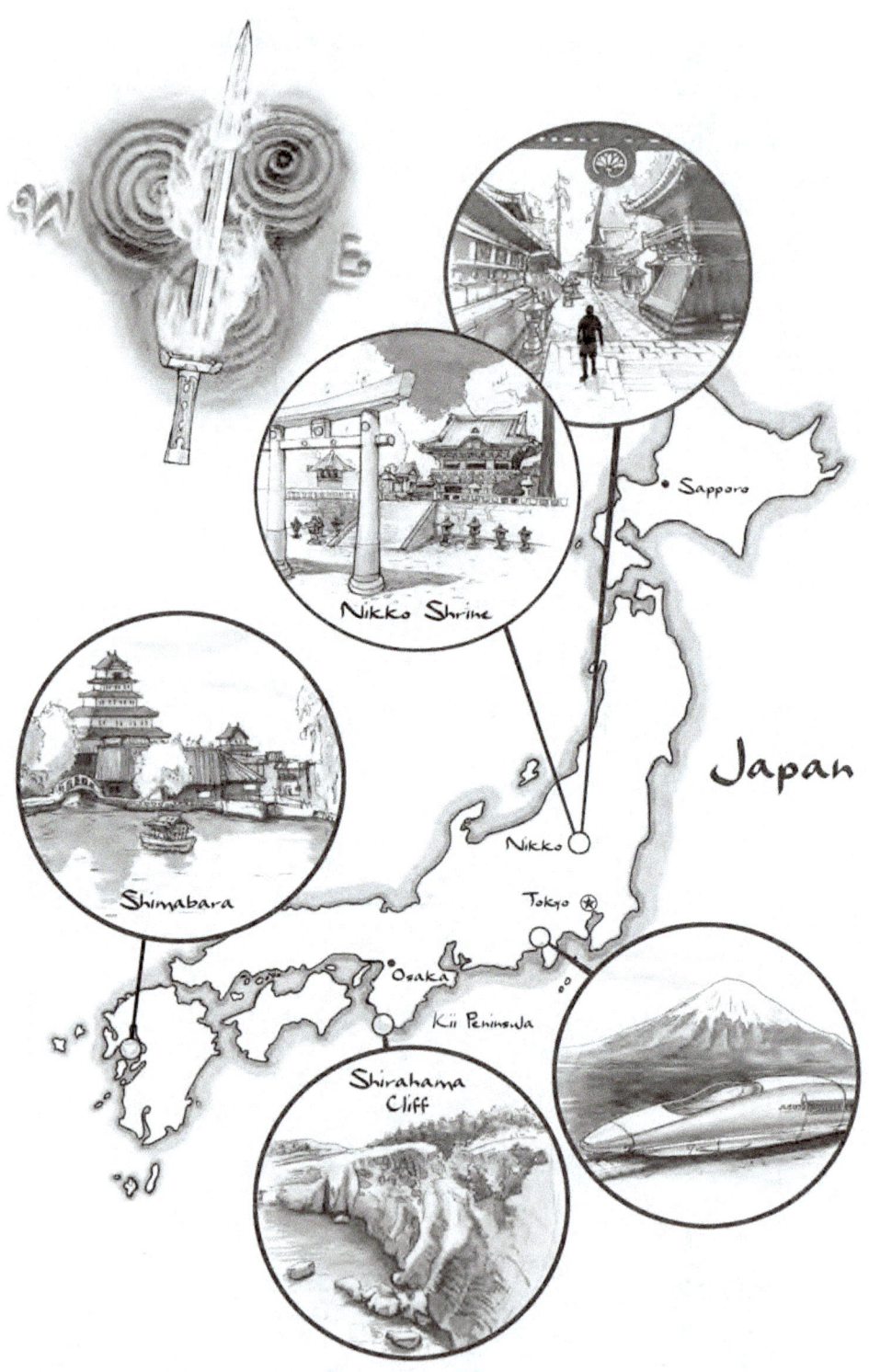

Sapporo

Nikko Shrine

Japan

Shimabara

Nikko

Tokyo

Osaka

Kii Peninsula

Shirahama Cliff

The grass withers and the flowers fall,
but the word of our God stands forever.
—Isaiah 40:8

CHAPTER 1

It was too quiet. The coming of spring marked more than a year since I'd made it out of Gilead, the isolated gorge in Telanoo where I'd nearly frozen my foot off and died of thirst. I'd also survived Abner's Latin class, a slower way of dying, stretched out over two whole semesters.

Reece's mom and Officer Taylor had gotten married. (A week before the ceremony, Reece's dad came back and hung around acting weird, but the whole police force was at the wedding, so there wasn't any trouble.) We four—Reece, Rob, Marcus, and myself—were all in various stages of driver's ed, constant reminders of Mei being gone. She was in Japan where getting a license costs thousands.

And I was back on the track team—Mom insisted. I had laid low for months, saying that I needed to give my foot time to heal, but I was more concerned with protecting the priceless Tear of Blood diamond by staying out of the limelight. After rejoining the team, my picture was in *The Magdeline Messenger* once for winning regionals, but I was just a big blur crossing the finish line, so that was good. Since nothing sinister had happened over the last year, I figured anyone hunting for the diamond had lost my scent. But just to be safe, my shadow rarely ever darkened Main Street in Magdeline, Ohio. If I had to go into town, I'd cut through Owl Woods, dodge Morgan's prize bulls, cross the tracks, and wind through back streets. Not that I was afraid. After Gilead, I couldn't think of one thing that scared me: not hunger or cold or nests of blue racers. Not even the voice of the evil one—which also had gone quiet. The whole Gilead nightmare had pretty much cleaned the cobwebs from every dark corner of my mind. Now, I don't recommend lying facedown under a two-ton stone slab in the dead of winter for any reason, but Reece said God worked it out for good. She called the fearlessness in me the work of the Holy Spirit. I didn't understand it, but I didn't doubt it. Reece had always known more about God than I did.

My clan of four got together every now and then to do Bible studies, which were sometimes interesting. But as far as the search for the sword was concerned? Zero. God wasn't giving any new clues. Mostly we went about life like regular kids while the belt of truth, breastplate of righteousness, shoes of peace, shield of faith, helmet of salvation, and right arm of fellowship hung on a mannequin collecting dust in the attic of The Castle. Sometimes I'd go up there and sit for hours in the dim light, just looking at the armor, wondering if this was how Dowland ended up crazy. But no, the waiting hadn't done him in; greed had. He'd really been searching for the Tear of Blood all along and never found it. For sure, Dowland would have rolled over in his grave to know his treasure had been in the helmet the whole time and was now in the sweaty palm of the kid he'd tried to kill, a kid named George Telanoo. (Which was really me, Elijah Creek. But after the sales manager in New York Jewelers went into a fever over the diamond, I'd gone incognito as the geeky George from Georgia, stashing the Tear of Blood in ever-changing secret places—just in case.)

Over the year the clan got a few chatty notes from the Stallards, asking about our progress on the search for the sword. They'd moved to Boston and told me to put off sending them any of my blood until they got established.

Rob and Emily were kind of a thing, though Rob followed Marcus's advice about not getting too cozy with a nonbeliever. Reece and I were still best friends and then some. She kept feeling that God was telling us to go to Japan and help Mei, but nobody had that kind of money except Marcus. Meanwhile, the armor sat in Rob's attic without its sword, a ragtag relic inscribed with words of power. Just standing there waiting ...

Camp Mudjokivi geared up for another summer. And except for the crazy fact that Florence's was now the new cool hangout— thanks to Marcus's addiction to grits and bacon—everything was the same old same-old.

I often wondered why we'd never found a left arm piece. Could it be a sign? Had God bared his arm for battle? Sometimes I'd imagine him waiting like an archer, his eye on a target, elbow locked, and I was the arrow drawn into the bow he was pulling back ... back ... ever so slowly.

An arrow never knows when the archer is going to release the bowstring and send it flying. I can tell you from my experiences with bow hunting that when you get a target in sight, it's best to stay in smooth constant motion from the second you draw until the second you release. It was making me crazy, my life moving slow and fluid like an arrow aimed and circling the target but going nowhere. So imagine my surprise when one morning in early June I heard a knock on the door and opened it to find the Stallards standing there.

They were dressed in tropical shirts, white pants, and sandals with white socks. (I guess compared to Boston, June in Ohio felt like the tropics.) Dr. Dale had his usual shabby briefcase. Dr. Eloise said, "We tried to call several times on our way down, but the line was always busy."

"My sisters live on the phone now," I apologized. "Um, come in."

"Is your mother home?" Dr. Eloise asked skittishly.

"Yeah, she's reading out on the patio."

"Might we speak with her a moment?"

When Mom came in, she was shocked and seemed embarrassed—probably because of the negative way she'd talked about the Stallards during the past year. But she sat the old archaeologists on the sofa in the living room and offered iced tea. "I'll have to make some."

While she clattered dishes in the kitchen, I sat on the ottoman and whispered, "What's up?"

Dr. Eloise beamed, "Everything, Elijah! Everything's up!"

"Is that ... good?"

She spread her hands out. "Who knows?" She leaned in suddenly. "The armor's still in your possession? The gem?"

"Yeah. But no sword."

"We have much news. Are the others available?"

"Rob's at acting camp, but he'll be back tonight."

"We have many things on our agenda: a peek at Gilead if you are agreeable to guiding us there, a discussion about The Window, and—at long last—details on the global conference! We've arranged for it to be held in Japan so that you and your friends may kill two birds with one stone."

"Actually three birds killed, my dear," said Dr. Dale. "Visiting Mei. The training. And the first battle."

"Okay, but we don't have the sword," I said, keeping my voice low. "Doesn't each piece have a lesson for us? Should we do a battle without our weap—"

She dismissed me with a wave of her fingers. "We've done our best; mustn't worry; have to move ahead."

Mom came back but stayed in the doorway as if she were afraid to get too close to the Stallards. "Tea's brewing." She paused awkwardly. "How can I help you?"

Dr. Dale said, "Perhaps your son told you that we requested a sample of his blood a while back, to help you trace your family roots."

Mom's jaw dropped. Her eyes drilled me. "No. He didn't."

Dr. Dale went on calmly, "Well, it's been ... has it been a year already? And we've been very busy—relocating. We have substantial resources at our disposal and have taken the liberty to check into the MacMerrit family line. Your genetic information will help greatly. But that is only one reason for our visit. I'm sure you know how badly the children have wanted to reunite with their friend Mei Aizawa."

Mom smiled blankly.

"We can be of help there as well. Our global conference is in August and takes place in the mountains north of Tokyo. Our associates were glad to adjust their plans—change the date and the location—for that very purpose. We apologize that it has taken us so long, but the conference involves many people spread out over sixty countries."

Having known the Stallards for more than two years now, I still had to snicker at their nerve. Even talking bloodletting and global meetings, how could Mom refuse? They'd gone to a bucket of trouble. She'd look like the jerk of the century.

Mom tried to smile. "Well, I certainly appreciate all the work you've done, but—"

"Yes, yes! The money," Dr. Eloise cut in, rocking back dramatically. "The money! Always a problem in this world." Then she chirped, "But! We can be of help there too. Our constituents—though their resources are slimmer than you would imagine—are chipping in. Granted, it won't cover the whole cost, but think of the financial perks: for three weeks you won't have to feed the boy!" The Stallards chuckled and winked at me. "And what an opportunity for the children's education. By happy coincidence, a team of young people known as the Students of the Seven Seas will be at the conference. High school age, like Elijah."

She pulled out a pamphlet with a cruise ship on the front and handed it to Mom. Sounding like an old-time encyclopedia salesman, Dr. Eloise gave her spiel: "Your child will have the chance to discover the world through others' eyes and experience fascinating cultures. And look there on page three: information about the conference. As a mother myself, I'd jump at the chance to give my child a visit to the lush mountains and teeming cities of Japan for a fraction of the regular exchange program cost. A real bargain."

Mom frowned at the pamphlet. The short leash she'd had me on for the last year was straining, ready to snap. I wanted to go! I could practically smell the salt air. I could taste the fancy little Japanese meals Mei made when we built the road through Telanoo. I could hear Marcus's running travelogue and Rob's smart remarks. I could see Reece at my side grinning from ear to ear.

"Russ and I will need to discuss this," Mom said doubtfully.

I scooted to the edge of the ottoman. "It's educational, Mom! For social studies this fall, I could do a paper on Japanese government or something!"

The Stallards smiled at me, their eyes glittering in a way that was always a little unnerving. Dr. Eloise stood. "Of course, Jodi. Of course, talk it over with your husband. We're in the area for a few days on several items of business." She turned to me. "While we're here, Elijah, we'd love to see the place where you nearly lost your life."

I went straight to Dad, spilling everything before Mom could talk him out of it. "It's three weeks at the end of summer, Dad. I can line up a replacement for my chores. And about them drawing my blood, okay, sure it's weird, but the Stallards know how to find things out. They tracked down Francine Dowland when the police couldn't! It might help Mom to know the truth about her past."

Somehow in the next few days, after a parent meeting with the Stallards and a late-night phone conversation with Dom Skidmore, my parents reluctantly gave the okay. I thanked them a zillion times. Especially Dad, because nowadays more than ever he depended on me to fill in the gaps at camp and—as he'd say with a sad smile—"Keep an extra eye on the twins, will you? Just until your mom is back to her old self." I could tell he was going to miss me.

. . . . .

The camp nurse gave me a strange look about drawing blood but went ahead. I'd done so much for her over the years—calming kids down when they got sand thrown in their eyes, carrying bigger kids up to her station when they sprained an ankle—she owed me big time.

My blood got sent off to who-knows-where, and then I took the clan and the Stallards—outfitted in safari shorts and mountain boots—to Gilead for archaeology and a picnic. We drove two carts through Telanoo until the road ended, then headed west, hiking the rough terrain. We guys took turns carrying Reece on our backs.

The little old scientists cooed over Gilead's wall inscribed in ancient *Ogham* script: "The right hand of God is a shield—a prayer." They took pictures and rubbings and insisted again that we keep my discovery quiet. I told the story of what happened there, and then we spread a picnic on the big slab of rock that had nearly killed me. Dr. Dale gave a prayer of celebration for my rescue, and we dove into the food.

Dr. Dale sat his skinny self on the ground cross-legged with his plate balanced on his knee, acting younger than he was, more spry. "You recall our telling you about The Window." On the ground in front of him, he spread a map of the world showing a wide strip of land above the equator, shaded in red. It reminded me of a map of Magdeline showing the path of damage after the tornado struck. "The Window encompasses almost sixty countries across ten thousand miles. To be sure, there are many dark and dangerous places in this sector, but millions of wonderful people and rich histories also. We choose to see it as a place through which the light can yet shine … until the clock ticks no more." As an afterthought he added, "We call it The Window, but it's also labeled the Zone of Despair or the Belt of Terror by some international agencies." He gulped from his canteen. "And rightfully so."

We ate and stared at the map—they'd get to the point soon enough. They mentioned that in Japan we'd be "storming a stronghold" and attending a few classes for "training." We'd meet other young people from all over the world: the Students of the Seven Seas—the SOS for short.

Reece said, "I called Mei, and she's so excited! She wants us to come to her house and visit her church. I promised we would; is that okay? The Trentons are missionaries there. Their church is small, and the people have terrible problems: sickness, accidents, and mental illness. I feel so bad for her, so I thought we could talk to the people."

The Stallards exchanged knowing looks. Then Dr. Eloise gushed to Reece, "Your very presence will bless them! Certainly we will go and fellowship together!"

Dr. Dale slurped a bite of melon. "A prayer journey may be in order there. We'll check on the—" he hesitated, "the spiritual climate of the place."

They coached us on Japanese customs—a lot of which Reece already knew—like shoe manners. In Japan they have outdoor shoes, indoor slippers, porch slippers, and bathroom slippers, and you have to know when to switch out of one and into the other. The Japanese are all about being clean. We discussed the customs of gift-giving and obeying rules of courtesy. The Japanese people always seem to act courteously, with one exception: getting on a train at rush hour—in which case you run like a maniac, push your way in, don't get separated from your group, and try not to get trampled or stuck in the door.

The Stallards gave Rob the location names; he wanted to help plan the itinerary. They told Marcus privately (though I overheard it) to make sure Dom stayed in contact with the rest of the parents.

As we finished up, Rob—fresh from acting camp and buzzed about going to Japan—exploded into a karate-ninja act. He took off down the canyon, hand-chopping trees on the way. He threw himself shoulder-first onto the ground, rolled and spun in one motion into attack posture, and faced us. Wailing a bunch of nasal, high-pitched vowels as a war cry, he came at us full tilt and took a flying leap at the slab—for a spectacular stunt jump over the picnic.

He almost made it. His toe caught the edge of the slab. One knee went into the potato salad, one hand scraped rock, the other slushed through cantaloupe as he hollered, "Yeeaam sorrreeee!" Dr. Dale leaped to his feet to escape the flying food. I was sure he'd be mad, since he'd paid for it all. But with a napkin pressed to his mouth, Dr. Dale bent double and slapped his knee for a good minute, while Rob—like a roast pig at a luau—lay there in the middle of the feast: ninja à la carte.

Marcus and I dragged him off to the little waterfall at the end of the canyon. We each grabbed an arm and stretched him under the falls to clean him off. While he howled like a torture victim, Reece cackled and Marcus yelled, "No more acting camps for you, man! You are out of control!"

Nothing more was said about The Window and what it had to do with our trip to Japan. On the long hike out of Gilead, Dr. Eloise drew me aside. "Elijah, the Tear of Blood?"

"I still have it."

"No sign of trouble?"

"Not yet."

She nodded. "Very good. Keep our contact information with you at all times. And don't take any chances."

We walked for a while. "Dr. Eloise, is my life in danger?" She paused for a long time—which to me was not a good thing. I said, "This problem won't ever go away, will it?"

"If you mean people wanting the Tear of Blood, no, dear. It is perhaps the most prized gem of all." She walked on, huffing and puffing as we headed back toward the golf carts. I helped her across the dry creek bed, and she thanked me. "We have not heard any more from our contacts in the diamond industry since the first … information leak." Her tolerant smile was worse than getting chewed out.

"I'm really sorry about that," I said.

"Concealing your identity was a wise move. Treasure hunters are probably checking leads in Georgia, which is why we've heard nothing. But … ," her smile went thin, "the silence is a little unnerving. Perhaps it will be good for all of us to be out of the country, even for a short while."

CHAPTER 2

"How are everyone's preparations coming?" Reece asked.

We were into July, hanging out in the Tree House Village doing a Bible study and eating ice cream. The Stallards had driven off waving and saying, *"Mata atode!"* Then life had gone quiet again, the same old same-old.

I answered Reece's question with a question. "Your mom's making crafts for us to take as gifts, right? So I'm pretty much ready: clothes lined up, passport and Quella. I sold off a few more snakes, and I'm working overtime at camp."

She said, "But is everyone reading the Bible and praying?"

Rob added to my answer, "Elijah and I are mowing yards too, so the money's coming in."

She huffed. "I know about the money. The church will take up an offering, and the Stallards sent a big chunk. But they said we should do a prayer journey at Mei's town."

"So?" Rob asked. "Don't you pray once you get there?"

She went ballistic. "You haven't been *praying!?*"

"I pray!" he defended.

Reece shot a questioning look at Marcus, who shrugged confidently, "We're in the kingdom, baby. Chill."

I said, "The Stallards didn't say we had to do anything special, Reece."

She raged, "But for Heaven's sake, we have to be ready! Marcus, didn't your dad always train before he went on a mission? Didn't he know who the enemy was?" She turned to Rob.

"And when you're starring in a show, don't you read the script first?" She turned to me. "Don't you get food, water, and a tent before you go into the wild?"

Marcus said coolly, "Preach on, sista!"

I couldn't tell if she was hyper about seeing Mei and helping her church, or nervous about her bone condition, or what. She was down to using a cane, but anything could aggravate it. I didn't want her getting upset. I said calmly, "We'll be staying in hotels and stuff. We won't need tents."

"I mean preparation for the *prayer journey!*"

Grunting in frustration, I muttered, "I've done prayer walks, Reece. It's the same thing … isn't it?"

Marcus was now in a mood. "I travel all the time, Elliston. A lot more than you."

"I don't mean the traveling part!" she snipped.

"Calm down, everybody," Rob said.

"We're in trouble, guys," Reece said dramatically. "I'm calling the Stallards."

Reece made good on her threat, and in a week we had a letter back marked "URGENT."

Children—Since ours is a spiritual journey as well as an international one, you must prepare on both levels. Perhaps we were remiss in not discussing this in detail. Take passports, lightweight clothes, and comfortable shoes, of course; travel light. But do please read your Scriptures and pray! Refer to Luke 9 where you will see that a change of clothes and pocket money are not so important as having God's power and your own testimony. Since we are not privy to the particulars of the adversary in the second stronghold we'll visit—on the Kii Peninsula where Mei lives—it might be wise to fast, perhaps once a week; let your heart lead, and do not go to extremes. The point is to make special time for the Word and prayer.

Perhaps we assumed too much, children. Do you even want to participate in storming a stronghold? Are you at all aware of the religion and culture of this country? Do you not believe in the power of prayer? If not, this trip could do more harm than good. Please talk this over among yourselves and reply immediately. There is still time to get a refund on the flight tickets.

In his service, The Stallards

With less than a month to go, we were suddenly cramming for finals. Practically overnight, Rob became an expert on Japan. I happened by the library one day to find him behind a stack of books. He perked up when he saw me. "Hey, Elijah, I've made a map of our itinerary: two days to get there because we lose a day over the international date line. Osaka to Nikko, a week at the conference, then to Kii Peninsula for five days. A day to get to Shimabara. The Stallards want to show us some archaeology there. Then car ferry to Osaka. We're going to be all over Japan!"

"Cool." I sat down and waved at Mrs. Otto, who was peering down the aisle at us.

"Hot, actually," said Rob. "The average temperature for August is eighty degrees; the average rainfall six inches. Possible typhoons. We should take clothes that dry fast."

"One backpack and a carry-on," I reminded him.

"Right. Here's what I know about the religion." He shoved a big picture book at me. "Those little oriental house-looking things are Shinto shrines. And this is a *torii*, a gateway to the gods. You always go through a *torii* to get to a shrine. It's mostly nature worship. Everything—even rocks and trees—has a *kami*, or a god, inside it. But people can be worshiped too." He shoved another book at me with pictures of big golden gods. "The other religion is Buddhism, following a man who lived around 500 BC. I skimmed several books, and I'm confused. It's about reincarnation and getting to nirvana, which means nonexistence. There's also ancestor worship—"

I interrupted him to show off what little I knew, "Which is why Mei used to pray to her grandmother."

"Yeah. Hey, are you taking your diamond?"

"It's not mine, and I don't know."

"My people!" Marcus appeared and slid into a seat beside me. He spotted the books on Buddhism. "I've known that stuff since my trip to Thailand when I was nine!"

"Shhhhhhhhhhhh!" Mrs. Otto went off like a steam train.

"There are a bunch of different kinds," Rob whispered authoritatively.

"It's all worshiping people and statues," Marcus said.

"Fear of spirits and demons. Idols. The same as where my ancestors come from in Africa." He leaned back with his hands knotted behind his head.

"We've heard about your voodoo a million times," Rob snipped. "Find something else to brag about."

. . . . .

Two weeks before we left, I was dashing out of the hardware store on a crack-of-dawn camp errand when I nearly collided with a cup of coffee—carried by the New York Jewelers guy. Our eyes locked. And even though I was taller, better dressed, and with a shorter haircut than when I'd first shuffled into his store and naively plopped down the Tear of Blood, he recognized me.

Muttering, "Excuse me," I sidestepped him and moved on. My heart sank. I ducked into an alley, feeling his eyes drill into my back. I dashed across the town's back parking lot, jumped a hedge, and scooted down the bank to the tracks—just as the 7:05 barreled past. A blast of hot greasy air, the rumble of heavy wheels, and an ear-splitting whistle knocked me back. *Close call!* I covered my ears and waited. I crossed the fence to Morgan's farm and leaped over. My foot plopped down into a fresh, squishy cow pile. *Drat!*

I was dragging my foot through the grass to wipe off the stinking stuff when I heard a snort and a heavy thud behind me. *Oh no ...* I knew without looking that it was one of Morgan's prize Angus bulls protecting his turf. Slowly I turned. The monstrous horned beast snorted, tossed his big black head angrily at me, and stomped the ground—his way of saying, "Get out!" My adrenaline kicked in, and before he could charge me, I went back over that fence, light as a fairy.

Trudging home along the tracks—the smell of hot grease and bull dung still in my nose, the sound of my feet crunching gravel, my veins still throbbing, and sweat collecting in my eyebrows—something in me snapped. It wasn't just the New York Jewelers guy or the train or Morgan's bull. It was the pressure of the "spiritual preparation" that I really didn't understand. It was Rob asking if I was going to take *my* diamond to Japan, me getting mad at him, when in fact I *had* formed a strong attachment to it. But I was tired of thinking up new hiding places for it, tired of wishing I could let Reece keep it to take the pressure off me (but afraid one of her nosy friends would find it). I was frustrated seeing Dad worried about money all the time while hidden in my room was a huge fortune in a bean-size rock. And another thing: the armor wasn't complete, yet we were supposed to "storm a stronghold." Without the sword of the Lord? What kind of sense did that make?

The icing on the cake was a cryptic note from the Stallards the day before, which ended with: *We realize this will sound silly, but our friend has had a recurring dream, and she is worried about our safety. In her dream there was a flower, a rather plain one, which had no fragrance or medicinal use. She knew—as one knows in dreams without understanding how—that if one moved*

*the flower or looked at it too long, it would die. And the flower said,
"Don't move me or try to change me!"*

*Our friend senses danger for our journey and will not be com-
forted by our reassurances that Japan is perhaps the safest country
in the world. Few Westerners understand this. The crime rate is
low. The people are immaculately clean, so there is little chance of
contracting a fatal disease. Public transportation is well maintained,
the food is carefully prepared, and the water supply is rigorously
tested. If this flower riddle makes sense to any of you, please tell us
so we can assuage our friend's worries. And please pass the reassuring
facts about Japan along to your parents. We are looking forward to
a grand time!*

That night I lay awake in bed. I held the red diamond to the
light, watching its triangular facets sparkle. Shaped like a tear,
the color of blood. *What am I supposed to do with you? Should I
take you or leave you? Why do you exist in the first place? Why did
someone centuries ago put you in the armor?*

It was priceless and useless at the same time. I couldn't sell
it. But it was only a matter of time before someone would rob
me or kill me to have it.

*What if New York Jewelers connects me to Camp Mudj and hires
hit men while I'm gone? Dad could get death threats and not even
know why.* My mom and sisters could be kidnapped. I pictured my
family bound and gagged, jewel thieves ransacking the house
while I was off in Osaka eating sushi, the gem stashed safely in
my belly button and sealed with duct tape.

What had the Stallards said about its meaning? That from the
ancient legend of the Tear of Blood came the Hindu custom of
painting a red dot in the forehead to show service and sacrifice.
Rob had discovered that, in Eastern folklore, a red diamond
symbolized a warrior. *It's in the helmet, so its purpose has to be
related to salvation. Its message has to be more than "People want*

me, and they hate you for having me. They're out for your blood!" I fell asleep with the gem in my hand and a prayer full of questions in my mind.

In the middle of the night, I woke up with a crazy idea. *It's insane. It's awful. It's great!* I sat up, found the stone under my pillow, and held it under my bedside lamp, deciding, *Whatever the others think about the Tear of Blood and what should be done with it doesn't matter. You're the one connected with it, Creek. It's your call. Not the clan. Not the Stallards. Not New York Jewelers. You answer to God about this and to no one else. After all, it is his armor, his tears, his blood.*

I was up the rest of the night sketching.

. . . . .

The next morning I showed up at Rob's in a shirt and tie and dress pants. "Your dad has a good camera, doesn't he?"

"Yeah," he answered. "What are you dressed up for?"

"Business. The camera has a macro lens?"

"Yeah."

We spent the next hour taking pictures of the stone.

"What's up?" Rob asked.

"Don't ask."

He scowled at me but went on helping with close-ups of the diamond in the sun, where its fire shot right into your eyes. We got pictures of me holding it in my hand, placed next to a ruler to show its size, and so on.

"Thanks," I said, taking the film and the gem. I went to the drugstore, told the photo girl to rush the pictures through, not caring whether she looked at them or not. I was done with the cloak-and-dagger stuff. I got a chocolate shake—breakfast—and waited on the pictures. Then I crossed Main Street and strolled into New York Jewelers, reminding myself, *The Tear of Blood is not about money. It's about salvation.*

The sales manager was waiting on a young couple. I dallied near the door at a watch display. When he saw me he dropped the ring he was showing and called out, "I'll be right with you." Another five seconds and he had excused himself to come wait on me.

"Take your time," I nodded toward the couple and lost the Georgia accent I'd faked the last time. "I'll wait."

"Interested in watches today? We have—"

"Diamonds," I replied. "I'm interested in diamonds." He went pale. In a minute he'd rushed the couple out. I pulled the diamond out of my pocket and laid it on the counter. "You want a piece of the action? You got it. A piece, that is. I need this cut into six pieces."

He gasped in air so hard he choked on his spit.

I went on. "Cut it into six small stones. I keep five; you get one as payment. Here are the specifications." I pulled out the paper with my sketches on it and laid it on the counter. "I know what this is, sir. It's the Tear of Blood, the Netsach Prism. The only pure red diamond ever found."

"Y-y-you can't—" he stammered, horrified at my idea.

"I can, and I will. But hey, if you don't want a piece of the one and only Tear of Blood, that's your business." I picked it up and held it in front of his face. His shoulders went stiff. His eyes glazed over.

In a stern voice I said, "My sources tell me you've created quite a stir in the global gem business. You spilled the beans." *Spilled beans?* I yelled at myself. *You sound like a kid, Creek. Talk businesslike.* "Unwise, sir," I continued. "With such lack of discretion, you're lucky I'm not taking my business elsewhere."

"You don't know what you're doing! It's a world treasure!" he said desperately.

I leveled my eyes with his. "I know exactly what I'm doing. The cutting will proceed in my presence; the stone is never to be out of my sight. If you don't have the skill to do it, call in a master gem cutter. I need the project completed in two weeks. Not a day later."

He looked doubtfully at the sketches.

I waffled. *Bad idea, Creek. You've done it again. He's not going to go for it—there's not enough time. What's more, he sees you cleaned up and looking like your regular self. He's gotta know you're from around here. He knows you're not from Georgia. Cover's blown.* I snapped the stone, enclosing it into my fist. "Too bad." I headed for the door thinking, *From this moment on, I officially have no life. Every moment I'll be jumping at shadows, imagining that I'm being followed, wondering if my house is being ransacked. I'll have to leave Magdeline and never come back.*

"Mr. Telanoo?"

I'll stay in Japan longer ... or move to Ireland and live at Murlough House and help out there ... maybe the Stallards would put me up in Boston for a while.

"Mr. Telanoo?"

He's talking to me! I turned.

Ashen-faced and short of breath, he said, "I have a friend, best in the business. I'll get him here Thursday."

"Tomorrow."

"I don't know if—"

"I'm out of time." I acted like I was leaving.

"All right!" he barked.

"Good." I paused a minute at the open door, giving him the steeliest look I could muster, and said darkly, "Don't underestimate me."

· · · · ·

I, George Telanoo, slipped into the back room of New York Jewelers every morning for the next two weeks, a few hours before the store opened. The salesman sent the regular guy on vacation. The master gem cutter shook like he had palsy when he saw the Tear of Blood and found out what I wanted him to do. Obviously, he'd agreed to do the work before he knew exactly what it was. I acted impatient and told him to get a grip or I was leaving. (I couldn't believe myself. But I just kept picturing how cool and brave the Stallards were at facing down Cravens in Dublin when he discovered they were looking for the armor of God. That's the only way I faked my way through. That, and a lot of praying.)

Once the initial cut was made and the Tear of Blood lay in pieces, the gem cutter breathed a little easier. There was no turning back now. Day after day I sat close, watched his every move. He'd stop working occasionally, breathe deeply, and mutter words like, "Utterly magnificent … Lights and perfections! It's the core of the earth afire!"

They played innocent and tried to squeeze information out of me, but I'd say, "When we're done here, you'll have a piece of the Tear of Blood. You want more? You ain't gettin' more." *Drats.* I'd meant to use business lingo like *breach of confidence* and *the firm's acquisitions* and *my fiscal year is in ruins.* They probably didn't buy it for a minute, that I was a whiz kid wheeler-dealer named Telanoo. Didn't matter. They wanted their tiny hunk of the treasure.

Every day I'd take the diamond pieces and head home right before the store opened for the day. I'd wind through Magdeline's back streets and backyards until I knew I wasn't followed. Then I'd cut across the tracks, ever watchful for Morgan's bulls. I'd work late at camp to make up the time I lost in the morning. And in those two weeks I often wandered out to the porch in the middle of the night and listened for footsteps of jewel thieves. In the tense silence I'd say in my heart, *El-Telan-Yah, I know you're there.*

I hardly slept.

CHAPTER 3

A week before takeoff, the clan got Bibles and water bottles and went up on Devil's Cranium for an official clan powwow. They knew nothing about what was happening with the Tear of Blood.

As I got the fire going, Reece said, "I've been studying Psalms because it's the *Warrior*. Here's my favorite verse: 'Lift up your heads, O you gates; be lifted up, you ancient doors, that the King of glory may come in. Who is this King of glory? The LORD strong and mighty, the LORD mighty in battle…. He is the King of glory.'"

"Gates …," Rob said thoughtfully. He pulled out a notebook and showed her a picture of a *torii* at a shrine. "This is a gate of the gods."

She blew a gasket. "That's … that's it then … the gates! I get it—why those words kept jumping out at me. When I see a gate, I'm supposed to pray those verses!"

Everybody said they were pretty much ready. I didn't want to make a big deal about Reece's condition because she seemed okay. I sure didn't want a repeat of the nerve-wracking days before Ireland when her prospects of making it seemed slim to none. I knew how she could have a setback any minute. From listening to Rob and Marcus, I also knew how much walking we'd be doing. In Ireland we drove everywhere; In Japan it's all buses and trains and lots of steps. She was probably worried about it. So when the guys were busy on another conversation, I looked across the fire to her and said in a tough voice, "Same as always, Elliston. If I'm going, you're going."

"Sure, Creek," she smarted off, saluting me like Marcus does sometimes, "over and out."

· · · · · ·

Operation Tear of Blood was completed the day before takeoff. I walked out of New York Jewelers for the last time, looked back at the sales manager, and said, "You have what you wanted, or as much of it as you're going to get. The rest is my business. Any hint of trouble my way and the police will know where to look." I tapped the store's name emblazoned on the glass door, then swaggered down Main Street, proud of myself for what I'd done. Relieved. Excited. Sick to my stomach.

The Stallards came to stay at the Wingate Bed and Breakfast and Tea Room the night before takeoff. They'd brought a ready-to-assemble packing crate for the armor of God. My clan and I were a little surprised. "We're taking it?" I asked.

"Oh, the conference must see it!" Dr. Dale insisted, more excitable than usual. "It will be the highlight! But first, might we have tea with Jodi and Dorian to discuss genealogy? Could that be arranged immediately?"

In twenty minutes we were sitting around two little tables in the tea room of The Castle. The Stallards complimented Aunt Grace's orange cake and raspberry tea, and then Dr. Dale began, "Jodi, Dorian, Rob, and Elijah, regarding your ancestry: genetic studies are making swift strides, so our conclusions might yet be subject to further refinement. But you are certainly an interesting mix of peoples. The MacMerrits can be traced back to Scotland where—and this is a striking point which will interest Elijah—Creek Indians were often taken, either voluntarily for the sake of getting an education, or by force as a curiosity for the Europeans. We've been able to sketch out the family line from Isabel's parents near the Isle of Magdeline—later named

Seven Avon Place—back to the MacMerrits of Scotland, who intermarried with the Creeks."

"You mean I'm a Creek!?" I cried. "I really am Indian?"

"Me too?" Rob asked weakly.

"Genetics and old church records indicate as much. You, Elijah, are perhaps doubly so. We've checked out your father's lineage as well, though with fewer resources. It appears that Russ's ancestors were also some of those Native Americans taken to Europe in the 1700s, who returned to the Deep South generations later with the surname they'd been given: Creek."

"I'm twice an Indian?" I said in a happy fog.

"And heavily Scotch-Irish too."

Mom eyed them curiously. "Goodness, you went to a lot of trouble."

Glancing at me, Dr. Eloise admitted, "Our motives are not entirely pure; we are immensely curious about the boy." She cleared her throat and went on. "Jodi, we were only able to find that your real father's first name was Simon, and that he worked with the newspaper or a dairy farm, perhaps one and then the other. Your parents' marriage license was destroyed, but your mother Isabel has a younger cousin, a Portia Ridley, who is still living in Ennis, County Clare. She works at a children's bookstore. She has cut ties with your side of the family, but we spoke with her directly, and she is willing to talk to you. Here is her number as well as numbers of a few relatives elsewhere in Ireland."

Mom was bowled over. She took the information into her outstretched hands as if it were gold. "Thank you so much! Dorian and I have been trying to find ... how did you ... ?"

Dr. Eloise said humbly, "One advantage of old age is that people are inclined to believe you are helpless. You ask a few questions, look pained and pathetic, wring your hands. Anyone with half a heart … !" She and Dr. Dale traded chuckles.

(It occurred to me then what dumb kids and old people have in common: we can get away with stuff. Full-blown adulthood with all its high expectations wasn't going to cut me any slack; and all of a sudden, I wasn't crazy about getting there. But at least I had senility to look forward to.)

"What about Dowland?" I asked.

"Stanford Dowland was a relative, yes," said Dr. Dale.

"We believe it was he who tried to rescue Isabel from that horrible church-run workhouse. Clearly he was not successful. We must give the poor man credit for his heroic effort."

Dr. Eloise looked around the tea room. "The politician who built this lovely house was one of a line of rescuers who stole or bought babies—sometimes at a high price—from the Isle of Magdeline in order to spare them a fate like Isabel's. He bequeathed his mission of mercy to others, who stashed copies of the paperwork in a secret room here in The Castle, the small space I believe Grace and Dorian found while remodeling."

She asked for more tea as if that were the end of it. Dr. Dale whispered, "The MacMerrits, dear."

"Ah yes." She cleared her throat and said diplomatically, "What a curious lot they were: rough and rugged, handsome and heartless. More than a few skeletons in their closets! They were known for occult practices and were greatly feared in their heyday." She shook her head. "We believe that they did, in fact, acquire the armor of God and hide it in Leap Castle, believing as their pagan forefathers that they could 'hide all the magics' from the followers of Jesus."

Dr. Dale said, "Foolish bravado led them into dark spiritual waters they were not prepared to navigate. Rare photos in Irish archives show the later descendants as stark, miserable, haunted individuals. They have all but faded from history." Grimly he added, "The lure of the evil one from the beginning is still an effective ploy, children. But to clutch at spiritual power apart from God will ultimately result in a downward spiral into Hell—as with Satan himself—with no chance of deliverance."

We ate cake. Mom and Uncle Dorian—not believers like us—gave each other looks. Their being brother and sister, I figured they had their own eye code and were talking things over.

Dr. Eloise broke the quietness. "Elijah, all of you, we have been able to trace the MacMerrit lineage much further back, much further, which you might find even more thrilling than the Indian connection. But that discussion will have to wait. We have last-minute packing to do. Jodi and Dorian, best wishes and blessings on you! And, Grace, a lovely dessert!"

Dr. Dale threw down a big tip.

We gathered in the attic. The Stallards put the crate together, all the while chattering to each other: "After all these years! … Speculations put to rest … What fun we shall have! … The skeptics and doubters brought to the light! … All revealed!"

When the crate was assembled and the bags of packing straw opened, Dr. Dale beamed at his wife romantically, "My dearest, dearest Eloise! We have done it!"

Reece grinned at me. The guys looked down at their shoes.

We wrapped the pieces of armor in linen. I checked the inside of the helmet, which I'd repaired to look like it did before I dug out the diamond.

Dr. Eloise asked me, "And the stone?"

"Packed. Safe," I said with a guilty lump in my gut.

She patted the helmet. "Excellent."

We couldn't get Rob out of ninja mode. With stiff poses and guttural sounds, he neck-chopped the attic mannequins and leaped from the couch, hacking at rafters. He kicked the air yelling, "Neen-jaaaa!"

Marcus shook his head, "Ninjas are masters of stealth, Wingate. Stealth. They don't go around screaming like banshees. You couldn't be stealthy if your life depended on it."

Rob stopped dead. "Can't be stealthy? *Me?*"

I'd seen that wide-eyed, fake innocent expression before: when we were kids and I double-dog-dared him. This trip was going to be interesting.

* * * * *

There was the traditional crying and hugs from our parents, including Officer Taylor this time. Mom drove us to the airport, tense and quiet. Once there, she waved us through the first gate until we got in a long line and signaled that we'd be there a while. She blew me a kiss and disappeared.

We piled our luggage around us, including the crate stamped "FRAGILE: Antiquities Research Center." I guarded it with a watchful eye because people in line kept looking at it. The Stallards weren't about to let it go into the cargo hold. They wanted it in a special closet in the cabin. One by one we put our backpacks on the conveyor belt and watched them go through security x-ray. Once everyone else was through, Marcus and I hauled the armor crate onto the belt and watched the x-ray screen, curious about what it would look like, wondering if the security people would question it. The shape of the helmet came into view. I watched the eyes of the security screener go on alert. He paused the conveyor belt for a few seconds. Next came the breastplate with the shoes, belt, and arm piece tucked inside. Suddenly he stopped the belt and came up off his chair ... because on the x-ray screen, mixed in with all the other shapes, was the perfect outline of a sword blade.

CHAPTER 4

"Please step over here," the guard said severely to Marcus and me. Two security people hauled the crate to a side table. "Please open this," one ordered.

The Stallards, who'd gone through and were talking with Reece and Rob, saw the problem and came right over.

I turned my back to the guard and mouthed, "Blade."

Dr. Dale didn't understand.

The guard asked, "Whose crate is this?"

"Mine," Dr. Dale stepped in. "I'm from Antiquities Research Center. Is there a problem?"

"Please open the crate, sir," the man said again.

Dr. Dale went to the crate and said calmly, "Certainly. We keep the tools with the box for convenience. Shall I?" He slid a small panel of the crate's wooden frame, which opened up a tray. Inside was a weird tool—a screwdriver on one end, a hammer on the other—and a few extra nails.

As he pried the lid loose, I caught a glimpse of Rob, Reece, and Dr. Eloise on the other side of the security gate, looking worried. I said to Dr. Dale, "I'll go tell the others."

The security guard stepped in my path. "Stay right here!"

"Oh, sorry. Sure."

Marcus shot me a "you idiot" look. The people going through the gate gaped at us like we were criminals caught in the act. My face burned. I wanted to tell Dr. Dale that there was a blade in the crate, but didn't want to arouse more suspicion. *Is there a secret compartment in the bottom? Did someone put a sword in the box to smuggle it through? How'd they do it with us right there? Or is it the sword of the Lord, invisible to the eye? Dr. Dale is so calm.... Does he know something?*

The lid came off. The guards lifted out the armor, spilling packing straw on the airport floor. They unwrapped and examined it piece by piece. Dr. Dale explained it was an antiquity and must be handled very carefully. He thanked them for wearing gloves. They emptied the crate to the last shred of straw. There was no sword. I kept my mouth shut.

"There was a weapon in here," said the security guard. Dr. Dale looked confused. "Excuse me?"

"A sword blade showed on the scanner."

Dr. Dale looked into the crate, baffled. "Impossible."

My voice trembled, "I saw it. There was a blade."

Dr. Dale looked at the dismembered armor scattered on packing straw. His face slowly changed from confusion to suspicion to astonishment. He whispered to himself, "He speaks the Word, and he is the Word. He has the sword, and he *is* the sword." He turned to the guard with a strange smile on his face. "Scan it again, please, piece by piece."

They moved us to an unused security gate so the other passengers could go on through. They fired up the scanner, laid the helmet aside, and ran the other pieces through, one at a time. The breastplate showed bits of metal: the torq, the brads. They ran the belt with its disc-shaped pieces, then the shield, which showed a metal piece roughly the size of a hot dog. One of the shoes of peace went through. Nothing. The last shoe went through. The conveyor belt stopped.

"There!" my voice cracked. "There it is!"

The guard looked at the shoe, then the screen. He pulled the shoe out and examined it.

Dr. Dale said with pleasant enthusiasm, "Why, this is wonderful! I'm sorry for the disturbance, sir, but we have been looking for this piece and thought it lost. Yes! Quite often the ancient warrior would conceal a weapon. Eureka!" He said lightly to me, "We have found it." Then to the guard, "If you kindly allow me a penknife, I'll extract the item so we may all have a look. If you need to contact a higher authority, please do. Again, I apologize, and I thank you."

Dr. Eloise looked worriedly at her watch and came over toward us, keeping her distance. "Dear, the flight leaves in fifteen minutes, and we are at gate thirty-three." She asked the guard, "Can you please let the children go on? This is an international flight, their first trip to Japan."

"Please stay back, ma'am," the guard barked. Two more guards showed up with handguns and walkie-talkies and made us all take seats—Dr. Dale, Marcus, and me separate from the others. I was ready to explode. *We have the sword!*

Borrowing gloves and a Swiss army knife from the armed guard who kept his hand near his gun, Dr. Dale studied the foot-and-a-half-long shin guard. He ran his fingers along the inside. At the bottom was a leather hem folded under metal trim. He snipped a few threads and stepped back while the guard carefully drew out a slim sword blade.

"There you have it," Dr. Dale said conclusively, and went on as if taking mental notes, "It is plain, but elegantly so, about fourteen inches long. Can't pinpoint the age from the style." To the security guard in charge he said, "Mystery solved. Once again I apologize. If I'd known, I would have certainly applied for special clearance."

"It's a concealed weapon, sir," said the guard. "You were taking it into the cabin." He looked at the Stallards' passports and asked questions about Antiquities Research Center. I wanted to offer to stay behind. I wondered where the rest of the sword was, if it was hidden in the armor. I wanted to touch the blade and test the edge for sharpness. It had to be the sword of the Lord. It just had to!

Everything happened in a rush. A supervisor told the Stallards they'd have to fill out some papers and go on a later flight. They ran us all through security again. Dr. Eloise asked again if we "children" would be allowed to go on. We objected, but Dr. Eloise pleaded with the guard, "Please, sir, let them make their flight. They are students, not employed by our business." She looked at her watch again fretfully.

"Oh, they have six minutes and a disabled girl!"

Dr. Dale turned to us matter-of-factly. "Mei will meet you in Osaka. We'll catch the next flight and come directly to Nikko. Here's the information you need." He pressed a note in my hand. "You have the necessary addresses and phone numbers. Remain calm. We'll see you in Nikko."

The guard let the four of us through and called ahead to hold the plane. He got Reece a shuttle cart; we guys threw our backpacks on and jogged along behind. They rushed us to the departure gate and hurried us onto the jet. As we were getting settled, I read Dr. Dale's scratched-out note, then passed it on for the others: *Excellent composure! Withhold judgment—and euphoria—until the evidence on our find is collected. Leave no related correspondence in the seat pockets.*

"Brilliant," Rob said, dropping into the seat beside me.

"Yeah!" I thought he meant the sword hidden in the armor of God. Way cool. The quest was complete!

Rob glared sourly at the seat in front of him.

"What?" I asked.

"I looked back one last time before we turned the corner to the concourse. The Stallards were shaking hands with the security guard and smiling."

"So?"

"I mean, like a mission-accomplished handshake." He looked at me and whispered, "Where's the diamond?"

"I have it."

"On you?"

"In my backpack. In the overhead compartment."

"Do they know that?"

I remembered how Dr. Eloise had patted the helmet when I told her the gem was safe. "Probably not."

He gave me a sly, sneaky look. "You outwitted them."

"No, I just … wait, you don't think it was a setup?!"

He roughly buckled himself in. "You saw how they pushed the idea of taking the armor at the last minute, so we couldn't say no. What if they'd already figured out where the sword was? Sometimes archaeologists x-ray artifacts in the lab. What if this was their way of getting the whole thing after all?"

Dr. Eloise had been so casual that we hadn't found the sword. How odd that had seemed. Maybe they were just trying to find a way to get the diamond. But … "No," I said solidly. "They didn't ditch us. They wouldn't. If they'd wanted it, they'd have taken the whole thing before."

Rob growled, "We knew where they lived before, but they've cleared out their Chicago office. They say they live in Boston, but all we have is a P.O. box. By the time we get to Osaka, they could be in Istanbul with our armor!" He snorted. "At least you have the diamond."

Seconds before the plane started taxiing, a young couple came rushing back and filled the two empty seats behind us, the seats which I'd thought were for the Stallards.

Preoccupied with getting her stuff in order, Reece leaned across Marcus and said to me, "Hey, remember what Dr. Eloise said taking off to Ireland: 'We're in God's hands now!'"

They're not ditching us in Japan. After all this? They're not!

Nobody mentioned the sword, because Dr. Dale had said to withhold judgment. Marcus and Reece hadn't heard Rob's comments about the diamond, but every so often he and I exchanged knowing glances. I could tell he was holding back all kinds of bad feelings, especially the kind of anger that goes along with being played for a sucker.

We changed planes in Chicago and then settled in for a long flight with headphones, inflatable flight pillows, and skimpy blankets. There was a meal and a movie. Over Alaska Reece switched seats and gave Marcus the end so he could sleep while she and I played cards.

"Hey," I said as she shuffled the deck, "that dream about the threatening flower. That mean anything to you?"

"No. You?"

"No."

"It's probably nothing," she said. "Japan's safer than the States. Everybody has weird dreams sometimes."

"Yeah."

"Changing the subject," she said, "a few more hours and we'll be there! I can't wait! Mei has a whole bunch of fun things for us to do. There's a resort town she wants to take us to, and we can swim in a stream near her house. Their church is having a picnic for us!"

Forgetting our troubles for a minute, I grabbed her ponytail, pulled her face toward mine, and rubbed noses with her. An Eskimo kiss.

She giggled. "What are you doing!?"

"We're over Alaska."

Eleven hours in the air. I couldn't sleep; my legs were cramped. Rob's suspicions rubbed off on me. *With so much at stake—all the time—will we ever trust the Stallards? Ever? Will I see the sword again? Get to hold it? What if, after all this time and danger and hard work and waiting ... "*

The only good thing about the long flight was Reece asleep on my shoulder.

The captain's voice came over the loudspeaker: "Afternoon, folks. We'll be coming in behind a typhoon as it veers north across the main island. Not a big one, but it's leaving an arm of fairly high winds. We can expect significant turbulence. Nothing to worry about; we're in touch with the tower and will get you to Osaka safely. You'll want to finish your drinks and buckle in."

No kidding. The flight attendants took their seats, and for the next half hour we got bounced around like a toddler on his grandpa's knee; only it was no fun at all, and nobody was singing "Pony Boy." Marcus forgot everything he'd learned at the Cliffs of Morte about height fright.

Rob grabbed the airsick bag from the seat pocket and read the names for *puking* in eight languages. A nice delicate shade of green, he said, "If they don't get us through this storm soon, look out for *luftkrankheit!"*

We dipped below the storm clouds, and a square of concrete the size of a postage stamp appeared in the bay of a huge gray city. The plane rocked and shuddered and dipped. I prayed that we'd make the runway in one piece.

CHAPTER 5

It was strange being in a country where everything was spoken in another language and where most everybody was shorter and darker than me. I began to see what Mei had felt, being a foreigner in a strange land. We followed the crowd off the plane into the terminal. We made it okay through customs by doing what everyone else did. Mei was waiting for us behind a wall of windows.

Marcus took one look at her and wheezed, "Whoa!"

She was taller, her hair longer and streaked with red. She had on skinny jeans, high heels, and a flowery top. Mei was a knockout. She waved wildly when she spotted us. Once through the door, Reece dropped her bag and crutch. They did the usual squealy-huggy girl stuff, and then Mei hugged us guys. We couldn't believe we were all together again.

Mei peered through the window back into the terminal. "Where are the Stallards?"

I shot Rob a "keep quiet" glance. "They're coming later." Mei helped us exchange our money for yen. Then she said to Marcus, "We are taking *shinkansen*, just like you wished in Council Cave! Our dream comes true!"

We hauled our stuff into the bottom storage bin of a big tall bus and boarded. It was so crowded there were no two seats together. For an hour we plowed through jammed traffic across the biggest city I'd ever been in, downtown in all directions as far as the eye could see. At the next terminal, I carried Reece's backpack while Mei led us through a swarm of people, like Christmas rush—times a hundred. At the bullet train office, we stood in line for a half hour and filled out papers for rail passes. Then we walked more, went through turnstiles, and climbed a crowded flight of steps to the train platform. Mei bought us way cool little drinks from vending machines and gave us gifts.

Watching down the tracks, Marcus grinned, "See what I mean, my people? Here she comes: classiest land transit in the world." An enormous, gleaming white, ultra modern projectile coasted in and stopped. The door of the *shinkansen* slid open. We hauled ourselves and our luggage onto the train, stashed our stuff in the overheads, and turned the plush blue seats around to face each other. I sat the other four together and I put myself right across the aisle. Reece was all smiles. Rob looked a little dazed. Marcus couldn't take his eyes off Mei.

"This trip is four hundred miles," Mei told us.

"I'm sleeping!" said Rob.

Not crazy about sitting for several more hours after a whole day on a plane, I went exploring. The bullet train had a dozen cars with restrooms and changing rooms, vending machines with all kinds of drinks, and even phone booths with desks where you could do office work—all super clean, super modern. I'd pictured countries in The Window as being primitive, people living in shacks and doing laundry in a river (not that I thought Mei lived that way). But this beat anything I'd seen in the States.

A voice over the PA said we were departing for Tokyo. Mei clapped her hands together. "I have three weeks with my friends! No school and only two papers to write."

"Homework?" Reece cried. "You have to do homework?!"

"It is okay. Not too much. Tell me what is happening in my American town and who has driver's license?"

"I do," Marcus said smirking. "We'll do a road trip when you come back: Yosemite, the Rockies, the Canyon ..."

Show-off.

By the time we'd told Mei about the blade discovered in the scanner at the airport—all of us sure it was the sword of the Lord—we were clipping along at one hundred seventy miles an hour. It didn't feel fast, just a supersilky ride, but fields and phone poles went by in a blur. When we passed another bullet train on a parallel track, it felt like our train had been swatted with a giant pillow. *Pfoom!* Rob was fascinated by the Doppler effect created by two trains passing at a combined speed of three hundred forty miles per hour.

"Don't stick your head out the window to study it, Rob," Reece joked sarcastically.

"I'm not an idiot."

Marcus smiled coolly at Mei. "No, he's a ninja."

She gasped at Rob. "You are studying martial arts?"

"Acting," Reece explained, and proceeded to tell about Rob's stunt in Gilead.

We cracked up all over again. Rob acted put out with us, but he was fine being the center of attention.

Smiling at Rob thoughtfully, Mei said, "We must give you a ninja name then: Shinobu." She wrote down the *kanji.*

"This means a person doing something secret, hidden."

Marcus snorted, "Oh, right. Secret man."

We all wanted Japanese names, and Mei said she'd think up some.

Zipping up the coast of Japan, we took turns telling Mei about life in Magdeline. Reece had written about my baptism, but I told her about Rob's rubber ducky trick.

A lady in a white uniform appeared at the end door of our car with a snack cart, said something in Japanese, and bowed. Mei bought us pricey snacks: green tea ice cream and sea chicken *onigiri*: rice balls with tuna inside.

Rob was all intrigued by the drink boxes. "These straws telescope out to twice their length and have a joint so they bend!" He put on a straw demonstration then grudgingly said, "Japan's straw technology is more advanced than ours. So is their train technology."

Mei and Rob took pictures. The landscape changed from mountains and seascapes to another enormous city, crammed together while spreading out in all directions: Tokyo. We switched out to another bullet train, hurrying through another crush of people in huge underground tunnels lined with shops and restaurants.

"Rush hour!" Mei yelled as we pressed through the turnstile.

I didn't think it could be more crowded than Osaka, but it was. For a guy like me used to being alone a lot, this was way too much city.

Shooting north across the Kanto Plain, we headed into a range of dark, misty mountains drilled through with tunnels that were miles long.

Mei gave us our Japanese names. "Reece, you will be Mayu. It means true and kind." She turned to Marcus shyly. "You are cool, so I call you Ryo. And, Elijah," she smiled at me, "you are Takumi. It means pioneer and sea, since you have led your clan to explore across two oceans."

As the bullet train slowed, Shinobu Wingate showed us on the map how far we'd gone in practically no time.

Mei said, "We switch trains now to a slow train. We will get to Nikko at night."

The local train was like a subway, with seats along the sides and empty space in the middle for people to stand. The rhythmic *clickety-clack* and the drain of jet lag (plus thirty hours with little sleep) suddenly got to me. I tried to stay awake planning what to do in case Rob was right about the Stallards. I personally couldn't believe they'd orchestrate a scam at the airport to give themselves a head start and make off with our armor into the wild blue yonder. True, they probably figured I'd stashed the diamond in the helmet for safekeeping. They thought they had it. But they didn't.

Rob nudged me awake as we pulled into Nikko; I'd fallen asleep on my backpack. Our train had emptied out along the way and we were the last ones in our car. The station was old and small, the opposite of the bustling stations of Osaka and Tokyo.

Mei got directions to the inn from the guy in the ticket window. "He said it is a short walk."

We stepped out into the dark—five high school kids in a strange village nestled in wooded mountains. Mei warned Reece, "The sidewalk has holes and a drainage ditch underneath. If your crutch goes in a hole, you will fall."

Rob was talking to Marcus in a low voice, and I knew why: he was spilling his suspicions, even though I'd told him not to. Their muttering stopped after a while when we had to use all our energy for hauling ourselves up the narrow sidewalk. Thirty minutes later we were still trudging. Mei stopped at an intersection and looked around uneasily.

"Are we lost?" Rob asked.

"I don't think so," she answered. "A little farther."

I could hardly see Reece's face in the dark and thought about stopping for a snack to give her a rest. But the town seemed closed down for the night.

Marcus came up and said under his breath, "Global conference, huh?"

"Hey, your dad okayed this!" I griped back. The lonely street was a far cry from Dr. Eloise's fancy pamphlet with the picture of a cruise ship on the front and aerial shots of mountains and seashore advertising the conference.

Rob asked worriedly, "Elijah, are we even in the right town?"

"It is there!" Mei said cheerfully. "The *ryokan*. The inn!"

I'd been imagining a convention center like in downtown Columbus. But across the street, wedged between little darkened shop fronts, stood a big, gloomy, unpainted house backed up to a steep mountainside. The parking lot had room for three small cars.

"That's it?!" Rob whined what I was thinking.

I nudged him and shook my head. I didn't want Mei to feel like we were slamming her country. But I was already thinking, *Okay, if the Stallards don't show, we hole up in the same room for safety's sake, then head back at first light for Osaka. Thank God we have Mei to help us get home.* I don't mind saying I felt more lost than being stranded in Telanoo in a soupy fog.

We hauled our gear across the street to the inn. *So what if I never see the armor of God again? The whole point has been about its message, right? Salvation and faith and peace? Truth and righteousness? But ... what if I lose that? What if the Stallards' story about the armor of God was all a big lie to get the diamond? Or what if this was a global kidnapping scheme and we never see home again?* Crazy, shadowy doubts swept through my mind.

Mei got us signed in while we dropped down and kicked off our shoes in the entry. The innkeeper, a friendly old woman with yellow teeth, talked Japanese a mile a minute as she led us up dimly lit back stairs. The guys' room was musty and low ceilinged, with tatami mat floors. Thin mattresses were stacked in the corner beside a low table holding the oldest TV I'd ever seen. We dumped our gear while the lady took the girls down the hall.

Inspecting the room, Rob suddenly burst out laughing. "Look at this sign: 'Prease keep door close. There is a bug.'" He eased open the paper doors, then the glass sliding doors beyond them. "Hey, there's a little garden out here. Wait … how can that be? We're on the second floor."

Foggy-brained and dog-tired, I peered out into the darkness and wondered if we were in another dimension.

Marcus said knowingly, "Guys, the inn's built into the mountainside."

"Oh yeah," Rob and I said in unison.

Rob tried the TV, and Marcus plopped down on the pile of mattresses. I put on the outdoor slippers, stepped out into the dark garden, and closed the doors behind me—to keep the bug out. Sounds of the guys talking inside faded. To my left was a little *torii* about three feet high. A few feet beyond it and surrounded by baby trees was a tiny building. It was a creepy sort of cute. I felt like a giant. *A gate to the gods. I'll tell Reece. Wonder what's in the little house?* I knelt down, ducked my head under the gate, and looked down the little path into the doorway of the building. Staring back at me was a living, blinking human eye.

CHAPTER 6

I fell back and gasped. A couple of seconds of hard breathing and staring at the building—which was big enough to hold a human head—gave me the guts to look again. The eye blinked! Just as I blinked. *It's a mirror! A reflection of my own eye!* Feeling skittish and dumb, I chuckled to myself and went back inside where the guys were making their pallets for the night. Then we went down the hall to the girls' room.

Mei obviously figured I didn't know what to do next and took over. "Now you are in my country, and I will be the host, okay? It is custom to take *ofuro* at night. The boys' bath is down the hall, the girls' bath is on the third floor. Then you wear *yukata*." She picked up a stack of folded, blue-patterned robes. "Use as a robe or pajamas—you can even wear it outside. We will have tea. And you can go to sleep while I wait for the Stallards to come."

Revived by a hot bath and feeling sort of spiffy in my Japanese getup, I walked down the hallway listening to see if the Stallards had come. Quiet. Even down in the lobby and up the old wooden stairs to the third floor, there was no TV blaring, no talking. *Where are all the other convention people? Are we the only ones at the inn?* I'd planned on spending some time alone with Reece that night but had second thoughts about splitting up the group. I figured Reece and Mei would be scared, but they were busy giggling at us guys in our robes. I warned Shinobu not to turn ninja and vandalize the paper screens. He did a few moves anyway and accidentally hit a low-hanging ceiling light, which went swinging wildly.

Marcus shook his head and said, "We can't take you any-where," and sidled up to Mei.

Honestly, I was fried. But sitting around a low table on a straw mat floor with matching robes and a pot of tea, we really looked like a clan. A strong hope welled up in me. *With or without the Stallards, I thought fiercely, with or without the armor, even tired and lost and sitting in a musty room, dead tired after thirty hours of travel, six thousand miles from home, still ... I'm living a dream.*

· · · · · ·

Morning comes early in Japan. Sunlight filtered through the paper door around 5:00. I lay there for a good half hour unable to sleep because, to my body, it was 4:00 in the afternoon. I got dressed, crept down the hall, listened at the girls' door, and heard two people breathing evenly. *Sound asleep. Safe.* I went downstairs to the entryway. The door was slid wide open to the street, cars and bicycles whizzing past. In the night, someone had lined up our shoes all facing out. I was surprised no one had stolen them. There were other shoes too, other guests. *So we're not alone,* I thought optimistically. Then I noticed next to my sneakers a familiar pair of sandals. *Dr. Dale! They're here! They're here, and the armor's here! They didn't ditch us!*

I stepped out into the sunshine and breathed in the smell of car exhaust mixed with fresh mountain air and frying fish. My shadows and doubts faded. I headed left down the village street to work the kinks out of my body from yesterday's travels. *Thanks, God, for the day and for getting us here. And for where you're going to lead us, thank you!*

Several blocks later the shops thinned out. Ahead in the morning mist was a bridge above a stream full of big boulders. I crossed the bridge, climbed down the bank, sat on a rock in the middle, and got out my Quella. Pearly light filtered through the trees. Clear water rushed past me, all around me. *Yep. Living a dream.* With no special devo in mind, I looked up the word *stream* and scrolled down to Psalms, the *Warrior:* "As the deer pants for streams of water, so my soul pants for you, O God. My soul thirsts for God, for the living God. When can I go and meet with God?"

Thirsting for God? I thought back to Gilead, the days without water, and tried to compare it with wanting to know God. *Just being honest here, El-Telan-Yah. Sure, I want to know you better ... but I can't say it gnaws at me like the thirst I had in Gilead. Is that wrong?*

Back at the inn, I was taking off my shoes when here came a pair of old bare feet down the steep steps at the end of the hallway. Dr. Eloise's whole self descended in a wine-colored dress and ran to me like she hadn't seen me in decades. "We are here! We arrived before midnight."

"How'd you get here so fast?" I asked.

"Direct flight," she said simply. "The others are awake."

Familiar voices came from the top of the steps. Pairs of feet, then legs, then whole selves came down, wondering where in blazes I'd been.

Reece cried, "We were worried!"

"I was down by the river talking to God. The coffee shop is two doors down. Let's go."

Our first meal in Japan was a traditional breakfast of miso soup, rice, a little fish (whole, with the head and eyes), a pile of cabbage, and green tea.

Rob made an eensy hat from his napkin and put it over the fish's head because, as he said, "I can't eat something that's staring at me."

Marcus said, "Try to blend in, Shinobu. Don't embarrass Mei."

"I'm not!" he snipped. "I'm just joking."

Six days in Gilead had taught me a lot of things, one being

to be grateful for anything edible. It was pretty good. Actually, I could have eaten two breakfasts, the way my body was whining, *Dinnertime was hours ago, Creek. Where you been?*

While the clan jabbered away about the rough landing and the bullet train, I worried over the Tear of Blood. I got ready to bring it up, but Dr. Eloise said, "Children, we mentioned in a letter about our friend's dream." She took a minute to retell the flower dream to Mei. "Our friend continues to be unsettled regarding our trip. She is quite the spiritual warrior, so we do trust her. If you have stumbled across anything in your preparations, we'd appreciate hearing it."

We looked blank. I said no for all of us.

Back at the *ryokan,* which looked more shabby than scary in the light of day, Dr. Eloise said with a wink, "I see we have stumbled upon another no-shamrock inn. But we shall make the best of it. Now we must prepare for the day. We'll examine our favorite relic and storm a stronghold!"

While we waited for the girls to fix their hair and stuff, I showed Dr. Dale the little building out my door. "Why's there a mirror in that little temple?" I asked.

He glanced at it and murmured something in a foreign language. "It's called a shrine, Elijah. The presence of a mirror comes from the legend of the sun goddess, the premier deity in Japan. She and her brother, the storm god, weren't getting along, so she hid in a cave, plunging the world into darkness. The other gods used a mirror and a pearl necklace to lure her out. She saw herself in the mirror, was overcome by her own splendor, and emerged."

"But when you look in that shrine, you see yourself. It's like you're the god."

Dr. Stallard said grimly, "Yes. And that's how it is all over the world."

. . . . .

The Stallards had already unpacked the armor pieces and laid them out on a sleeping mat. I knelt down and carefully picked up the blade in my two hands. I felt the cold metal, ran my thumb across the sharp edge. "Clean, efficient, the perfect size."

"Amazingly sharp," said Dr. Dale. "If the blade was in one piece of the armor, we may speculate that the other parts are hidden as well. Why don't each of you take a piece and examine it."

Rob said authoritatively, "We'll be looking for a scabbard, a hand guard, and a hilt."

Casually I picked up the helmet. I needed to see if the diamond's former hiding place had been dug out again. Because if it had, it would prove to me that the Stallards had followed us to Japan to get what they were really after: the Tear of Blood. In a way, I didn't want to know. But I had to know. I looked inside. The cavity behind the center of the forehead was smooth, intact. Nobody had messed with it. I sighed in relief and glanced at the Stallards. They were smiling over us kids like we were their grandkids and it was Christmas.

Mei picked up the belt, holding it carefully in the same way as when she first found it on Devil's Cranium.

Rob reached over and touched the disc-shaped ornaments of the belt. "Hand guard!" he said. "The metal pieces are hand guards!"

Reece cried, *"Sugoi*, Mei! *Sugoi!"*

Marcus said deeply, "The whole sword has been with us the entire time... ."

Mei loosened the metal pieces from their leather laces and nested one in the other to make a solid piece with a hole in the middle where the blade fit through. "It is the hand guard!"

Marcus took the breastplate and felt along the back. "Hand me the blade, will you?" He slipped the sword tip along the side seam, cutting a few stitches to get a couple of fingers in. "There are leather reinforcements fastened in the back, but one piece moves." He cut a few more stitches, slipped his hand in, and drew out a piece of thick leather. It was shaped almost like a pair of pants with pointy legs. He folded it, lining up the points and old stitching holes. Losing his usual cool, he said, "Look, people, see the slits where it can be connected to the belt of truth! We have a scabbard!"

Dr. Eloise got out a travel-size sewing kit to stitch the scabbard together.

I couldn't find any removable piece on the helmet.

Reece cut a few stitches along the bottom of the shin guard and worked out a long strip of folded leather.

Rob said, "That's for winding around the grip. Who has the grip?"

A little more searching and Marcus found the hot-dog-shaped hand grip inside the shield, masquerading as armband reinforcement. For the next hour Rob and Dr. Dale put the sword together piece by piece. They knew a lot about how to assemble it. (I was always a bow and arrow guy myself.) Every part had been hidden in the armor.

When it was together, Dr. Dale laid it across my open hands, me being the head of the clan. "The sword of the Lord, Elijah."

For a long moment I just stared at it. Sure, the sword wasn't a whole lot to look at. It wasn't huge, didn't have much in the way of ornamentation. Just a no-nonsense blade to be used at short range. "It's easy to handle, lightweight."

Reece reached for the hilt. "Even I could use it." She held it up in front of her and smiled at me so deep it felt like a slug in the chest. "We did it, Elijah, we did it! We have the full armor of God!"

"Who can know," Dr. Eloise whispered eerily, "what fires

have forged its steel?"

While the others passed the sword around, I excused myself, went to my room, and closed the door. I'd never cried from joy before. Never. But I cried like a baby.

. . . . . .

When I'd collected myself, I went back. Reece was quoting a verse, "'In the beginning was the Word, and the Word was with God, and the Word was God.' He speaks the Word, and he *is* the Word. It's so mysterious."

Marcus thought out loud, "Every piece of God's sword is made from every piece of his armor. And vice versa."

Rob said, "Except for the helmet. You didn't find anything, did you, Elijah?"

"No. But the sword is complete."

"Where's the word on it?" Reece asked.

We looked but couldn't find it. Reece scowled.

Rob said, "The hand guard is a little loose."

Mei studied it. "Maybe I don't have it put together right. It needs tighter."

"But it is the sword of the Lord," I announced. "It has to be, even without a word inscribed on it."

Reece looked doubtful. "The other pieces were inscribed."

Rob suggested, "Maybe it's microscopic. Those words engraved on the mesh were small—"

Dr. Eloise broke in, "We never would have found them without the linen tester," and went fishing in her luggage again. Unfolding the little square magnifying glass, she gave the sword a quick once-over. "I see nothing in the way of letters or symbols."

We took turns reexamining the sword.

Mei said, "With samurai warriors, the secret wisdom of the clan might be carved in the blade in very small letters or hidden inside, even inside the metal on a piece of paper."

"Inside the blade?" I asked. "How would you get it out?"

"You must break the blade."

"We're not doing that," I barked. "No."

For a long minute we sat on the mat floor with armor pieces scattered around, the sword gleaming in the morning sun.

Rob asked hesitantly, not wanting to seem dumb, "So … what's it mean, now that we have the whole armor of God?"

Putting away the linen tester and sewing kit, Dr. Eloise said, "Actually there is one more piece."

Our mouths dropped open. Our eyes got wide.

Rob whined, "Another piece?! You gotta be kidding me!"

We were on the brink of freaking out. Reece grabbed her Bible and flipped it open to Ephesians chapter 6. "Okay, it says belt of truth, breastplate of righteousness, shoes of peace, shield of faith, helmet of salvation … 'and the sword of the Spirit, which is the word of God.'"

"Read on," said Dr. Eloise.

"'And pray in the Spirit on all occasions with all kinds of prayers and requests.'"

"Prayer's a *piece?*" Rob asked.

"Oh. Thank goodness." I dropped back onto the pillows. No more vague clues, no more digging in hard clay or scuba diving in Silver Lake, no more reaching into burning cars, or run-ins with creepy guys like Dowland or Theobald.

Dr. Dale said to me in a fatherly tone, "Not so fast there, Elijah. You've given your life to the almighty one, all of you children have. You left the enemy camp for the eternal kingdom. You have blessing and power in this life and glory in the life to come. But now you have become the enemy's enemy. There are hazards."

Dr. Eloise jumped in. "To take your communiqués with the Almighty too lightly is to be unprepared for the trials. Prayer is like this stitching that holds the armor together. Drop a stitch here and there and finally the thing unravels."

"So the armor won't work without prayer," Reece said.

"Correct," answered Dr. Dale. "To use another metaphor, what good is a lamp if you don't plug it in?"

Dr. Eloise pressed her hands together. "Not to intrude on your spiritual journeys, children, but we would like to hear about the preparations you made and what you have learned."

Reece said, "I've been fasting one day a week. I read through Psalms several times. I prayed."

"And what did you pray about, dear?"

"That I'd be able to come, that I'd be ready for whatever happened. I prayed for Mei a lot. For her church."

"Very good." Dr. Eloise looked around at all of us. "You know what to expect when you engage in spiritual warfare?" She waited for an answer.

Marcus said, "We take 'em down!"

Dr. Dale smiled patiently. "Yes. That's exactly what we do. But it is an invisible war. Our ultimate goal is rescuing people, not wielding power. Faith, not force."

Marcus said, "Got it. Our battle isn't against flesh and blood, but against the powers of the dark world and evil forces in the heavenly realms."

Mei sat listening.

Rob said sheepishly, "I gave up snacks and drinks like pop. Is that fasting?" He added for extra bonus points, "And I go to church and Bible studies. And I know Japanese history!"

Dr. Dale said, "There are no hard-and-fast rules for preparation except that it must be done in the right spirit. Fasting and prayer are about discipline, thinking more about God than you do yourself."

Dr. Eloise turned to Mei. "Dear, we know you are very new

to all this. We don't expect for you—"

Mei broke in, "Yes, but Reece talked to me in letters. I read the Bible and prayed at my church or in my room. I did not change my eating because my aunt will worry about me. And many girls in Japan starve themselves to be thin, so I couldn't stop eating at school; it would be a bad example."

Dr. Eloise looked at her sympathetically. "Your walk with God is a lonely one, isn't it, child?"

Trying to hide her sadness, Mei said, "A little bit."

"Courageous girl," said Dr. Eloise. "Most excellent girl!"

The Stallards wanted to hear about my preparations next. I gave them a pat answer: prayer and Bible study and stuff. Hey, after Gilead I figured I was ready for anything.

Dr. Dale instructed, "Today you will all observe. Take your Bibles—your swords. Don't engage if you don't want to. It's a fascinating cultural site with spectacular architecture; you can simply be tourists."

"A few from the conference will join us!" chirped Dr. Eloise. "You will meet the SOS, and we predict you will get along splendidly." She stood—a signal that we were on our way. "Expect the unexpected, children. We must put on the full armor of God in our hearts and minds. For today we go through the gates. Today we begin."

CHAPTER 7

We headed out from the old mountainside inn and made a left through town. We stopped for vending machine drinks, and Dr. Eloise warned Reece about the holes in the narrow sidewalk. She cautioned all of us about the traffic as if we were grade-schoolers: "When crossing a street, remember to look right first, then left, then right again. Traffic comes from the right because they drive on the left."

"To the left, to the left!" Dr. Dale made fun of himself, strolling along with a skinny can of coffee milk. "As much international driving as I have done over the years, I still get confused. In the Orient one drives on the left. In America it's the right. Most of Europe is right, but Britain is left. Turkey is right. Pakistan is left. Or is it the other way?"

We went down the street singing to help Dr. Dale remember which side to drive on: "To the left, to the left, to the left left left... ."

Nikko was an old, quaint mountain village. Dr. Eloise said, "It has a bit of morose, nostalgic appeal, I suppose. The valley setting is superb, isn't it, Dale? Couldn't we live happily here? Fresh air, fresh food, mountain strolls. Good for the constitution. Mei, the Japanese are the longest-lived people in the world, are they not?"

Dr. Dale asked what we knew of the history of the place.

Rob piped up, "It's a shrine to a dynasty that unified Japan under one government four hundred years ago."

"Exactly, and that was a good thing," commented Dr. Dale. "But in the process, they tortured and executed untold thousands of people, particularly believers."

"Not a good thing!" Rob huffed.

"Certainly not. At this shrine those very leaders are worshiped as supernatural representatives of the sun goddess. To worship a created thing—whether man or beast or element of nature—is breaking God's first Commandment: 'I am the LORD your God.... You shall have no other gods before me.'"

Dr. Eloise broke in. "An offense to the creator. But he does not forbid such a thing simply because he needs our adoration."

Reece said, "He just knows how the universe works."

"Precisely. When you worship something, you give it your power—the power and love meant to grow between you and the Father, to give purpose to life. Worshiping other gods is the absolute worst thing you can do!"

Rob asked, "I'm not disagreeing, but ... why the worst?"

"Because making something your god opens the door."

"The door?" I asked.

"The veil! The veil to the evil one and his vast hordes! No human should give his power to a created thing. The spiritual world is not a safe place, no matter what naive seer, diviner, or medium says to the contrary. Those on the dark side are shape-shifters, mask-wearers. Do not be fooled."

We crossed the bridge where I'd had devos that morning and stopped at an intersection at the foot of a broad mountain. From the right came a group of foreigners.

Dr. Eloise waved and said, "There are our early birds!"

We joined up at a wide spot in the path overlooking the stream. We milled around and introduced ourselves. There were a handful of adult conference people and more than a dozen teens, the SOS. I caught a few names: Robin was a tall, pretty girl with brown hair. Karinna had green eyes, wild red hair, a long skirt, and bare feet. They were from the States. Eva from Germany was short and athletic. The guys were Li, a Taiwanese with perfect English; Dmitri from Ukraine; a scrawny kid from Hawaii named Cody; and Mahesh from India. The leader of the SOS was a blond woman in her forties wearing a navy T-shirt that said "Pilgrimage" on the back. Her name was Veronica.

Dr. Dale—by far the oldest guy—led the way. We followed a path above the stream for a few blocks, and then he turned and stopped us. "This is where we engage and turn the battle over to the Lord."

Suddenly I got nervous. I had no idea what was about to happen. For the sake of my clan, I acted relaxed, slugging down the last of my skinny can of peach nectar.

He read from 2 Chronicles 20, where a king facing an unbeatable army made singers form the front lines to praise God. Before the battle even began, the enemy troops got confused and turned their swords on each other. When the good army got to the battlefield, all they saw were corpses.

Dr. Dale read, "'This is what the LORD says to you: "Do not be afraid or discouraged because of this vast army. For the battle is not yours, but God's."'" Then he lifted his eyes to the skies and powerfully barked, "'The word of God is living and active. Sharper than any double-edged sword, it penetrates even to dividing soul and spirit.' Your Word is truth!"

Walking up a winding road, the conference people softly sang the names of God and the power of Jesus. I'd heard some of the music at my church and in Ireland. We had no weapons, but it sort of seemed we really were going into battle.

Veronica reminded the SOS kids and us too, "This is a tourist site, and we are guests in another country. We respect their beliefs even if we do not agree with them."

Marcus whispered to me, "She sounds like my mom."

"And don't draw attention to yourself. If fear overtakes you, pair up, stop, and pray. Use the weapons he gives you."

I glanced questioningly at Reece.

"We're observing," she said uncertainly.

Then we were on a long, wide gravel avenue lined with huge evergreens. Ahead stood a *torii* like the one outside my room. Only this one was stone, thirty feet high, and massive.

"'This is the gate of the LORD, through which the righteous may enter,'" Reece said shakily.

Li, the sharp-looking Taiwanese, came up beside her: "'Lift up your heads, O you gates; be lifted up, you ancient doors, that the King of glory may come in. Who is this King of glory? The LORD strong and mighty, the LORD mighty in battle… He is the King of glory.'" He smiled. "That's my job here—to pray that verse."

Shocked, Reece said, "I think it's mine too."

Dr. Dale overheard and glanced back. "Reece, Li, you have your weapons."

Anyone who wanted could stay at the gate, so Reece paired off with Li and Veronica. Hesitantly I went on.

It didn't take long to get what was happening. A couple of the SOS kids zoned in at the purifying basin where people were washing their hands and mouths. They quietly flipped through their Bibles. "Here," one said to the other. "Isaiah 41:17."

I found it in the Quella and read to myself: "The poor and needy search for water, but there is none; their tongues are parched with thirst. But I the LORD will answer them; I, the God of Israel, will not forsake them." With open Bibles they prayed for the people trying to get pure enough to go into the shrine and worship a man.

Mingling among the tourists, admiring the cool buildings and ancient forest around us, we passed through another gateway to the gods, then another.

Ever the history buff, Rob whispered, "Can you believe it? These buildings have been here longer than America has been a country!"

Small groups casually split off and drifted in different directions. Inside one small building sat three beautiful gold and black containers about three or four feet square. Tourists were bowing and praying to the boxes. Mei was there, but she wasn't bowing. She felt me come up beside her and said, "The presence of the three gods is there."

"In those boxes?" I asked.

She nodded. We were quiet for a long time.

Finally she struggled to say, "It is very hard not to believe what my ancestors believed for many generations."

"I know. My parents don't believe the same as me either. And my ancestors were the MacMerrits."

I strolled on to the last gate, which was unlike the others, a massive gatehouse with a roof. It was carved all around with hundreds of creatures, horned and fanged with bulging eyes; writhing dragons and demon dogs painted green and white with gaping, bloodred mouths. I didn't understand it. I couldn't take my eyes from it. I felt frozen in my tracks—rooted in the spot the same way I'd been two summers ago when I couldn't find Mei and was worried she'd gone over Lover's Leap, when actually she was right there. *Am I supposed to do something here?*

I looked around for someone else from the group. Several yards away and sitting on a step, Robin was reading her Bible. She looked up and spotted me. I motioned her over.

"Look at this," I said. "What's it mean? Why are there monsters in a temple?"

"Wow ... ," Robin said, gazing up at the threshold to the

inner shrine. "Wow."

"Yeah," I said grimly.

"I don't mean *them*," she nodded to the demon dogs and dragons. "Guess what I just found, what I was just reading?"

"What?"

"'To the arrogant I say, "Boast no more," and to the wicked, "Do not lift up your horns. Do not lift your horns against heaven; do not speak with outstretched neck." No one from the east or the west or from the desert can exalt a man. But it is God who judges.'"

I got it. Now it was my turn. This was my battle post, and that verse was my weapon. I thought about the words. Then I said them ... and said them again—still quiet but with more authority. I felt out of place and surrounded by an eerie quiet. Nothing happened—no earthquake or lightning from Heaven. Robin wandered off, but I stayed and prayed for a long while that no one would make a god of himself or for himself. I wandered among the shrine buildings, past clumps of people reading or talking to each other seriously. A few strolled around with deep, thoughtful expressions on their faces. They were activating the armor in their hearts, using the sword against an unseen enemy. Dr. Dale kept looking up toward the trees, as if listening.

We met back out under the first massive stone *torii*, everyone still drifting around, talking quietly. Dr. Dale asked, "Are we ... finished?"

Most everyone nodded.

Karinna frowned at her bare feet. "Not yet. I keep remembering a phrase—*build up, build up*—but that's all I know. It seems important."

"Coming up." Marcus flipped open his Quella and scrolled through a couple of verses. "This must be it. 'Pass through, pass through the gates! Prepare the way for the people. Build up, build up the highway! Remove the stones.'" He looked up at the giant gate towering over our heads, then at me with a wild twinkle in his eye. "Orders straight from headquarters, Takumi. How cool is that."

Dr. Dale smiled. "I believe we are finished here. We pass through the gates."

We walked back down the ancient tree-lined avenue. I felt like I was floating on air. *That was it? That was spiritual warfare? It was so easy! No blood and guts, no screaming, at least not that I could hear. Just a peaceful spot in the mountains with big gates and cool old buildings.* We stopped at a snack shack. Dr. Dale bought himself an ice cream and a water bottle and sat down on a bench.

"So," I asked half joking, "did we win?"

"We've already won, Elijah. Good is eternal, evil is temporary, and that score was settled two thousand years ago. But the great deceiver, while he is permitted, still lusts for victims. His appetite is insatiable. Demonic insurgents under his control feed on pain and destruction. So, yes, the war is won, but the battles are not over. We press on with search-and-rescue missions, clearing the ancient rubble of fear and superstition. I believe that's what the verse meant about passing through the gate, building the highway, removing the stones." He glanced at the white sky above us.

"How do we know we accomplished anything?" I asked.

"First, we know by faith. You were wearing the shield of faith, weren't you?"

"Uh, yeah."

He finished up the ice cream. "Did you have any forebodings?"

"No."

"Some people do. Some don't." He sort of glowed with quiet confidence, smiled at the sky again, and said lightly, "I didn't think you would. Not today."

"Why?"

He wiped ice cream off his chin and leaned over to me. "See that open spot in the sky, beyond the gate?"

"Surrounded by the big trees? Yeah."

"The whole time, we had protection. There."

"What do you mean?"

"An angel I suppose," he said wistfully. "In a circle above us."

"You saw it?!"

His eyes reflected white light from the sky. "With spiritual eyes, you might say."

He took a slug of his water bottle and said matter-of-factly, "If we succeeded, then we have aroused the enemy's anger. I can say with a fair amount of certainty that we will be attacked." He stood tiredly, gripping my shoulder to help himself up, and then looked down at me firmly. "Regardless, Elijah, you must pass through the gates and prepare the way. Remove the stones blocking the way of the people."

Down at the main road, most of the crowd was talking lunch, but the mountain stream was calling me. I got Dr. Dale's permission and headed down the bank, yelling at the others, "Come on! Let's cool off first!"

Soon, even the Stallards were picking their way down the bank and yanking their shoes off. The sun blazed, and there was no breeze in the valley, so my clan and the SOS cooled off by horsing around in the stream. We climbed on the warm rocks. Rob kept trying to sneak up on Marcus and get him in a hammerlock, but he had zero luck.

In a short while, one of the men came down the bank with a bag full of *bentous,* Japanese meals-in-a-box like Mei used to make for us. Drinks were passed around. Cars on the street above slowed down, people gawked at us foreigners lying around on rocks, barefoot and wet, with our shoes and socks and lunch boxes strewn everywhere.

Mei giggled and cried out, "All around me are *henna gaijin!* Strange foreigners. Help!"

Soaked to the skin, Marcus, Rob, and I dropped down to eat our *bentous.* We overheard Mei asking Reece, "This baptism, does it happen in a church?"

Feeding herself with chopsticks like a pro, Reece answered, "You can be baptized anywhere there's water."

Mei looked down the stream. "Even there?"

Reece's eyes lit up. "Totally."

"You must have a priest or minister?"

Marcus said, "Yeah, a priest. But you're lookin' at one."

Rob screwed up his face at Marcus. "Oh brother!"

Marcus tossed his head casually. "No joke, Shinobu. We're priests. You too—hard as that is to believe." Full of the same giddiness we were all feeling, Marcus stretched out on a big flat boulder and cried to the sky, "A holy nation called out of darkness into light. 'Once you were not a people, but now you are the people of God.'" He thrust a lazy fist to the sky, "My people!"

Mei said to us, "I want the baptism too."

I scouted out a deep, quiet pool downstream, and in a few minutes all of us had gathered. Dr. Dale did the honors of baptizing Mei. Everyone clapped and sang while cars on the highway slowed and people stared. Reece and Mei hugged and cried to each other, "My sister! My new sister!"

. . . . .

Jet lag—and what Dr. Eloise called spiritual fatigue—hit us like a strong drug. Back in our rooms we slept like logs. Next thing I knew it was dinnertime; our days and nights were all screwed up. We joined the SOS—and several more new faces—at a restaurant where you cook your own meal on a grill at your table. The specialty was *okonomiyaki,* a sort of big pancake with vegetables and any kind of meat you want to throw in. Reece and I sat with the Stallards and the SOS kids we'd hung out with at the shrine, Li and Robin.

While everyone was dumping ingredients onto their pancake batter and letting it grill, Dr. Eloise said to me, "Elijah, we told your mother that there was more to your ancestry than we had time to discuss. It's quite fascinating if you want to hear it."

"Shoot," I said.

"You do have some Native American roots, but you are more heavily and originally Basque."

"Basque? What's that?"

Dr. Dale explained, "They are a unique people group who have occupied an area in western Europe for millennia. As we traced your lineage from the Isle of Magdeline further and further back in time, we discovered that Scottish and western Irish genetics are very similar to Basque."

I looked blank.

"We find it fascinating that your ancestors on both sides are the oldest and most intact people group known. Since the earliest days of humanity, the Basque have occupied parts of France, Spain, and North Africa."

Rob, my history buff cousin, would find this interesting. But for some reason, only food and spending time with Reece were on my mind.

Dr. Elise said dramatically, "Before Rome became a world power, before the Goths invaded Europe, those called Basque had claimed a place in the world. And Mei will find this very intriguing—you must remember to tell her—there are striking linguistic similarities between the Basques and Mei's ancestors, the *Ainu.*"

Li jumped in and explained to Reece, "They're like the Indians of Japan."

"The word *ain'u* is an abbreviated Basque word meaning 'scattered or disappeared.' Your and Mei's people may have been forced apart due to a severe climate change: ice age or famine. Mei's clan migrated east across the entire area that's now The Window and settled in the islands of Japan. Your clan moved north into the British Isles."

"I'm related to Mei?" I asked.

"Veeeerrry distantly," Dr. Eloise joked, then said to Li and Robin, "We've been wondering if he is the third Elijah and, therefore, interested in everything about him. We're archaeologists; we dig down."

Robin suddenly stopped cooking her pancake and gaped across the table at me. "The third Elijah? *You're the third Elijah!?*"

Li's narrow eyes popped. "The one who'll preach on the streets of Jerusalem at the end of days? Drama!"

Dr. Eloise put up a corrective hand. "There's no way to know until the time, dears. But we discovered another curiosity ... oh, my pancake needs flipping. There ... easy, easy... ah, perfect! Now where was I?"

"The third Elijah," I reminded her. "I wondered about that when I was stuck in Gilead." (I didn't mention that I'd bargained with God to get me out of Gilead alive, even if it meant dying in a foreign country later. I was buying time.)

"Here's the surprise. Elijah, you are from Magdeline, Ohio—no news there. Your grandmother spent her days on the Isle of Magdeline—common knowledge now. But this prehistoric culture to which you can be traced is called ..." She leaned in over her steaming pancake, "Magdelinian. By startling coincidence, you are connected to that name since the dawn of mankind."

My pancake looked done. I scooped it onto my plate and poured on the "bulldog sauce."(I was pretty sure it wasn't made from bulldogs; it smelled like barbecue sauce.) I tried not to get creeped out at the Stallards' poking into my history and bringing up all sorts of weird details. "What's that mean?"

In her usual flippant way, Dr. Eloise said, "Only God knows! But it is very curious indeed, isn't it? Three times over, you are a Magdelinian."

"Like Mary Magdalene in the Bible?" Reece asked.

Dr. Dale refilled our teacups and smiled at me. "The woman from whom Jesus extracted seven demons. Slightly different spelling and no traceable genetic connection to our Magdelinian. But, yes—"

An explosion of cackles came from across the restaurant. Rob was making little hats for the fish heads at his table.

I had my Quella and looked up *Mary Magdalene.* "It says she was from Magdala on the southwest coast of the Sea of Galilee. Jesus cast seven demons out of her. She was one of a few devoted followers at the time of his death, and the first to see him alive after the resurrection."

Dr. Eloise said, "Having been a captive of the dark side and come face-to-face with the Son of Light—to see him risen from the dead—I suppose one would be entirely devoted!" She pointed at my Quella with her chopstick. "There you have Mary Magdalene's entire history. But what a great lesson we have from her life: anyone can be snatched from the very gates of Hell."

"How did she get the demons?" Robin asked.

"Dabbling in the occult, most assuredly—like Elijah's forefathers, the MacMerrits; opening the forbidden doors; parting that veil between the worlds."

Dr. Dale shook his head. "It was your former path, Elijah. Your openness to the spirit world without guidance from the Word, ancestors immersing themselves in the occult, your parents' own disinterest in the things of God ..." His eyes drifted out the dark window. "Your chances for ever meeting him were slim indeed."

"Slim to none, without me!" Reece nudged me, grinning.

I thought of how I'd always believed in a Great Spirit of some kind without understanding anything about him. How I'd wanted to visit the Crystal See even when the minister preached against it. How much I'd wanted to see the dark side when I was in Ireland. "So what does it mean that I'm a Magdelinian?" I asked.

Dr. Dale chuckled heartily. "Apparently, it's up to you to find out, Elijah."

CHAPTER 8

After dinner we walked to a community center a few blocks away on a side street. On the second floor was a big Japanese-style room with paper screens and tatami mat floors. We took off our shoes and sat on big square pillows.

Dr. Eloise padded over to me in bare feet. "We will show the armor tonight. Would you like to model it?"

I looked around at the crowd. "Um, I'll pass."

There were over two hundred people there, way fewer than I expected for a global conference, but people from all over: Baruti from Egypt, Paulo and Ramona from Brazil, the Bremmer family from Switzerland, and so on.

Dr. Dale put up the map he'd spread open at Gilead, showing The Window. After announcements and prayers for the world, we sang a bunch of songs. There was a guitar and bongos and a flute player sometimes. A guy named Fred played banjo. Not all the songs were in English, but nobody seemed to care; they hummed when they didn't know the words. I was trying to figure out the purpose of the conference when Dr. Dale asked my clan to stand so he could introduce us. Turns out that we were the visual presentation for an hour lecture. (The whole time we were up there, I knew they'd want to see the Tear of Blood before the night was over. The pancake with bulldog sauce lay in my stomach like a rock.)

Dr. Dale began the introductions with Reece, describing her has having "extraordinary spiritual vitality," that she was "quite unsinkable." He explained in clinical terms why she had to use a crutch. "Unfortunately, even with current medical technology, there is little hope she will completely recover. But that does not stop her!"

He went on. "Mei Aizawa is a new believer. She acclimates well to changing surroundings, is gifted artistically, highly intelligent, cooperative—an excellent team member. She has lived in the States and visited the British Isles, is willing to work alone if necessary. Mei is quite the brave one. And after only a few years in the States, she was in the ninety-five percentile range for language comprehension!"

People clapped. Rob was next in line. He stepped forward stiffly and beamed. It sort of felt like we were beauty contestants without a runway.

Marcus barked, "Go, Shinobu!"

Dr. Dale said officially, "Rob Wingate is the whimsical one, if you haven't guessed," Twitters went around the audience. "He is naturally curious, a researcher, a detail man. Good navigator. Rob stood up to his father during a family crisis and single-handedly turned the situation around."

A few oohs and aahs. Rob's eyes shifted shyly to us. He murmured, "I had help."

"And Marcus," Dr. Dale said warmly. "Street-smart and charming. An excellent fact finder. He's familiar with diverse cultures, comes from excellent parental stock. Marcus would make a good detective, I think. Just enough intimidation in his manner to get information when needed."

Excellent stock?! Now I was feeling like one of Morgan's prize bulls up for auction. I caught Marcus's eye and brain-waved, *What gives?*

He shrugged, caught Karinna's admiring eye in the audience, and winked.

I whispered to him out of the corner of my mouth, "Do the words *Miranda Varner* ring a bell?"

Dr. Dale stepped over to me. "And finally, Elijah Creek. Emotionally and physically tough. You must hear his story about surviving six days in freezing temperatures, trapped under an enormous rock—without food, water, or shelter." (More oohs and aahs.) "Elijah has received a clear call from the Almighty, has demonstrated the gift of discernment, and has encountered one of the dark forces while in Ireland."

My clan looked at me questioningly.

Dr. Dale went on, "And it is through Elijah and his friends that we are able to make the next presentation."

The lights dimmed. Dr. Eloise and a dummy covered with a white sheet appeared in the back corner of the room from behind a paper screen. One small ceiling light beamed down on Dr. Eloise's ghostly sidekick. She announced loudly, "The Magdeline children—" (I wondered if she'd still be calling us children when we were in our fifties and she was a hundred.) "—found the armor of God, which" (she adjusted the ghost to face the crowd) "we have brought for everyone to see. Some scoff at the armor of God, its power and protection. Skeptics have doubted its existence, called it a mere metaphor, but ..."

The flute and drum began a mysterious tune—haunting and tribal-sounding. Dramatically, Dr. Eloise threw the sheet off with a *whoosh*. The crowd gasped. There, for the first time in ages, stood the whole armor of God with all of the pieces—including the sword—gleaming in the spotlight on a dummy wrapped in black, like Rob had done in his attic.

Everyone applauded.

Then the armor moved.

Another gasp went up from the crowed. One girl screamed. A real person was wearing the armor! Nervous giggles followed, but the effect was pretty awesome. Slowly, silently, the armor floated through the crowd, pantomiming a battle, lifting the shield of faith against invisible projectiles, thrusting the sword into unseen enemies. Light flashed off the helmet and sword; the black-clad arms and legs and face practically disappeared. It moved to the rhythm of the drum as smooth and liquid as the flute melody.

I scanned the crowd to see who was missing, who was wearing the armor.

Marcus leaned over and whispered, "Dmitri."

I nodded agreement. The dark warrior matched Dmitri's muscular build.

The Stallards had made their big splash. The lights came up, and for the next half hour people swarmed around the armor, touching it ever so carefully. The old archaeologists had the time of their lives showing how each piece was created from fragments of history: from the Viking torq around the neck to the scraps of the tabernacle lining the breastplate; from the *Ogham* inscription of faith on the shield to the worn sandals of ancient mariners sailing from Europe to America and back.

The Stallards had us sit up front, like a panel. Mei was asked to tell how she and Rob had found the Chinese letter hidden in the breastplate, how the symbol for *righteousness* means "lamb over me." Reece explained that finding the belt of truth had uncovered one of Magdeline's darkest lies.

Marcus demonstrated how word-searching the Quella led us to a burning car where the shield of faith was stashed. The SOS kids grumbled; they wanted Quellas too.

I told how even when I was trapped in Gilead, God had led me to find the helmet of salvation, which I'd lost the year before.

The armor-clad phantom went back to the corner and stood like a castle guard under the spotlight. Dr. Dale summed up,

"Friends, we have gathered here to retreat from the battle this week. We will share our stories, salve our wounds, rearm and reconnect with our God, our source of strength. He assembled this armor as surely as he made the spiritual armor we wear. These pieces were crafted across continents and through millennia from the histories of true warriors: worshipers in the Holy Land, pilgrims who died alone and lie in unmarked graves, spiritual wanderers venturing into the unknown to serve him. Nameless heroes lost in jungles and locked in dungeons.

"These precious pieces of leather and metal armor—like God's real armor—have been stashed away unused for too long. We shall not be able to show our amazing relic to the world for it to be dismembered and disputed over. But no matter. The full armor of God is not a relic; it is a reality."

During a coffee break, the SOS hung out with us. We kicked back and relaxed. But the knot in my stomach jumped to my throat when Dr. Eloise came over. "Elijah, when we reconvene, might we have a look at the Tear of Blood? It will be a moment they will never forget!"

. . . . .

The audience sat down with hot drinks and smiles of antici-pation. I stood, let out a long, slow breath and began. I told them about finding the red diamond in the helmet of salvation, how I'd assumed it was glass and spilled the beans to New York Jewelers, how in a few weeks' time, news had reached around the globe. And how that made me a marked man. Though I'd passed myself off as George Telanoo from Georgia, I still feared that roughly half the human population was ready to slit my throat to have the diamond.

The Stallards sat there beaming. They thought I was leading up to big drama like they had done. My heart pounded in my ears. "If that armor of God is a symbol of spiritual things," I pointed to the pieces now spread out neatly in the corner, "then so is the Tear of Blood. I've been thinking about its purpose for over a year. It was in the helmet of salvation, so its message has to be about saving people. I think it stands for God's tears over his lost children and the drops of blood Jesus gave. The triangle facets stand for Father, Son, and Holy Spirit. Mind, body, and spirit. Birth, death, resurrection. Yesterday, today, forever … a hundred meanings."

I cleared my throat. My face felt hot. "But instead of a great treasure, it ended up being a burden, heavier than that two-ton rock in Gilead. It was only a matter of time before I'd be found, my family would be robbed or kidnapped, and it would be lost forever. My family, they're not believers yet. How could I risk their lives over a rock? Yeah, I know it's priceless and forged from fires in the bowels of the earth and all that … I lost a week's sleep deciding what to do with it."

The Stallards turned somber. Their backs went stiff.

"After Gilead, and after I'd preached to my high school, a new kind of fearlessness came over me. But at the same time, I was going back into fear because of the diamond. I couldn't walk down Main Street for thinking I'd be mugged. God wouldn't want me living like that."

The smiles completely faded from the Stallards' faces. They knew something was up.

Pulling four velvet pouches out of my jacket pocket, I heaved a breath. "Well, this is as good a time as any." I handed out the pouches to my clan. When they poured out their jewelry, it took a moment to register what I'd done with the Tear of Blood. Every kind of expression washed across their faces: shock, excitement, disbelief, anger.

"I had to," I looked at the baffled audience. "I had to." I said to the clan, "I had the Tear of Blood divided. I designed the jewelry like I thought you'd want. Mei, yours is a pendant that looks like a compass. Wherever you go, God will guide you.

"Rob, yours is a ring. The spiral design is the whirlwind that wrecked your house but worked things out with your family for the best. Marcus, yours is an ID bracelet. The stone is in a sand dollar design, which tells the story of Jesus. You can have anything you want engraved on the bracelet. Reece, the last piece broke in two when the gem master was working on it, so I had it made into earrings. They're eagle feathers. You know what they mean." I explained how I'd used the sixth cut for payment.

"The metal is electrum—gold and silver—like Job 22:25-28 says: 'The Almighty will be your gold, the choicest silver for you.' We'd looked at this verse, but never read the rest. Get this: 'Surely then you will find delight in the Almighty and will lift up your face to God. You will pray to him, and he will hear you, and you will fulfill your vows. What you decide on will be done, and light will shine on your ways.'"

I looked at the Stallards pleadingly. Their expressions were blank with shock. "If we think this diamond was valuable, just think how much power is in every drop of God's blood, how much his tears cost: enough to save millions of people in every single drop. I couldn't hide it away, Dr. Dale! I couldn't be on the run the rest of my life because of a priceless piece of rock. *It's just a rock!* All the world wants it, but the world doesn't understand what it's really worth—what it really means. The Tear of Blood isn't for a museum or some filthy-rich woman to wear at big parties. It's supposed to help truth go out to the whole world before the Day of Evil comes. It's about salvation."

I looked back to my clan. "You each have a piece of the Tear of Blood. You have a job to do, a vow to fulfill. If you don't want to do it, pass along your treasure."

Marcus fastened the heavy bracelet around his wrist and got

choked up. "Thanks, man. Thanks."

As the others put their jewelry on, I finished up. "If the Day of Evil comes and you need to sell it for food or to help people, do it. Don't feel bad. I don't know how much the jewelry is worth, but it's a lot."

"Where's yours?" Reece whispered.

I grinned. "I'm not much for jewelry."

She looked horrified, "You don't have one?"

"Yeah, I do."

She reached over, tugged on my earlobe, and frowned. "Where is it?"

I yanked the waistband of my khakis down and showed them my belly button.

Rob guffawed. "You had it pierced?!"

I looked over the crowd. "If anyone wants mine, if you need it right now, it's yours."

For a minute there was dead silence. People glanced around uneasily to see how other people were reacting. Then Dr. Dale pulled his old, arthritic self up off his floor cushion and limped over to me. Deliberately he put his hand in mine. "Wisdom," he said deeply. He raised his other hand to Heaven. "'I praise you, Father, Lord of heaven and earth, because you have hidden these things from the wise and learned, and revealed them to little children.'" Then he put his hands together. One clap, then two, then another. Slowly everyone in the room stood and clapped and smiled at us. Waves of relief washed over me. The old scientist nodded to the crowd. "'The price of wisdom is beyond rubies.'"

I realized in that moment how much the Stallards' respect meant to me.

Dr. Dale and Dr. Eloise admitted they were shocked but applauded my "uncommonly clear perspective." Whatever. I was just glad not to be clobbered for committing some crime of global proportions.

The clan was all over me with thanks, saying how they liked the jewelry and how they'd honor its purpose. Then Reece nailed me. She got right up under my nose and demanded, "Okay. What's this about the dark forces? Spill!"

CHAPTER 9

My clan was on a huge high. We'd stormed the gates without a scratch, had a great meal (Rob renamed it okeydokey-yaki because he liked the taste but couldn't say the word). We'd shown off the armor of God to people from all over the world. The Stallards were pretty okay with my breaking up the Tear of Blood into pieces—huge relief. So we five wanted to go out on the town, even though there wasn't much town to go out on. While the Stallards were in meetings, we went to the *ofuro* and then called the SOS to come over. While we hung out in the girls' room to wait, I explained about the dark forces, how in that bookstore in Ireland the clerk had said in a demon voice, "You'll never find it," and how it rattled me—especially after our futile search for the sword. The clan was stone sober taking it in. Even Marcus, who'd bragged about his knowledge of the dark side—stunned speechless.

Finally, Rob said in a creeped-out way, "You mean demons are really real?"

"But God's more real," Reece said earnestly.

Marcus looked at me curiously. "Something my dad said, Takumi, about your needing spiritual backup … you told him about this, didn't you?"

"I had to get it off my chest. But we did find the sword though, so the evil voice was lying."

Reece said doubtfully, "We haven't found the word on it."

"We will," I insisted. "It's got to be there."

The SOS came over with dripping hair and dressed in blue *yukatas,* just like us, and for a second I imagined them all as my clan. We strolled through the village, sporting our new jewelry, dodging sidewalk bicyclists every few minutes. Nothing was open but bars, so we found a bunch of vending machines and dug out pocket change for royal milk tea. Mei was our resident expert, and people kept asking her what foods were good. Li worked his way over to her and said, *"Moukari makka?"*

Beaming with surprise, she went all coy and answered, *"Bochibochi denna."* She translated for us. "He said, 'How's business?' and I said, 'So-so.' He speaks my Osaka dialect!"

Mei and Li went off in their own little world, using a bunch of languages. I couldn't read Marcus, but he sure kept an eye on them, at least until Karinna and her friends swarmed him.

We strolled along in the warm evening breeze. A starry sky spread over the looming black mountains. From what Reece and I picked up, the Students of the Seven Seas were kids with an interest in global spiritual problems. Some had parents in the same business; others had to go to church alone or in secret. Mahesh was kicked out of his family for his beliefs and wasn't sure where he'd go after his SOS tour of duty was over.

It wasn't long before Rob was goofing off doing his Ohio version of a ninja. Even if he'd had the traditional black getup, he'd have looked goofy enough. But a block away, dancing around Marcus in his long tight robe, chopping the air, he was an old, bald lady fighting off a nonchalant mugger.

Reece giggled, "They're at it again. Will it never end?"

Their stark silhouettes highlighted by streetlights, Rob thrust stiff hands in front of Marcus and cried, "AaeeeeeAH!"

Marcus eased back and said coolly (to impress Karinna), "Don't want to hurt you, buddy." Rob froze for a second, then whirled around and skittered with baby steps across the street.

Reece asked, "Where's he going?"

"Running start. He's getting steam for a karate kick at Marcus … but … oh no … no, Rob. Wait! Your skirt!"

Hands in a chop-chop position, he loped sideways across the street toward Marcus, hollering, "Aaeeeah-HYA!" and kicked. That *yukata* bound him up below the knees; his left leg shot out, the other leg came up with it, and he went sailing sideways in midair, like a cartoon. Marcus eased out of the way, and Rob disappeared into an alley—followed by an awful racket of trash cans, bikes, and who-knows-what echoing down the street.

Eva from Germany ran into the alley to retrieve the body of my crazy cousin; the rest of the SOS lost it. They hung off each other clutching their stomachs; they leaned against street poles in hysterics. One guy dropped to the street on his knees and howled like a coyote. In a minute Rob emerged to the wild applause of the SOS and made a deep curtsy.

Reece hugged my arm. "I'm so glad he's one of us."

. . . . .

"'Lijah!"

My head jerked off the pillow, the urgent whisper jarring me awake. The room was pitch-black. "What time is it?"

"'Lijah, pretend you're asleep!" Rob wheezed.

"I *was* asleep!" I moaned and dropped back on the pillow.

"I know, but pretend you are!" Frantically he piled pillows and clothes on his pallet, covering them with a blanket until it looked like a body asleep. He jumped over me onto Marcus's pallet. Marcus wasn't there. "Restroom," Rob explained. Hurriedly he hid himself under a pile of dirty laundry beside Marcus's backpack.

Retribution, I thought and snickered, "Got it."

"Shhh!"

Turning toward Marcus's pallet, I pulled my covers around

my face, closed my eyes, and waited for the show to start.

The door clicked open; feet padded on straw mat. I adjusted my breathing, slow and regular. He plopped down on the pallet … a rustle of sheets, then all quiet. My eyes opened to slits, and because I'd trained myself to see in the dark, I could make out his profile. For a few minutes, it was quiet except for steady breathing. I bit my lip with anticipation. Then from the other side of Marcus came a low, guttural, "Mmaarrccuuss …"

Half awake, Marcus wailed like a siren with weak batteries, "OooooowhatISIT!?" He came straight up off the floor like he'd been detonated, and flung himself over me. Landing on Rob's squishy fake body, he made a sick cat sound of disgust. To keep him from hurtling through the paper screen, I grabbed his arm; he thought the thing had him and squealed like a girl.

Rob exploded from the pile of dirty laundry, raised his fists, and cried victoriously, "I am Shinobu! Master of Stealth!!"

Once we'd peeled Marcus off the ceiling, we lay there in the dark, too wired to sleep. Ryo, the "cool" one, had blown his cover. In the end he didn't really mind the prank: "Shinobu, you'll always get the last laugh. You're a dangerous man."

It seemed like life couldn't get any better, like nothing could ever go wrong.

· · · · ·

The next morning the SOS joined us on the busy sidewalk outside the inn. The day was already heating up. The Stallards came down in matching brown suits. Rob couldn't wait to tell everyone how Marcus "went soprano" on him last night. In talkative clumps, we made a left and headed into town, dodging oncoming bicyclists.

Dr. Eloise said, "Careful there, Reece, watch those tricky holes in the sidewalk. Now where is that bakery I noticed yesterday? Ah, across the street. And some of our people. *Ohayou!* Good morning!" She waved and then chirped, "Dale, assist Reece if you will."

We started crossing the busy street a few at a time. Dr. Dale took Reece's arm. She smiled and sang, "To the left, to the left, to the left left left."

Dodging traffic, Rob and Marcus danced across, trading karate moves. Mei was looking up, explaining a road sign to Eva. Reece was right in front of me. It happened so fast, I didn't see it coming. There was nothing I could have done.

CHAPTER 10

A sickening thud. A horrible, hurtling black blur. Shattering glass. A heavy crunch shook the ground. The car didn't even slow down. It plowed right into our group. Dr. Eloise fell back. Her arm shot out in front of Reece, who stumbled back into me. Dr. Dale, who'd been standing at right angles to Reece and guiding her steps, took a direct hit and disappeared. He was there, and then he wasn't. Screams. Tires squealed. Other cars screeched to a stop. Cries of horror. The hiss of air: blown tires, engine steam. A razor-sharp flashback cut through my mind: the grill of the black coupe had slammed into his legs, his shoulder hit the hood, he went into the windshield, it shattered, the car careened full force into a utility pole. *God …* A quiet voice that was mine came from a deep place inside me, a knowing place. I was already past wishing *no, please no*. It had happened in the blink of an eye. There was nothing anyone could have done.

Reece was chalk white, her eyes glazed and confused. I put my arm around her, scanned the crowd to locate the guys, and ordered them back across the street. "Marcus! Come on, but watch out! Rob, you too!" Then Mei had hold of Reece. The guys dashed across the stalled traffic and stared in horror at the car. I stepped into their sight line. "He's gone. Take the SOS and Reece and go back to the inn … unless anyone saw the whole thing—they should stay. I'll need Mei here. Reece, go with the others." Adults from the conference were running toward us.

"Anybody else here speak Japanese?" I asked them.

Li was there. "I know a little."

"Hang close." I'd gone into camp counselor mode without realizing it. Where was Dr. Eloise? There, at the crushed, steaming car. I went over to her. The whole front of the black coupe had collapsed on impact, Dr. Dale thrown into the front seat. He was curled up, his face pressed against the back of the seat. As if he'd fallen asleep in the car. Peaceful, still. Dr. Eloise reached her hand into the car's shattered side window and patted the familiar brown suit, now covered with pebbles of broken glass. *No blood. Not a drop. Probably didn't want to inconvenience anyone,* I thought with a strange, crazed detachment. *Didn't want to be any trouble.* I put a hand on Dr. Eloise's shoulder.

Eventually she looked up at me, her eyes glittering with tears, her thin lips quivering. "It was painless, wasn't it?"

"Yeah. It was."

She kept patting his back. "He never did relish the thought of lingering … some long, slow disease … he never wanted that… . He didn't even feel it."

"Not a thing. Why don't you go to that step and sit down?" I suggested. "The police will be here soon."

She didn't hear me but leaned further into the car, reaching over her husband to the man slumped over the steering wheel, motionless. "Oh dear," she said sadly. "Oh dear, sweet man! Lord, take his spirit if you will. He didn't know what he was doing. I'm sure he didn't know." She touched his head as if to give him a blessing, then straightened up and sniffled. "Sit where? Over there by the little garden? Don't the Japanese do wonders with their small spaces? Thank you, Elijah. Are the others all right?"

"We're good. You should sit down."

People from the conference encircled her. I edged myself out and found Mei. Crying but calm, she explained what would happen when the police came. It was pretty much the same as in the States. They'd want to talk to every witness. (But since Reece didn't see a thing, what good would it do for her to be here? I'd seen the look on her face. I knew, probably better than she did, what she was thinking.)

Others had seen the fatal black car run a red light and swerve for half a block, not once putting on the brakes. Mei said that drunk driving was a big problem in her culture.

"In America too," I said.

The conference people stood around sniffling, lips moving. While the police took statements, I weaved through the crowd, dazed but alert. They were crying and thanking God for the accident in the same breath, asking him to use it. To use them. To shine through the loss. They might have been speaking in a foreign language, it seemed so strange to me. Why weren't they bawling and asking why, why, why?

For a moment I stood there in a haze, remembering three years ago when Reece had first mentioned God using you. The idea had really turned me off. Getting used had seemed like a lame way to live. I looked around at the group, a hundred calm, sad people wearing their peace and faith … like armor. Getting used by God was Dr. Dale's reason for being. Theirs too. Yesterday they'd used words as weapons, now for comfort. Random thoughts floated through my head. *Dr. Dale's gone. He went down inches from us. We were inches from death. Reece. Inches. Like on the Cliffs of Morte … like me in Gilead … Dr. Dale was here. Now he's … somewhere in eternity.* A kind of quiet bubble surrounded me, and it seemed I heard his old, gentle voice say, *"The walls between the worlds are always thin, Elijah. Always thin."*

Reports were filed, two bodies taken away. Traffic was diverted to let the tow truck through. A crowd of hushed villagers milled around, not caring if they were late for work. My clan and the SOS wandered back out. As the car was being hauled off, a youngish Japanese woman came running down the middle of the street, her apron flying, her house slippers flapping, a look of terrified expectation on her face. One glance at the car and she stopped and crumpled to the street.

I didn't need an English translation to understand what was happening: the drunk man was her husband. A woman storekeeper came into the street and knelt down to comfort her; the wife asked how it happened; the storekeeper explained. Then the storekeeper nodded to Dr. Eloise who had stepped to the curb. The young Japanese wife got up, her face frozen in shame and fear; her husband had killed that foreign woman's husband.

Dr. Eloise stepped into the street, and the two women locked eyes. The wife stepped back, bracing for the foreigner's rage. The whole town stood still. Dr. Eloise stretched out her arms and called out, *"Daijoubu!* It's all right!" The wife stiffened as Dr. Eloise grasped her shoulders, looked into her face, and said, *"Daijoubu,* my friend!" Alone in a huge circle of onlookers, the widows clung to each other and cried and cried.

· · · · · ·

News spread among the conference people that regular meetings were postponed until further notice. There'd be a get-together tonight, a cremation in the morning.

All day Reece didn't come out of her room. She wouldn't talk to anyone or eat anything. Mei's face was strained and sad. As dinnertime approached, I knocked on their door. Mei opened it slightly. Over her head I saw Reece on her pallet, facing the wall.

Mei stepped into the hall and whispered, "She thinks it was her fault because she was joking to Dr. Dale about 'to the left

left left,' and he was supposed to look to the right. The cars come from the right."

"Reece?" I called into her room.

"Go away."

"Reece, come on—"

"Go away!"

CHAPTER 11

We gathered in the meeting room at the community center. Fred played his banjo, easy and gentle and full of hope. People hovered around Dr. Eloise like guardian angels; they sat at her feet like children. We four sank down in a corner watching like outsiders for a while, with nothing much to say until Veronica came over. "How are you kids holding up?"

"We're okay," I said halfheartedly. "Reece is back at the inn. She's tired."

She sat down next to me. "I came to say thanks, Elijah."

"For what?"

"You took over. You started handling things seconds before the rest of us—adults included—could even register what had happened."

I shrugged. "I was right there."

"You have amazing presence of mind in a crisis," she said, studying me.

"My dad owns a nature camp. I help him a lot because there's always something."

She agreed, "Yes, there's always something, isn't there? Sounds like you have lots of experience."

The evening wore on. Food was brought, floor cushions handed out. Blankets came and Dr. Eloise rested. I worried about Reece. Then who should walk in with a woman at his side but Donovan.

Mahesh said, "Look, it's Donovan and Hester."

I knew without asking that the woman was the daughter of Dale and Eloise. Hester was every bit a Stallard, just thirty years younger: slight build, energetic, bright eyes, short brown hair, and clothes so old-fashioned they were cool again. They hugged and cried with Dr. Eloise; then Donovan came over. We all stood and shook hands.

"How's that foot?" Donovan asked.

"Good."

He looked us over and asked kindly, "How's everyone doing?"

"Okay. Reece is sleeping."

He nodded toward Dr. Eloise. "I need to get back to the family. We'll talk later."

Mahesh leaned over, amazed. "You know them already?"

"Yeah."

"Wow. They're *parabolani*," he said. I must have looked blank. "They didn't tell you?"

Now I felt really stupid. "No."

"They will, I guess. Once you're in."

When we sat down again, I looked to Rob, the smart one. *"Parabo … ?"*

Marcus had a strange look on his face. "Mom and Dad have used that word. I thought it was spy stuff."

When the swarm of people cleared around Dr. Eloise, she caught sight of us in the corner and came over—her eyes red-rimmed, a strong smile on her face. "We are not going home, children. He wouldn't have wanted that. After the cremation, I will need to tie up a few loose ends here. I'll join you in Shimabara. But I'm afraid you will have to do the prayer journey at Mei's on your own. Are you prepared?"

"We can handle it," I said confidently. "Same as at Nikko."

No one wanted to leave the meeting room. It was looking like an all-nighter, so I slipped out and went back to the inn. I knocked on Reece's door.

"Go away."

I went in anyway and sat beside her on the floor. She knew I was there but didn't say anything. After a long while, I said, "Reece, get up." She ignored me. I waited a few minutes then barked, "I said get up!"

Startled by my harsh tone, she sat up and wobbled but wouldn't look at me, her eyes cast down, hair hanging over her face. I pulled her to me and hugged her hard. "You didn't do it, Reece! It wasn't your fault."

She leaned against me lifelessly and whimpered, "I said, 'to the left,' and he looked left. He didn't look to the right. I knew he always got it confused, but I was joking around."

"He was an old guy," I said nonchalantly. "He wasn't going to last much longer anyway. And Dr. Eloise said he would have wanted to go that way. It was better for him than to have a lingering disease and suffer a lot."

She was limp as a dishrag in my arms. Wouldn't say a word. Where was the feisty, optimistic, outspoken, unsinkable Reece Elliston? Where had she gone? I wondered if I'd lost two people.

The next morning I went by the girls' room. Mei came out alone and closed the door. "She is so sad she can't lift up her head."

"You guys go on. I'll catch up."

I went in, knelt down beside her, and grabbed her shoulders. "Reece, look at me!" She wouldn't. I made her sit up. "Hey, girl, if you believe anything that you yourself have told me over the past three years, then Dr. Dale is in Heaven and having the time of his life. If you don't believe that—if you've been making all this up—then you're a big fat liar, and you need to go home!"

Her eyes drifted up to me. She was hardly breathing. "He died because he was helping me."

"No, Reece, he died because he got hit by a drunk driver. It happens every day in every country in the world. Come on, this isn't like you. It was horrible, but we gotta get a grip, okay?" I brushed the hair out of her face. "Hey, there's a world out there that needs protecting, and we have the whole armor of God, remember? That's why we're here. I'm not leaving without you. Remember what I always say? It's our motto: if I'm going, you're going."

Donovan's memorial speech gave details of Dr. Dale's life I never knew. He was born and raised in Nebraska, lost his parents young, served in the military, had degrees in history, archaeology, and anthropology. Married at twenty-one, he had one daughter, Hester. "Dale Stallard made significant discoveries in the field of Near Eastern studies before his life purpose changed course. My father-in-law was an atheist until he began to compare the ancient history he knew so well with the Word of the living God. He found that Word to be true. More than true. Dad discovered it was *the* truth."

He paused and looked around at the crowd sitting informally on cushions. "A friend of mind once said that each person you meet comes into your life with an encrypted message from God. So instead of me rambling, I'd like anyone who knew Dale Stallard to briefly tell the message you received from him."

Dozens of adults took turns saying stuff about his radical faith, his quiet courage, about times when they were ready to give up and then Dale and Eloise showed up out of nowhere and talked them through it. Then Donovan nodded to me. My clan stood together.

Choking back tears, Reece started, "I'll … I'll always remember how he fought for us in prayer. And how he died helping me."

Dr. Eloise said, "Reece, dear heart, it was his time, not yours. Don't grieve. He would gladly have gone in your place."

The room got quiet.

I spoke up. "When we were in Ireland and he quit eating, that's what I'll remember. He was worried about us and wondered why God had chosen a bunch of dumb kids to find his armor. But he didn't lecture or point out our faults. He took the burden on himself. I'll never forget how he helped me build a fire—" my voice cracked, "a fire on the Hill of Slane and how he read from the *Warrior* against the darkness that night."

Rob spoke up next. "I guess he taught me that it's cool to be a nerd, even an old one. So there's hope for me."

Everyone chuckled, and for a minute the sadness eased up.

Mei sniffled. "Our tradition in Japan is to honor the old ones. So I couldn't believe that Dr. Dale was happy to be my friend. He honored *me!* Dr. Stallard was a very honorable man."

Marcus stared at the floor, his jaw was clenched. He couldn't speak.

"Marcus," said Dr. Eloise, "it's all right."

"The last thing he said to me—" he turned away and swallowed hard. "After the day at the shrine up there, I was going off on how cool it was to be bringing down pagan gods with words. He said, 'Humble yourself before the Lord, Marcus, and he will lift you up. Don't exalt yourself. Let him raise you up.'" Marcus gulped hard, wiped his eyes. "I'll work on it."

Dr. Eloise called out, "Oh, how he believed in you children! Dale called you his Magdeline Five. In like manner to the Cambridge Seven, those courageous young people of European history, journeying to the very ends of the earth! Why, just yesterday morning as we lay in the quiet of our room, he said to me, 'Eloise, God has not spared our Magdeline Five the pains of this life, but he has certainly called them out of their lives into his work. How fiercely he must love them!' He sat watching the morning come with a glorious smile on his face and said, 'Long after we're gone, God will use them.'"

My clan sat down. Except for sniffling and clearing of throats, it was quiet for a long time. Then Fred started playing his banjo again. Someone started singing. We joined in where we could—songs about Heaven, how God reigns there, and how the rhythm of his power echoes throughout the world. Guitar and bongos joined in. For a half hour, people sang in all kinds of languages. At the end there was a standing ovation to Dr. Dale and to the God he served. My throat was so tight I couldn't talk afterward.

Everyone was wrung out, but again no one could leave the community center. It started looking like a lock-in at church: people eating, some singing, playing cards, or sound asleep on pillows. Marcus called his dad to tell him the news; Dom Skidmore offered to bring us all home. We said we were fine, that we still had a prayer journey to make. He promised to call our parents and tell them the sad news.

Some of the SOS kids came over and wanted to know more about us being the Magdeline Five. As we went around the circle reliving the past three years, I myself was shocked, even though I'd lived it. Rob told about his parents almost splitting up, how he'd almost drowned on Farr Island, how a tornado slammed his house. Reece told how she went down at Hermits' Cave looking for the shoes of peace, and how God had taken away her pain the night of her operation. I explained how the quest had led us to the grave of Kate Dowland and stirred up the whole town and uncovered why Old Pilgrim Church had died. It was great to talk about it openly after so long. No secrets.

While Marcus was telling about how his parents' friendship with the Stallards had got us connected in the first place, Mahesh started looking at him weird. "Your dad knows the Stallards?"

"Yeah. They met in the Middle East."

"Is he part of the network?"

Marcus said uncertainly, "He knows about it."

Mahesh asked at the others, "Doesn't Marcus look a lot like Metatron?"

· · · · ·

Through that night—in a foreign country, at the foot of a mountain ruled by pagan gods, with that dream of the threatening flower at the front of my mind, and having lost our adopted grandpa—in all that strangeness, the Magdeline Five learned some surprising facts. Number one: Dom—aka Metatron—and Donovan were *parabolani.*

Sitting cross-legged with a cup of coffee in his hands, Donovan explained it this way: "In the early days of the church, there came to be a group of people who rescued fellow Christians in danger and retrieved the bodies of those lost in spiritual warfare. They were the *parabolani,* the riskers, who gambled with their lives to help others. Today they do everything from smuggling Bibles to outfitting and equipping missionaries."

Li added, "Some are experts in security systems and high-tech communications."

Rob interrupted, "Like Dr. Eloise's binoculars with a secret recording device?"

Mahesh said, "And escape techniques, like jumping out of buildings blindfolded."

Karinna added, "They have hiding places all over the world for when the Day of Evil comes."

"Dunluce Castle was one!" Reece cried. "The Stallards were starting to show us!" It was good to see her sparkle a little.

Li said, "My country has thousands of places. I even know a few."

I said to Donovan, "So when you and Dom rescued me, you were being the … the *para*—?"

"*Parabolani.* We prayed for rescue. Thank God for that little fire you set."

I winked at Reece, remembering how I'd burned her poem. "Without that piece of paper I'd have had no fire."

Donovan said, "Without that fire you wouldn't be here. You had two days left at the most. Now, the *peregrini:* these are pilgrims who move often and acclimate to other cultures quickly. At the first level of spiritual warfare, they pray at strongholds. Like you already saw. On the next level, they go into the dangerous places and preach the gospel in homes, churches, on street corners. The *peregrini* venture into hostile areas for short periods, do their work, and clear out to avoid capture. The apostle Paul is the model of a *peregrini.*"

"And Patrick of Ireland," I added, "and Columba and Brendan. Dr. Dale told us about the *peregrini*. And about seraphs."

He nodded. "Seraphs—the burning ones—are the third category: missionaries. We call them seraphs when we're in high-threat situations. These are preachers, teachers, and doctors who settle in a place for long periods of time—even for life. Theirs may be the least dangerous but the most lonely, difficult work. They stay because of a burning passion for the lost. No matter what, they stay."

Mahesh turned to Marcus. "I met your father once. He is *parabolani* and has no fear. Big and scary. Tough talker."

"Where? How?" Marcus looked miffed that a stranger could know more about his dad than he did.

Li said, "At orientation in Alaska. He told a story about a guy named Metatron going into a jungle to rescue a captured missionary. The missionary was cut loose and escaped. Metatron disappeared. Everybody was sure he was killed, until he showed up two weeks later—just walked out of the jungle hungry as a horse. Then your dad explained how he did it. He's a legend."

Rob gaped at me. "Farr Island, guys! Dom and his two buddies hiding in the trees, teaching us jungle warfare! He said it was a refresher course, to keep his reflexes on alert!"

"Saving the world," I muttered, dumbfounded. "When we visited that military base, Peck and Yancy said they had to get back to saving the world. They're *parabolani*?" I asked Donovan. "How big is this network?"

"Nobody knows because it's invisible." He grinned. "Well, God knows. But he's the only one. Commander in chief, you see. These three branches of the network form what we call the helix."

"People in churches—do they know?" I asked.

He shrugged. "Some of them get it. Some don't." Donovan excused himself and went back to Hester.

"So who is the SOS?" I asked Mahesh. "Are you guys seraphs or *peregrini* or *parabolani?*"

"We don't know who we are yet, or if we qualify. That's why we're SOS—basic training."

Leaning against the wall angrily, his green eyes hard as stone, Marcus demanded, "How many of you—ballpark figure?"

Li said, "Three hundred on our ship."

"Where are the rest?" Mei asked.

"All over Japan ... working. We'll set sail again in September for survival training in Samoa. Don't ask me how many ships. I don't know. The inland teams are in the thousands, maybe millions. I'm not sure. But what about you Magdeline Five—are you joining?"

. . . . .

Dr. Dale was cremated the next day. Dr. Eloise invited us to go along with Donovan and Hester, Veronica, and a few other adults because, as she said, "You five were the closest to grandchildren he had."

His body was in a box with a glass lid. Flowers were around his face. Donovan said a prayer for us and for the Japanese woman who also lost her husband. Then a door in the wall opened and the casket slid into another room. We went down to a waiting area.

Dr. Eloise sat next to us. "Perhaps this is not the best time, children, but a decision must be made about the armor. Now that its existence has been confirmed, our problem is Cravens and others of his ilk. He doesn't know that the Tear of Blood has been dispersed. Dividing the diamond was genius and so very brave. But it does not solve our problem entirely. The armor is still a legendary relic. It contains pieces of the ancient tabernacle of God and remnants of spiritual history from all ages. And the sword of the Lord, as plain as it looks, is a thing from the mists, origins unknown—a magic charm to some who don't understand. In the wrong hands, the armor of God would be dissected and fought over. Claims, hot debates, backroom deals, tests and more tests ... it would inevitably be enshrined in a museum or cathedral and prayed to!" She clicked her tongue. "Elijah, you are unusually logical about such situations. Do you have a suggestion?" Before I could think, she went on, "I had thought of burying it with my husband's remains back home."

I looked around. None of us liked the idea, but out of respect we considered it.

Mysteriously, Rob said, "Guys! 'Piece by piece they will rest in peace. Like the loved ones, in the ground.' Dowland's prophecy comes true!"

Dr. Eloise said, "My reasoning was this: I would select an aboveground crypt and use a casket—as if there were a body. The casket could hold the ashes and the armor. It is illegal to exhume a body without a court order, so our treasure would be safe—should we have need of it. The armor has served its purpose: to inspire you and the network, the fountainhead of this generation ... perhaps the final generation." Wistfully she added, "I wish the whole network could see it somehow. Ah well, if memory of it grows dim, it can be circulated. But only a handful of us will know where it is."

"We never found the word on the sword," Reece said. "What about the legend that the sword speaks?"

She made a thin smile. "The Bible, which is the Word of God, speaks to us. That must be the answer."

I wasn't keen on the idea of burying the armor—not at all—but since we couldn't come up with a better idea, we agreed to go along with her decision—as long as we knew where the armor was.

We got called back to the first room. Dr. Eloise gasped as if she'd remembered something important and said in a rush, "Cremation is the Japanese custom, so do not be shocked. He is in Heaven and cares not a whit about his mortal body. He will put on a resurrection body as Jesus did when he came back from the grave. Are you prepar—"

Donovan whispered, "Brace yourselves."

The door in the wall opened and out came a huge tray carrying the skeleton of Dr. Dale—or most of it. Mei was the only one in our clan who wasn't a breath away from freaking out.

We stood there horrified as they picked up pieces of his bones with chopsticks and put them in a big urn. Mei quietly said to us, "I am sorry if this scares you. But I must be honest—we Japanese think American funerals are terrible. People touch a dead body! How awful!"

Rob had turned that nice shade of green again. I whispered harshly, "No *luftkrankheit,* Cuz, got that? No *luftkrankheit!*"

Dr. Eloise didn't flinch through the whole ceremony. I thought back over the two years I'd known her, how easily—even cheerfully—she coped with morbid stuff. Like Reece, she was stronger than she looked.

When Dr. Dale's remains were in the urn, Donovan shook

our hands. "Thanks for being here with Eloise. It meant a lot to her. Each culture has its way of dealing with death, all pretty gruesome in one way or the other. I've seen my share. But it has to be done; people die. Sorry we didn't give you advance notice."

Rob murmured glumly, "It wouldn't have helped."

We met the rest of the people back at the mountain stream, but the spirit wasn't the same as before. Mei cried to think that Dr. Dale had baptized her a few days ago. We lay around on rocks like lazy walruses, listening to the stream, watching clouds float by, not saying much. Reece and I shared a rock, held hands, and stared at the sky.

In a daze she said, "Birds … cars … water … clouds … people … everything's rushing past us so fast, going away."

The next day the conference resumed at a quiet pace. There were Bible studies and discussions on science and archaeology—and "training." The training included group games to test how people worked together and handled stressful situations. We heard testimonies from around the world about miracles and brushes with death, updates about secret churches meeting in basements and forests and caves, stories about angel appearances, people rescued from torture, children "kidnapped" out of slavery. All of this stuff happening in The Window—and it was spreading.

I sat there on my floor pillow surrounded by my clan and people from every corner of the planet. *Where in the world have I been? Off in my safe little corner, oblivious.* Sure, I appreciated Mom and Dad protecting me from this kind of stuff when I was a grade-school kid—more grateful than ever. *But now*—I could hardly believe I was thinking it—*now I'm old enough and strong enough to do something about it. To be a part of it.*

We had dinner at the okeydokey-yaki place. Hester had gone with Dr. Eloise to rest, so Reece and I sat with Donovan, Li and

Mei, and Baruti from Egypt. Baruti was a rugged, dignified man with gray hair, a wide face, and piercing eyes. As he poured batter on the grill, a chain around his neck swung forward with a medallion engraved with the tri-swirl design I'd seen on the tomb at Newgrange in Ireland.

"What's that?" I asked.

"The helix."

"What's it mean?"

He glanced at Donovan who gave him the go-ahead. "It's a universal symbol, claimed by Celts, Buddhists, Wicca, and Hopi Indians, to name a few. But in truth it is older than them all and refers to tribal migrations, homecomings. It is the symbol of our network. You see, three times God commanded mankind to go into all the world. He gave Adam and Eve the whole earth to fill and subdue. Centuries later he told Noah's three sons the same thing." Baruti's voice boomed through the restaurant, "Go! Fill the earth!

"Instead, humankind gathered to build a tower with the hopes of installing a one-world government and reaching Heaven, making themselves gods." He fixed his eyes on Reece and me. "To spare mankind an early demise, the Lord confused the people's language and scattered them across the face of the earth."

Li said, "The third and final order came from God the Son: "'Go and make disciples of all nations.'"

Baruti fingered the medallion. "Correct. Three commands. Three people groups from the sons of Noah. Three types of warriors: riskers, wanderers, and those who stay."

Donovan pulled his medallion out from under his shirt and showed us. "Each is personalized, encoded with information: how many coils in each spiral, which direction they spin. Each element refers to a global position, a people group, and so forth. You probably didn't know this, but since you young people found the *Ogham* script on the shield, the Stallards suggested we add those markings to denote names and meeting places. Each medallion contains much more information than a military dog tag." He smiled. "And this symbol is a great conversation starter. People think it means everything from alien abductions to genetic mutation to prehistoric sun worship … which gives us an opportunity to talk about our mission: to fill the earth with God's truth and rescue his people."

"Most Christians wear crosses," Reece said skeptically.

Baruti stirred meat on the grill and said grimly, "Not all countries have the freedom you enjoy in the United States. In some places, if we wear crosses, we are sitting ducks."

CHAPTER 12

The whole next day my clan withdrew. Marcus brooded. As far as I could tell, he was ticked that he'd been kept in the dark about his dad's secret career. Mei became Reece's shadow again, quiet and helpful, mostly because Reece still felt guilty about Dr. Dale's death. She was in a lot of pain because of the stress. Rob lost his comic edge and slept. I spent the afternoon at the stream. I'd gotten a glimpse of the big picture and needed time to take it in.

When Donovan and Hester left Nikko, Veronica kept Dr. Eloise company. Every morning I'd wake before sunrise and go for a run. Thoughts of the threatening flower nagged at me. The next few days of training with the members of the helix were something I'd never forget and can't really describe. These average-looking people knew everything about science and language and the Bible and spy-type stuff—all rolled into one. And there was this light in their eyes.... .

At the final send-off, we gathered in a tight spiral so everyone was hugging everyone. As powerful prayers went up, the feeling of the Presence was so thick you could cut it with a knife. But for me personally, God was silent.

On the final morning at Nikko, I got dressed at dawn and headed downstairs, planning to go to the stream to think and pray. I was getting my shoes on when Veronica appeared. She'd been waiting for me.

"Good morning, Elijah. Out for a run so early?"

"Yeah. I'm still on American time, I guess."

"Mind if I tag along?"

"Uh, not at all."

Answering my doubtful expression she pulled a form out of her pocket and said, "Don't worry, it's good news."

. . . . . .

Late morning we checked out of the inn. The SOS came by to say good-bye, which was hard. It seemed we'd known them forever. Time had gone strange after losing Dr. Dale.

Apologizing for not going with us, Dr. Eloise sat a big suitcase down in front of me: the armor. "Where you are going next, you will not be welcome. I am speaking of the principalities and powers, not the people. This is a reminder of the power you have at your disposal. Know your enemy and, more importantly, know that in your weakness God is strong. Whatever happens, don't be afraid."

"What could happen?" I asked uneasily.

"Anything," she said with a sad smile. "Anything could happen. Pray the armor on. Follow the procedure that Dale set out for you. Enjoy your time with Mei. She can bring you on to Shimabara. I'll meet you at the castle there in a few days."

Rob chimed in knowingly, "Southern island. Eight hundred miles."

My clan got a taxi to the old station and tickets for the train. Marcus had seen all this before in his travels, but we three Ohio *gaijins*—Rob, Reece, and myself—were impressed that kids, even grade-schoolers, could go all over a country by themselves on mass transit. The slow train took us back down through the dark mountains to the station where we picked up the bullet train again: a double-decker, even bigger and sleeker than the first.

"Honestly, Mei," I said as we boarded, "this is better than driving. You can sightsee, eat, sleep, go anywhere in luxury. Who needs a car?"

She grinned slyly. "Me."

For the next few hours, Rob and Mei chatted and ate *onigiri*. Marcus brooded. Reece slept against the window and didn't even flinch when other trains whooshed past just inches from her face. All the walking had been a drain on her, but she hadn't complained. She'd kept up.

We got off in Osaka and wound forever through the huge station. Without Mei, the Magdeline Five would have been lost lambs in a wild stampede of humanity. Snarfing down convenience-store meals, we caught a local for Kii Peninsula. For an hour we stood, packed like sardines, zipping through the humongous downtown again. I tried to imagine how all those people could live crammed together, so different from the wide-open spaces I called home. I felt small. Swallowed up.

As our train headed into the country, the crowd thinned out, and we found seats. Then it went dark. Not a darkness you see with your eyes; the August sun was blazing hot out there. I turned to Rob. "Did you feel that?"

"Feel what?"

"We just crossed over into ... something. I don't know." Reece was writing postcards. I asked her, "Hey, Reece, did you feel something just happen, you know, spiritual?"

She sat still, as if listening. "Not really."

Marcus was asleep sitting up.

I moved over to Mei. "Remember the Stallards talking about that dream? Is there anything about a flower in your old religion?"

"I have been thinking about it, after Dr. Dale ... There is the *Lotus Sutra*, a Buddhist scripture. In the temples many gods are standing or sitting on lotus flowers or holding lotus flowers. And we have prayer chants to the lotus."

Reece said, "But the dream said the flower had no fragrance or purpose. Lotus flowers are useful."

I said, "I don't think it's a real flower. It's symbolic."

· · · · ·

At the station, Mei's aunt picked us up in a van. She told us in Japanese that she was very happy we'd come and hoped we enjoyed Japan. Mei said nothing about losing Dr. Dale. We all wanted to lay the horrible memory aside for a while, to relax and hang out on Mei's home turf. Marcus was pleased to have her all to himself again, no doubt about that.

Reece sniffed the air as we unpacked the van. "I smell peaches or apricots!"

"The valley is full of orchards, and it is harvest season," said Mei. "Our area is famous for fruit, especially *ume*, plums, which are made into wine and pickles. We will have fresh figs—my favorite!"

The house was small and old-style Japanese-y, with paper screens and dark wood and a garden out the back. It was way cool. I warned Rob not to go ninja and demolish it.

Reece settled into Mei's room. Mei's two little cousins— Kenji and Taka, ages seven and ten—moved out of their room so we guys could have it. Mei had been teaching them a lot of English, but Marcus had to show off his Japanese. "Hey guys, *moukari makka?*"

They burst into guffaws and yelled, "*Bochibochi denna!*"

Mei acted like it was the coolest thing.

We sat around a square coffee table and had sandwiches and fruit. None of us *gaijins* had ever had fresh figs, and Rob snarfed up way more than his share. When her aunt went into the kitchen to get more, Mei whispered to us, "We will visit the mission house soon, but don't talk about it."

It was a short walk down a dirt lane to the Trentons' mission house. I guessed this was where the prayer journey would start. But I didn't know; this was still new to me. Marcus hung his arm around Mei the whole walk (which I don't mind saying bothered me; he wasn't doing right by Miranda). The Trentons had a nice American-looking place—two stories with a big yard. Mei introduced Paul, a short, friendly guy in his early forties, with light hair. His wife Lenora—small with dark hair and eyes—served tea in the living room. We did the small-talk stuff and then told about losing Dr. Dale. The Trentons had heard of him.

Reece explained that we'd come to visit Mei. "And we want to pray about the problems at your church."

He chuckled at us with that "they're just kids" look and said, "Mei mentioned that."

"We're here with the armor of God," I said seriously. "We need to know what to pray about. A soldier should know who the enemy is."

"Soldiers, huh?" Paul dropped down on the couch and smiled as if he were going to have to humor us.

"We mean it," Reece said toughly.

She's back, I thought with relief. *Unsinkable Reece is back.*

"Okay. If you want it, here it is," said Paul frankly. "Our numbers are few, our problems are many and severe: mental illness, cancers, abuses, suicide attempts, panic attacks, you name it. For years we've struggled... ."

"We'll pray for a whole day. Two days even," Reece said.

"Thank you," he said. Then after a long, curious pause, "I have to say ... we get a lot of tourists from the States. They want to see the sights and sample the food. But we've never had any praying tourists." He smiled at us. "How 'bout you kids? Prayer warriors, huh? Okay, sure."

Remembering Dr. Dale's plan, I said, "We want to go to the temples and shrines around here and pray to God in places where he is ignored. But we won't be obnoxious."

"Is this a new kind of mission work?" Paul asked.

Marcus repeated what he'd heard at the conference, "It's very old. Like when Moses stood on the banks of the Red Sea with Pharaoh's army advancing. A bad fix they were in. Millions of people between the enemy and the deep blue sea. That's when you pray like crazy and let God do his stuff."

"What's causing the problems here?" Rob asked.

Paul entwined his fingers. "The problems are enmeshed, one tangled up in the other. They are offerings to idols—which are actually demons. There's praying to many buddhas who are seen as men or gods, depending on whom you ask. There's nature worship: sun, mountains, trees. The nation's leaders were once considered descendants of the sun goddess. There's ancestor worship and the fear of displeasing the family, living and dead, if you don't perform certain rituals. Do you see how complicated it is?" he said sharply. "It's all intertwined! How does a citizen respect his culture and get untangled from its spiritual darkness?"

Reece said, "Mei did!"

Paul smiled. "But at great personal cost. Her family is not pleased. Her friends make fun of her."

Reece's face screwed up in a sad frown. "They do?"

Mei smiled. "It's okay. We are taught to do what the family decides." Her eyes dropped. "I know that God is real; I know the Bible is true. But my mother is right that it is scary to believe in one God. Many little gods to choose from are easier than one big, powerful God."

Marcus nodded, "He's untamable, all right. Unstoppable."

Mei went on. "I believe I can be a good Japanese and good daughter and a Christian too. I have a little more courage every day with the armor of God."

Paul studied his interwoven fingers defeatedly.

I asked, "How about we start tomorrow?"

"Sure," Paul said agreeably. "Mei wants to take you to the

swimming hole, and today's a good hot day for it. The water is still swift from the typhoon," he warned, then chuckled, "which fortunately washed out the road to the local saloon. Their business has dropped off considerably!"

Rob said, "Hey, we flew in on that typhoon's tail!"

While the others made plans, I skimmed Paul's bookshelf.

"Looking for some reading material?" he asked.

"You have lots of religion books."

"It's my life's work."

"Do you have anything about the lotus?"

· · · · ·

A short walk through a great-smelling plum orchard brought us to a clear stream bordered by marsh reeds.

The shady swimming hole was deep and calm, but in the narrow, shallow places, the current would sweep you right off your feet. It was as good as any water park! Needless to say, we guys did a lot of wrestling each other into the narrows. Several times Rob got washed downstream a hundred yards and dumped into a pool. (Funny how his brave ninja cry and his "I'm pretending to drown" cry were exactly the same.) Reece said we should use our new names and pretend to be Japanese high school kids enjoying break. We guys tossed Mei and Mayu around and made them giggle. Shinobu, Ryo, and I—Takumi—forgot all our troubles for a while. Fresh air and countryside—it suited me fine.

After the swim Mei fixed barley tea and had us take a rest. Kenji and Taka went with their mom to the market. We stretched out on our pallets with the electric fan rotating across us, the smell of fruit on the hot afternoon breeze. In no time the guys were snoozing on either side of me. Out of nowhere it hit me like a load of bricks: Dr. Dale was gone, crushed right before my eyes. I suddenly felt sick. He'd left me in the lead for spiritual warfare, and I didn't even know what that meant yet. Dr.

Eloise and the SOS were hundreds of miles north. Sure Paul was an expert on religion, but since we were just teenagers, he was skeptical of our mission.

Staring at the ceiling, I got to worrying about the lotus again. On a whim I grabbed the Quella from my backpack and punched in the word, expecting nothing. But it came up: "Under the lotus plants he lies, hidden among the reeds in the marsh. The lotuses conceal him in their shadow."

Conceal *who?* I sat up, scrolled up a few verses to see what the passage was talking about. "Look at the behemoth.... . He ranks first among the works of God, yet his Maker can approach him with his sword."

Behemoth? I looked it up: a powerful beast. *A beast hides under the lotus, concealed in its shadow? What beast?*

· · · · · ·

Mei's Aunt Sachiko fixed the best steak dinner we'd ever had, cooked with vegetables outside on a Korean-style grill. We stuffed ourselves then kicked back in the living room and played with Kenji and Taka, swapping English and Japanese words, tossing a ball around.

I took Reece for a bike ride so we could be alone for a while. We stopped at a bamboo forest and decided to explore it, squeezing through the dense stalks, not saying much. Reece commented, "Mei said this is the best place to be in an earthquake. The roots hold the ground together."

"That's good to know."

We went deeper into the grove until the road behind us disappeared. She stopped and looked at me. Her normally blue eyes had changed in the light of the forest to pale green.

"Elijah?"

"Uh-huh?"

"Do you think that lady's dream had anything to do with

Dr. Dale?"

"I don't know."

I gave her a hug and half joked, "Hey, you're feeling okay, aren't you?"

"Yeah," she answered, a few seconds later adding, "There'll be a lot of walking tomorrow, I guess."

"Probably, but there's no hurry. We have all day. It's awesome in here, isn't it?"

"It's beautiful. Hey, what's your favorite drink so far?"

"Between the peach nectar and the royal milk tea," I said.

"Me too. I want to take some back on the plane for Mom and Darrell."

"Good idea."

A long time passed. The breeze swayed the lacy tops of the bamboo trees and gave us a feeling like we were at the top of Great Oak again. Only this time we weren't in the middle of a big fight when I kissed her and she kissed me back.

"Elijah," she asked quietly, "what do you think of the SOS, about what they do?"

"Sounds hard. But cool." I changed the subject. "You know, Dad should add a bamboo grove in Owl Woods." I didn't mention the long talk with Veronica—or the application form in my backpack.

Reece kept staring up at me until I took my eyes from the swaying treetops. Her expression was deep and unreadable. "About the SOS—you'd be good at it, Takumi."

· · · · ·

I should have had a powwow that night to pray, but everyone was involved with the family: Marcus and Rob played hide-and-go-ninja through the neighborhood with the boys; Reece and Mei made a craft with Aunt Sachiko. I was out of it, thinking about the beast hiding under the lotus.

Did that mean anything? I took a stroll through a plum orchard, watched the sun go down over one mountain and the moon rise above another. I wondered whether the danger was over—if Dr. Dale's death was the end of it. Part of me was relieved it had been him and not one of us. I felt like dirt thinking that, but I was up front with God and said I was sorry. I asked him to please break the silent treatment. *I'm not seeing your point. Are you silent because we don't have the real sword? Will you speak when we find it? What am I doing wrong?*

Wandering through the rows of plum trees in blue-green twilight, I noticed little shrines like the one I'd seen at the inn. They were everywhere: next to houses, along the road, in the lanes between the fields. Remembering the darkness I'd felt when we crossed into the peninsula, I had an inkling—more than an inkling, a knowing—that it was all around me now, even under me. *If there are gods in each of those shrines ... but wait ... they can't really be gods ... because there's only one God ... then ... what are they? What is worshiped here? What has power? The lotus?*

Fighting the dread of going to the temples the next day, I pleaded, *God, where are you? Why did you take Dr. Dale and leave me on my own?* I wanted to back out but couldn't—I was the leader. I went back to Mei's house and tried to join in the fun everyone was having, looking at pictures and playing games ... until Mei's uncle came home drunk and ordered everyone to bed so he could sleep in peace.

Mei was embarrassed. "I am sorry. It is like many businessmen. They have work pressures, and they all drink together."

Kenji and Taka wanted to stay in the room with us *gaijins,* and Aunt Sachiko said it was okay. I figured they were afraid of their dad. I was beat, but having kids around reminded me of Camp Mudj—not that I was homesick.

In no time Marcus and Rob were out like lights; the boys

horsed around in a wide beam of moonlight shining through the window, quiet because they didn't want to wake their dad. They looked like skinny little ghost monkeys playing, showing no signs of winding down. Figuring they'd be fine, I started to drift off myself, my eyes closed, my muscles relaxing. My mind was calm. Why was I worried about tomorrow anyway? The Nikko prayer walk had been awesome, everyone praising God together, Bible verses popping up like magic. Easy. Way cool …

Then I felt his breath in my ear and a growling, hissing whisper: "I told you to leave!"

A cold chill erupted along my spine and spread around my chest like long fingers, clamping around my heart. Not for a millisecond did I think it was Rob pulling a prank. I recognized the voice. With awful assurance I knew. *It's him. Again. Or another one like him.* I willed my eyes open. Hovering over me on his hands and knees like a dog—his eyes drilling into me with the same undiluted hate I'd seen before in a bookstore in Ireland—was Kenji. He glared at me ferociously, his head tipped, his lip curled.

My mind spun, my heart thudded. "No," I whispered firmly, "you … didn't." *You didn't tell me to leave, whoever you are, even if you're Kenji—which you're not. No one told me to leave.*

For a few more seconds, he hovered over me. I lay there washed in moonlight, his small black eyes pinning me down. Then he backed away, sat down, and glared at me sideways out of the corner of his eye. The expression went away—just dissolved—and he was Kenji again, a kid sitting there not wanting to go to bed early.

What do I do?

Slowly, cautiously I reached over to him, afraid he'd bite me, wondering if he'd recoil. I put my hand on his back, like Dr. Eloise blessing the man who killed her husband. I prayed protection on both Kenji and me from whatever that thing was. Then I said, "Kenji, go to sleep now … Kenji."

He lay down and stared at the ceiling.

Over my short life, I'd had a lot of people mad at me: Dowland and his dog Salem, Theobald, the Mad River Boys, Miss Abner, the Brill brothers. And sometimes it was pretty scary. But all that was nothing to me now. It—whatever it was—hated that I existed, in this life or the next. That was clear as a bell.

All night I sat under the window and watched that patch of moonlight crawl across the room. Raw-nerved, exhausted, I stayed calm by thinking about home far away … teaching survival classes to grade-schoolers at Camp Mudj, horsing around with Nori and Stacy, building campfires for Dad, climbing Great Oak, wandering Council Cliffs, jogging down to Florence's for bacon and grits with the gang.

CHAPTER 13

It was a clammy, misty morning. Mei's aunt woke the boys up early for their morning exercise class, so I got to sleep for a couple of hours. At breakfast Marcus sat with Mei and acted all smooth again. For some reason it irritated me—bad. I guess I was just tired, but with a tone that annoyed even myself I sneered, "Mei, you should have seen Skidmore and Varner at the masked ball last year. They were Lawrence of Arabia and Queen Nefertiri. A regular Hollywood couple, they were!"

Innocently Mei said, "Oh, I would love to see it! Rob, did you take pictures?"

Reece gave me a look.

Marcus eyed me and asked Mei, "Hey, Aizawa, how do you say *Get lost!* in Japanese?"

Mei said, *"Dokka ike!"* then changed the subject. "When I graduate, I want to study the travel in America so I can be in tourist business. Then I can work in the whole world if my grades are good and my parents will help me. I hope so!"

Mei and Rob went off talking about colleges and scholarships. Reece kept glancing at Marcus and me.

After breakfast when Reece and I were alone, she asked, "What's going on?"

"What do you mean?"

"I mean you and Marcus. It's like you're fighting over Mei."

"I don't want her to get hurt. He acts like he likes her."

"Maybe he does."

"What about Miranda?"

Reece huffed. "Mei can take care of herself. She's smart." She snipped, "You're not her mother."

Miffed, I stormed off to get ready for the prayer walk.

On our way to Paul's, I was thinking, *So who cares about Skidmore and Mei? Big stinking deal! And who cares what Reece thinks about what I think?*

Reece got in step beside me. "I'm sorry about earlier. Now tell me what's really wrong."

"We lost Dr. Dale; that's what's wrong." I couldn't tell her about Kenji. He was Mei's cousin, a seven-year-old kid. How could an entity be inside a kid? And anyway, we had a few more days at the house, so why freak everyone out when I could stand watch? Maybe I'd dreamed it. But I knew I hadn't. Maybe I'd gone loony.

"You're not the only one who's sad," she grumped.

"I know. What's that got to do with anything?"

"You're being all distant and moody," she huffed.

Rob said, "Yeah, Takumi, and don't keep telling me not to 'go ninja' every place. You keep forgetting that I'm older and make better grades … so *dokka ike!*"

"You *dokka ike!* Fine, make a fool of yourself in another country. You're a *henna gaijin* anyway!"

Marcus scowled at me and muttered, "Creep."

By the time we got to the Trenton house, no one was speaking to me.

Paul loaded us into his van and gave us wary looks; you could cut the tension with a knife. I rode shotgun so I wouldn't have to talk to the others. Paul said, "Elijah, you were asking about the lotus. I did a little research last night. The use of the lotus in worship goes back thousands of years to ancient Egypt. And in Greek mythology, eating the lotus lulls a person into a state of dreamy forgetfulness." He paused uneasily and handed me papers. "I'd never read the Buddhist teachings of the lotus before last night. You might want to look over those excerpts of the *Lotus Sutra*."

I skimmed a few pages and didn't know whether to laugh or be completely creeped out.

Getting us back on track, Reece said, "Hey, let's sing first like we did at Nikko."

Winding through narrow village streets, the Magdeline Five tried to make the best of it, singing and waving at fruit farmers while Paul greeted them in Japanese. We turned up a steep, narrow street to a temple on the hill and parked beside it. Facing out over the city, the brand-new temple of natural wood had big pillars, a curved roof, and fancy gold trim. The landscaping was awesome, with sculpted trees and stone paths and fishponds. Up the terraced hill behind the temple was a cemetery. The place seemed deserted. Paul got out, uncertain as to what to do.

I said, "We split up. Everybody take your Bible. Don't make a scene or talk loud. We respect their property. And everyone stay where I can see you."

Paul chuckled at me in a fatherly way. "It's safe here."

Reece said to Paul, "Everyone wanders and stays open to what God wants him to pray. That's how we've seen it done. I'll stay here by the entrance, okay?"

"I'll go on up through the cemetery," said Rob.

"Far side," said Marcus and took off.

Mei said, "I will walk through the garden."

"What god is worshiped here?" I asked Paul as we wandered around the front of the temple.

He smiled. "Good question. Oriental cultures are known for their many gods." He picked up a rock and sat it on a bench. "If I bow to that, it becomes *kami*, a god. A god can be anything.

There are millions."

"Millions?"

Along the edge of the curved roof of the temple were round tiles with a flower design on each one. "There's your lotus," he said, "an object of importance, though I'm not sure why. In some sects the *Lotus Sutra* itself is worshiped. And the symbol of the lotus supposedly has great power."

"Why would people worship a book?"

"As a ritual to get to nirvana—which we Westerners think means Heaven."

"But it really means extinction," I recalled Rob's research.

"You'll read in that excerpt that dragons and other nonhuman creatures supposedly protect the religion. Ten demon daughters and the Mother of Devil Children pronounce curses on anyone who fails to heed their spells or tries to disrupt the teaching of the lotus."

I read aloud, "'Their heads will split into seven pieces like the branches of the arjaka tree.'" I skimmed more pages and added dryly, "Nice. So these curses are against us? It says that anyone who tries to stop the spread of this worship will go into Hell and be reborn as a scabby dog and plagued with starvation, or as a donkey to be whipped and beaten, or as a serpent to be devoured by insects, or as a blind, deaf, dimwitted, hunchbacked human. There are pages of curses."

Paul smiled grimly. "All this in allegiance to the Thus Come One, most honored of two-legged beings." He quoted, "'I am the World-Honored One! None can rival me!'"

"Is this for real?"

"To those who believe it, yes."

"Who is the Thus Come One, World-Honored One?"

He shook his head. "Supposedly an enlightened being. But we know from the Bible that Satan is the honored prince of this world, even though he leads it astray."

"This was Mei's religion?" I asked in disbelief. "Extinction and curses by demons?"

"She probably never read the *Lotus Sutra* or understood the rituals. Religion is more like tradition here, for good luck."

There were no gates at the temple, so I circled the whole place, praising God for his power and for using me and my friends for some great purpose, even if I couldn't see it yet. Even if I didn't feel it. Even if I didn't like them very much right now. It was lonely up on that hillside—just us five, a bunch of dead people, and Paul, one of the few believers in the whole city. I missed the big youth group at home. I missed Dr. Dale's calm presence, and wondered if he'd been taken out because he was our leader.

I wondered if I was next.

Mei was reading her Bible in the garden. I sat down with her. "Did you ever read any lotus sermons or worship them? Did your aunt ... or cousins?"

She thought. "I don't know ... but one of the favorite goddesses in Japan—*kannon*—has a lotus prayer for good luck. We say that prayer."

I left Mei in the garden so I could find a place to be alone and think. *Lotuses in stone and bronze. Flowers with no fragrance or purpose. Threats from dreams: don't move me or try to change me. Lying threats: I told you to leave! Demon eyes glaring out of the head of a nice little kid.* Shaken, I looked up the familiar armor passage and read it thirstily: "Our struggle is not against flesh and blood, but ... against the powers of this dark world and against the spiritual forces of evil in the heavenly realms. Therefore put on the full armor of God... ." I put on, prayed on, every piece and wondered stupidly why I hadn't done it sooner. Wondered why I hadn't prayed it on the Magdeline Five.

· · · · ·

Paul drove us to a second temple on another hill after we crossed a bridge and saw the saloon and its washed-out road, a casualty of the typhoon. We passed a children's graveyard with a guardian god standing on a lotus. "This is one of many pilgrimage places," he said. "Last night while doing research, I realized for the first time that this whole peninsula is dedicated to religions involving the lotus." He looked at me curiously. "What made you ask?"

I told him about the lady's dream and about feeling a huge darkness as we entered the peninsula. He listened but had no comment.

Mei and Reece found a spot in the shade and read Scripture to each other. Paul joined Marcus and Rob as they walked a path lined with idols. I wandered the parking lot, pacing below the huge temple, trying to think about God, trying to call on his power. But I didn't feel any power. My heart wasn't in it. All I could say was, *God, you are God. I know that. There is only you. The other gods are no gods. There is only you.* Finally I dropped down on the curb, tired and sweaty, punched in the lotus Scripture on my Quella, and dwelled on it a long time. This prayer journey was nothing like Nikko's. It was lame, and we were glum and hot and tired.

· · · · ·

By the third day without sleep, I was running on fumes. I couldn't sleep for imagining what that thing—Lotus—might do to me in my sleep. It was Sunday. Kenji and Taka were still asleep when my clan grabbed breakfast and walked down to the Trenton house for church, their red diamond jewelry glinting like fire in the morning sun.

The downstairs of Paul's house was fixed up with metal chairs and a pulpit. A dozen people came; the only girl our age had an odd look about her. As she sat down by us, Mei whispered that she had a mental problem. The service was simple, but everything was in Japanese. We four Americans were pathetic singers; we didn't know the words or tunes.

Paul introduced us and asked us to say a few words about ourselves; he would translate. Reece took center stage first, saying how we'd come from America to visit Mei and to pray for their church. She was her usual upbeat self; they loved her. My spiel was brief. It was hard to concentrate, fighting off sleep like I was. The people were appreciative and nice, but honestly, I was glad when church was over.

They set up tables in the front yard, brought food out, and we had a picnic. One older lady had handmade purses for the girls. We guys got kites with samurai warrior designs on them. By mid-afternoon the church people had gone home. We went back to Mei's. My head felt like it weighed a ton; I wanted to find a spot under a tree and sleep, but Mei wanted to take us to the coast for dinner. *Okay, Creek,* I told myself, *be excited or you'll look like a jerk.*

A half-hour drive got us to the Pacific Ocean. The overlook was so much like the Cliffs of Morte, it was spooky; everyone said so. We got quiet, gazing out over the thrashing sea with the late afternoon sun behind us, a sheer drop-off yards ahead. This was the suicide cliff Mei had told us about at Cathedral Cave, the beautiful place to die.

Reece said, "Okay, we all stay waaaay back."

"Got it!" Rob agreed.

"Where are the fences and warning signs?" Marcus griped. There was no rail and only one sign in Japanese with a cross on it.

Mei translated. "It says 'The Phone Call of Life. Before making a final decision, please talk with us! We are waiting for your call.'" She read the verse at the bottom: "Jesus said, 'I am the light of the world. Whoever follows me will never walk in darkness, but will have the light of life.'" Mei paused seriously. "I have been here many times, but I didn't understand this verse. I was blind to it, but now I see." Unexpectedly she threw her arms around me, then around each of the others. Considering that Japanese don't touch much in public, it was a shock. She cried, "Thank you again for saving my life at Cathedral Cave. I would have missed my whole life with my friends!"

"It's okay," I said, "we're the Magdeline Five. Nothing will ever change that."

· · · · ·

I told you to leave!

Yeah, right. It was a big fat lie to scare me off. And it almost worked. I wished Dr. Dale was here. I wanted to call Dom Skidmore. What time was it in the States, 5:00 in the morning? Nope, I had to handle this myself. *God, talk to me. I need an English translation of what's going on.*

I kicked back through dinner while the others chatted and wondered what was wrong with me, why I was so quiet. When the rest went to sleep, I propped myself against the bedroom wall. Mei's uncle had come home drunk again, so if I had tried to make Kenji and Taka sleep in the living room, I'd have looked like a totally mean *gaijin*. And I'd have worried about Reece and Mei all night. Kenji had acted like a normal raucous kid except for that one moment, but I didn't trust him. It was my job to protect my clan. I started thinking about how to get Mei out of here once we left the country.

By 2:00 in the morning, my eyelids were lead weights; my eyes sandpaper. Throwing on shorts and a T-shirt, I took the armor in the suitcase out to the front porch. I unpacked it in moonlight, keeping an ear toward the open front door. Handling each piece, I imagined my clan back around a campfire at Silver Lake where we'd first analyzed it—things had been simpler then. I put on the right arm of fellowship, made a fist of the ragged glove. *We need to go back to the beginning, get* koinonia *again. We still have a day of spiritual warfare at the town's main torii gates and at those little farm shrines. For whatever good it will do. Really ... what's the point of praying and reading? Nothing happens. Yeah, yeah, I know faith is being "certain of what we do not see," but how are we supposed to believe what we can't see? Oh ... oh great! Now I'm losing my faith—with the shield of faith lying here right in front of me. That's just terrific. Peachy as peach nectar!* I lay the arm down and sat gazing at the full moon. I silently called up to Heaven, *Why won't you talk to me? This prayer journey's almost over and getting lamer by the minute. Where are the magic Scriptures and the happy floaty feelings?*

No answer. I wanted to run, blow off some steam, but couldn't. I had to stand watch over the house in case that thing came back, an ageless, evil thing I didn't understand, didn't know how to deal with. At home I could have climbed Great Oak to clear my head, but here I was stuck. Trapped. Suddenly I just stood up and screamed inside, *Hold on a minute! Satan may be prince of the world, but you're the big king of the universe, so you baby-sit for a while!"*

Angrily I took off. Down the lane past darkened houses and creepy little shrines I ran barefoot, pretending I was in Owl Woods and knew every dip and curve in the path. My curses raged at God for leaving me high and dry. *Yeah, I'm cursing. So I'm bad now! Just lost the breastplate of righteousness, I guess. I'm soooo bad!*

The moon cast my own swift shadow ahead of me. I wanted to run over it, stomp it. Stomp myself. Shadowy arms and legs pumped; my fugitive self was flat and formless and slithering ahead of me. No matter how hard I ran, I'd never stomp it.

I zigzagged blindly through the neighborhood, past orchards

and rice fields. The swimming hole came into view—black as ink
under the tree-lined bank, dark as Gilead on a moonless night.
I didn't pause to think. I ran full force and dove in. Baptism
into nothingness. Nirvana. Extinction. Swallowed up by the
cold inky water, I forced myself to stay under until my lungs
burned. *No peace, no faith, no truth, no nothing! I didn't want to
hear from you anyway. Keep your words and your wordless sword!
It's just a hunk of metal anyway. Probably not even the real thing.
No word on it … no word from YOU!*

When my air-starved lungs couldn't take it anymore, I jet-
tisoned myself to the surface and hungrily gasped air. I threw
myself back and floated in the swimming hole like a dead man,
eyes open, seeing nothing. Nothing but leaves, low and black and
lacy with the moon a silver disc beyond. I'd seen moon shadows
a million times, seen stars in a charcoal sky above Great Oak,
but this time it was different. Everything was alive, watching me.

Slowly the current began to move me across the swimming
hole and toward the narrows. I drifted. The current picked up,
faster, faster, shooting me across the narrows … and into a tangle
of reeds. I found myself caught in a kind of whirlpool. I tried
to paddle but got nowhere, the reeds thick and slimy hindering
me. *Hidden in the reeds of the marsh, under the lotus he lies. The
beast.* Frantic, corkscrewing to free myself, I paddled like crazy
but got nowhere. *I'm going down!* My feet couldn't find bottom
to push off, only slimy tangles—below, above, all around. Fingers
of terror tightened around my ribs again. *I want up. Up! Get me
back in the current, in the current. Don't let me drown! I'm close to
the current, but which way? I need you! Which way is out? I need you!*

Then I looked up. I caught sight of the watery moon and
got my bearings, all the while thrashing wildly until the current
grabbed me like a cool, strong hand. I was shot through the narrows like an arrow, dumped downstream into the next quiet pool.

I squished all the way back through the sleeping neighborhood, the moon casting my shadow behind me now. I plopped down on Mei's porch, my mind strangely quiet. I repacked the armor. *Talk to me, sword.*

"Elijah?" came a voice behind me. I jumped. Mei came out on the porch. "Are you okay? How did you get wet?" she laughed. "Did you fall into the *ofuro?*"

"Can't sleep," I said wearily. "I went for a swim. Jet lag, I guess." Which was a lie. I lied with the belt of truth at my feet. I was slipping backwards on every count. *I need help.*

She sat beside me. "I finished my papers for school, and then I was thinking of the word on the sword. There was no piece of the sword from the helmet."

"Right."

"May I look again?"

"Sure. The armor's yours too."

I followed her inside with the suitcase. We sat on the floor near an end-table lamp. She examined the helmet, her delicate fingers running over every edge. "I think it must be inside, like the other pieces."

"We all looked. Rob even used a magnifying glass." Her patient examination of the helmet brought a calm over me. I started to breathe again. "Hey, um, it's none of my business, but you and Marcus ..."

She got shy. "He is so kind to me."

"Uh-huh."

"He is helping me with a problem. I ... I like a boy at my school, but he makes fun of me for worshiping the American god. Marcus has a problem with Miranda who has no belief too. Marcus talks to me about it and makes me feel better." She giggled. "He promises—but it is a joke—he promises that he will not get married until I do. And if I can't find someone, then he will marry me. He's great."

"Yeah," I said guiltily, "he's pretty cool."

Mei said, "You and Reece—uh, Mayu … you are very lucky. You have the same beliefs."

I grinned. "Yeah."

Her fingertip stopped on one of the lines etched into the helmet. "This cut is deeper. I think there is a separate piece." She dashed to the kitchen on tiptoe (while I sat there feeling like a big clod of dirt about Marcus) and came back with a paring knife. She slipped the point into the crack, working it ever so gently until it lifted a fraction of an inch. "Ah! I think this is like our secret boxes. You must move it just the right way to get it open." Patiently she worked, moving and sensing, a hair to the right, then left, cleaning bits of mud that we'd missed after fishing it out of Silver Lake.

The piece rose by degrees and finally lifted off. Inside was a secret compartment barely an eighth of an inch thick and lined with wool. Pressed into the cloth was a layer of glitter. She lifted it out. "It is like chain mail only—aaahh!" She dropped it into the compartment and looked at her open hand. Her fingertips were covered with blood.

"What in the world?" I said.

Mei got a hankie from her pocket and blotted her fingers. I reached in to pick up the mesh.

She cried, "It hurts you!"

I picked up the very edge with my fingernails. It was mesh, a long, ragged scrap of woven metal made of what you might call flat metal threads—fine and sparkling and razor sharp.

"Should we wake the others?" she asked excitedly.

I suddenly remembered Kenji, how I'd left the others in God's hands while I stupidly half tried to drown myself. "I'll go check on 'em." I looked in on the guys and the cousins, then Reece. I went back out to the living room where Mei had spread the piece over the arm of the couch. I said, "They're sound asleep. Maybe the words are engraved here like they were on the chain mail."

We had no magnifying glass. Carefully, I picked it up and held it under the light. Mei and I were excited. I was sure we'd found the word.

· · · · ·

That next morning we showed the others the shiny ragged mesh and brainstormed over it. The others were as excited as Mei and me, but no word could be found. We needed Dr. Eloise's linen tester.

We did the last maneuvers of the prayer journey in better spirits, strolling the lanes between farms, smelling the fruit drying, watching misty clouds drift up the mountainside. *Fresh air close to the Pacific coast, homegrown food, a swimming hole—a perfect place to live.* Except for little shrines to gods of agriculture and who-knows-what-else lurking throughout the village and orchards. At every little *torii,* Reece would say her verses from the *Warrior.* Honestly, it was a little embarrassing to sing songs about Jesus by ourselves in a plum grove. But we did. We followed an overgrown set of stone steps up a hillside and found a newly planted shrine in the bushes. They were cropping up everywhere.

Paul took us downtown to the largest shrine in town with a gate as big as the one in Nikko. We paused while Reece did her thing. This time I said it with her. The shrine was a large, open area ringed with awesome red and gold buildings of different sizes, fishponds, and arched bridges. I circled the space and opened my heart up to God. Then I put on the spiritual armor I'd thrown off the night before.

Paul chatted in Japanese with the Shinto priest. I stood beside him, taking in the rhythm and complexity of the language. Having suffered through Latin, I was impressed at how Paul had mastered another language.

We left after Reece had put her hand on the giant pillar one last time and said tiredly, but with determination, "'This is the gate of the LORD.'"

CHAPTER 14

Shimabara—on Kyushu island. I've never had such trouble getting to a place in my life.

After good-byes at the station (I gave Kenji a bear hug while praying in earnest, *God, whatever you do in this demon situation, do it, okay?*), we waited for the train. Rob complained about the driving rain.

Marcus said, "Count your blessings, Shinobu. We're under a roof. You Americans are spoiled. In some places in the world, just walking across the street could get you shot."

"No more arguing please," Mei said firmly.

Suddenly cheerful, Rob said, "Mei and I have figured out the cheapest way to get there: overnight bus. We head back toward Osaka, get a taxi at the fifth stop before Sakai, and catch the bus there."

I didn't care as long as I got some sleep.

Only that didn't happen.

The local train was packed. We got off at the right stop for a taxi stand, but there wasn't one. The street was deserted, with one convenience store open. Mei asked for directions at the counter and turned to us, flustered. "The closest taxi stand is in that direction." She pointed down a dark street. "Not far."

"Let's hope so," I said. We set out into the warm, sloppy night.

We took turns carrying Reece and her luggage for the next twenty minutes. Wheezing, Rob cried, "Not far? Hogwash! Don't people here know what *not far* means? Does *not far* mean *not near* in Japanese, 'cause that's what I'm getting."

"The Japanese walk more and talk less," Marcus said with threat in his voice. "That's why they live longer."

Ignoring him, Rob said, "I see streetlights over there."

"The store clerk said this way," Mei argued.

I whispered to Reece, "Pray, Mayu, pray!"

We stopped in a pedestrian tunnel under a highway to get out of the weather and take a breather. I offered to scout ahead, but the others were afraid we'd get separated. Out of nowhere a businesswoman appeared in a suit and high heels. She stopped dead at the sight of us *gaijins* lurking in the dark tunnel. Mei stepped out, apologized, and asked directions. A couple of lefts and rights and we were on the main street. Rob frowned at his watch. "We have fifteen minutes to get to the bus terminal. Start flagging taxis!"

"Here comes one!" Reece stepped toward the curb.

I barked at her to get back. "Let Mei and Shinobu do that. Ryo, you guard the luggage."

"I can flag!" he barked back.

"You're too scary."

Mei got us a cab and ordered the driver to hurry. He barreled through traffic, pulled down a side street, and screeched to a halt at a lonely open-air bus stand thick with spiderwebs and big gnarly spiders.

"Where's the station?" Rob whined.

Mei handed bills to the driver. "No station. We get out." The cabbie unloaded our luggage, pulled out, and once again we were by ourselves on a dark road at night. The time came and went for the bus to come.

Rob eyed his watch. "I bet it was early, and we missed it."

· · · · ·

The overnight bus barreled in ten minutes late; we cheered in relief and sloshed up the steps. It was nice and super clean with a TV up front. Down a few steps were a restroom and a tiny tea station half the size of a shower stall. We got free blankets, bitsy pillows, and paper slippers, and then we took turns opening our backpacks in the aisle to get dry clothes and change in the little restroom. The others on the bus—mostly businessmen—politely ignored us.

Our chairs only reclined so far, with no way to turn over or lie flat. It was a long, achy night, but at least we were dry and going somewhere. After Gilead, I'd vowed never to complain about accommodations again.

At daybreak, Rob woke us up and fixed tea at the little tea station, mostly so he could make the same lame joke over and over: "If anyone needs me, I'll be *downstairs in the kitchen.*" (And I have to say here that Japanese people can get more stuff into a tiny space and make it work than I've ever seen.)

The overnight bus dumped us out at a sweet station in Nagasaki with an ocean view and tons of vending machines. We were on Kyushu island! Marcus and I ran around the parking lot to get the kinks out. We all grabbed a Japanese breakfast, brushed our grungy teeth, and washed our faces.

"To the next train!" said Rob, waving his map, his face dripping and shiny.

Easier said than done. The stop where we could catch a bus for the next station was half a mile. I could tell that Reece was beyond worn out. But it was a clear, sunny day; we were dry and full of tea and *onigiri;* the rain and the overnight bus ride had beaten all the complaining out of us.

The local to Shimabara was slow and old, *clackety-clack*ing along. We didn't care; our car was half empty with plenty of space to stand, sit, or stretch out. We didn't know why the Stallards had wanted to end our trip here—and didn't care. The darkness had faded, and we were on our way to a shogun castle with hours of nothing to do but hang out. Rob snapped pictures of rice fields. I made myself swear if he went into ninja mode in the castle, I'd keep my trap shut. Marcus was in another world. Mei wrote in her journal.

Reece curled up on the seat next to her, using her backpack as a pillow. I watched her sleep and thought about a million things: *How far was it to Samoa? How many days by boat? If I worked it so the others could go, who'd pay for their tickets? The SOS kids were great, but we were the Magdeline Five. Would we need different clothes? Biggest question of all, what would our parents say?* I read over the application form stashed in my backpack and thought of Mom and Dad and the twins and Camp Mudj. I wondered what it meant to be a Magdelinian, what it might mean to be the third Elijah, and why I'd been targeted by Lotus. Questions were as thick and tangled as those spiderwebs four hundred miles ago.

As the town came into view, Mei chirped to Marcus, "We need a travel talk, Ryo, like you made in Ireland!"

Straightening an invisible tie, Marcus came back to planet Earth and said with flair, "As the traveler approaches the quaint village, he will pass verdant countryside panoramas. Brilliant rice fields in August make a veritable patchwork quilt. If one is alert, one may catch a glimpse of sun-washed sea. And looming ahead, the jagged peaks of—what's that mountain, Mei?"

Rob answered, "It's Mt. Unzen, a volcano; and there's a hot springs spa there."

"Ah, the famous Mt. Unzen," Marcus droned on. "Road-weary wanderers flock to its healing waters and breathtaking view. Daring mountain climbers hazard its steep slopes. At the foot of the mountain rests Shimabara, a quaint village—"

"You already said 'quaint village,'" Rob jabbed.

Marcus ignored him, his eyes locking on something ahead. "Whoa ... get a load of that!"

Hogging the whole center of town, a huge, white Japanese castle rose up above modern houses and businesses, strangely out of place in this century.

We hauled ourselves and our luggage off the train and up a short hill through the outer wall of Shimabara Castle. Acres of low gardens and pools where the moat used to be surrounded the stone foundation wall.

And waiting for us on a bench and admiring the lily pads was Dr. Eloise. "Hello, children. Who's ready for some exciting history?"

· · · · ·

The castle was way cool, a big square hallway on each floor with displays of samurai weapons and armor, paintings of battles and burning castles—lots of war stuff. Rob kept a pretty good lid on his primal screams and air-chopping.

Faking disappointment, Marcus said to him, "Sorry, Shinobu, but it's just not the same without the skirt."

"This town was the last stand of Christianity in Japan in the old days," explained Dr. Eloise. "Dr. Dale wanted very much for you to see it." She smiled a faraway smile. "The year was 1637. Faith in one God was spreading through the country when the leaders, for many reasons—some political, some purely evil—saw belief in Jesus as a threat. To make matters worse in this region, there was a very high tax oppressing the farmers, the government taking up to eighty percent of their crops. Those who didn't comply with the tax law or the religious prohibitions could anticipate torture or death. Believers were beheaded, crucified," she pointed out the window toward Mt. Unzen, "or thrown into the volcanic crater. Children were killed beside their parents. Each torture was devised to be more horrible than the one before.

Many thousands died. It was in the thick of this persecution that a boy of sixteen named Amakusa Shiro, a young believer who sympathized with the farmers, led a rebellion against the fierce shogunate.

"For months the rebels held off the more powerful army, but eventually they ran out of food and ammunition. Thirty-seven thousand died in one battle. This castle museum gives us the story; we'll take a shuttle to the actual site. And we must see the statue." She smiled at me mysteriously.

"This is *fumie*," Mei said, pointing into a display case at a small square piece of wood engraved with something. "It is a picture of Jesus. The leaders made Christians step on Jesus' face. If they did not do it, they were killed." She turned to us. "This is why it is still hard to be a Christian here."

Rob's eyes got wide. "You mean we could be killed?"

She laughed. "It is safe now. We are civilized country. But our culture says it is better to do the same as everyone else. We have a saying, 'The nail that sticks up will be hammered down.' Being the same is very important to us. We will gladly give up personal wishes to be part of the group. To be a Christian is to be different."

Rob said, "Sorry, Mei, I couldn't do that: be the same."

Marcus snorted, "You got that."

Dr. Eloise said, "Our cultures are different for good reasons, Rob. America is a young country; the Europeans who settled America were adventurers—risk-takers with individualism and grit. The Japanese, on the other hand, have lived on a small island for many centuries. Yet they have found a way to maintain peace in close community."

"Makes sense," Marcus said. "My people have their own ways too." He did a jiggy dance. Rob chopped his neck. The girls rolled their eyes. I laughed and then got a pang in my gut. *The*

Mag Five. My clan, together … for how much longer?

There were other buildings to see, but Dr. Eloise steered us through the gardens to a bronze statue of a young warrior wearing old-style Japanese clothes, a cross, and a sword. His hands were folded, his face lifted to Heaven. "This is Amakusa Shiro," she said, "the boy who led the rebellion in hopes of stopping the persecution. He risked everything for his convictions. Can you imagine that kind of courage?"

I glanced at Mei, wondering what she thought of him, a kid like herself killed by his own people.

But Reece was looking at me.

· · · · ·

We caught a shuttle to the Hara fortress ruins where the final stand actually took place. It was an overgrown hill ringed with remnants of stone walls. In spots the ground was raked clean and measured off for excavation.

"Why are we here?" Rob asked.

Dr. Eloise said, "Children, remember the metal cross at the center of the shield of faith? Dale's research has led us to conclude that it came from here. There at those bare spots where the fortress once stood, scientists unearthed a carpet of bones dating back to the rebellion. In the final days of the siege, the rebels were unable to hold off their enemy any longer. All hope of victory vanished, and thousands chose to burn rather than surrender. But in the fortress ruins along with the bones, several crosses were found, apparently cast from the last of the bullets. Some of those crosses were even found under skulls, suggesting that believers placed their precious crosses in their mouths so they would be the last things to burn."

Silently we looked across the quiet field, its tall grass blowing in the breeze under a sunny blue sky. Hard to believe it had been a battleground.

Rob said, "Someone who knew about the armor of God was here on that day?"

"Someone survived?" Reece asked.

Dr. Eloise said, "He would have taken his cross, gone underground, and become one of the 'hidden Christians,' those who worshiped in secret for generations under threat of death." Her voice hardened. "Souls as indestructible as those little crosses. Children, you must grasp this: in spite of the carpet of bones, they all made it through the fire! As will the millions who stand their ground to the end. We must remember—not that they died, but that they live!"

Dr. Eloise pulled a small plastic bag from her purse. She raised it high and whispered, "'Can these bones live?'" and poured out a handful of ashes. The ocean breeze carried the little cloud across the grassy field. She dusted off her hands and smiled. "They will live, when the number is complete, when the bones of martyrs carpet the earth."

CHAPTER 15

"I need to rest," said Reece on the shuttle back to town. Her face was strained and red from all the stair climbing.

"The youth hostel is four blocks from the castle," Mei said. "Should we rest before checking in?"

Reece took a ragged breath. "I can make four blocks."

We made it to the hostel, but the door was locked. A sign in Japanese hung over the door. Mei worried over Reece. "Oh, Mayu! They are closed and will not open until 6:00!"

Reece strained to say, "That's okay. Let's go to a restaurant, get something to drink … sit down."

Rob studied the map. "Hey, the waterfront is that way. There's a park. It'll have benches."

Mei said cheerily, "I will bring food and drinks. A picnic!"

"How far?" I asked.

"Two more blocks," Rob answered.

"Two blocks," Reece grimaced. "I can do two blocks."

I stooped. "Hop on. Piggyback."

The park was a huge waterfront lawn with a playground on the far side. Fishing and tour boats lined the pier. Not a soul was around. I spotted a short tree with a trunk that looked like a bunch of vines twisted together. I slapped my hands together and went into Camp Mudj mode. "Okay, kids, nap time! On your bunks!"

"What bunks?" Marcus said flatly.

I ran to the grassy spot under the tree, tossed down my

backpack, pulled out my jacket, spread it on the ground, and started blowing up my flight pillow. "My bunk's ready. Anybody need help with theirs?"

They bought the idea.

"Perfect," Reece said with relief. "Let's rest then eat."

We settled ourselves under the thick viney tree, which Dr. Eloise identified as *ficus superba*. Rob named it the Elf Tree. We were exhausted from the complicated trip and dazed by Dr. Eloise's story of Amakusa Shiro and the carpet of bones. We were tired of bickering and relieved the prayer journey was over. I was fried from night watches for Lotus. The cool afternoon breeze felt great. Magdeline, Ohio, was a galaxy away. Soon we were all flat on our backs staring up at the Elf Tree. Mei felt funny being there. Only homeless people sleep in the park, she said. We told her it was okay to do weird things; she was with *henna gaijins*.

Rob said quietly, "Right now we *are* homeless."

"Not bad, eh?" I observed.

"Not bad until the next typhoon," he said darkly.

"Aw, it's just water," I said flippantly.

We lay there snickering about old times—me getting dunked with the ice chest on Devil's Cranium, our last powwow with Mei. Dr. Eloise was snoring already.

"Open air—no boundaries. This is my turf," I murmured. Lured by the sounds of seagulls and light traffic, a warm breeze, and a magic tree ... in minutes we all were asleep.

An hour later I woke, every muscle in my body at perfect rest. I looked around. The others were out like lights. Here we were: homeless teens asleep under an elf tree with an old archaeologist in an empty park in a foreign country, with the armor of God wadded up in a suitcase. *Traveling freak show.* I chuckled to myself for a long while at how ridiculous it all was. I was dead tired but wide awake, relaxed but braced for another surprise attack from Lotus. *How'd I ever get here?*

My thoughts drifted to Amakusa Shiro's statue, how he wore a cross and a sword, with his eyes on Heaven and a smile on his face. I wondered if he really was glad to die young, or if that was just the sculptor's idea. He and thirty-seven thousand snuffed out, his dreams up in smoke, his rebellion crushed. *Bummer.* Here I thought this trip was going to be a fun visit with Mei and a chance to see Japan. Instead, I'd been chewed up and spit out; set up, singled out, chosen by God? For what—to eventually be bronzed and stuck beside a castle with a pretend smile on my face for future generations to stare at? I sat up, miffed. *Were those prayer journeys meant to make me strong for some future trial? Well, they didn't. Nothing happened. Three years searching for your armor. A trip around the world. Why? To see Dr. Dale die? To be sneered at by this Lotus thing from the ancient past? You've shot me into the air like an arrow, and I don't know where to land. Don't I get a say?* I begged, *I need a word from you, El-Telan-Yah! I am thirsty to hear from you!*

I got up and quietly staggered to the water's edge. Cruise boats bobbed, the smell of saltwater filled the air. I was back in Low Country, where we'd gone shrimping and had fought unseen boo-hag enemies in the dark. Everything seemed to be coming full circle. I looked back at my clan, like fairy-tale characters under a magic spell. *I gotta make a decision about the SOS. I gotta get Mei out of that house. I gotta talk to Dad. And Reece.* My mind a wreck, I got the Quella out of my pants pocket and punched ON. Nothing. *Battery's dead.* I laughed darkly. *Figures.* I went back to the tree where Reece's study Bible lay beside her. I picked it up, stuck my finger in a page and threw myself onto my jacket faceup, with an umbrella of leafy green above me. *Whatever you have to say, I'll listen,* I thought grudgingly.

My finger had stuck in Isaiah chapter 28. Oh great. Old

Testament, the dull stuff: "Woe to that wreath, the pride of Ephraim's drunkards, to the fading flower, his glorious beauty, set on the head of a fertile valley—to that city, the pride of those laid low by wine!"

I stopped. *Fading flower? Glorious beauty on the head of the valley? Hold on!* I remembered the temple on the hill at the head of the valley. *Who's Ephraim?* I looked it up in the notes. The word meant "fruitful"? Like the Kii Peninsula, smelling of plums, used to make wine and get people drunk. Like Mei's uncle and the guy who'd killed Dr. Dale. I looked up *wreath.* It meant "an entwined crown." In a flash I saw Paul entwining his fingers to explain how religions and traditions control the culture. *Woe to the fading flower ... Lotus.* Chills rolled over me like waves as I read on down, details about where we'd been and what we'd done in clear detail. He was speaking to me right from the page! From an ancient book alive in my hands! I dropped the Bible on my chest and covered my face with the back of my hand. "Unbelievable!"

A whisper hissed in my ear, "What's wrong?" I jumped. It was Reece, her eyes sleepy and scared. "Elijah?"

"You gotta hear this!" I sat up and woke the others. In the warm, windy park I read the verses, explaining as I went.

"'Woe to that wreath, the pride of Ephraim's drunkards.' It's a warning to the culture that keeps people from believing in God and to the peninsula that prays to idols for wine that ruins people's lives. 'To the fading flower, his glorious beauty, set on the head of a fertile valley—to that city, the pride of those laid low by wine!' That's Lotus and his temple on the hill overlooking the valley. "'See, the Lord has one who is powerful and strong.'"

Dr. Eloise broke in. "Ah yes! Originally this passage was a warning to Israel around 750 BC that the Assyrians were attacking. It was God's judgment against Israel, often called Ephraim because their fruitful valleys were filled with vineyards. But go on, tell us what it means to you."

"'Like a hailstorm and a destructive wind, like a driving rain and a flooding downpour, he will throw it forcefully to the ground.'" Excitedly, I said, "It's like the stream where we waded, the swift stream from the typhoon that washed out the road to that old saloon. It repeats the phrase: 'That wreath, the pride of Ephraim's drunkards, will be trampled underfoot. That fading flower, his glorious beauty, set on the head of a fertile valley.' It says this twice; we went to two temples on two hills. It 'will be like a fig ripe before harvest—as soon as someone sees it and takes it in his hand, he swallows it.'"

Rob sat up. "That's like me grabbing up the figs?"

"Yeah, just like you gobbled up the figs, that's how God is going to destroy Lotus. It's our prayer journey, guys, the whole thing here in facts and symbols. Our prayers were an actual war against Lotus, who rules the peninsula, who keeps people lulled senseless by booze, who controls them with the fancy temples built in his honor and the little shrines dedicated to him."

Marcus's green eyes flashed. "You're saying that God knew we'd make this prayer journey almost three thousand years ago?"

"I'm just saying it's written here exactly the way we did it. I stuck my finger in the Bible, and there it was. Here's the rest: 'In that day the LORD Almighty will be a glorious crown, a beautiful wreath for the remnant of his people.'

"That's your little church, Mei, the ones who belong to him no matter what. The left-outs and the leftovers. The remnant. 'He will be a spirit of justice to him who sits in judgment, a source of strength to those who turn back the battle at the gate.'" I beamed at Reece. "That's you praying at the *torii* gate."

Dr. Eloise looked totally lost, so we backed up and went through those days again: how I'd felt a huge darkness going into the peninsula, how Rob gobbled up all the figs, how we swam in the typhoon-swollen stream that had washed out the road to the saloon, how we'd flown into Osaka on the wing of that very typhoon. We told her how the woman's dream of the threatening flower must have meant Lotus, represented in temples carved with useless stone flowers. All of which was just a symbol for what hides beneath it: the beast.

Then, as nice and easy as I could, I told Dr. Eloise about Mei's uncle coming home drunk, how it embarrassed her and bothered the boys. I braced everyone for what happened next: Lotus had spoken through Kenji, demanding I leave. "Now I know why. He didn't want us invading his turf with the sword of the Lord." I held up Reece's Bible. "He saw it coming."

Dr. Eloise stopped me there. "Dear, not to put too fine a point on it, but since we are talking about an entire peninsula here, this Lotus is probably a principality, a high-level arch-demon over a territory. Dear Heaven."

I explained how I had stood watch and didn't get any sleep. I apologized for being moody and figured that was part of Lotus's evil plan to mess with our spiritual warfare. Lotus had got me so got caught up in thinking about it, I almost forgot to concentrate on God. I realized I'd messed up our *koinonia* over Marcus and Mei, which was none of my business. The evil one had tried every angle to wreck us.

As Reece told her part, I pictured her leading us around the gates with her little hand on the huge posts, commanding those ancient doors to let the Lord in, telling the universe that the king of glory was coming through.

Marcus dropped back against the Elf Tree. "This totally rocks. We were following precise ancient marching orders and didn't know it!"

Dr. Eloise shook her head eerily. "My word, children. I have done many of these journeys in my life and have never seen the likes of this."

Rob grabbed the Bible and read it for himself. "It's a play-by-play, all right. Spooky."

Dr. Eloise said, "You understand why he led you to this chapter, Elijah? The answer is in verse 6. The Lord promised to be a source of supernatural strength to those who fight his battles. Sometimes we do what God says without understanding why until later. It's a walk of faith."

I sank against the Elf Tree beside Marcus. "I messed up."

Dr. Eloise smiled at me. "The entity told you to leave, but you didn't."

"I wanted to."

"But you didn't. We may feel thoroughly out of sorts doing the right thing. One cannot count on feelings."

I looked over my clan, and suddenly every moment with them was as priceless as the red diamonds they wore.

The park was still deserted, the breeze cooler. In three short weeks, we'd fought off typhoon fears, the shock of Dr. Dale's death, bone-aching weariness, dumb spats, and demon threats. Now, in a matter of minutes, everything had changed again. In six little verses, he'd given us back everything we'd lost. No one was tired anymore. I raised my heart to him. *You really are the king of glory, strong and mighty in battle. Your weapons are the words.*

· · · · ·

Mei and Marcus bought *bentous*. We hung out in the park like a bunch of regular Japanese kids: Mei and Mayu, Shinobu, Ryo, and me—Takumi. We were lounging around in golden afternoon light and sea breezes. Paradise.

Over noodles and peach nectar, Mei said to Reece and me, "I understand the kind of war we fight with the armor of God and a sword, which is his Word of power. I see it now."

"Yeah, and about your cousin," I said protectively, "I think we need to get you out of there—back to Magdeline."

"I think I've got it." Rob was fiddling with the suitcase of armor pieces to show our mysterious new piece to Dr. Eloise.

"Got what?" I asked.

"There are two bigger rings on that glittery stuff. I think I know why." He'd gotten Mei to pry open the secret compartment, and with the tail of his T-shirt he lifted out the strange mesh. He raised it to eye level. "This goes on the sword," he said. "It may help us find the word."

"How? Where?" I asked.

"I'll show you." He disassembled the sword very carefully.

"How can putting that on get us the word?" Marcus asked him skeptically.

"I don't know, but see these bigger rings at each end, like on a necklace? Well, you can't put it around your neck; it would cut you to shreds. It's too small for a waistband. But hold it this way, and it's the same length as the blade." He fit one loop over the blade tip, stretched the mesh, and then hooked the other loop over the tang, the tab that goes down into the hilt. It was a perfect fit. His fingers bled a little from reassembling the sword. Then he held it up. The piece hung like a ragged flag, limp but sparkling like a waterfall, shaped like flames.

Rob handed it to me. "Try it out."

"Whaddya mean? Try what?"

"I don't know. Just try."

I stood and took the sword handle cautiously with both hands. I drew it back and forth slowly. The others leaned away from it. The piece quivered silkily, glimmered, and sparkled. It was strange and beautiful. I brandished it with easy sweeping movements. When it caught the sun, it almost seemed to disappear, leaving a trail of light.

I brought it up, took a swipe at a small branch of the tree. The sword sliced the branch, the trailing flame shredded the leaves, which fell like confetti on the clan.

Dr. Eloise said powerfully, "'The word of God is living and active. Sharper than any double-edged sword, it penetrates even to dividing soul and spirit, joints and marrow; it judges the thoughts and attitudes of the heart. Nothing in all creation is hidden from God's sight. Everything is uncovered and laid bare before the eyes of him to whom we must give account.'"

It might be my last chance. With only the clan around, I wasn't shy anymore. I put on the whole armor. I moved out to the open lawn of the park, brandishing the sword of the Lord full force with all my might. Back and forth it went, catching the light, becoming light as it sliced the air. Wind whizzed through the mesh and made a sound. Not a *whoosh* like you might think. A strange sound like a human whisper.

I stopped. "Did you hear that?"

Marcus's eyes locked on the blade. "Heard it. Do it again."

Spellbound, the others listened as I swept the sword back and forth through the breeze faster and faster, watching the mesh spiral around the blade like a whirlwind of flame. The sound was always the same, something like *heee-ahhh-ooo-ehhh* but all connected, like a *hyahwheh.* Suddenly Dr. Eloise cried out and clasped her hands to her chest. I stopped.

Mei ran to her. "Oh, are you sick? Is your heart okay?"

Dr. Eloise asked, "Did you not hear it?"

I said, "Yes, but—"

"It speaks the name, children! It speaks *the name!*"

Reece cried, "It's the word, Elijah! Do it again!"

I raised the sword with both hands, unable to breathe for a moment, eyes locked on the sword, a sheet of fiery light dripping from its blade. I brandished the sword again and again.

Hyahwheh … Hyahwheh …

Next thing we knew, we were all hugging and laughing and being all squishy. Beside herself with joy, Dr. Eloise went all teacherly and said, "Children, you remember your vowels from grade school? A, E, I, O, and U. They are the current on which all language flows. Just try to say something and leave out the vowels. Try saying '*bentous* are delicious' without vowels. Go ahead, try." We tried and sounded stupid. "Do you see? Without vowels, no spoken language works. Now here is the beauty of his name: it is formed from the vowels IAOUE, spoken *eeaaoouueh.* Yahweh."

We all tried it.

She repeated, "See, children? The name—his name—is the current on which all language flows. He is the word and he is *in* every word. Please, let us hear it again as it was spoken perhaps from the very Garden of Eden, the name that grants entrance into paradise, or blocks its path forever!"

With the late sun shining, the sea breezes blowing, and my clan watching with pure joy, I whirled across the park like a warrior fighting invisible foes, brandishing the flaming sword of the Lord, listening to it sing his name. I danced and spun in the wind until my arms ached and I was dizzy and drenched in sweat. The verse about the lotus came to me: *"Look at the be-hemoth…. He ranks first among the works of God, yet his Maker can approach him with his sword."*

Only with the sword of the Lord had we been able to confront Lotus, an alias for the satanic creature concealed in the shadow of temples and statues. As I brandished the sword, I wondered what God had protected us from. *Had Reece been targeted for death on that street in Nikko? Had Dr. Dale taken the hit for her? Should I have drowned among the reeds at the swimming hole, my body washed out to sea downstream at the suicide cliff? What other disasters had God saved us from?* We'd probably never know. Hearing his name fill the air around me, I remembered cursing at him, raging that I wanted nothing to do with him or his sword. My heart hurt. He should have held me under in those stupid reeds or let me get hit by the car and save himself some big trouble. But he didn't. He let me live, let me have his sword; he'd forgiven me and made everything right. Better than right. He'd called me out of my life and into his. Me, Elijah Creek. All I had to do was say okay.

I spun across the lawn—I didn't ever, ever want to stop—and reclaimed the name which he had hidden in *my* name from my birth: *My name is Elijah: El is Yah. My God is Yahweh!*

If the police had come by and seen me—a *henna gaijin* swinging a deadly weapon in a city park—I'd have been arrested for sure.

CHAPTER 16

We got our gear together, walked back to the youth hostel, and got our bunkrooms. The hostel was cheap but nice, with crazy decorations in the lobby that were great for a laugh: a stuffed mongoose wrestling a stuffed rattlesnake in a glass case, a foot massage chart, and faded art of zoo animals by a guy named Ivan Itch. We were giddy about everything. We got cleaned up and went out for beef teriyaki.

As we waited for the food to come, Reece said, "Guess what! Mei killed a giant centipede in our room. Careepy! But she doesn't believe in reincarnation anymore."

We gave her high fives.

Mei said, "All of a sudden, it didn't make sense to me anymore. I should not kill a spider because it may be my grandmother, but I eat fish and chickens and cows? If reincarnation is true, then we could be eating our grandmothers. But no, I am not a carnival!"

Rob fell off his chair. *"Cannibal.* You're not a cannibal!"

When our meals came, Dr. Eloise said sadly, "After tomorrow we shall not see one another for a long while." Her eyes flickered on me a second before she went back to breaking apart her chopsticks. "If you have issues, let us discuss them."

Issues? We five drew blanks.

"Let me reiterate then: Lotus is—I suspect—a principality. In other parts of Asia, especially in the north, grotesque worship practices involve the lotus. Yes, children, for whatever reason, you have come across a very ancient power and have ruffled his nest to the point that he has manifested." She looked around at us with a kind of worry and awe. "Who *are* you children in the Almighty's eyes? I would love to know. But … one must not be so enamored with mysteries that his heart drifts from the Almighty himself."

While we ate, I mentioned how I'd been confused about God's silence during my prayer journey—why he waited until the end to explain things.

"His silence means you are to listen and wait. Twice in history God was silent for an entire epoch: four hundred years of slavery and silence in Egypt followed by an explosion of miracles. And Israel was freed. Four hundred years of silence before Jesus' birth and another explosion of miracles. All of mankind was freed from death." Dr. Eloise looked kindly at Mei. "From the Shimbara Rebellion when most believers were exterminated to the present is nearly four hundred years. Some say God has been silent in Japan. I believe, dear heart, that the silence is ending. When he speaks, there will be both judgment and rescue. There is much work to do and not much time."

"What should I do?" Mei asked earnestly.

"Live your life and grow in your faith. Wear the armor and protect yourself with the Word."

I cleared my throat, "Uh, Dr. E, I was sort of thinking we should get her out of here. Because of … Lotus."

"Hmm," Dr. Eloise said thoughtfully. "We shall pray and weigh our options."

Strongly, Mei said, "My little church needs me for now. I will be like Amakusa Shiro. I will not retreat. But I pray that my parents let me visit Magdeline and see my friends."

Dr. Eloise served up tea all around. "Now about your astonishing revelation from Isaiah 28. Highly unusual!"

I said, "I'd already figured that the Quella was three-dimensional."

"Indeed. You may find many levels of meaning in one passage. This is an unfathomable mystery, how the living Word of God teaches and reveals to one and all in a billion ways and at any moment at any place on earth. It is a powerful gift! One must take great, great care not to misquote or misinterpret it."

"How can you be sure you're not?" Rob asked.

"By a relationship with the author. When you know him, you'll know what he means. You pray, listen, read, and observe. Discuss your ideas with others; learn from those with more experience. Keep in mind that the evil one knows Scripture too and is adept at twisting it to suit his purpose. One final matter: what shall we do with the armor of God?"

Mei said, "Keep it with Dr. Dale's remains? You wanted to put it in a casket to keep safe."

"I am rethinking that idea." She looked at me.

Marcus said, "One thing's for sure, we can't haul it through airport security more than once. I'm not having my name connected to a string of international incidents."

Through the meal, Reece kept watching me in a strange way. I could hardly look her in the eye. She was reading me like a book. Always could.

· · · · · ·

Dr. Eloise came pecking on our door late that night. She wanted to talk to me. "Have you decided?" she asked when I'd closed the door behind me.

I didn't know. I'd had this wild idea about tracking the armor across the world, uncovering its history, seeing where it led. But it had been just a dream.

She handed me the suitcase. "Take the armor, Elijah. Find a good hiding place … in Magdeline, perhaps?"

"Well, I was thinking that Mei's parents would more likely let her visit the States if they knew the clan had disbanded … if the ringleader was gone."

"I see," she smiled.

"But if I'm on the move—if I go with the SOS—there's the problem of getting a sword through security everywhere."

"Ships have safes for the crew's valuables. Wherever you might disembark, your treasure could stay on board. When difficulties arise—and they will—it will remind you. His name must be proclaimed throughout the world."

"You're sure you don't want it?" I asked.

Her small, glittery eyes drilled into me: "Our Mr. Dowland was in error, child. The armor of God must never again rest in peace!"

After a long pause, I said, "Could you help me make an international call?"

She smiled, pulled something metallic out of her pocket, and folded it into my hand. "Follow me."

· · · · ·

It shouldn't have been hard for a bunch of teenagers to say good-bye to an old person like Dr. Eloise, who'd always been a little left of center. But we all had a tough time that next morning. We promised to keep in touch.

On the slow train from Shimabara to the seaport, I plugged in Mei's music and watched the rice fields go by. What she said in Ireland was right: there's no other green like rice fields in August—nature's neon. I watched my clan. Rob was asleep on his backpack. Marcus was talking to Mei. Sitting on the opposite side of the train, Reece locked eyes with me in a way that sent my heart into my throat. She'd been watching me awhile. I smiled at her. She smiled back.

It seemed like a scene from a movie: blue mountains and sky

whizzing past behind her, background music floating through my brain. I was suspended between worlds, between going and staying. I was in Ireland on the Hill of Slane where Marcus had said we were the new wave. Ireland, where I'd first heard about the *peregrini,* the wanderers, where we'd searched for the sword when we had it all along.

But no wild-goose chase there; I'd needed to build Patrick's fire. Like I needed to see the statue of Amakusa Shiro and hear about the carpet of bones, so I'd have the courage to stand against whatever was to come. In that look that passed between Reece and me, we relived it all: a three-year quest from Magdeline to Farr Island to Ireland and beyond.

My whole life is in Magdeline. How can I leave?

It seemed that God had chosen the Magdeline Five to go into all the world and spread his Word. (Actually God meant that call for everyone, but only a few are listening.) To start with, I wouldn't need anything but a transcript of my grades and my parents' permission. Dom had already been talking to them. Mom and Dad had cried on the phone with me the night before. Mom apologized for being a bad mom, and I told her to cut it out. That wasn't the reason I was going. I had to go; it was a God thing. I had all I needed for Samoa: a few changes of clothes, a toothbrush, and the Quella with fresh batteries. Bare necessities.

· · · · · ·

Mei treated us to the world's best ramen in a little shop on the Hakata station platform. The end of the line. We slurped ourselves silly, ate out the noodles, and lifted our bowls to not miss a drop of the broth.

While Reece and Mei looked at postcards, I bequeathed my weapons to Marcus and Rob: "In my closet are my bow and arrow, a Bowie knife, a few other things. Use them while I'm gone." Rob almost blew a gasket. I figured he sort of already knew. "I'm thinking about going with the SOS. I'm not sure yet." He looked like he was going to cry. Marcus stared down the train tracks, his jaw muscles clamped.

I was their leader. How could I leave?

A bus dropped us off at the harbor. Huge—and I mean huge—car ferries were backed up to pier ramps so that cars could drive into the lower level.

Mei pointed up to a row of windows near the top deck. "We stay up there." She took care of business at the counter, then led us up a fancy winding staircase with gold rails to a big room lined with mats and pillows. "Family room," she apologized. "The sleeping is not too comfortable for you, I think. But food and the *ofuro* on ferries are very good."

The ship set out. The wind picked up, and I started feeling what life might be like for me. Open sea. Survival training. Adventures. Danger. Taking the armor of God around the world. No family, no home, no Camp Mudj. No clan. No Reece.

I was ripped in two.

The cafeteria was packed. We laughed and chitchatted like old times, but everyone had a kind of scared sadness behind their eyes. My heart was in a big knot. I couldn't think about climbing Great Oak with Rob in summer. Or driving the golf cart through Owl Woods with Reece when yellow leaves fall like flakes of light. I wouldn't be running into the house smelling like campfire and have the twins jump on me and Mom take care of me like she used to. I wouldn't be working with Dad or hanging out at Florence's.

Mei wrote a *kanji* symbol on her napkin and gave it to Rob. "This is ninja. It is made of three symbols: sword, heart, and person. The sword and heart together mean either 'hidden' or 'endure.' So," she sniffled, "we are all ninja. We hide or we endure, for the sake of the sword."

Reece looked out the window at the sea, "We hide the sword in our hearts."

· · · · ·

She was on deck watching the sun go down, her hair blowing in the wind, the big ship engines roaring underneath the deck. I came up beside her and saw tears running down her cheeks.

"This is way cool, huh?" I said stupidly.

She nodded and there was a strangely unnerving expression on her face.

A lump formed in my gut. "Reece?"

"Elijah, I'm letting you go."

I knew what she meant, but then I didn't. "What do you mean?" I asked.

"I'm letting you go, as simple as that."

I waited for more.

"That's your destiny, out there with the Students of the Seven Seas."

"It only lasts two years. Then I'll graduate. I'll be back."

Her head shook fiercely. "You're meant to go into all the world. It's your calling to trace the path of the armor. Everything's falling into place—" her words caught in her throat, "just like I planned."

"You can go with me. We can all go, as soon as there's an opening. Hey, remember what I always said: if I'm going, you're going. I said it on Devil's Cranium. And when we went to Ireland. And coming here to Japan. And ... and out there too." I nodded to the sunset making red streaks across dark water.

"Not this time."

"Reece ..."

"I'd just hold you back."

"No, you won't. You're the reason I'm here. Who knows where I'd be if you hadn't ... if you hadn't prayed?"

"You'll be going into dangerous places where you should travel incognito. American girls on crutches stick out like sore thumbs."

"You'll get more surgeries."

She turned to me with conviction. "It won't help."

"You don't know that."

"Yes, I do." She turned back resolutely to the red sky.

She was scaring me. "What are you talking about?"

"It's settled between God and me."

"If you know something, you can't leave me out of the loop," I tried to joke. "It's my life."

"Yes. It is."

I spun her around. "What's settled? You have to tell me."

She bit her lip to stop it from trembling. "When … when you got hurt in Gilead, and the doctors considered amputating your foot, that day I prayed for God to work a miracle, like he did for me that night I was in the hospital and in so much pain." She cried, "They were talking about cutting off your foot!"

A terrible feeling welled up in me. "What did you do?"

"I made a deal with God. I prayed for him to take what was wrong with you and give it to me. That if you were never to walk again, that it would be me instead."

"What are you talking about? The doctor said the frostbite wasn't that bad."

"That was later. Things changed … after I prayed. You got better."

"In another couple of years, doctors will have new technology."

She shook her head. "It's settled, Elijah. You're the Magdelinian."

"What's that mean, Reece? I don't even know what that means!"

"I think it just means that God has had his eye on you from the first. That he brought you to this place and time for his purpose. He's given you the ancestry of the first Magdelinians, made you to know the Indian ways to survive, let your mom be adopted from the Isle of Magdeline so you could live free in Magdeline, Ohio. And now you're like Mary Magdalene because you're fighting off demons and following Jesus. It's how he does things, bringing all the details together across time and space. Like he did with us and Isaiah 28. It's his way of showing us he knows what he's doing and that we should pay attention."

"Why should God answer your prayers and not mine?" I huffed. "I'm the head of this operation."

She just shook her head, her lips trembling. "He told me." She looked out at the sea and with her strong Scripture voice said, "'A voice of one calling in the desert, "Prepare the way for the Lord, make straight paths for him."'" That was written about the second Elijah and maybe the third too. 'Pass through the gates! Prepare the way for the people.'"

The past three years spread out … me climbing through the broken basement window of Old Pilgrim Church; that moment when Reece held the helmet for the first time, all aglow in my campfire, a look of mystery in her eyes; her bringing Marcus into the clan against my objections; how she supported me all through the trouble about the Kate Dowland mystery, saying, "If anyone can solve it, you can." Reece calling me at Farr Island to tell me she had Dowland's journals, telling me to hurry back. The tornado, how we all clung together in the dark while God tore through The Castle, his backhanded way of putting Rob's family back together and uncovering the truth in that closet about the MacMerrits. Which had led us to Ireland. Which had traced my roots as a Magdelinian back to the dawn of history. I pictured Reece and Rob in their silly green elf outfits at the Christmas Village. I remembered playing the eagle-bone whistle on a frosty night in Owl Woods. It was Reece's gift to me so I could play songs to God.

Her prayer had helped Mei and Rob decode the breastplate. It was her courage and faith that kept me calm when she went down at Hermits' Cave. Her prayers gave me peace when I was trapped in Gilead. If it hadn't been for Reece Elliston pressing the authorities to sweep Telanoo at night to look for me, I'd be a pile of bones in Gilead.

I remembered how on the plane to Ireland she was willing to give me up if I liked Emma. "I want us to always be friends," she'd said. And when Mom and Dad weren't excited about my baptism, Reece had squeezed my hand and told me I had courage. I'd circled the planet, and I was wearing the armor of God because of her. Without Reece showing me God, I'd have stayed at Camp Mudj and had a real nice ordinary life.

Her voice broke into my thoughts. "Mei named you Takumi—explore the ocean—even before she knew! You should run free, Elijah—it's what you love."

"I know … but … it's not the only thing I love."

• • • • •

Sometime around midnight Rob came on deck to look for us. Reece was asleep and wrapped in a blanket in her deck chair, her head on my shoulder, her hand in mine. Rob crossed the deck, hands in his pockets, arms stiff against the brisk wind. His eyebrows went up when he saw my drained expression. He slowed, stopped, and stood frowning at us, the wind whipping his jacket. I gave him a look and shook my head, which meant *dokka ike*.

Shrugging, a little embarrassed, he left. I reminded myself to give him my samurai kite to take to Nori and Stacy.

God had pulled me into his bow, stretched me to the breaking point, and then released. *I'm going*, I said, amazed. *All I'm asking is one thing. Why can't you heal her?*

The sky was so black and clear the stars didn't even twinkle.

As the early sky brightened, I looked up *leave home* in the Quella to see if God had anything to say about it. "No one who has left home or wife or brothers or parents or children for the sake of the kingdom of God will fail to receive many times as much in this age and, in the age to come, eternal life."

I know, God, but what about your verse saying that a cord of five strands is not quickly broken? Yeah, it actually says three strands, but you know what I mean. We five were supposed to stay together, the Magdeline Five. Does one verse cancel out another?

My Word is truth.

I sat staring into the night. Never—not in my wildest dreams—did I ever imagine that an innocent peek into an old church would change my life forever, turning me into the wild vagabond that I was now. But it did.

Over the sound of waves and ship engines he called me, *Elijah…*

I'm here, I answered. The wind whirled around me. A thin string of lights twinkled from a distant island shore. In a few hours we'd be in Osaka port. Mei would take the others to the airport. I'd wait at the dock for the SOS ship. I was alone, and I guessed that's how it would be. My mission, I figured, was somehow to prepare the people for the war to come. I'd have to stay on the move to get the word out, my piece of the Tear of Blood pierced to my belly, the armor and sword in my keeping. I'd have to keep the last bit of advice Dr. Eloise had whispered in my ear: "Steer clear of treasure hunters." She probably meant that Cravens and his kind wouldn't give up. Some people would never get it about the real armor of God: the *omen* truth which sets things right; righteousness to protect your heart; faith in unseen powers to ward off the evil one's fiery arrows (like whatever demons would be slithering out from behind the veil next);

unexplainable peace; salvation and hope no matter what; the flaming sword as powerful as any weapon devised, for storming the gates of Hell.

I pulled out the medallion on the chain around my neck—the metallic thing Dr. Eloise had slipped into my hand. I ran my fingers over it, feeling the strands of the three coils: migration. God's command given three times to the world: go, go, go fill the earth with my goodness.

I'm going.

Elijah …

I'm here, Master of Breath.

Take heart. A cord of five strands is not quickly broken.

ANCIENT TRUTH

(Page 14) "He will save his people from their sins."

Matthew 1:21

(Page 14) "Whoever wants to save his life will lose it, but whoever loses his life for me will find it."

Matthew 16:25

(Page 14) "What good is it, my brothers, if a man claims to have faith but has no deeds? Can such faith save him?"

James 2:14

(Page 14) "For it is by grace you have been saved, through faith."

Ephesians 2:8

(Page 14) "If you confess with your mouth, 'Jesus is Lord,' and believe in your heart that God raised him from the dead, you will be saved."

Romans 10:9

(Page 37) "Then the LORD said to me, 'You have made your way around this hill country long enough; now turn north.'"

Deuteronomy 2:3

(Page 44) "Take up the shield of faith, with which you can extinguish all the flaming arrows of the evil one."

Ephesians 6:16

(Page 45) "You, who through faith are shielded by God's power until the coming of the salvation that is ready to be revealed in the last time. In this you greatly rejoice, though now for a little while you may have had to suffer grief in all kinds of trials. These have come so that your faith—of greater worth than gold, which perishes even though refined by fire—may be proved genuine."

1 Peter 1:4-7

(Page 49) "At that time many will turn away from the faith and will betray and hate each other, and many false prophets will appear and deceive many people. Because of the increase of wickedness, the love of most will grow cold."

Matthew 24:10-12

(Page 49) "When the Son of Man comes, will he find faith on the earth?"

Luke 18:8

(Page 54) "I am your shield, your very great reward."

Genesis 15:1

(Page 58) "You are a shield around me."

Psalm 3:3

(Page 58) "My shield is God Most High."

Psalm 7:10

(Page 58) "We wait in hope for the LORD; he is our help and our shield."

Psalm 33:20

(Page 71) "These are the words of him who has the sharp, double-edged sword. I know where you live—where Satan has his throne.... Repent therefore! Otherwise, I will soon come to you and will fight against them with the sword of my mouth."

Revelation 2:12, 13, 16

(Page 106) "When you look up to the sky and see the sun, the moon and the stars—all the heavenly array—do not be enticed into bowing down to them and worshiping things the LORD your God has apportioned to all the nations under heaven."

Deuteronomy 4:19

(Page 113) "Why do the nations conspire and the peoples plot in vain? The kings of the earth take their stand and the rulers gather together against the LORD and against his Anointed One.... The One enthroned in heaven laughs; the Lord scoffs at them.... O LORD, how many are my foes! How many rise up against me! Many are saying of me, 'God will not deliver him.' But you are a shield around me, O LORD; you bestow glory on me and lift up my head. To the LORD I cry aloud, and he answers me from his holy hill!"

Psalms 2:1-4; 3:1-4

(Page 157) "Faith is being sure of what we hope for and certain of what we do not see."

Hebrews 11:1

(Page 158) "I will give you the treasures of darkness, riches stored in secret places, so that you may know that I am the LORD, the God of Israel, who summons you by name."

Isaiah 45:3

(Page 161, 235) "The god who answers by fire—he is God."

1 Kings 18:24

(Page 168) "A sword for the LORD and for Gideon!"

Judges 7:20

(Page 221) "The Rock of Israel ... blesses you with blessings of the heavens above, blessings of the deep that lies below."

Genesis 49:24, 25

(Page 221) "The LORD is my rock, my fortress and my deliverer; my God is my rock, in whom I take refuge. He is my shield."

Psalm 18:2

(Page 222) "Elijah was a man just like us. He prayed earnestly that it would not rain, and it did not rain on the land for three and a half years. Again he prayed, and the heavens gave rain, and the earth produced its crops."

James 5:17, 18

(Page 226, 256) "Naphtali is abounding with the favor of the LORD and is full of his blessing; he will inherit southward to the lake."

Deuteronomy 33:23

(Page 244, 246) "Even though I walk through the valley of the shadow of death, I will fear no evil, for you are with me."

Psalm 23:4

(Page 244) "In the beginning God created the heavens and the earth."

Genesis 1:1

(Page 244) "God is light; in him there is no darkness at all."

1 John 1:5

(Page 246) "Jesus answered, 'It is written: "Man does not live on bread alone, but on every word that comes from the mouth of God."'"

Matthew 4:4

(Page 246) "For our struggle is not against flesh and blood, but against the rulers, against the authorities, against the powers of this dark world and against the spiritual forces of evil in the heavenly realms."

Ephesians 6:12

(Page 267) "Then the Almighty will be your gold, the choicest silver for you."

Job 22:25

(Page 277, 471) "A cord of three strands is not quickly broken."

Ecclesiastes 4:12

(Page 292) "And they were calling to one another: 'Holy, holy, holy is the LORD Almighty; the whole earth is full of his glory.'"

Isaiah 6:3

(Page 293) "Then I heard the voice of the Lord saying, 'Whom shall I send? And who will go for us?'"

Isaiah 6:8

(Page 297) "The LORD will lay bare his holy arm in the sight of all the nations, and all the ends of the earth will see the salvation of our God."

Isaiah 52:10

(Page 301) "The LORD said, 'What have you done? Listen! Your brother's blood cries out to me from the ground.'"

Genesis 4:10

(Page 301) "Who is this, robed in splendor, striding forward in the greatness of his strength? 'It is I, speaking in righteousness, mighty to save.' Why are your garments red, like those of one treading the winepress? 'I have trodden the winepress alone; from the nations no one was with me. I trampled them in my anger and trod them down in my wrath; their blood spattered my garments, and I stained all my clothing. For the day of vengeance was in my heart, and the year of my redemption has come.'"

Isaiah 63:1-4

(Page 302) "I will make your forehead like the hardest stone, harder than flint. Do not be afraid of them or terrified by them."

Ezekiel 3:9

(Page 309) "Be silent before me, you islands! Let the nations renew their strength! Let them come forward and speak; let us meet together at the place of judgment."

Isaiah 41:1

(Page 309) "The islands will look to me and wait in hope."

Isaiah 51:5

(Page 311) "He put on righteousness as his breastplate, and the helmet of salvation on his head; he put on the garments of vengeance.... So will he repay wrath to his enemies ... he will repay the islands their due."

Isaiah 59:17,18

(Page 330) "He gave them power and authority to drive out all demons and to cure diseases, and he sent them out.... He told them: 'Take nothing for the journey—no staff, no bag, no bread, no money, no extra tunic.'"

Luke 9:1-3

(Page 339, 372) "Lift up your heads, O you gates; be lifted up, you ancient doors, that the King of glory may come in. Who is this King of glory? The LORD strong and mighty, the LORD mighty in battle… . He is the King of glory."

Psalm 24:7-10

(Page 361) "As the deer pants for streams of water, so my soul pants for you, O God. My soul thirsts for God, for the living God. When can I go and meet with God?"

Psalm 42:1, 2

(Page 365) "In the beginning was the Word, and the Word was with God, and the Word was God."

John 1:1

(Page 366) "… and the sword of the Spirit, which is the word of God. And pray in the Spirit on all occasions with all kinds of prayers and requests."

Ephesians 6:17, 18

(Page 367, 431) "Our struggle is not against flesh and blood, but … against the powers of this dark world and against the spiritual forces of evil in the heavenly realms. Therefore put on the full armor of God."

Ephesians 6:12

(Page 370) "I am the LORD your God… . You shall have no other gods before me."

Exodus 20:2, 3

(Page 371) "This is what the LORD says to you: 'Do not be afraid or discouraged because of this vast army. For the battle is not yours, but God's.'"

2 Chronicles 20:15

(Page 371, 457) "The word of God is living and active. Sharper than any double-edged sword, it penetrates even to dividing soul and spirit, joints and marrow; it judges the thoughts and attitudes of the heart. Nothing in all creation is hidden from God's sight. Everything is uncovered and laid bare before the eyes of him to whom we must give account."

Hebrews 4:12, 13

(Page 372, 440) "This is the gate of the LORD through which the righteous may enter."

Psalm 118:20

(Page 372) "The poor and needy search for water, but there is none; their tongues are parched with thirst. But I the LORD will answer them; I, the God of Israel, will not forsake them."

Isaiah 41:17

(Page 374) "To the arrogant I say, 'Boast no more,' and to the wicked, 'Do not lift up your horns. Do not lift your horns against heaven; do not speak with outstretched neck.' No one from the east or the west or from the desert can exalt a man. But it is God who judges."

Psalm 75:4-7

(Page 375, 468) "Pass through, pass through the gates! Prepare the way for the people. Build up, build up the highway! Remove the stones."

Isaiah 62:10

(Page 377) "... a holy nation, a people belonging to God, that you may declare the praises of him who called you out of darkness into his wonderful light. Once you were not a people, but now you are the people of God."

1 Peter 2:9, 10

(Page 388) "The Almighty will be your gold, the choicest silver for you. Surely then you will find delight in the Almighty and will lift up your face to God. You will pray to him, and he will hear you, and you will fulfill your vows. What you decide on will be done, and light will shine on your ways."

Job 22:25-28

(Page 389) "I praise you, Father, Lord of heaven and earth, because you have hidden these things from the wise and learned, and revealed them to little children."

Matthew 11:25

(Page 389) "The price of wisdom is beyond rubies."

Job 28:18

(Page 405) Humble yourselves before the Lord, and he will lift you up."

James 4:10

(Page 413) "Go and make disciples of all nations."

Matthew 28:18

(Page 422, 436) "Under the lotus plants he lies, hidden among the reeds in the marsh. The lotuses conceal him in their shadow."

Job 40:21

(Page 422, 458) "Look at the behemoth.... He ranks first among the works of God, yet his Maker can approach him with his sword."

Job 40:15-19

(Page 430) "Satan ... leads the whole world astray." "The prince of this world now stands condemned."

Revelation 12:9; John 16:11

(Page 433) "I am the light of the world. Whoever follows me will never walk in darkness, but will have the light of life."

John 8:12

(Page 435) "Faith is being … certain of what we do not see."

Hebrews 11:1

(Page 448) "[Ezekiel] saw a great many bones on the floor of the valley, bones that were very dry. [The Lord] asked … , 'Can these bones live?'"

Ezekiel 37:2, 3

(Page 448) "[The martyrs] called out in a loud voice, 'How long, Sovereign Lord, holy and true, until you judge the inhabitants of the earth and avenge our blood?' Then each of them was given a white robe, and they were told to wait a little longer, until the number of their fellow servants and brothers who were to be killed as they had been was completed."

Revelation 6:10, 11

(Page 452-454) "Woe to that wreath, the pride of Ephraim's drunkards, to the fading flower, his glorious beauty, set on the head of a fertile valley—to that city, the pride of those laid low by wine! See, the Lord has one who is powerful and strong. Like a hailstorm and a destructive wind, like a driving rain and a flooding downpour, he will throw it forcefully to the ground. That wreath, the pride of Ephraims's drunkards, will be trampled underfoot. That fading flower, his glorious beauty, set on the head of a fertile valley, will be like a fig ripe before harvest—as soon as someone sees it and takes it in his hand, he swallows it. In that day the LORD Almighty will be a glorious crown, a beautiful wreath for the remnant of his people. He will be a spirit

of justice to him who sits in judgment, a source of strength to those who turn back the battle at the gate."

Isaiah 28:1-6

(Page 468) "This is he who was spoken of through the prophet Isaiah: 'A voice of one calling in the desert, "Prepare the way for the Lord, make straight paths for him.""""

Matthew 3:3

(Page 470) "No one who has left home or wife or brothers or parents or children for the sake of the kingdom of God will fail to receive many times as much in this age and, in the age to come, eternal life."

Luke 18:29, 30

CREEK CODE

Delaware

Langundowagan—(lahn-goon-do-wah-gahn) Peace

Irish Gaelic

Cathach—(kah-thukh) Warrior

Creidim—(kred-im) Faith

Lough—(lockh) Lake

Ogham—(oh-yam) Ancient system of writing to keep records

Samhain—(sow-en) Irish holiday comparable to Halloween

Greek

Koinonia—Fellowship

Machaira—(makh-ahee-rah) Short sword, dagger, or saber

Parabolani—The riskers

Rhomphaia—(hrom-fah-yah) Large brandishing sword

Soterion—Salvation

Japanese

Arigatou gozaimasu—(ah-ree-gah-toh go-zah-ee-mah-su) Thank you very much

Amerika-jin—(ah-meh-ree-ka-jeen) American(s)

Bentou—(ben-toh) Box lunch

Bochibochi denna—(boh-chee-boh-chee den-nah) So-so

Daijoubu—(die-jo-boo) It's all right

Dokka ike—(doke-kah ee-keh) Get lost!

Fumie—(foo-mee-eh) Picture of Jesus to be stepped on by suspected Christians to prove they were not believers.

Gaijin—(gah-ee-jeen) Foreigner

Gi—(ghee) A kanji character meaning righteousness

Henna gaijin—(hen-nah gah-ee-jeen) Strange foreigner

-Jou—(joh) Castle

Kowai—(ko-wah-ee) Scary

Mata atode—(mah-tah ah-toh-deh) See you later

Moukari makka—(moh-kah-ree mak-kah) How's business?

Obon—(oh-bone) Japanese festival of the dead

Ofuro—(oh-foo-roh) Japanese bath

Ohayou—(oh-hah-yoh) Good morning

Okonomiyaki—(oh-koh-noh-mee-yah-kee) Pancake filled with meat and vegetables

Oni—(oh-nee) Demon

Onigiri—(oh-nee-ghee-ree) Rice ball with salty or pickeled filling and wrapped in seaweed.

Ryokan—(ryoh-khan) Japanese-style inn

Ryokou—(ryo-koh) A trip

Souzousha—(soh-zoh-shah) Creator

Torii—(toh-ree-ee) Shinto gateway to the gods

Ume—(oo-meh) Plum

Yukata—(you-kah-tah) Lightweight kimono-style robe

Latin

Peregrini—(peh-reh-gree-nee) Pilgrim

Veni, Vidi, Vici—(weeny weedy weeky) I came, I saw, I conquered

Hebrew
Omen—(aleph, mame, noon) Truth, faithfulness
Yahweh—Jehovah, the Lord

German
Luftkrankheit—(looft-krahnk-heit) Air sickness

ABOUT THE AUTHOR

 **"Go far, Go light"** is Lena Wood's mission. She's an author, speaker, adventurer, mom of two, and grammy of seven. Lena's been **going far** her whole life: to Asia (seven times), South Africa, Egypt, and Ireland. She climbed Mt. Fuji, slept at Everest base camp, and recently emptied her bucket list on a 5600-mile drive across the US.

Going light means traveling light, seeking simplicity, and writing books that enlighten. And Lena uses her home, The Ridge, to host friends who share a passion for taking the light of Jesus to the uttermost.

Her *Elijah Creek & The Armor of God* series sprang from a desire to prepare kids—and adults—for the dark stuff. To that end, she became an unwitting expert on occult mysticism. She speaks on the topic around the country.